THE DARKEST PLACE

Also by
DANIEL JUDSON

The Bone Orchard
The Poisoned Rose

THE
DARKEST
PLACE

DANIEL JUDSON

St. Martin's Paperbacks

This is a work of fiction. All of the characters, organizations, and events portrayed in this novel are either products of the author's imagination or are used fictitiously.

THE DARKEST PLACE

Library of Congress Catalog Card Number: 2006040532

ISBN: 0-312-35515-7
EAN: 978-0-312-35515-9

Printed in the United States of America

St. Martin's Press hardcover edition / June 2006
St. Martin's Paperbacks edition / May 2007

St. Martin's Paperbacks are published by St. Martin's Press, 175 Fifth Avenue, New York, NY 10010.

10 9 8 7 6 5 4 3 2 1

*For Sara Bassett and
in memory of Doris Barton*

THE
DARKEST
PLACE

ONE

He didn't mind the cold. he was wearing his heavy Carhartt jacket and leather gloves and wool hat, the hat he had once seen in that movie about corruption among longshoremen, the one with Marlon Brando, the one from the fifties. What was that movie called? He couldn't remember. But he had liked the look of those hats, the look of the men who wore them. Tough, self-reliant, beat-but-still-standing. He liked that, wanted those who looked at him to see that, see a man still standing. As he drove his van through the dark he remembered that he had also liked the woman in the movie, the blonde in the white slip, the one with the sad eyes. He liked the way she looked, he liked her voice. There was something about it, something about her. He had been born in Brooklyn, lived in sight of those very docks, surrounded, he was certain, by women who talked like she had talked. He hadn't ever known his father, didn't know what the man had done for a living back then, if the man had in fact been one of those men who worked the waterfront or had done something else to earn his money. But what that something could have been he didn't know.

His father had left before he was born, and his mother had found a house farther out on the island, in the town of Riverhead. This was when he was four. He could barely remember that day, his first in the new house. Men came and went. He remembered that. His mother never spoke of his old man, but there wasn't a day when he didn't think about his father, about the things this unknown man might have done to survive, the places he might have lived in and the women he might have been with and maybe even loved in the years that followed his leaving them. He thought about that, gnawed on that, a hundred times a day—at work, at home, at night, down in his basement, and then later on in bed. He was thinking of all that now, as he steered his van through this cold night, looking calmly for a place to deposit the body.

He had lifted weights before he left his house, the rusted bench press set up in the basement, beside the large furnace. The furnace worked continuously against the cold, against a wintry wind that pressed like a shoulder again and again against the windows, bending and rattling the panes. He could see through the small glass window in the hatch of the furnace the fire that raged inside. It was the only source of light, and he stared at it as he briefly rested between sets. He had made a point of doing slow, forced repetitions with heavy weight, filling his thick muscles with blood and raising his heart rate to one-twenty. This had warmed his core up plenty, and the engorged muscles in his torso, quivering beneath his jacket now, were like an added layer of living insulation packed around him. Even after the half hour it took him to reach Hampton Bays, the van's engine had yet to heat the radiator fluid enough to affect the heater coil. It was that cold outside, that raw. Arctic. The air rushing through the vents under the dashboard was still cold, but he didn't mind that. He liked the feel of it on his face. It was something for him to stand against, something to prove his resilience. And anyway, his heart and lungs and gut, the deepest parts of himself, only seemed warmer by contrast to what was touching his large, unshaven face like a dead hand.

No, this cold was fine with him.

He was a big man—six-five, two-ninety. He wasn't yet thirty. Beneath the heavy jacket he wore dirty coveralls, rarely wore anything else, even on his days off. This cold snap dropping into the double-digits-below when the sun went down, was only two days old. Before that the weather had been mild—a long Indian summer in October followed by a mild November. The first day of winter was just a week away, but until two days ago, it hadn't seemed really possible to him. Despite this sudden cold, he wasn't worried that the bay would be frozen over. Even the lakes around town had yet to freeze. Only the small ponds on the back roads of Bridgehampton had a thin sheet over them. No, there was nothing for him to worry about, nothing to stand in his way. This was easy money. Easy money.

He entered Hampton Bays from the north and headed his van east along Main Street. He drove slowly, the way he had driven in from Riverhead, through the desolation of the pine barrens. No need to attract the cops, though he was ready for what he'd have to do if one dared to stop him. A few blocks east, in the heart of town, he turned the van south and headed through a working-class neighborhood called Ponquogue. It wasn't late, not much past nine o'clock now. He didn't feel that he needed the protection that a later hour would afford him. He'd done this before, was getting good at it, better and better each time. Besides, there was elegance in this, in what he was doing. There was elegance in his being daring, being efficient and confident. Elegance was a sad-eyed blonde in a slip, elegance was Brando in his checkered jacket, standing up, his face bloodied. This mattered to him, elegance. As he rode past the houses he knew that those hidden inside were watching television, just killing time till sleep called. Without straining he could see through the front windows, see from the corner of his eye the flickering blue light cast against the walls, the ever-moving shadows, action without motion. The people occupying these houses were getting fatter, he knew this, growing weaker by the day, wasting away as they waited on soft couches for their precious hours of unconsciousness. What was the point in living, he thought, if living was only this?

As he steered down the dark street he found himself looking at the upstairs windows, splitting his attention between them and the familiar road ahead. Some windows were dark, others lit. He watched them all as closely as he could, concentrating. One night not too long ago he had seen a woman crossing a well-lit bedroom, saw her turn and face the window just as he rode past. She was undressed. Lean and strong, from what he could see in the second or two that he had. She had aroused him, not only sexually but deep in his heart. He imagined her lonely, like he was. He imagined her seeking perfection in everything she did, defining herself with every gesture she made, the way he was trying to define himself by what he did. He thought of her working out every day, unashamed of her body, tending to it. Neat and clean. He thought of her with him, naked in his basement, on his bench, the heat from the furnace touching them, the orange glow from its flames reflecting off the sweat that covered their skin . . .

He was more than what he seemed, much more, and the woman he would love would know that. He would know that about her, too. He would have her when he wanted, she would undress for him, without him having to ask. She would walk before him freely, never doubt him. She would have him, too, whenever she wanted, and he would walk before her for her to see.

A few miles later he was pulling over to the side of the road. There weren't any houses here, just a wooded lot to the right and the shimmering edge of the bay on his left. He was focused now. Sharp. He killed the lights but left the motor running. He wouldn't be long. He got out and stepped around to the back, opening the rear doors and leaning in. The body wrapped up in the sheet of clear plastic had begun to stiffen. It was heavy now, in that way dead things are heavy. But he curled more than that weight every other day, so his muscles didn't strain a bit as he pulled the body out and carried it to the water's edge.

He knelt, letting the body down onto the bank. With both hands he held the jagged edge of the plastic so the body unrolled down the bank and into the water. At this time of night Shinnecock Canal was closed, so the current would be a lazy one. Still, the body, facedown, immediately started to drift away from the bank. Fully dressed, per his orders. An air pocket was probably caught inside the nylon jacket, enough to give it buoyancy, or close to it. He had thought he might have to give the body a shove, and there was a broom handle in the back of the van for that reason. But he could see he wouldn't need to do that. The body was twenty feet from shore and still moving by the time he was back at the van. He tossed the clear plastic through the rear doors, then looked at the bay for a moment longer. He watched till he couldn't distinguish the body from the surface chop that was stirred up by a steady wind that all but cut his exposed skin.

He closed the doors, walked around to the front, and got in. Heat was coming finally from the vents, but he didn't want it, nor did he need it. He felt good just as he was and switched the heater off. It was to him a sign of his greatness, his strength. Then he pulled the column shifter down, made a U-turn, and drove back as slowly as he had come.

He watched the houses as he went past them again, watching windows for a glimpse of a woman who might think as he thought, know what he knew. Maybe a blonde, maybe with a quaver in her voice and sad eyes and the willingness to do what needed to be done. He thought then of driving past the house where he had seen the naked woman nights ago. But that was in a town farther east from here, on Peconic Bay, and anyway, there was a phone call to make and money to collect.

He left Hampton Bays and started north through the darkness of the pine barrens, heading back to Riverhead. For the longest time his van was the only vehicle on the road.

In Southampton, thirst woke Tommy Miller. He got out of bed, the floorboards cold beneath his bare feet, and walked lightly toward his bathroom. The windows were frosted, the small room lit tonight with a ghostly blue wash. He found that he was out of the little paper cups he used when he brushed his teeth, so he drank from the tap, filling the palm of his hand and bringing it to his mouth. Then he dried his hand on a towel and went back to his bed and to the woman he barely knew lying still and quiet beneath his blankets.

It occurred to him, though, as he eased in beside her, that she was awake, that maybe she had been even before he got up for some water. Her breathing wasn't low and regular, and he knew enough about a sleeping woman to know that what he was hearing wasn't the sound of someone comfortably at rest. By the clock on the nearby table he saw that it was just past midnight. They had fallen into bed together around ten, after too many drinks at Barrister's and a quick ride to his house on Moses Lane, and made love as best they could, then lay side by side in awkward silence for a while. He must have dozed off soon after because the next thing he knew he was awake and in desperate need of some water.

He moved carefully as he settled back into his bed, saying nothing to her. If he was wrong about the meaning of her breathing pattern and she was in fact asleep, he didn't want to disturb her. He was awake now, though—the beer he'd drunk had worn off in his nap. He was awake and thinking, not a good thing in this dark hour. He wondered if she had enjoyed herself, if he had acted properly. He wasn't very experienced with this kind of encounter. He hadn't been with a woman in a while, well over a year. He'd needed time, needed to put distance between himself and a relationship that had ended quite badly. Before that, before the previous relationship, his only experience with women had been violent encounters. It was this, his past, when finally it was revealed, that had ended that relationship a year ago. As he lay beside this woman, he wondered how he would tell her, if it ever came to that, if this wasn't just a one-night thing. What words, if any, would keep her from hating him, from leaving him, too. He was inclined now, with these thoughts in his head, these concerns and questions, to remain silent beside her even if she was awake. He'd spent a year in such silence, was safe there. Her presence beside him wasn't enough yet to veer him from this habit.

His house was old and drafty, his bedroom cold. He had lived there with his mother and father before they died, lived there for all of his twenty-two years. The only source of heat in the whole place was a large square grate in the floor of the living room downstairs, the only access to the rooms above the narrow stairwell at the far end of the hallway. Miller had left his bedroom door half-open, but very little warmth had found its way up to them. Outside was a solemn winter night. He could sense the killing cold beyond his windows even from his bed. He and Abby had talked about the cold as they drank at Barrister's. It was all anyone talked about. They had raced through it to his car when they left, laughing, just a bit tipsy. She had teased him about his cold feet when they first got into his bed. Her hands had felt almost like those of a dead person's in his. But their bodies had warmed up fast enough, for the most part anyway, and had remained warm for as long as they both stayed under the protection of his heavy blankets.

He heard her sniffle now, once, and then again, and knew for certain that she was awake. He waited awhile, but the silence, broken only by their shallow breathing, rang. Eventually he said the only thing that he could think to say, a rehearsal for the day he, or someone else, would tell her his secret. Southampton was a small town, and notorious pasts weren't quickly forgotten.

"Sorry," he said.

"What for?" She spoke in a whisper.

"I woke you."

"No." Her voice, soft, deep for someone so young, was anything but groggy. He wondered how long it was he had slept beside her as she stared up at his ceiling. An hour? More? Their lovemaking had hardly been epic. They were little more than strangers to each other, and with so much at stake, he had been nervous.

"You okay?"

She answered with a quick nod. Then, after a moment of more silence, "Is there a TV or something on downstairs? I hear something."

He tuned into it then. On a bureau he kept in the hallway, just outside his half-open door, was a police scanner. It had belonged to his father. Miller kept it turned on with the volume set close to zero. The voices, unless you really listened, were little more than murmurs. He had adapted the ability to tune out the low voices and the occasional squawking, only listening closely when something important came through. Somehow he knew the difference; it was something in the tone of the dispatcher's voice that told him when to listen. It was a skill he had spent a lifetime developing, one that had also belonged to his father. But while this noise was little more to Miller than the sound of street traffic to a city person, to Abby it was something she could not easily ignore.

Miller told her what it was and that he'd turn it off.

"You'll only bring more cold back to bed if you get out again," she said. "It's okay for now."

"Are you sure?"

"Yeah. Maybe you can talk to me for a while."

"What about?"

"I don't know. You can tell me why you have a police scanner. Why do you leave it on?"

"For work."

"You run a magazine store," she said. It was how they met. His small shop, magazines and prepackaged bags of gourmet coffee, was next door to the gourmet deli where she worked. They had been on friendly terms since she started working there three months before, but in that time hadn't exchanged anything more than small talk and pleasantries. She had mentioned in passing that she was about to turn twenty-one, and somehow he got the nerve to suggest that they go for drinks some night after work to celebrate. It all happened so quickly, really. He had always assumed, up till the point tonight when she told him otherwise, that she had a boyfriend. Attractive women were rarely single. He didn't ask her why she happened to be unattached, and she didn't offer. He was careful not to ask questions about a person's past. They often led to questions about his own.

But she wasn't asking about his past now, just his present. Why did he listen to a scanner? The question was unsafe territory for a number of reasons, the chief among them being that, whether she knew it or not, it was connected to his past, and could lead them places he didn't yet want to go.

"Sometimes I do some work for a guy," he answered.

She was looking at him now. His eyes were fixed on the ceiling above.

"What guy?"

"It's nothing major."

"Tell me."

"I'm not supposed to talk about it."

She smiled, glad that they were at least talking. She wasn't used to men staying around after sex. Being there in that strange bed, awake while he had slept, she had started to give in to feelings of loneliness. But now that was gone. "You brought it up," she said, teasing him.

"I'm just not supposed to talk about it. It's nothing to worry about."

"I wasn't worried."

"I'm not a criminal or anything."

"I didn't think you were." She wanted to keep the conversation going. "So you live here all alone?"

"Yeah."

"You own it?"

"My parents left it to me."

"Oh. Lots of space for just you."

He nodded. His attention had drifted. She sensed it.

"What?" she said.

"Wait a second."

At first she thought maybe he had heard something, a noise downstairs. She could tell that he was straining to listen to something.

"What is it?" Her voice was a whisper still, but there was an edge of urgency in it now.

"Did you hear that?"

"What?"

"On the scanner."

"No."

They both listened now. Neither moved or even breathed. His head was lifted off the pillow, and he was looking in the direction of the door.

Then came a soft squawk, followed by a burst of murmured words. She could barely make them out.

"What?" she asked.

"He said something about a body."

"What?"

"Hang on."

They listened together. After a moment there was another soft squawk, followed by more chatter she couldn't understand.

"It's a patrol car calling in," he told her.

"What's he saying?"

"They found another body."

"Another?"

Miller nodded. He was sitting up now. She was leaning on one elbow. They were both naked under his blankets.

"You mean another one of those boys?" she said.

One morning eight weeks ago a fisherman had found a body adrift in Mecox Bay. A month after that another body was found in Peconic Bay, this time by an old man as he took his early morning swim. Both victims were young men, the older of the two only twenty. The coroner had, in both cases, listed drowning as the cause of death, and the police had first considered these deaths suicides, finally ruling them as accidents. Miller, among others, wasn't so convinced of that.

Abby knew of the dead young men—boys, really. Both deaths had made the local papers, and for days after each body was discovered, no one in town seemed to want to talk about anything else. Everyone who came into the deli had a theory, to believe that something other than what the cops were saying was actually going on. One of her regular customers, an old German professor who claimed to have known Einstein as a youth and smelled always of garlic, was convinced that this was the work of, as he put it, "dark forces." Such talk made her uneasy. Though she had a roommate, she was often alone at night, and the idea of something sinister roaming the quiet streets of her town disturbed her deeply, kept her from sleeping, and made her wish for someone, anyone, to be in bed beside her.

Miller was sitting on the edge of the mattress now. He

was a big guy, had once played football, had once been bound for the University of Michigan on an athletic scholarship. But his knee went, or, rather, was taken from him, and that all changed. Abby sat up, the blanket falling away, exposing her breasts to the cold air. She could barely see Miller in the outside light filtered deep blue by the frosted windows. But she could sense that he was listening now even more intently than before. She waited for whatever was coming next.

A moment more, and then a final squawk and murmur of words. She heard some of them this time. *Shinnecock Bay. Reservation.* The instant the transmission ended, Miller was standing, searching for his clothes.

"Where are you going?" she said.

"I have to check something out."

He found his jeans, then his shirt, and finally his boots. He dressed beside the bed, quickly. She felt threatened by his abruptness but fought hard not to let this trigger her old insecurities.

"How long will you be?"

"I don't know. I'm sorry. You can wait here, though. I mean, I'll be back eventually."

"Do you want me to wait here?"

"Yeah. I'll have my cell phone. You can call me if there's a problem."

"Where are you going?"

"I just need to check this out."

"Why?"

"I won't be long. I promise. An hour, tops. If I'm going to be any longer than that, I'll call."

She nodded despite her uncertainty about this. Her car was back in town, parked in the lot behind the deli, a mile or so away. Walking distance in the summer but not in this weather, not with her uneasiness about things that lurked, both imagined and real.

"You can watch TV if you want. And I have food downstairs. I'm sorry about this." The words echoed in his head. He would be saying this again soon, if things got that far.

"It's okay," she said. "Just hurry back."

He was dressed now, tucking in his shirt, tightening his belt. His army field jacket and down vest he wore beneath were downstairs, by her coat. They had begun in his kitchen, kissing as they had walked through the door. It seemed at the time that throwing themselves at each other before they sobered up was the thing to do. It had seemed she needed that as much as he had. For both of them it was nothing short of a leap into darkness.

He left her in his bed, in the cold room, and, as best as his bad knee would allow him, hurried down the stairs. He grabbed his vest and coat and gloves. He was zippering up the field jacket as he hurried out the back door, his muscles flexing against the harsh, cold air. He paused to make sure the door was locked, then rushed to his pickup.

He sat behind the wheel a moment, allowing the engine a few seconds to warm up, then shifted into gear and pulled out of his driveway. At the end of Moses Lane he turned right, heading west on Hill Street. He wondered as he drove down the empty two-lane road if he had been maybe a little too eager to get out of there. Had he jumped at the chance to get away? He needed to do this, to find out what he could. But he was also feeling grateful for the diversion from conversation. The more things they talked about, the more small talk they used up, the sooner there would be nothing left for him to say but to tell her the things he had once done.

His breath was a white mist that burst from his nostrils and mouth. Steady, long bursts. He could smell her on him, taste her still. He thought about her, the warmth of her beside him. In the distance were police sirens. He was moving toward them.

M iller's hope was to arrive before the cops were able to get organized. Moses Lane wasn't more than a few minutes' drive from the reservation, even at the posted speed limit, so there was a good chance of making it before the scene could be secured. Miller made the sharp left-hand turn from Hill Street onto Little Beach Road not

much more than a minute after leaving his house, but once
he did, he was forced to ease back on the accelerator. The
roads that ran through the reservation were narrow and unlit,
not at all well tended or even marked. His pickup, though
one of the smaller trucks of its line, wasn't designed for high
speeds, certainly not high speeds through this kind of envi-
ronment. So he forced himself to drive more cautiously despite the excitement building in his gut, mounting like a
storm inside him. He needed to keep his emotions in check,
to govern himself better; he'd been told that several times
before by the man from whom he wanted to get more work.
Miller wanted to show that he could learn, that he could
change, that in fact he had changed. The last thing he needed
was to roll his truck over on a turn and not even reach the
scene. That would hardly be impressive, he thought, hardly
serve to help make his case for being worthy of full-time
employment by the only PI in town.

Miller made a second left turn onto Church Street and
was approaching Cemetery Road when he caught sight of
something up ahead. Bright lights flickering in the darkness.
He continued on toward the end of Church Street even
though he knew by these lights that he was already too late.
It was only a few seconds later that the first patrol car came
into view. Then another, and then a third. They were parked
together in a cluster, their red and blue bubble lights blinking, each one out of sync with the other and illuminating
with a kind of unrelenting chaos the tops of the bare trees
that lined this back road.

Two of the cars were parked nose to nose across Cemetery
Road, blocking it to traffic. The third car was directly beyond
these two, facing toward the bay, its headlights lighting the
way down the empty road. A uniformed cop with a flashlight
standing at the corner of Cemetery and Church waved Miller
off, making it clear that he wanted Miller to turn left onto
Cemetery and not right as Miller had indicated with his turn
signal. But Miller didn't make the left, just stopped at the end
of Church and sat there, waiting. The cop quickly approached
Miller's truck, showing his impatience in the way he moved.

Miller didn't know the man. Half of the force now was made up of recruits who had been hired after Miller's father had been killed five years earlier. Those who remained on the force, who had once been blindly loyal to Miller's father, were too worried about their jobs these days to ever be of much help to Miller those few times when he could have used it. The police chief the town had brought in to replace Miller's father was as against corruption as a man could get, easily as against it as Miller's father had been for it, a part of it, at the head of it for most of his career.

This cop was wearing a fur-lined leather jacket and a cap with earflaps. It wasn't anywhere close to being enough against this cold. But nothing short of a parka and full-face mask would have been enough tonight. As the cop approached, Miller rolled down his window and felt a blast of cold air rush into his truck. It all but shoved into him with the force of a crowd.

"Road's closed," the cop said. He spoke quickly. It wasn't a conversation opener. It was the conversation, as far as he was concerned.

But not as Miller was concerned. "What's going on?" he said.

"Do you live down this road?"

"No."

"Then I'm going to need you to turn around."

"What happened?"

"You're going to need to turn around and leave."

"Was there an accident or something?"

"Please turn your vehicle around. This is a crime scene, closed to the public."

The cop backed away, giving Miller room to turn. He kept his eyes focused on Miller. Miller nodded and rolled the window up, then made a U-turn, heading east along Cemetery. The next street over was Old Point Road. He turned onto it and pulled over again. Through the woods that separated these two streets, Miller couldn't see the cop cars, just their light show in the trees a block over. Of course this meant they couldn't see him, either. He shut off his motor and killed his headlights and stepped out into the cold.

It grabbed at him right away, hard. The wind was coming from the south. He looked into it, his eyes quickly drying. He tilted his head down, tucking his chin against his chest, and walked into the wind, cutting through the small woods that stood between him and the bay. He always carried a small penlight in the pocket of his jacket. He used it now to find his way. The larger flashlight he kept under the front seat of his truck would have certainly made the going easier, but it also would have attracted attention, which of course he didn't want. After a minute of trudging through the woods, he lifted his head and could see the bay. He wasn't far from it now, just a few yards. The dark water shimmered under the black sky. There was nothing else to see. To his right he could hear cops, their voices but not what was being said. By the way they spoke he could tell that they were talking into their radios, reporting in. He heard the same squawking sounds he had heard back in the warmth of his bedroom, the same cross-chatter.

The woods gave way and he was in the open finally, standing on the edge of the bay. The beach was narrow, only a few feet wide. The sand was filled with rocks and bits of broken shells that crunched beneath his boots. He looked to his right and saw two cops, or the shape of two cops, anyway, standing together. They were looking out over the water, shining their flashlights into it. Miller tried to follow their line of vision but couldn't make out anything but chop. The water was black, except for where it was touched by the flashlights, and then it looked like tarnished silver. So far the cops hadn't seen Miller. He was a good hundred feet from them. But he needed to know what they knew. He needed to know something, anything. He needed specific information to report. And he wasn't going to get it standing where he was. He turned off his penlight and started toward the cops. He didn't want to have come out in the cold for nothing.

Miller closed about half the distance between where he

had exited the woods and where the cops stood. But he still couldn't see what they were looking at. Another cop joined them, and then another still. After about a dozen steps along the sand, Miller stopped. The last cop to arrive had what looked to be a handheld floodlight. He shook it several times, then whacked it with the heel of his palm, once, then again. The other cops gathered around him, and it was then that the light finally came on, casting a clear circle of bright white at their feet. The other cops stepped back, opening a clear run to the water, and then the light swung very quickly down the beach, the wide beam cast finally out over the bay.

Miller could see it then, see what it was they were all looking at. A body was floating facedown. It was about fifty feet from the shore, maybe less. The tide was low, and the body wasn't moving. Miller figured that its feet must have dragged along the bottom as it drifted into shallow water. He imagined the toes acting as anchors. The body probably wouldn't be coming closer, or going out any farther, for that matter, not till the tide shifted and the water got higher.

Of course who it was floating in the freezing-cold bay Miller didn't know. Nor did he know if it was a male or a female, and that mattered, that much he would need to report. He wanted to show himself to be helpful, someone not to overlook, and the news that someone had been found floating in the bay wasn't going to do that. Anyone with a scanner would know that much. Anything more than that the police would sit on for as long as they could, but not out of courtesy to the victim's loved ones. There was a bigger agenda in play here.

Miller waited, watching. He was shivering, his teeth starting to chatter, but he wasn't going to leave now. He was close enough finally to hear not only voices but words. He heard one cop wonder if they should call the fire department to help retrieve the body. Another asked if the town had a diver on call, someone with a dry suit who could just wade out. Then a third cop pointed out that half the kids enrolled at the college were marine biology majors. They'd have wet suits, and the college was less than a mile away. Another cop, the one who had brought the floodlight, said that Roffman, the chief of police, was on his way, and that policy was to contact the coast guard, which had already been done. There was a station just across the bay. Someone would be there in fifteen minutes.

A short while went by and nothing much else happened. The cops waited, stomping their feet against the cold, their hands in the pockets of their coats, their shoulders held up as far as was possible. No one said much of anything, and all the radios were now silent. Miller wondered if the cops had been able to determine from where they were standing if the dead body was that of a man or a woman. Young or old? Maybe the clothes, maybe the hair would give it away, something. After a moment Miller decided that it was probable that at least one of those cops knew him, had in the past worked for his father. Certainly if Miller walked up to them and was recognized, he would be taken away, but not without first learning more, if he was lucky. He decided that it was worth the shot, easily a better thing to do than just standing around in the freezing cold, too far away to see anything but the floating body and five bored cops.

Miller started walking toward them. They were facing the water, standing in a cluster, but it didn't take long for one of them to turn his head. Maybe he had heard Miller, or caught sight of him from the corner of his eye, or maybe just sensed him out there in the dark, sensed his motion. For whatever reason, the cop turned suddenly.

"Hold it," he said. There was anger in his voice. Not authority but anger. Miller knew then, coming out of the dark as he was, that he had startled the cop, caught him off guard. The man's anger was a reaction to the fear that had cut through him like a shot. Miller had seen that a hundred times in his life, seen cops covering up their emotions in that exact way.

The other cops turned too. Several flashlights cut into Miller's eyes at once. Miller just stood there with his hands held out from his side. He didn't take another step.

"Anything wrong?" he said. He made sure the tone of his

voice was even and calm. He wanted to appear as innocent as possible. It was necessary despite the fact that he was innocent, more or less. *Just a man out for a stroll, nothing to worry about. What's all the fuss? No, I love this cold, are you kidding?*

But the cops weren't swayed by his act. Miller had snuck up on them, had strayed into a crime scene, and not just any crime scene. They acted quickly, three of them moving toward Miller. Without hesitating they led him away from the water's edge. There wasn't any woods here to climb through, just an open parking lot, empty except for patrol cars. Miller turned his head to look over his shoulder as they escorted him away, trying to see what he could, but there was no light on the body now. He could barely see the shape of it in the water. Once they reached the parking lot, the cops led him to the nearest patrol car. None of these men was someone Miller knew all that well, certainly not well enough to expect anything close to favorable treatment. None of these men had worked for his father, had come to the Miller home for meals, had been there to congratulate Miller when he won his scholarship to Michigan.

At the patrol car Miller was questioned. He understood that the cops' first reaction would be to assume that Miller had something to do with the body floating in the bay. Maybe he was returning to the scene of the crime, feigning innocence, just to mock the police. Their need for a break in this case would lead them to such a wild hope. The cop who asked the most questions was in his thirties, not that much older than Miller himself. His name was Spadaro, and he had been hired three or four years ago. It was hard for Miller to keep track, though he tried to, tried to keep all the players and their stats straight in his head. It seemed important to him, worth the effort required.

Spadaro pressed Miller to explain what he was doing out here, at this time of the night, in this weather. Did Miller live around here? Miller calmly replied that he took this walk every night. He didn't live far, and he liked this beach, liked that it was secluded. The Shinnecock didn't seem to mind that Miller came here. As for the cold, he didn't much mind it, and anyway there wasn't much he could do about it, was there? He needed his walks, they cleared his head. He thought about mentioning something about doctor's orders but stopped himself. Keep it simple, don't say too much.

Of course everything Miller said was a lie. He never took walks on this beach, or any beach, for that matter. Walking on sand was particularly hard on his bad knee. And he hated the cold, despised winter. He spent his evenings thinking of summer nights, the ones past and the ones to come—open windows and swelling curtains, crickets chirping, the sound of cars on Hill Street. He craved all that. But Miller wasn't really worried about being found out. He wasn't worried that any of the early suspicions the cops had about him would lead to anything serious. He had spent all day working at his tiny shop on Main Street. Regulars had come and gone at the rate of five or six each hour, had seen him, spoken to him, handed him their money. After work he had gone for drinks at Barrister's, and plenty of people had seen him there, seen him leave with Abby. Then of course there was Abby to back up what he had done with his time after that, and the cop watching the perimeter who had seen Miller drive up just moments before. No, he wasn't worried about this going too far. He was covered. And, besides all that, he was the son of a cop, had grown up in the presence of cops. He could read one of them better than he could read anyone. He had already seen in Spadaro's body language the exact instant when hope of a lucky break fled from the man.

Soon enough Spadaro ran out of questions. Or maybe it had become clear to him that Miller wasn't going to run out of answers. He left Miller at the car, under the watch of another cop, and went to confer with his colleagues standing near the water's edge. Miller waited, listening to the conversations around him, to the squawk of the radio. He listened for anything that would tell him more than what he had seen. But he heard nothing. His face was numb now, and he knew that the inside of the car by which he was standing would be warm, that relief from this brutal cold was so close. But he tried not to think too much about that. He imagined instead the nights he craved, those bouts of humidity that come and stay around for a few days in August, hanging heavy over the town, unaffected even by the ocean breezes. He wondered if Abby would be around next summer, if she would still be in his life, coming to see him after work and lying beside him, her skin silky and cool. He imagined beads of sweat collected on the bridge of her small nose, and how her hair, after a late night shower she had taken to cool off, would smell spread across his clean pillowcase.

Another car pulled into the lot then, its headlights swinging toward Miller. He turned his head so he could not be recognized. When the light passed, he looked and saw that this car was an unmarked sedan, the same make and year as the patrol cars. Roffman, the new chief of police, was arriving on the scene. Miller watched as the car came to a stop and Roffman climbed out from the passenger seat. A man of average build, Roffman was in his midforties. At first glance, there was nothing very distinctive about him, nothing threatening or, for that matter, inviting. Miller's father would have summed Roffman up in one word: *administrator*. But Miller knew better, knew the man to be more than he appeared to be. Roffman was a politician first, good and getting better every year, and a cop second. Compassionate human being was somewhere much farther down that list.

Another cop climbed out of the sedan. A woman, from behind the wheel. Miller knew her. Her name was Barton, and she had been the last cop hired by Miller's father, back when the man was under investigation by the FBI and trying to give his department at least the appearance of being something less than corrupt. But her appearance here now was too little, too late. Miller's chances of learning anything more had disappeared the moment Roffman arrived.

Spadaro hurried up from the beach to meet Roffman. He must have seen the headlights. At first it looked like Spadaro was going to be successful in leading the chief past Miller, which was clearly his intention. It wouldn't be good—for anyone—for the chief to see Miller. But Roffman spotted

him just as he reached the end of the parking lot. He stopped
short, fifteen feet from Miller, regarding him the way he
might regard a stray dog that had wandered into his yard
with the intention of digging a hole.

"Christ. What is he doing here?" Roffman said.

Spadaro answered that Miller had walked into the crime
scene from somewhere down the beach—or at least Spadaro
started to say that. Roffman cut him off mid-sentence.

"Get him out of here. If he shows his face again, arrest
him."

"Yes, sir."

"This isn't amateur night." This wasn't said to Spadaro but
to Miller. Roffman waited a moment more, staring at Miller,
then finally turned, sharply, and continued toward the shore.
To say anything else would have been to give Miller more attention than he deserved, the exact kind of attention the kid
desired. He was just a wannabe, a busybody, and Roffman
wasn't worried about him. There were plenty of ways to handle him if he got out of hand. His past could revisit him. All it
would take was an accusation, or the threat of one. The kid
would crumble, run. But that fuck the kid worked for sometimes, he was a different story. He was a problem, something
to worry about, especially now that a family had hired him. If
it came to it, Roffman would send him a message by locking
up his little scout, kill two birds with one stone. If it came to
it, which it looked now like it had.

Roffman reached the beach and started down it. Barton
was following behind, but Spadaro stopped her.

"Take Miller to his car and make sure he leaves the area,"
he said. "If he doesn't go or tries to come back, cuff him and
take him in. Understand?"

Spadaro hurried after Roffman then. He didn't look back
at Miller. Together, the two men headed down the beach.
The cops waiting at the water's edge all turned to face them.
The floodlight came on again, aimed at the sand, a circle of
light as white as a summer moon.

Barton led Miller to the unmarked sedan. He didn't make
her say anything to him. He'd pushed his luck as far as it

would go. They reached the car and got in, Miller in the back seat, like a criminal. But he didn't care. *The warmth.* Barton sat behind the wheel. Miller told her where his truck was, and she started toward it, passing a few hundred feet later the cop's standing point on Cemetery Road. She made the turn onto Old Point Road and parked at the curb, bumper-to-bumper with Miller's pickup. She yanked the column shifter up and turned her head to look at Miller through the cage that separated the back seat from the front. She spoke over her shoulder to him.

"You working?" she said. "Or has this just become a habit of yours?"

"I was just out for a walk."

Barton smiled. She was twenty-seven, maybe twenty-eight, Miller wasn't sure. She certainly wasn't over thirty. She was tall, fair-skinned, slight even in her cold-weather jacket. Miller couldn't recall ever seeing her outside the company of Roffman. She was his driver whenever he left Village Hall on business, and at the end of the day, when it was time to go home. During the day, while in the office, she was his assistant, rarely pulling any other duty. There were rumors about the exact nature of their relationship, but Miller wrote most of those off as nothing more than the griping that usually occurs whenever a woman is brought into what has for too long been a boys' club. Still, Barton *was* attractive, had a natural beauty, didn't wear a lot of makeup, didn't try to call attention to herself, not that she needed to. Her hair was brown and straight, done up in a bun when she was in uniform but down the one time Miller had seen her in civilian clothes. If there was anything more to Barton's relationship with the chief, Miller knew he couldn't really blame the man, though maybe she had some explaining to do. Barton had a smile that was quick and warm, even when she was using it to let you know that she knew full well that you were lying, like now. Few men could resist a killer smile.

"You're out here for that friend of yours, aren't you?" Barton said.

Miller didn't answer. Instead, he asked, "Is it a man or a

woman out there floating in the bay?" It was what he had come out into the cold to learn.

"Tommy," she half-scolded. She had always treated Miller in a sisterly kind of way. She had stood beside him at his father's funeral five years ago. She'd only been on the force for a few months then but had already become like family. Two years after that she'd stood beside him again, when his mother was buried. In the years that followed there really hadn't been a day when Miller didn't think of her. And there hadn't been a week when she didn't call to check up on him.

"Just tell me, Kay."

"Why do you care?"

"It's a man, isn't it?"

"You should go home. I mean it."

"I just need to know."

"So you can impress your friend?"

Miller nodded.

"Then he isn't really your friend, is he?"

"You shouldn't believe everything you've heard about him. He's not what a lot of people think."

Barton waited a moment, watching him. "So what is it with you two anyway? I mean, the real story."

Miller ignored the question. "It's a young guy back there. Isn't it?"

She nodded. "Yeah, that's what they say."

"How do you know?"

"They called the chief on the phone and told him. They didn't want it going out over the radio."

"No, I meant how do *they* know. The body is a pretty good distance from the shore. Facedown, from what I can tell."

"There was a phone tip. An anonymous woman. She said there was the body of a young man floating in Shinnecock Bay. Units went looking and spotted it."

"That's weird. I mean, how did she know it was a young man if it's offshore?"

"That's what I was wondering, too."

"Were there phone tips before? For the other two?"

Barton shook her head, but he knew she was refusing his question, not answering it.

"That's all I can do for you, Tommy. Anyway, you're going to want to stay out of this. Roffman is under a lot of pressure. The mayor, too. There are people who don't want this to get out, who are afraid tourists will think twice about coming out here if they're worried about ending up face-down in a bay. Do yourself a favor, okay? Stay out of this."

Miller reached for the door handle. He needed to call this in, needed to do that now. "Thanks for the tip. And for the advice." He yanked at the handle but the door was locked. There was no way to unlock it from the back seat. He looked at Barton through the metal screen. She was still looking over her shoulder at him. He looked at the side of her face.

"I mean it, Tom. Stay clear of this. Tell your friend, too. This is serious business."

"We've always thought so. Let me out now, Kay."

"Don't like being locked up?"

"Not really."

She nodded and pressed a button in the console in her door. The back door unlocked.

"See you, Tommy."

"I'll see you, Kay."

Miller swung the door open and got out, hurrying to his truck. He climbed behind the wheel and started the engine for the heat. Barton made a U-turn, then stopped, the sedan standing alongside Miller's truck. Miller waved to her. She nodded, then drove off.

He dug his cell phone from the pocket of his field jacket and punched in a number, then waited. It was late, but there was nothing he could do about that. Three rings, and then a female voice, low and breathy, the accent French. It was hard for him to tell if he had awakened her; she always sounded a little dreamy, a little far away.

"Hello."

"It's Miller. Is he there?"

The female voice said, "One moment," then disappeared. A few seconds later Miller was listening to a male voice.

"Yeah."

"They found another body," Miller said.

"We heard."

"It's the same as before, pretty much. Except this one didn't just wash up. They found it because some woman called in an anonymous tip."

There was a pause, then: "You're certain about this?"

"Yeah. What do you want me to do from here?"

"Nothing."

"I can help."

"Don't need it."

"I know the family has hired you to find their kid. I'm trying to be a good citizen here. I didn't have to tell you any of this."

"Call Reggie tomorrow. He'll give you the usual hundred bucks."

"I don't want snitch money. I want to help you guys."

"If you want to help, do what you can to lose my number. Understand?"

The line went dead. Miller closed his cell phone and looked out his window. Through the bare trees he could see the bay, a dark void in the expanse of dark night. The Long Island horizon was low, just so much sky over so much water. Beyond the bay was a narrow strip of land. Dune Road. It separated the bay from the Atlantic. Fantastic homes were found there, and secluded beaches. Why not toss the body into the sea? Miller thought. At the right time, it would be carried far away, wash up somewhere else, if at all. The two bodies before this one were also found in bays. Why?

Miller stared at the string of greenish lights that ran the length of Dune Road. Streetlights, but from where he sat, a long bracelet of pale emeralds spread out unevenly against a soulless black. A thing of beauty, thin, frail, not much really against so much dark. The only sign of life, aside from the cops back at the shore's edge, and Miller's own breathing.

Now he thought of the girl waiting for him in his bed. Her warmth, her smells, her breath. There was nothing more he could do here, nothing more that could be done tonight. So he started back toward home, vents blowing heat against his legs, as he drove rehearsing in his head what he would say and what he would not say.

A late moon was rising in the northeast, in the sky over town, cresting the long line of trees. It added very little light to the night.

TWO

Deacon Kane drifted toward consciousness, or what passed for it, at eight in the morning. He had arrived at Meg's bayside house the evening before, after dark, just to be safe, and they had gone through two bottles of Merlot and then some vodka before falling into bed together sometime around midnight. An hour or so later, drunk and exhausted, Meg slipped into a deep sleep beside Kane. He remained awake, however, listening to the wind pressing against the long windows of her home and feeling the alcohol rush frantically through his bloodstream. He eventually gave up altogether on the idea of sleep and sat up in the dark, moving to the edge of the mattress so he could look out the window nearest to the bed. Meg and he only slept together in a small room at the front of the house, never in the bedroom at the back, the bedroom Meg shared with her husband. The reasons for that were obvious to Kane.

A hundred feet below the bluff on which the house stood lay Great Peconic Bay, and Kane had no choice when he couldn't sleep but to sit and stare at it. Sleeplessness as such wasn't at all uncommon for him; it plagued him often enough both here and back at his dingy two-room apartment in town. But at least when he was here, when Meg reached her limit and passed out beside him, he had something to study other than an empty parking lot—the view outside his own bedroom window—as he let his mind drift toward his grief. He was never all that far from it anyway. It might have been better if he'd had a different view outside her window, anything but water, but there was nothing he could do about that. So he had sat there for a while, silent in the dark, watching the late moon rise in the northeast, grieving.

Kane had eventually climbed in beside Meg again. Her breath was both sweet and foul. It and the wind outside was all he could hear. Gradually he found sleep. This took awhile, though, coming finally out of nowhere. When he awoke again, his head aching, he was alone in the bed. It was morning, and the five tall windows that ran the length of the room let in the bright morning. The comforter that covered Meg's bed was white, as were the walls and ceiling, all flawless white. The floors were highly polished pine. The light from outside seemed to almost echo around the bare room like a harsh noise.

Kane rose slowly. He was thirty-five, certainly not a kid anymore. But he felt old. His lower back ached. The mattress was too soft, but you take what you can get. The only exercise he got lately was fucking Meg, and though that wasn't without its demands, it wasn't enough to keep him from feeling that he was growing weaker and weaker in this exile of his. What he had thought would be a few months of wandering had somehow become two years—two years—with nothing much to show for it but an attachment to a woman he could never have, and ever-increasing debt. He hadn't written a word since he started teaching, hadn't thought much of anything but his need for Meg and everything he'd lost.

He found his jeans and sweater and pulled them on. The morning sun did nothing at all to warm the room. It was as cold now as it had been during his dark vigil. Kane stood, felt the floorboards beneath his feet. His shoes and socks were elsewhere, but where exactly he wasn't sure. The house was an old cottage that had over the years been built onto, the latest addition having been made some fifty years ago. Drafts could be felt coming off the windows and, in some places, through the walls. The place, covered in dark, weathered cedar shingles, looked sturdy enough from outside. Kane never would have expected such chill could be found inside a bayside house like this. They were all, he had imagined, as tight as ships. And it was worth, what, millions? But then this unusual and sudden cold seemed to have the ability to find its way to wherever it wanted to be, find its way in and stay.

Kane paused to look out his window once more. It was *his* window now, or so he felt. You spend hours alone with something in the dark and it becomes yours. This window, Meg, his grief. The bay reflected the overcast sky, its gray surface looking like ice. But Kane knew it wasn't frozen over. Every morning, in the time he'd been coming here whenever Meg's husband was out of town, the old man who lived next door made his way down from his back porch to the beach below. There he'd rush into the water—fall and spring, summer and winter. The old man was lean and tall, balding, with silver hair and beard, and he took his morning dip without fail, as far as Kane could tell. The last few days, despite this arctic cold, the old man held to his routine. And this morning, not at all to Kane's surprise, the old man was out again.

Kane watched him emerge onto his back deck and make his way down the long stairs to the beach. He was wearing a white terrycloth bathrobe and unlaced boots. Once on the beach, the old man walked to the water's edge and threw off the robe and stepped out of the boots. Kane watched this, waiting. He muttered, "You've got to be fucking kidding me." And then there it was, the old man rushing into the water, plunging into it with a dive. He climbed out as fast as he had jumped in and hurried into his robe and boots. Then he headed back up the stairs to his deck. Kane watched till the old man was back inside his home. He wouldn't have believed it if he hadn't seen it. He *had* seen it and still didn't believe it.

Of course this only reminded Kane of his grief. He hadn't gone near water since his son died four years before. Meg's place was the closest he ever got to it. And that wasn't without its cost to him. But of course his child wasn't the only one to have died that way, to have drowned. It wasn't his grief and his alone, he knew that, though the knowledge helped him little.

Just two weeks before, while Kane was asleep in his dingy apartment in town, and Meg was beside her husband in the other room, that very same old man had, during his morning plunge into the bay, found the body of a dead young man. When Meg had phoned Kane later at the college to tell him about this, her first concern was that this would be big news and that the cops and reporters would be camped out, as it were, around her place, maybe even for days. Kane would have to stay away if that was the case; they were that cautious. Meg's husband had been home for a week, longer than was normal, and would be leaving that afternoon for five days. Both she and Kane craved each other, deeply, and people nosing around would mean they would have to wait. It seemed intolerable. But in the end, the cops had come and gone quickly, very quickly, and no one except a curious neighbor or two came around. Even that only lasted into the afternoon. Kane showed up after dark, a little haunted, and threw himself into Meg, into the pleasure of too much drink and her soft flesh. They tore at each other for hours. The next morning, watching the water, seeing it differently, Kane had observed as the old man came out for his morning swim, though this time he entered the water with obvious trepidation. According to Meg, the old man hadn't seen the body but instead bumped into it shortly after diving in. This was back during the long Indian summer; the water was not yet freezing, and the old man's swim would have been much more leisurely than the ones Kane had seen of late.

Kane left the front room then and entered the kitchen. The glare wasn't going to be any better here, he knew that, but this was where he would find Meg. She painted there, had two easels set up at all times, two paintings going at once. As he entered she was standing beside the butcher block island in the center of the open room, her back to the wide window, the morning sun on her shoulders, a steaming mug of tea in her hands. She was wearing a fisherman's sweater and white socks—nothing else. The sweater hung to the top of her thighs, barely hiding her ass. Normally she spent her mornings undressed, sipping her tea with the sun on her as she looked over the work she had done the day before. She claimed there was something about being naked at the start of the day, being naked in front of her work. It both focused and opened her mind, she told him. He didn't care why; he liked the look of her, her short red hair alive in the morning light, her pale skin just a little golden. But these last two mornings, when Kane emerged from the front room, he had found her in one of her husband's ratty sweaters. Oddly enough, that was somewhat more distracting to Kane than the sight of her in all her glory. He wasn't really certain why but didn't much care.

She didn't look at him at first. This was her time to be silent with her paintings, to look at them with rested eyes and a mind not too far removed from the landscape of dreams. Kane sat at the small dining table, just inside the room, and watched her as she stood in profile to him. She was tall and thin, built like an Olympic swimmer—long legs and lean arms, a sleek torso and flat stomach. She had that kind of refined look that comes with having money, or marrying into it. She was tired now, that was obvious. A morning person by habit or necessity but not by nature. By nature she was a night person, like Kane was. A drinker, yes, but not big on parties or get-togethers. Her husband dragged her to those, or used to. He liked to be with his friends, maybe to show her off. Kane could understand that. But she said that most of her husband's friends were awful people. She was an awful person, too, but at least she knew it and didn't impose it on others. She preferred to be at home, with her work, or at least within sight of it, within reach of it. If there was no paintbrush in her hand, then there was a glass of wine, sometimes, just now and then, a joint when she needed to get away from herself; the kind of away that leaving the house or taking a walk wouldn't bring her.

She watched her two paintings now, looking from one to the other, trying to decide which one, in her words, needed her more. Holding the steaming mug in her right hand, she reached up to rub the heel of her left hand into her eye, to further wake herself up. Her arm up like that raised the sweater enough for Kane to glimpse her bare ass and tufts of her strawberry blond pubic hair. His heart rushed then, his throat tightening. In his gut, he felt a dozen fists. More than anything now, he wanted her.

She let her arm down, the sweater covering her lower half again. Kane spoke, breaking the silence. "I was thinking about calling in sick today, hanging out. What do you think?"

She smiled. She knew what he meant by "hanging out."

"I need to get some work done this morning. And you need to go to work. We can 'hang out' all you want later."

"I had a bad night again, that's all."

"I'm sorry."

"There's only one more week left to the semester anyway. I think the damage is done, missing-classes-wise, don't you? What's one more day?"

"I really need to get work done. I don't work well with you staring at me the way you do."

"I could wait in the other room."

"I don't work well with people waiting for me, either. You need to go to work, Deke."

Kane said nothing to that.

"You weren't able to fall asleep last night?" Meg asked.

"No."

"Sorry I passed out on you. You tired me out."

"It's okay."

"So what did you do?"

"What do you mean?"

"Last night, when you couldn't sleep."

"I just sat up."

Meg nodded, her eyes on one canvas now. She was zeroing in on which one needed her, getting ready to approach it.

"You should go into the other room when that happens," she said. "Watch TV, listen to music. Do anything but sit there and look out at the water. I mean, there's no point in torturing yourself."

"I'm not torturing myself."

"I didn't mean it that way, Deke. Maybe you should see someone. A doctor or something. Talk about it."

"Talking makes it worse."

"It shouldn't."

"It's got to break soon, you know. That's what I keep thinking. It's got to end soon."

"It's been a bad few years for you."

"It hasn't been all bad."

"That's sweet of you. But you still have to go to work."

"You're a hard woman."

"To know me is to love me."

She was ready, ready to begin, knew what needed to be done. She looked at Kane then, as if from a trance. Her mouth dropped open immediately at the sight of him.

"Oh my God," she said.

"What?"

"Your face."

"What about it?"

"Did I do that?" Her hand rose to her mouth then, to hide a sheepish smile she couldn't suppress, or didn't want to. She turned, facing him fully. Kane saw her pubic hair. She shaped it for swimming but let what remained grow full. He'd seen this, what, a hundred times now, maybe more? *And still, this thrill.*

"Did you do what?" Kane said.

She walked toward him, the mug of tea in her right hand. It was filled to the top, so she moved carefully, holding it away when she reached him. She stood over him and placed the fingers of her left hand under his chin, lifting his head up a little to get a better look at the four fresh scratches on his face, long ones running from cheekbone to jaw.

"You don't feel that?" she said. "Doesn't it sting?"

"What?"

"I must have scratched you last night."

"What?"

"I must have scratched you."

"How bad?"

"Bad enough."

"Shit."

"I don't remember doing that."

"Let me see."

Meg moved aside so Kane could stand. He walked to the small bathroom on the other side of the kitchen and looked at himself in the mirror over the sink. He saw four long marks running right through the stubble. The cuts were bloody, shiny in the bright morning light. Meg came in and stood behind him.

"Shit," he said again.

"Sorry." But she wasn't, not really. By her tone he knew she was more amused than ashamed.

"This isn't good, Meg."

"I really don't remember doing that. And obviously neither do you."

"I'm supposed to go out like this?"

"No one will care."

"Yeah, says you."

"Wear them like a badge. Don't give a shit."

"Jesus, Meg. People will think I'm a rapist."

"You were close enough to it last night."

"This isn't funny. I can't go in, not like this."

"What?"

"I can't teach looking like this. I'm going back to sleep."

"I need to be alone to work, Deke."

"You won't know I'm here."

"I will, though."

Kane ran some water and washed his face. He could feel the stinging now. When he was done he dried his face, careful around the scratches, and then his hands. He took one last look at Meg's handiwork, looked at her in the mirror, and walked back out into the kitchen.

She followed him, but not closely. He glanced over his shoulder at her. She looked worried, even a little bothered. But Kane knew it was more than the loss of privacy in which to work that was bugging her.

He stopped and turned to her. "Just cut me some slack today, okay, Meg?"

She opened her mouth to speak but said nothing. She was like a mother uncertain what to do with a child who didn't want to go to school. Kane turned again and headed toward the bedroom. He didn't look back.

"You curl up into a ball too easily, Deke," she said to him as he walked away. "Every little setback just knocks you down. I don't think that's good."

"I just need some sleep, Meg. That's all this is. You won't see me all day, trust me."

"Don't you have to call someone and let them know?"

"My students will figure it out. I think they know the drill by now."

"Deke—"

He closed the door and sat on the edge of the bed. He barely noticed the cold now, or the glare, for that matter. He didn't look out the window but down at the palm of his hands. What was the line? *The useless things these hands have done.* The last thing he needed was to see the water, to be reminded yet again. He knew Meg was right. Of course she was right. But being right, knowing what was right, well, that didn't really help matters any. He'd come back to his alma mater to teach when the money ran out, when he had found it impossible to put words onto paper. This was what, his fourth semester now? *Four semesters, two long years.* He'd missed more classes than he had taught. Too tired, too much to drink, drowning in grief. How long would they put up with this crap? How long before he was fired for cause? Yes, Meg was right, of course she was right. He should go, should show his face, no matter how he felt or looked. It had taken a lot of wrangling to get that job. And what exactly would he do for money when it, too, was lost?

But knowing all this didn't change anything. Kane continued to just sit there, staring at the palms of his hands. If the place had caught on fire, he probably wouldn't have moved. He wasn't sure how much time had passed when he heard the phone ringing in the kitchen. It could have been awhile. His thoughts were a maze, and he had long since gotten lost in them. Meg picked up in the middle of the third ring. Kane listened to her voice, and he knew even before she came to the door that the call was for him.

She opened the door and leaned in. He looked up from his hands. She wasn't a beautiful woman, her face was angular, her blue eyes were too narrow. Still, it was a face most people couldn't help but stare at, men and women. It was like a painting just a few strokes from greatness.

Kane looked at her face and immediately wished she was coming back to bed. He wanted to kiss that face, wanted it to kiss him, to see her with her eyes half-closed as she rocked slowly above him, eclipsing out the rest of the world. But he knew that wasn't going to happen this time.

"It's a guy named Mercer," Meg said.

Kane nodded. "Okay."

"I thought no one was supposed to know you're here."

"Mercer's my department head. I had to give him the number, just in case. He knows to say he got a wrong number if a man answers."

"What else does he know?"

"He's cool."

"Do you want to talk to him?"

"Yeah."

Kane went back into the kitchen and picked up the receiver off the top of the butcher block. The phone was corded; all of the phones in Meg's house were. Her husband was security conscious, and cordless phone calls, he had told her, could be picked up on certain kinds of radios. For whatever reason, that mattered to him.

Kane said, "What's up?"

Mercer had a voice that sounded as if it was coming at you through a barrel of oak. He had been born and raised outside of New Orleans but left there some forty years ago, when he was fifteen, to join the merchant marines. Along the way he had earned a PhD in American literature. He'd been teaching at Southampton College for the past twenty years.

But to listen to him speak, you'd think he'd just come up from the French Quarter maybe a day or two before.

"It's Mercer," he said. "Listen, you need to come in today. You need to come in right now."

"What's going on?"

"There are two cops in your office. Detectives. They want to talk to you."

"What about?"

"Listen, Deke, one of your students is dead. I'm sorry to be the one to break it to you. His body was found last night."

"Jesus."

"Yeah, that's what I said."

Kane's first thought was to ask which of his students had been found, but that really wouldn't have mattered, he barely knew any of them—any of the males—by name. Instead he asked another question. It was one he almost didn't want to ask. "Where'd they find him? I mean . . ."

"Shinnecock Bay."

"Shit."

"The detectives want to ask you some questions. They went to your place but you weren't in. They're waiting for you in your office."

"Tell them I'll be there as soon as I can."

"You might want to get here a little faster than that. Dolan is with them. And he's got that look on his face."

"Great."

"Hurry on in, buddy. I'll try to keep them busy till you get here."

The line went dead. Kane hung up and looked at Meg. She was standing by her easel with a paintbrush in her hand, watching him. She had turned on a small quartz heater. It purred by her now-bare feet. Kane knew that anytime now the fisherman's sweater would be coming off and she would be standing naked in front of her work.

He headed toward the campus in his '94 Wrangler, wondering as he drove about the student who had been found dead. It both was and wasn't hard for him to imagine, someone being there, then not being there ever again. His classes were informal, small, twenty students tops. Yet that didn't help him picture all the faces. He could see many of the girls but only a handful of the men, the ones who spoke up or kept company with the girls who had caught Kane's attention. The rest of his students just slipped into the background, where it was clear to Kane they wished to be. Had he been one of them, the dead boy? Which class had he taken? How often had his and Kane's eyes met? *Had* their eyes ever met?

Kane thought about all this only for a moment or two. Meg's house was fifteen minutes from the college, on the Southampton side of the Hampton Bays line. Most of the time he spent driving away from her house was spent thinking about her, about getting back to her. Kane thought he'd meet with the cops, go to his two morning classes, sit around for his office hours, and then cancel his afternoon classes and catch Meg while she was taking her four o'clock nap in the bed they had left in shambles. There were only a few days left before her husband was to return, and after that Kane and Meg would have to go without each other for an unknown period of time. Meg never knew what her husband's travel schedule would be. He only mentioned when he was to leave next at some point after his return. Meg never inquired about his schedule, pretended not to really care. She was focused on her work. It was her cover. Only after she and Kane had already gone a day or two or three without each other, talking only briefly on the phone, would Kane learn when he would next see her, and for how long; for how many days or sometimes just hours, they would be free, as Meg put it, to make good use of each other. It was a hard way to live, considering she was all Kane had, and all he wanted.

He rode east on Sunrise Highway, then made the right turn onto Tuckahoe Road. He followed that narrow street along the eastern edge of the campus, driving from north to south. He passed the gym, thought briefly of his general lack of activity, then pushed it from his mind. A half mile down

Tuckahoe Road, Kane turned into the parking lot of the Fine Arts building. He parked. His office was in the Humanities wing of the single-story building, but on the other side. He could not see his window from the parking lot. And those waiting for him in his office couldn't see him.

He climbed out and hurried through the cold and entered the building. Dolan was waiting for him inside the door. Kane stopped short, startled at the sight of him. Dolan was slightly built, as tall as Kane, maybe a little taller. He wore bad suits and polished black shoes, was the head of campus security, took his job seriously, made certain everyone knew that he took it seriously. He had held his position for twentysomething years, held it when Kane was a student fifteen years back. Dolan didn't like Kane then, though Kane right now couldn't remember why. First he couldn't remember how he got the scratches, and now this. Was his mind slipping? Too much drink, not enough sleep, grief eating away his gray matter. His first thought was that it had been a run-in over something Kane had written about Dolan in the college newspaper, something meant to be funny, something that *was* funny, that everyone but Dolan thought was funny. But no, wait, it wasn't that. It didn't start there. There was a small stone outbuilding behind the gym, out by the skeet shooting range. It had been a chapel, back when the college was a working plantation a few hundred years ago. It was abandoned, off limits. Very few students even knew about it. Kane used to go there with girls, sneak in with them. Break in was what Dolan had called it, slapping Kane with a semester of probation. Then the article came. *And still, all these years later, Dolan unwilling to forget.*

Dolan's eyes went straight to the scratches on Kane's face. He let his stare linger there, taking this chance to let his disdain show. *Never miss a chance to do that, you old fucker,* Kane thought. Then Dolan turned and led Kane down the hall, as if Kane didn't know the way to his own office. He saw that his door was open. When he was near enough to see into it, he glimpsed the two men waiting inside. Across the hall was Mercer's office. Kane glanced toward it, maybe a little panic in the way his head turned, with a snap. Had Dolan seen that? The guy had eyes in the back of his head. Mercer wasn't behind his desk. He was sitting on the ragged couch that faced it. He never sat on that couch. It was for visitors. Their eyes met for a moment, and then Kane was ushered into his own office by Dolan. Dolan pulled the door closed and stood beside it like a guard, his arms folded.

Kane remembered the article now. While he was a student the college had become part of the Long Island University system. The position of college president had been vacated and replaced by a chancellor. Kane had quipped that it was a good thing that the "little man in the bad suit" hadn't gotten the position because one fanatical chancellor in human history was enough.

Kane's office was small, barely enough room for the desk and two chairs and bookshelves that lined two of the walls, let alone four grown men. Without enough seats to accommodate them, they stood—Kane just inside the door, Dolan behind him, and the two detectives in front of him, beside Kane's desk. They stood with their backs to the single window, their gray overcoats blending nicely with the gray sky beyond. The detectives introduced themselves. Ligowski and Donahue, both in their fifties, both healthy-looking men. They could have been undertakers, by their dress and their manner. Still, Kane knew they were cops. They had that air of authority, of no-nonsense courtesy. Ligowski had a round face and large head covered with short salt-and-pepper hair. Donahue had a thinner face and a small mouth with slight lips. Deep creases cut through his pale skin. Maybe a fellow drinker, Kane thought. The room smelled already of three different aftershave lotions. Joining those scents now was the raw smell of Kane's sweat.

Ligowski and Donahue each studied the side of Kane's face as he shook hands with them.

"You're a professor here?" Ligowski started. Donahue removed a notebook from a pocket inside his overcoat and opened it, ready to write.

"I'm an instructor," Kane corrected.

"Sorry?"

"I'm an instructor, not a professor. I only have a bachelor's degree. Technically, I'm a visiting lecturer."

Ligowski nodded. "And you teach writing? Creative writing?"

"And a course called Forms of Fiction. Also, Intro to Film."

Ligowski smiled. "Nice work. And you're a writer, too, right?"

Kane nodded.

"Books?"

"Yeah."

"Published?"

"Yeah."

"How many?"

"Two."

"Working on another?"

Kane said nothing, wondering why the cop cared, unless of course, like so many other people Kane had met, this cop thought he had a story that needed to be told, that he himself couldn't tell, that maybe Kane would be interested in telling for him.

Donahue swung in then. His voice was hoarse. Maybe the cold, maybe too much bourbon.

"We understand that a young man named Larry Foster was one of your students," he said.

Kane remembered the name, but just barely. No face came to claim it. Kane knew that the kid had been in his afternoon writing workshop, though. He could remember that much, and told the detectives that.

"Did you know him well?" Donahue said.

"No, not really."

"What does 'not really' mean?"

"I guess it means I didn't know him at all."

"Did you notice that he had been missing from class the past two days?"

"No."

"Why not?"

"I don't take attendance. And the workshop he's in only

meets on Tuesdays and Thursdays for an hour and a half. And since today's Tuesday . . ." Kane didn't feel the need to complete that sentence.

Donahue nodded, writing something down. It seemed to Kane by the amount of writing Donahue was doing that he was probably writing something more than what Kane had just said.

Ligowski took another turn. "Do you remember seeing him on Thursday?"

"No. I mean, I don't really remember if he was there or not."

Donahue was still writing away.

"Do you remember when the last time you saw Larry was?"

"No." Kane hoped again for a face to place with the name, but still nothing came.

"I'm sorry to be the one to have to tell you this, Mr. Kane, but Larry Foster was found dead last night."

"I know."

"How do you know?" Donahue asked.

"Mercer told me."

"Who?"

From behind Kane, Dolan spoke. "Dr. Armstrong Mercer. He's the head of the Humanities department. I asked him to get Kane on the phone, to make sure he was coming in today." Dolan's tone was that of a man trying to be helpful, till the end anyway, when the subject of Kane's attendance came up. Then he sounded like what he was: a little man with a grudge eager to point out shortcomings. As if Kane's needed to be pointed out to anyone.

"Don't you normally teach today?" Donahue said.

"Yeah, I do. But I was running late."

Ligowski spoke next. His tone changed, he was acting more casually now, as if the official part of their visit had come to an end with the breaking of the bad news. *Just men now, trying to figure out what happened and looking for all the help we can get,* was what he was trying to convey. But it didn't make Kane feel any more at ease.

"We were wondering if you had any of Foster's writings

around your office here, anything that might help us understand him."

"What do you mean? What do you need to understand?"

"It's how we approach cases of possible suicide."

"You think he killed himself?"

"We just need to cover all the angles. You can understand that."

Kane thought about it, then nodded and said, "I don't keep students' writings."

"You have to grade them, don't you?"

"The students hand me their papers, I give the pages to the Humanities office with a work order. From there they go to Office Services, where copies are made for the number of students in that particular class. When I get the copies back, I hand them out to the class and give the original back to the student. From there the student reads aloud and we all make comments as a group."

"Could any of Foster's writings be in the Humanities office, or out being copied?"

"It's possible. I don't know."

Dolan said, "I can check into that for you." Kane had almost forgotten that the man was behind him, listening, watching.

Donahue wrote something in his notebook, something of length. Ligowski was staring at Kane's scratches. Kane waited. It didn't take long at all.

"How'd you get those?" Ligowski said.

Donahue looked up from his pad then.

"It's a long story."

Ligowski smiled. "We always have time for a good story." There was nothing at all friendly about his smile.

"It's nothing, really," Kane said.

"Lady friend, maybe?"

Kane said nothing.

"They look fresh. Were you with her last night?"

Kane hesitated, then said, "Yeah."

"Care to give us a name?"

"No, not really."

"Why not?"

"Because it's none of your business."

Ligowski shrugged, smiling again. "Okay. If you say so. Is there anything more you can tell us about the Foster boy? His mood of late. Maybe his writing was on the morose side, something like that."

"No, not really."

"Not sure who he is?" Ligowski offered.

Kane said nothing. It seemed to him suddenly that the less he said, the better.

"Big class?"

Kane shrugged. "Twenty kids."

"I have a hard time keeping my own kids' names straight sometimes," Ligowski said. "Don't worry about it."

Donahue flipped back several pages in his notebook. He didn't seem all that interested in what Ligowski was saying.

"I was wondering, do we have your right home address?" he asked. "We went by your place this morning but you weren't there."

Donahue found the page he was looking for and tilted the notebook so Kane could see what was written. Kane told him that the address was correct.

"You said you were running late," Donahue said.

"Yeah."

"But you weren't home."

"That's right."

"We were there maybe a half hour ago. We asked your neighbor, and she said she hadn't seen you around in several days. You take off like that, she said, for days at a stretch."

"Yeah, so?"

Donahue shrugged. "Care to tell us where you go?"

"Not particularly."

Ligowski was still smiling. "I believe he goes elsewhere, Donny," Ligowski said. "The French have a word for it, I think, though I'll be damned if I know what it is." He extended his hand. In it was a business card. "Thanks for your time, Mr. Kane. If you think of something that might help us, please don't hesitate to call, okay?"

Kane waited, then took the card without looking at it. Ligowski nodded once, and immediately Dolan opened the door. He held it as the two men filed past and out into the hall. After that Dolan paused, looking at Kane.

The hate was there, so clear. Kane just looked at Dolan. There was nothing at all to say, or so Kane thought.

"You might want to wash before you come in," Dolan said. "You smell of cunt."

Then he was gone, following the detectives down the hall. Kane looked across the hall, toward Mercer's office. But Mercer wasn't sitting on his couch now. He was nowhere to be seen. Kane waited till he heard the door at the end of the hallway open and shut, then left his office and went to the men's room. He ran cold water in the sink and splashed it on his face, then looked at his reflection. The scratches shimmered.

After a moment he started to wash his hands with warm water and soap. As he did this the door opened and someone entered. Kane didn't look to see who it was, but soon enough someone was standing at the sink beside him. Kane didn't need to look to know that it was Mercer. He could tell by the thermos Mercer began to rinse out.

Mercer was almost sixty now, but with the exception of the deep wrinkles in his face, no one would have known that by looking at the man. He was solidly built, had gotten that way by working labor jobs on his summers off from teaching. Sometimes he worked road crews, other times he signed on with a contractor and did construction work. His deep wrinkles were the result of decades of summers in the hot sun, digging ditches or hammering at something. His thick, dark hair always seemed to be in need of a cut, hanging often in front of steady blue eyes. He seldom wore anything to class other than flannel shirts and jeans and work boots, and he carried his papers and books around in a military-style knapsack. But you could get away with that kind of behavior when you'd earned your PhD by the time you were twenty-three, and when your personal life wasn't so obviously set on self-destruct. Still, Mercer wasn't a Boy Scout. His fourth wife, Joanne, wasn't much more than a third his age and had been a student in the MFA program only a few years back. Mercer had been her adviser, and they had gotten married not long after she graduated. The administration looked the other way, if it had even looked at all.

"I think you did well enough in there," Mercer said.

"You could hear that?"

He nodded. "A closed door doesn't do much in this building. Dolan smells blood."

"I've said it before, I'll say it again: the guy's a Nazi."

"He's a clean freak, at least. But people listen to him here."

"That's scary."

"You'll get no argument from me. He wasn't all that fond of the idea of you being hired. You know that. He almost queered the whole thing."

"You know why, right?"

Mercer nodded. "I know your history with him. The guy has no concept of right and wrong beyond what he learned in Sunday school. If he had his way, everyone who wanted to work here would have to submit to a drug test *and* baptism. He's a born-again fool, but you don't want to play into his hands. That'd make you an even bigger fool."

Kane turned off the water. He was still staring at his reflection, not so much at the scratches now as the look in his eyes, the sadness, the despair, always there—except when he and Meg surrendered to their need to collide, and then of course, at least from what Meg has told him, *something else entirely*.

"What are you telling me, Doc?"

Mercer gave his thermos a final rinse, then stepped to the paper towel dispenser beside the sink, tore off a piece, and began to dry the outside of the thermos.

"I know what you've been through. Believe me, I know. But you're going to need to walk a straight line for a while, or at least a straighter one. You're going to have to do that if you want to keep your job."

Kane looked at him. "I take it you've heard something."

Mercer shrugged that off. "I don't need to hear anything.

I've been here almost thirty years. I know how it goes. I've seen it happen before. You're a good teacher, Deke, and the kids like you. But there's more to it than that, and you know it. You know it but you just don't seem to care."

"I care, Doc."

"There's what people say, and then there's what people do. You don't want to end up like Bill Young, do you?"

Kane thought about that. Young was his favorite teacher back when Kane was a student at the college. Young had been his adviser, the first published novelist Kane had ever met. Five novels published, reputation established. Kane was in awe. But then, what, insanity? A desire for chaos certainly. And where was the man now? Teaching at the community college in Riverhead, something like that, last anyone knew. All but slipped off the face of the earth. Not that Kane wouldn't mind that himself, not really, not now. To disappear, from others, from *yourself*. Could a man who never existed really have lost anything? If a tree fell in the woods . . .

"Is it that bad?" Kane said. Young's self-destruction was epic, and more or less common knowledge, out there for all to see. Kane had watched it, had, or so he liked to think, done what he could to stop it, or at least slow it. And, now, here, being talked to the way Young had certainly been talked to, and more than once.

Mercer shrugged again. "Why didn't you tell the cops the name of your lady friend?"

Kane hesitated, then said, "You know why."

"And she's the one who gave you those scratches?"

Another hesitation. "Yeah."

"You don't sound so sure."

"Apparently, there are some holes in my memory regarding last night. Hers, too."

Mercer thought about that. "You might want to stay away from her for a while, Deke. Get a good night's sleep and lay off the drinking. Normally I'd tell you to go home, looking like you do, but you need to finish out the semester right. You know what I mean? You need to show them that you can do it, show them you want to keep this job."

Kane nodded. He heard it all, heard the sense in it. Still, Meg beckoned. It was all Kane could do to think of something other than her.

"Thanks, Doc," he said. It sounded hollow even to his own ears.

"Listen, you're welcome to stay with Joanne and me. For as long as you need. She'd love to keep an eye on you. She worries about you. You know she loved your books. She's read them several times. Loves how you write women."

"That's good to hear. But I'll be fine. I pay enough for my apartment, I might as well use it, right?" Still, he had no intention of going there. It was cold and dark and lonely. There was enough of that inside of Kane, he didn't need his surroundings to be that way too.

"I had to fight like hell to get you this job, Deke. I'd like to see you at least fight like hell to keep it."

"Maybe I should talk to Wilson, let him know I want to do better."

"I think you should just stay out of his sight for a while. It's a matter of attendance now. You won't do yourself any good walking into the chancellor's office looking like that."

"I appreciate this, Doc."

Mercer crumpled up the paper towel and tossed it into the garbage can. "I've got some Old Spice in my office. Why don't you stop by and splash some on."

"Okay."

Mercer looked at his watch. "Time to get to work now."

Kane nodded. "Yeah. Thanks."

Mercer left. Kane waited till the door closed, then tore off a piece of paper towel and dried his face with it. He moved carefully over the scratches, then dried his hands and tossed the damp towel into the trash. He glanced at himself in the mirror again. He looked like all kinds of hell, there was no way around that. But the outside was nothing compared to what was on the inside. He had that much going for him at least. What couldn't be seen was the part of him that wanted—needed—to skip out early so he could slip into bed beside Meg as she napped, naked, dried paint on her hands, calm now that she'd got some work done. But he couldn't ignore what Mercer had said. There wasn't much that Kane could do to earn money; there weren't a lot of people clamoring for his particular skills. A BA from a lesser-known college, two novels soon to fall out of print, this was about all he had going for him.

Before he'd sold his first novel and had been able to write full time, Kane had made a living tending bar. But he couldn't go back to that, couldn't make his living by getting people drunk. That was bad karma. And he wasn't like Mercer. After Kane's year in exile, a year of relative inactivity, just the idea of physical labor was enough to kill him, never mind what *actual* physical labor would do. But aside from that, the East End of Long Island wasn't the place to go looking for a job, any kind of job, not in December. What could he do that would make him enough money to remain living near Meg except teach?

Kane thought of Bill Young again. He could see the man, see him clearly, remember the day he last saw Young, just before he disappeared in disgrace, before they fired him. Kane's own office had once been Young's, and Kane had come there so many times to visit the man, to talk about everything; about books and about women—finding them, lying with them in the dark, then losing them again. Kane had come to that office to tell Young about a woman Kane had met, a woman named Patricia. Months later Kane had come back there to tell Young that Patricia was pregnant and that they would be getting married. Kane had even named his son Will, in tribute to the man who had meant so much to him.

Kane knew right then that he needed to keep this gig. He couldn't bear yet another loss. The first step was, as Mercer had told him, to stay the whole day, to show the administration what it needed to see, to give Mercer something with which to fight for Kane. Still, Meg was there, was in his head, front and center, clouding his thoughts like a bad cold. Kane hadn't lied to the detectives when he told them that was why he had missed classes one day last week, whatever day it had been. He hadn't lied to them about anything. He had nothing to hide, nothing except who Meg was and where she lived. And who could blame him for that? He'd made a promise to her back when they started their affair, a promise meant to keep her from losing everything, the way he had lost everything. No matter what, he would keep that promise. No one—not her, not anyone—should have to lose everything.

THREE

In the village of North Sea, just as the sun began to fall behind the bare trees that bordered the tiny yard behind his apartment, Reggie Clay awoke. Though it was only four-thirty, dark wasn't that far off. On his stomach, his massive arms and legs hanging over the edges of his sagging mattress, Clay watched through tired eyes as shadows collected in the corners of his small bedroom. Night came suddenly this time of year, the twilight leading up to it brief. It took only fifteen minutes for the shadows in the corners of his room to grow in size and begin to spread out across the floor. They moved slowly but steadily at first, like ice melting into a shallow puddle of dark water. Clay, mostly awake but still facedown, watched the gradual transition carefully. He didn't really need to, he'd seen it enough times already. But still he watched. He rarely got to see more than a few moments of sunlight this time of year. It was an occupational hazard, the nature of the business. So he'd take all he could get, even if it was only these few moments of dying light. The first day of winter was less than a week away. The shortest day of the year would be followed by the longest span of winter night. Clay was eager for it to come, to have that day behind him for one more year. He'd felt that way since autumn arrived three months before, since the days started getting shorter and shorter and the darkness of night was about all he ever got to see of the world.

A little before five all trace of blue was gone from the sky outside his window, and the shadows in his corners had grown into the surrounding darkness. Clay finally got up then. He was beat, and there was stiffness in his back from having spent most of the night before sitting behind the wheel of his car. How long since his last day off, he wondered. Fourteen days? Fifteen? He couldn't remember. After seven or eight days, though, did it even really matter? He wasn't looking forward to what awaited him tonight, to the job that needed to get done. But there was nothing he could do about that. He was in motion now, heading yet again toward something he'd be better off not having seen.

He weighed himself first thing, like always. Still two-sixty, still the same solid build, more or less, that he'd had in high school ten years before, when he was a champion wrestler. His size and power were important to him, always had been. First as a bouncer at a bar called the Hansom House, then as a security guard at the hospital. Together his size and power had stopped things before they could even get started. Certainly now they both made this job easier, for the most part, anyway, at least in certain situations. After weighing himself he brewed some coffee, did some push-ups, three sets of fifty, while he waited. Then he drank a cup while standing in his boxers and T-shirt in the kitchen. The linoleum was cold beneath his bare feet, and he knew by this that the weather hadn't ended. Not that he had expected it to. The radio had said this record-breaking cold was going to be around for days. He thought about this as he finished his first cup of coffee, thought of the people, for one reason or another, who were lost in this cold, forced out into it, stuck in it. Then he showered, lingering under the hot stream for longer than usual, and picked out his clothes—dark slacks, a blue dress shirt, plain dark shoes. He only wore a tie when it was absolutely necessary, when he was required to appear in court for a client. But that was seldom enough. He knew, though, that the boy's parents would need to look at him to-night and see a professional, without a doubt a capable man. They would need that even more so now that they were grieving. So it was the least he could do for them, looking the part, particularly since any information he gathered at this point would probably do little to ease their suffering. If anything, in fact, it would only deepen it. He was more certain of that than he was of anything. Five years on this job had taught him nothing else the way it had taught him that.

Usually Sophia was up now, the two of them trying to get ready for work at the same time. But she was covering for a day-shift nurse who had gone on vacation this week, so Clay had the place to himself for the first time since they had moved in together three years before. He wasn't at all accustomed to it, but then again they usually just got in each other's way and ended up bickering, so as strange as it was to be alone now, he didn't mind the freedom of movement and the quiet. Once he was dressed he poured another cup of coffee and sat with only the kitchen light turned on, the rest of the apartment in darkness. Sophia had the bad habit of switching on lights as she entered rooms, and then leaving them on as she exited. It was one of the things they bickered about, one of the many things. Now, though, without her present to turn lights on as she went about getting ready for work, Clay was confronted by even more darkness than he was used to. It closed in on him, or so he felt, crowding him. All he thought about as he sat there was that this coming week couldn't pass fast enough for him.

Eventually he finished his second cup, took it to the sink to rinse it out, and caught his reflection in the window before him. He stared at it for a while. His skin was dark, not as dark as the night sky beyond, but he could see that he came close to blending in with it. His hair was buzzed to the scalp, his head the size of a crash helmet. The nice clothes he had chosen were an attempt at negating this, negating the color of his skin and the fact that he generally filled every doorway through which he moved. As much as his size and the color of his skin were helpful in some situations, in others they were a handicap. He had noticed that people reacted to him differently when he dressed down, those few times in the beginning when he wore jeans and a sweatshirt and sneakers while on a case. This was probably the first thing he learned when he had gotten into this business. A well-dressed black man seemed to have less explaining to do, struck those inclined to be intimidated by such a thing as less of a threat. Clients, cops, the people from whom he needed to get particular pieces of information, they all seemed to let their guard down, at least a little, when he dressed like a bank teller.

Clay looked at his reflection for a moment longer, then eventually refocused his eyes and looked at the nothingness beyond. The night was silky black, drained of all light. There was a thermometer outside the window. He looked it and didn't want to believe what he read. Six below. *Shit*. What he wouldn't give for the phone to ring, he thought, for tonight's job to be called off. He could stay home, stay warm, watch TV. But the local cops would have to do their job for that to happen, and Clay knew all too well that that wasn't likely. No, the family wasn't going to cancel. The need to comprehend what was incomprehensible was a need that overrode the desire to keep out of the cold. It overrode even grief. As much as he wished they would, for their sake and for his, the family wasn't going to cancel. At six Clay put on his winter coat and gloves and hat, grabbed his briefcase, and headed out.

The deli below their apartment was closing up already. Winter hours. Normally Clay picked up something to eat from there for later on but didn't bother tonight. He'd be close to town all night, and anyway, he hoped to be home sooner than later. He climbed in behind the wheel of his silver Dodge Intrepid and followed North Sea Road south to Sunrise Highway, then crossed Sunrise and followed North Main into Southampton. The village was dead, most of the shops already closed for the night. Restaurants were the only sign of life. About every fifty feet along the wide redbrick sidewalks that lined both sides of Main Street stood lighted, six-foot-tall Christmas trees. The town had put them up the week after Thanksgiving. But the trees had remained there for too long now, or at least so Clay felt. A case of too much too soon, and for too long. The season felt tired, played out. Clay rode along Main Street, looking as he went at the shops to his right—the Golden Pear, on the corner of Nugent and Main Street, and next to it a gallery, and next to that the bookstore, cleverly named Bookhampton South. A few doors down from the bookstore was the frozen yogurt place, and next to that, the magazine shop owned by the Miller kid.

Clay slowed so he could get a good look inside. Miller's shop, like the others in town, was closed. But Clay knew that two nights a week Miller stayed late, packing up boxes in the back, preparing the out-of-date magazines to be returned to their distributors. Whenever Miller did that, the light that burned in the back room was visible from outside. But Clay didn't see any kind of light at all tonight coming from inside. He knew by this that Miller was already gone. Miller had a history with Clay's boss, and Clay knew all about it. It was because of this history that Miller felt he had something to prove. He'd been the worst sort of punk when he was younger, but, it seemed, had put all that behind him. He wanted to "be on their team," to help out in any way he could. It had the feel to Clay of the zeal of a crusader at times, of a play for redemption. This was dangerous, Clay thought. They had hired Miller a few times to get information they needed and that the kid could obtain without raising too much suspicion. He did good work, was thoughtful and capable. And, being the son of the former chief, he probably had it in his blood. But that was as far as they had let it go. Both Clay and his boss were in agreement on this. Maybe Clay had wanted to protect the kid, keep him from seeing the ugliness Clay himself had seen in the years since he got into private investigations. Maybe the kid's eagerness clashed with the dread and hesitancy that plagued Clay of late. Or maybe Clay, deep down, just questioned anyone willing to rush into other people's dirty business. Clay hadn't expected things to be the way they were, to have seen the things he'd seen. If he could get out, he would. That would make Sophia happy. But he couldn't, not now, not yet.

Clay hoped to avoid Miller tonight. But with the kid not busy at his shop, there was no knowing where he was now, no being certain that he wouldn't show up. The last thing

Clay wanted was to have to make a scene in front of the family. He wanted tonight to go as smoothly, and as quickly, as possible, to make things as easy for them as he could. He wanted to be on his way before Miller had time to find them.

At the end of Main Street, Clay turned right onto Job's Lane, heading west now. After a block Job's Lane became Hill Street. Clay continued westward. To his left were mansions, to his right smaller, more modest homes, or at least modest by comparison. A mile to the south was the Atlantic Ocean. Clay imagined it, imagined the icy water crashing onto the shore with a roar, receding with a hiss. It was difficult for him to picture anyone willingly walking into that, no matter what their frame of mind. After two miles Hill Street became Montauk Highway and ran along the edge of the Indian reservation. Clay followed that for another half mile, then pulled into a dirt parking lot on the left-hand side of the desolate road. On the edge of that lot was a narrow, two-story building—a bar called The Still. A dozen cars were gathered around it. On the far side of the lot was a red pickup truck. It was Vicki's truck. Clay could see her waiting behind the wheel. The black Infiniti was there as well, not far from the truck. Clay pulled in between the two vehicles and parked.

The driver's door of the Infiniti opened first. A tall man in jeans and a leather jacket over a hooded sweatshirt got out. The jacket looked expensive but his face was unshaved, his short hair mussed. He hadn't looked any better when Clay met him and his wife two days before, when they had come to hire Clay to find their missing son.

The driver's door to the pickup truck opened next. Vicki climbed down, then led her dog, Ginger, out. A purebred bloodhound, Ginger was old, but she moved briskly enough, her tail wagging wildly. Free from the confines of the cab of the truck, she immediately shook her head. Strands of drool went flying. Then she shook her entire body. Vicki held on to the long leash with a strong hand. It had clearly been, for the bloodhound, a long ride out from Huntington.

Clay joined them, shaking hands, patting the dog on its

head. The man in the expensive leather jacket was named Foster. His eyes were bloodshot, a little glassy. He moved stiffly, as if he had only moments before broken from some deep daze. Clay wondered how long the man had been here waiting, sitting behind the wheel of his car, nothing to do but think.

He introduced Foster to Vicki. She was an energetic woman, in her late fifties, Clay guessed. Deep wrinkles lined her face, the result of a lifetime spent outdoors. She had worked for Clay several times before, always showed results. But more than that, she was good with the families, smiled warmly at them, as if to tell them that everything was going to be okay. Clay appreciated having someone like her with whom he could share that particular burden. Tonight Vicki was wearing a long barn coat, jeans, and Timberland boots. A wool cap hid most of her short, graying hair. She shook hands with Foster, then patted the bloodhound on her head to keep her still.

"My wife wanted to be here," Foster said. "But she just wasn't up to it. A doctor gave her something to calm her down."

"She's back at the motel?" Clay said.

Foster nodded. "Her sister came out today to help us out."

"I'm very sorry for your loss," Vicki offered.

Foster thanked her, but it really wasn't much more than an automatic response. He seemed almost spooked, like maybe he wasn't even sure where he was or what was being said to him. Clay wondered if Foster could even feel the bitter cold wind that at times buffeted him.

"Did you bring a piece of your son's clothing?" Clay said.

Foster reached back into his car and retrieved a clear plastic Baggie. He handed it to Clay. Inside was what looked like a T-shirt.

"His roommate said that's what Larry slept in the night before he disappeared," Foster said.

"That's fine," Clay said.

Vicki nodded. "It's perfect."

Clay handed the plastic Baggie to her. She zipped it open

and bent down, holding the Baggie so the bloodhound could smell it. The dog went for it almost hungrily, digging her snout inside and sniffing. Vicki waited patiently till the dog abandoned the Baggie on her own and tore off on the scent. She towed Vicki with her, heading toward the bar, stopping outside its front entrance. Clay and Foster followed, staying a few yards behind. At the doorway the bloodhound paused, sniffing frantically. Then suddenly she tore off again, heading across the dirt parking lot and toward the dark two-lane road.

"She's got it," Vicki announced.

Clay and Foster followed. The bloodhound was tugging hard, straining against her harness. At the edge of the parking lot she paused for only a second, maybe two, before turning to the left sharply. She moved along the shoulder of the road, heading west, toward the college. The campus was only a half mile away.

"So he did head back to his dorm," Foster said. He spoke absently. "That's where he told his friends he was going."

Clay said nothing. He watched Foster, whose eyes were fixed on Vicki and the dog, on everything they did. Foster seemed as much fascinated as he was bewildered. Maybe it was simply the fact that he was following what were most likely the last steps his son had taken. What parent wouldn't react the same? Clay thought.

The bloodhound had her snout close to the ground, following a dead-on course along the shoulder of the road. The cold only made the scent stronger, easier to follow.

"The dog doesn't ever get . . . confused?" Foster said to Clay.

Vicki answered, "No. It's definitely your son's scent."

They covered half the distance between The Still and the campus without the dog's once wavering from her course. There were no side streets along this part of Montauk Highway, no turns that the Foster boy could have made that would have led him easily down to the edge of the bay. To their left was nothing but scrub oak and pine, a barren, sandy area of rough terrain. Not what a drunk would chose to stumble across, Clay thought.

The only turnoff was West Road, still a quarter mile up ahead. That road was unlit but did lead through the reservation to the water's edge. If the cops were right in thinking that the Foster boy had decided to walk to the bay instead of back to the campus, then his trail would certainly veer off there. But if the cops were mistaken, if their theory wasn't much more than wishful thinking, then the dog would continue past West Road. What would happen after that Clay didn't have a clue.

Foster said, "His friends said Larry had had a lot to drink before he decided to walk back alone. Maybe he went for a swim. It was Indian summer here, wasn't it? That's what the lady behind the desk at the motel said."

"It was," Clay told him. The air had been unseasonably warm, nights in the seventies, but the water would have been very cold. The Foster boy would've had to have been very drunk indeed, Clay thought, to have gone for a swim.

"So it could have been an accident," Foster said softly. "He could have gone in or maybe stumbled in or something and drowned."

"It's possible," Clay told him.

"You don't sound all that convinced."

Clay was surprised the man had even noticed the questioning tone in his voice. "It's not that I don't think that could have been what happened," Clay said.

"But?"

Clay didn't answer. He didn't want to say what was on his mind. Not yet, not till he was certain. Foster had come in from out of town, from far upstate. Maybe he didn't know about the other two boys. It would be in keeping with the cops' agenda, Clay thought, for them to have elected to keep Foster and his wife in the dark regarding those facts. And, anyway, aside from all that, if Foster's son *had* gone for a late night swim and simply drowned, then it would not have taken two days for his body to be discovered. Shinnecock Bay was shallow, and clam diggers worked its shores regularly. Add to that the fact that there had been a phone tip by some anonymous woman. Clay and his boss both wondered why someone who had innocently spotted a body floating in a bay would need to remain anonymous. So Clay had plenty of reasons to have his doubts about this being an accident, or, for that matter, a suicide. He knew, though, that now wasn't the time to share such thoughts with Foster.

When Clay didn't answer his question, Foster said, "I just can't believe Larry would kill himself. He was a happy kid, had lots of friends. It just doesn't make any sense to me. None of it does."

They walked on in the cold, covering several more yards in thoughtful silence, before Foster finally said what was really on his mind.

"We're Catholic, you know that, right?"

He didn't say anything more than that. Clay was the son of a Georgian Baptist preacher, but he knew enough about the concept of mortal sin to understand what Foster was getting at.

"We should know something in just a minute," Clay told him.

They were still a hundred feet or so from West Road when the bloodhound suddenly came to a stop. Clay and Foster came to a stop behind her. Clay was holding his breath. The bloodhound sniffed at the ground determinedly, backtracking several times. Then she caught the scent again and guided Vicki across the street. On that shoulder the bloodhound starting making broad sweeping motions, broader than any before. Clay watched this. The bloodhound moved around in circles several times, quickly, almost frantically. Then she barked once, a low, almost mournful bark.

Clay and Foster had remained on the south side of the road. Vicki was waiting, watching the dog carefully, giving her every chance to pick up the boy's trail again. Finally, though, after a long moment, she looked up and said across the empty street, "She's lost the scent, Reggie. It ends cold right here."

"You're sure?"

"Yeah."

"What's that mean?" Foster said.

Clay turned and looked back toward the bar. He didn't say anything at first.

"What does that mean?" Foster said again.

Clay saw no reason not to tell him.

"It means your son didn't walk to the bay, or back to his dorm, for that matter. The only reason for scent to come to a stop like this is that your son had gotten into a car. His trail crosses to that side of the street, so that means whoever stopped to pick him up had been driving west, driving that way." He pointed toward the campus.

"Someone coming from the bar," Foster said. It both was and wasn't a question.

"Yeah, maybe," Clay said. He stopped short, stopped by a sudden thought.

"What?" Foster said.

Clay didn't answer. He didn't see the point in saying aloud what was on his mind, what was to him now painfully clear. Two boys dead, and now a third. Lost for a week, then found floating in a bay. This was a pattern, the start of something, something that would prove to be very ugly, that already was. Clay knew this, felt it like a stone in his gut. His mind went then from that thought to yet another one, a thought no less disturbing.

The cops were wrong, dead wrong—or else lying. Either way, none of this was good news, except for the fact that it gave hope to what Foster was so clearly desperate to hear.

"What!" Foster said.

Clay looked at him. It took him a moment more to find the words, then a moment more to find what it took to speak them aloud.

"Your son didn't kill himself, Mr. Foster. And his death wasn't an accident. Nobody goes swimming in December, I don't care if it is Indian summer or how drunk they are."

Foster said nothing at first. He turned his head and stared at the spot where his son's trail had ended. He stared at it for a while.

Finally, he muttered, "What are you saying?"

"I think someone killed Larry."

Foster looked back at Clay. "You think he was murdered?" He was clearly completely unprepared for this possibility. He stared at Clay with his mouth hanging open. Clay realized then that Foster hadn't allowed himself to come anywhere near considering that his son's death had been anything other than a freak accident. He had been as set on that explanation as the cops had been set on the boy's death having been suicide.

"It's beginning to look that way," Clay said. "I'm sorry. I know this must be hard to hear."

Foster spoke quickly, almost cutting Clay off. "Can you prove that?"

"I don't know."

Foster took a step closer to Clay and spoke softly but firmly. "We can't have suicide as the cause of death on our son's death certificate. My wife is devout. She believes everything the church tells her. It's bad enough that he's dead. But the idea that he's condemned to hell will just kill her. It'll kill her. I'll pay whatever it takes for you to prove that he was murdered. You find out who, and why, and you can name your price."

Clay nodded, but his mind was elsewhere again, on the ugliness that clearly awaited them all, that was right now hiding somewhere in this dark, maybe even somewhere nearby. Someone was killing young men, killing them and leaving their bodies in bays to be found. Clay had never before dealt with anything like that, faced anything like that. It wasn't just the killings that left him chilled, that three had already occurred and more were certain to come. It was the confidence the killer displayed, the apparent carelessness with which the bodies were disposed of. He wasn't trying to hide his crime. He wasn't concerned with that. That implied arrogance, the kind of confidence that comes with repeated success. It also implied high intelligence, a boldness and fearlessness.

Clay now understood why the local cops were doing everything they could to keep all this a secret. The idea of such a monster lurking in the dark would certainly send panic through the town. Clay felt it in himself, felt it moving through him, scurrying up his veins and rushing his heart. It wouldn't be much different for anyone else who knew.

"We bury our son in three days, Mr. Clay," Foster said. "Will you be able to get the proof you need by then?"

Clay looked toward the bar one more time. It was the only place he could think to start. The bloodhound barked again, the sound echoing down the empty road. But then it disappeared suddenly, swallowed up by the winter wind.

"I need to make a phone call," Clay said then.

Kane finished teaching his last class and was back in his office getting ready to leave when his phone rang. It was seven-thirty, the Fine Arts building almost empty. At first he just stood there by his desk, looking down at the ringing phone. He was fairly certain who was on the other end—who else would be calling him here, at this time? He was fairly certain, too, of the reason why she was calling him. It was the only reason she'd have to do so now, and that was reason enough for him to consider not answering at all.

His mind raced then. He figured he could easily tell her that he must have already been on his way when she called. It was no one's fault, what would happen next. He was in the mood for a confrontation—after the detectives and Dolan this morning, after his talk with Mercer, after the dozens of students staring all day at his scratches. He was in the mood for everything to be out in the open now, finally, after more than a year of this. Kane had only one thing in his life that he needed to hide—her—and yet he was tired of it, so tired of hiding. *To have her all to himself, to never have to leave her, to watch her paint naked all day, keep her naked all night.* Quickly enough, though, Kane remembered the promise he'd made to her, and that she'd lose everything if he broke that promise. As much as a part of him wanted to do so, needed to do so, he was bound. And anyway, a confrontation with her husband would not guarantee that Kane would get what he wanted. He couldn't support Meg, and she was used to being supported. His apartment wasn't big enough for two people—not big enough for two people madly in love, never mind two people with an act of such betrayal between them.

But if a confrontation would guarantee that he and Meg would end up together, that she in fact wouldn't lose everything, would he then force such a confrontation, or allow one to happen, maybe by a happy accident, by fate, by purposely not taking an important phone call? Kane really couldn't say.

He picked up the receiver after the fourth ring. He wasn't in the mood for a scene after all. "Hello."

It was, of course, Meg. "I've got some bad news."

"He's back, isn't he?"

"Yeah."

Kane looked out his window, at the pitch-dark night beyond. He could feel the cold coming off the panes of glass. He thought of his tiny apartment, the heat turned down to save money. He thought of walking into it, waiting the hour or so it would take for the place to warm up. "When?" he said. It didn't matter, but he was curious.

"This afternoon, just as I was about to take my nap."

Close call, Kane thought. *Missed chance?*

"Where is he now?" he asked.

"I sent him out to get some Chinese food, so I could call you."

"How long is he back for?"

"I don't know. I'll call you tomorrow, though. I'll send him out for something in the morning."

"If I'm not at my place, I'll be here."

"I know."

"Maybe you could find an excuse to get out and come by. Maybe later tonight. We could warm up my apartment together."

"Too dangerous. You know that."

"I could use to see you, that's all."

"I know. But get a good night's sleep, Deke. You need that more than anything else right now. You don't sleep well here, you've said it yourself."

Kane thought of the view from her window, the expanse of

the bay, like a silent, still void night. He saw himself then staring out the window in her front room, *his* window. He didn't imagine the view out her window, just himself sitting there on the edge of her bed, in the dark. He'd never thought of himself in the third person before, not that he could remember, anyway. He wondered what, if anything, that meant.

"You there?" Meg said.

"Yeah."

"I should go. I have to change the sheets in the front room still, and take a shower. Evidence, you know. But I wanted to call you first. It's a good thing I caught you before you left. That could have been sticky."

"I would have seen his car from the road. I would have kept on going."

"Promise."

"I promise."

"I'll call you as soon as I can tomorrow."

"I'll see you."

She hung up. Kane held on to the phone for a minute, then laid it down on its cradle. He stayed where he was for a while, standing still and staring out his window. Eventually he grabbed his coat and locked up his office and stepped outside. There was nothing else for him to do, nowhere to go but his cramped apartment. He'd make something to eat, he thought, maybe be lucky enough to fall asleep quickly, and to sleep through the night and wake in the morning with no memory at all of his dreams.

He hurried through the cold to his Jeep, starting it, shivering behind the wheel as he gave the engine a moment to warm up. The cold was like a grip clamping around him. The harder it held him, the more he shuddered within it. Finally he shifted into gear and steered out of the parking lot, heading east on Montauk Highway. The road was empty, except for a woman walking a dog, and two men walking shoulder to shoulder behind her, just outside the bar where Kane had gone with a few students one night. Kane followed that road into Southampton Village, to his apartment on Nugent Lane. It was above a secondhand jewelry store, across from the IGA parking lot and around the corner from the Golden Pear, where Kane sometimes had breakfast before class and bought pastries to bring to Meg. Just two rooms, his apartment was narrow, the second half of the top floor. The view from his back room, from his bedroom, was of the large municipal parking lot that stood behind the buildings that lined Main Street and Job's Lane. Kane parked in that back lot, in the spot designated as his by the landlord, and entered through the door at the front of the store. He started up the thirteen steps to his apartment, walking on his tiptoes. His neighbor was an older woman who seemed to believe that all people should live in total silence. He hated that; it felt too much like more hiding. But if not silence, he at least wanted peace, and his neighbor, Mrs. Wright, was more than willing to make a racket when she heard one, or what to her ears was one, so he moved as quietly as he could.

Near the top step, though, Kane stopped short and stood frozen. At first what he saw didn't make any sense to him. His door was open, ajar by several inches. How could that be? He waited a moment, his heart beating fast, staring at the opening. Had he left his door like that? Had it hung open for days? He tried to remember when he had left his apartment. Had he been in a hurry? But he couldn't remember. He could barely think. He continued to stand there and stare, then realized that along with his confusion was the feeling of fear, real fear. Maybe someone was inside.

It was then, with a rush, that Kane remembered the one thing he possessed that he couldn't lose, that no one could ever know about. Suddenly he climbed the rest of the steps and paused at his open door, listening. He heard nothing. He pushed the door open with the back of his hand and peered inside. He saw nothing but darkness. After a long moment he stepped through and into his front room. He found the light switch on the wall and flipped it upward.

Everything looked exactly as he had left it. He was prepared for just the opposite, and not finding that carried as much of a shock as finding it would have caused. He moved through the front room quickly and into the small hallway

that separated that room from his back bedroom. The kitchenette was here, to his left. It, too, was undisturbed. Across
from that was a tiny bathroom. He looked quickly inside.
Nothing. He checked behind the shower curtain. Nothing
again. From there he hurried into the back room and
switched on the light. He had left his bed unmade, the bed-
ding tossed to one side of the narrow mattress. Beside his
bed were several milk crates filled with books. Beside them
was a small TV with a built-in VCR. Everything was just as
he had left it.

Kane checked the closet next. It was hardly big enough
for someone to hide in, but he had to be sure. There was
nothing but his few clothes and some empty hangers. He was
alone in his apartment, he was certain of that much. But still
he didn't feel safe. A chill spiraled up his spine and into his
shoulder blades. He shuddered violently. Someone had been
here. *Someone had been here*. But who? Why? He couldn't
even begin to answer those questions, couldn't come anywhere near reasoning through this. He felt unsettled, riled
up. *Someone had been here*. This was the only thought he
could focus on. He thought of Meg's husband, how Kane
himself was an intruder in that man's house. Could Meg's
husband sense when he came home that another man had
been there? It was all Kane could feel around him. *Someone
had been here, stood here, walked through here*. Kane
pushed those thoughts from his head, as best he could, anyway, and hurried to check on his one valuable possession.
He was safe now, no one was going to jump out at him. This
was now the next order of business. He kept the item in his
bureau and almost didn't want to open the drawer for fear
that the thing wouldn't be there. What would he do then? His
mind was frantic, his heart pounded. But when he reached
the bureau he did open the drawer, quickly. He had to know
that the item was there, that the videotape he and Meg had
made a while back was safe. It was all he cared about now.
He stored the tape among the dozen or so copies of Holly-
wood movies he had bought years ago from a video store
that was going out of business. To camouflage it, he kept

their tape in the slipcase of a movie he believed no one would ever want to watch, let alone steal. Kane found the tape right off, just where he had left it on top of the others. He stood there, holding it firmly, looking at it. Relief washed through him. After a moment he put the tape back, this time at the bottom of the drawer, beneath all the other tapes. Then he closed the drawer and decided to check his front door.

There were scratches on the brass plate of the lock. He didn't remember having seen them before. He shut the door. It closed fine. Then he flipped the deadbolt lock. It just turned freely and then spun back without locking. Kane tried again. The same thing happened. He flipped it several times in a row. Each time the lock sprung back to the open position. Kane was convinced then that someone had busted his lock. But why wasn't anything missing? The only thing Kane was certain of now was that with the lock on his door useless, all hope of getting a much-needed good night's sleep was long gone.

It took Kane a while to even begin to calm down. He'd never felt such a violation before. Of all the things he had lost in his life, none had been taken from him in this way. The idea that someone could have found the videotape and taken it disturbed him deeply. It was all he could focus on now. If that had happened, if the worst had happened, how would he get it back? Where would he even start to look for it, for those who had taken it? What could they do with it? He didn't even want to think of that, or of the trouble it could make for Meg if it fell into the wrong hands.

Kane struggled to control his thoughts, to push the fear out of his head. But it held strong. Eventually he started to think that maybe he should call the police, if not to report the break-in then to at least ask for one of the detectives who had come by this morning and find out from him if his door had been hanging open. He assumed they would have told him if it had been. Weren't they looking for odd, for out-of-the-ordinary? A door ajar was certainly that. So was a busted lock. Still, Kane needed to do something, anything, and calling the police was something, the only something he could think of right now. Kane walked back into his bedroom and was looking at his phone on the table beside his bed, wondering whether or not to go ahead and make that call, when suddenly the phone rang. The sound startled him, and a fresh dose of cold fear burst through him again. He thought quickly of Mrs. Wright on the other side of the paper-thin wall and lunged for the phone, picking it up at the tail end of the second ring.

"Yeah," he said.

"Hello. I'd like to speak with Deacon Kane, please."

Kane didn't recognize the voice. A student, maybe. But not young-sounding enough. And it was a deep voice, with a touch of something Southern in the accent. He'd remember a voice like that, he thought.

"Yeah, speaking," Kane said. "Who is this?"

"My name is Reggie Clay. I'm a private investigator. I was wondering if I could ask you a few questions."

Kane waited a moment. A guilty mind moves slowly. A confused mind moves even more so. The words *private investigator* made Kane immediately think of Meg's husband. But his busted front door also came to mind. The only certainty to come from this confusion for Kane was the fact that he should speak carefully.

"What about?" Kane said finally.

"I've been hired by the family of one of your students, a boy named Larry Foster. I understand you've been informed what happened to him."

"Yeah." He thought he should say something more, something about how horrible the boy's death was. But he didn't. Caution won out over compassion.

"I thought maybe you and I could meet in person," Clay said.

"When?"

"Well, now, if it's convenient. I'm a bit pressed for time. The boy's funeral is in a few days—"

"How did you get this number? It's unlisted."

"From the college. A man named Ed Dolan."

Kane thought about that for a moment, thought about

Dolan, then said, "And you've been hired by the boy's family?"

"That's right."

"The thing is, I've already talked to two detectives this morning. I told them everything I knew."

"Our investigation is independent of the one being conducted by the police. I understand that it's a pain in the ass for you, but it's important for the family that I try to find out everything I can about their son's death. It's important to them that I find out what I can as soon as I can. You can understand that, right?"

Kane thought of his son. He nodded once, even though there was no one there to see it. "Yeah, sure," he said finally.

"Foster was a student of yours, correct?"

"That's right."

"I thought maybe you might know something that could help us put things together. Something the detectives didn't think to ask you."

"I didn't know Larry very well." *Don't even remember which one he was, can't even see his face,* Kane thought. "I didn't even know him at all, to be honest."

"Still, I'd like to talk with you, if I could. I'm right around the corner. I could come by in five minutes. It won't take long."

Kane's thoughts wandered. He couldn't help that. Thoughts of his own son were never that far away. But he didn't want to think of that, to be reminded of his boy, not now, not with Meg on the other side of town, stuck at home with her uncaring husband. Meg's skin, the smell of her hair, the feel of being inside her world, inside her—these things and only these things kept those painful thoughts away, or at least made them close to bearable when they wouldn't leave him be. The last thing Kane wanted was to talk to some private dick about a dead boy he barely knew. The last thing he wanted was to think of someone drowning, of the thoughts that must go through the mind at that moment when reflex takes over and water, against all wishes, against all instincts, is drawn into the lungs. He didn't want to think of the terror his own son must have felt in that second, and in the horrible, torturous moments that led up to it. He didn't want to think that way, of his own son, of someone else's son, of anyone.

At that point Kane's mind, or part of it, anyway, came back. He looked around his room, at his few things. *Still, nothing out of place.*

"What did you say your name was?" he said.

"Reggie Clay."

"I'd like to help you out, I really would. Now's just a bad time. Maybe tomorrow. You can come by my office."

"Mr. Kane, I'd consider it a favor if you'd talk with me now. And I've got a very good memory for favors."

Kane thought then about the useless lock on his door, and of the sleepless night that loomed ahead now because of it. He thought, too, of Meg's husband. Maybe a private dick who owed him something wouldn't be such a bad thing to have.

Kane took in a breath, then let it out.

"Yeah, all right," he said, "why don't you come by now. I live on Nugent Street."

"I have the address."

"The door's at the front."

"I'll be right there."

Kane hung up, then sat on the edge of his bed and waited. Not even three minutes had passed when he heard the sound of footsteps, heavy ones, on his stairs. He listened to them climb toward the top but waited for the knock on his door before he stood.

Kane wasn't expecting what he found waiting for him on the other side of his door, not by a long shot. The man in his hallway was huge, easily one of the largest men Kane had ever seen. This stranger, black, with a shaved head, was built for nothing less than pulling freight. He was almost as tall and as wide as the doorway itself. Maybe Kane should have known by the way the man's voice sounded over the phone. But he didn't. There was always the chance that this wasn't the man who had called, Kane realized, a little too late, so he asked to see identification. He was holding the door with his right hand, ready to swing it closed if came to that, not that it would have mattered much. The door was thin, nothing much more than panels of light wood. The freight-train stranger could have easily made his way through if he'd wanted to. He held up his credentials for Kane to see. It was the only move the man made. This seemed deliberate to Kane, like maybe this man was used to people reacting to him in this way and had long since adopted this manner because of it. According to the two licenses—driver's and PI—the man standing patiently outside his door was in fact the Reggie Clay who had called a few moments ago. Still, Kane didn't take his eyes off the man as he stepped back from his door, letting Clay inside. Once through, Clay closed the door, and suddenly Kane's tiny front room seemed smaller than it ever had.

Kane stepped back till he was standing in the narrow hallway that connected the front room with the back room. He stood facing the front room, his bathroom to his left, his kitchenette on his right. But he stood closer to the stove, and the heavy pot that sat empty on the front burner.

Though he didn't want it to show, Kane was still jumpy, still edgy from coming home and finding his front door open and deadbolt broken. Somewhere inside his troubled mind he was considering the possibility that maybe this Clay fellow had something to do with the break-in. What wild ideas will spring from a guilty conscience, Kane thought then. Still, anything was possible, and some coincidences aren't coincidences.

Clay stayed in the center of the front room, his back to the door. He stood with his hands hanging open at his sides. He didn't make a survey of the room in which he was standing. He was still consciously not making unnecessary moves. But he did glance at the scratches on Kane's face, though he did so only quickly and didn't look again. Whatever it took to put a man at ease.

Kane watched his visitor. The handle of the pot was just inches away from his right hand. He kept it in his peripheral vision, calmly ready to grasp it if he needed to. *And then what?*

"You said on the phone the family hired you to find out about Larry's death," Kane began.

"That's right."

"Like I said, I didn't really know the kid. I wish I had, though. If I'd known he was suicidal, maybe I could have done something to help him."

"Well, actually, Mr. Kane, we have reason to believe that the boy's death wasn't a suicide, or an accident."

"You think he was murdered?"

"Yeah."

"I didn't know what he was into outside of class, if that's what you're looking for."

"I was able to talk to his roommate a few moments ago. He said Larry was crazy about some girl in one of his classes. He couldn't remember her name, said it was fancy or something like that."

Kane nodded. "Yeah, that would have to be Colette."

"What class of yours is she in?"

"One of my writing workshops."

"So I could get her address from the registrar's office?"

"Actually, no."

"Why not?"

"Because she isn't signed up. I let her sit in."

"Why'd you do that?"

"She asked. She was working on an extended piece and wanted some feedback. I read what she had, and it wasn't half-bad, so I told her it was okay with me."

"Do you do that a lot?"

"No. But I'd probably do it for anyone who was a serious writer, and who asked me." *And female. And attractive.*

"So she and Larry were friendly?"

Kane shrugged. "Everyone was drawn to her. Men and women."

"What do you mean?"

"Just that. Colette is . . . special. Magnetic. Alluring." He shrugged again. "Everyone was drawn to her," he repeated.

"Did you get the idea that she and Larry were involved?"

"This is a bit awkward," Kane said. "But I really don't have a mental picture of which one Larry is—was."

Clay thought that was a little odd, to say the least. A whole semester spent teaching the Foster boy and Kane couldn't put the face with the name. But Clay didn't say anything about that. He looked at Kane. The guy was ragged, past ragged, even, clearly the worse for wear, whatever his wear happened to be. Clay had been around drunks enough to know a man intimately familiar with the inside of a bottle when he saw one. But more than that, this Kane fellow, scrawny, hair mussed, eyes badly bloodshot, looked lost, the kind of lost that comes to men who spend their time wishing they were somewhere other than where they were. Where was it Kane wanted to be right now? Clay wondered.

"Maybe you could describe him to me," Kane said.

"He was a freshman. Thin, built pretty much like you, about your height. Dark hair, blue eyes. I've never met him, but I'm told he was friendly, always quick to laugh at a joke. He was from up around Rochester. Always wore the same ragged blue sweater."

Kane nodded. He could see him now, see him sitting beside Colette, hanging on her every word, waiting for her in the hallway whenever she stuck around after class to talk to Kane, to ask him questions about writing, about getting published. If it hadn't been for Meg, and for Kane's own laziness, *maybe something there . . .*

"Yeah, okay," Kane said. "I remember him now. Of course. Larry. Wrote bad poetry, was working on his first short story."

And now he was dead, Kane thought. But Kane didn't want to think about that. It would lead his mind into shadowy places best avoided, or at least put off till drinking dulled his memory.

"So did you get the idea that Colette and Larry were involved, maybe seeing each other outside of class?"

"I got the idea that Larry wished they were. But whether they were or not, I couldn't say."

"What else can you tell me about Colette?"

"Her last name is Auster."

"Auster?"

"Yeah."

"How old is she?"

"About twenty-five maybe."

"What does she look like?"

"She's tall, a few inches taller than me, but athletically built. Maybe a hundred and thirty pounds. Dark hair, pale skin. She wore black a lot. And these thick leather bands on her wrists. She was kind of like this rock 'n' roll chick, but there was something about her that was refined. You know what I mean? Refined, classy. I don't know, maybe even elegant. She had muscles in her arms and back, sleek. I figured she'd been a dancer at one point, or maybe she just did yoga or something like that."

"Was she enrolled at the college?"

"No."

"Had she ever been?"

"At some point she was. But a while back, I think."

"You don't have her number, or know where she lives, anything like that?"

"No. She'd usually sit in for a few classes in a row, then disappear for a week, maybe two. She just came and went. That was her thing. She was secretive. Like I said, men and women were drawn to her. When she wasn't around, people used to wonder about where she was, what she was doing. One kid even wrote a poem about that. It was pretty amusing, actually."

"When was the last time she sat in on your class?"

"I don't know. A week or so ago."

"Did you happen to tell the detectives about her?"

"No. She didn't come up."

"What did they ask?"

"Not much. They wondered if I had any of Larry's writings in my office. They seemed set on the idea that he had committed suicide."

Clay nodded, thinking about that. Kane waited, watching him.

Finally, Clay said, "Can you tell me anything more about Colette Auster?"

"That's about all I know. Like I said, she was secretive. It was her thing."

"What's her novel about?"

Kane didn't have to try hard at all to remember that. "It's what they call a confessional."

"Memoir?"

"Not strictly. It may be autobiographical, I don't know. I wouldn't be surprised. It's erotic, but literary, and it reads like fiction."

"Like Anaïs Nin maybe?"

Kane was surprised by this. "You've read Anaïs Nin?"

"Yeah, sure. I'm big on the French intellectuals."

Kane thought about all that, nodding. He looked Clay up and down.

"Anything else?" Clay said.

"I think she works at a bar. She invited me there for drinks one night. On her, she said. But I don't remember the name of the place."

"Do you remember what town it was in?"

"No."

"Was it by any chance a place called The Still?"

"I really don't remember. Sorry."

"Anything else?"

"Not that I can think of right now."

Clay looked at Kane for a moment, was about to say, "So what happened to your face, man?" But he didn't. Honestly, he didn't want to know, didn't want to have to care.

"Listen, you've been very helpful," Clay said instead. "I appreciate this. If there's anything you need, please don't hesitate to give me a call."

He reached inside his coat and removed a business card. He placed it on the arm of the short sofa. That sofa, and a standing lamp, were the only pieces of furniture, the only *anything*, in that tiny room.

Clay nodded goodbye and turned to leave but stopped when Kane spoke.

"How are his parents doing?"

"Not very well."

"I wouldn't think they would be. Give them my sympathies, okay? Their son was a good kid. They must be going through hell right now."

Clay nodded. "They are, yeah."

"The funeral's up in Rochester?"

"Yeah. In three days. They're leaving with the body in the morning, once it's released from the coroner."

Kane thought about that, about the coroner he'd met when he identified his son. *"Yes, that is my son," Kane had said.* On a metal table in a cold room, the boy's body lay lifeless. He would never move or speak or laugh again, would never become what he wanted to be, what he was *supposed* to be. *How can that be?* Kane had once believed in God, had been raised to, had said prayers all his life in the dark. But he lost that comfort in his early twenties. Blame it on college, on a semester spent studying the existential writers. Bill Young had taught that course, taught it with a kind of fury, had helped lead Kane astray. A few years after that Kane made a point of reading everything he could on the teachings of the Buddha. Existentialism had taken him only so far. In Buddhism there is no god, only actions. Karma made sense to him, explained a number of things, made life less random. Kane needed that. Everyone needs that. But his son's death took that comfort from him as well. The world was without scheme. Why drown a smiling boy? Mercy was a currency of man, Kane realized then. It did not exist on its own in the universe. It would not be handed down from above to those who need it, who deserve it. *We were therefore at the mercy of each other, and at the mercy of dumb luck.* Kane found that a less than promising thing. Still, the least he could do was offer it when he saw it was needed, for whatever good it would do.

"Listen, I hope you can help them out," Kane said. It was all he could say, all that could be said.

Clay waited a moment, sizing this Kane guy up. "Yeah, me too," he said softly. This guy, this Kane guy, seemed decent enough—knee deep in some kind of shit, obviously, by the look of him, by the way he lived, by the scratches on his face. But decent enough nonetheless. Clay waited a moment more, debating whether to say what was now on his mind or to just let it go, just get out of there while he could. It wasn't any of his business, what he was thinking, and a part of him, a big part, wanted to keep it that way. But he couldn't not warn the guy, not point out what he had seen. What if something happened, something bad? Clay didn't want to have to carry that around. He had enough on his conscience. He'd seen enough lives fall into ruin.

He held back for a while longer, debating all this in his head. Finally, though, he came out with it. There was just no way he couldn't.

"Listen, man, it's none of my business, but it looks to me like maybe someone's been messing around with your lock recently. I noticed scratches on the lock face. They look pretty fresh to me."

Kane nodded, glanced at the door, then back at Clay. "Yeah. My door was open when I came home tonight."

"You remember closing it behind you?"

"Yeah."

"Anything missing?"

"Not that I can tell."

"You're positive about that?"

"Yeah. Everything is just as I left it."

Clay nodded toward the wall to his right. "What's your neighbor like?"

"A little old lady."

"You two get along?"

"As long as I sit in total silence while I'm home."

"One of those, huh?"

"Yeah."

"Do you have any enemies? Flunk a student, maybe? An angry ex, or a girlfriend with an angry ex, maybe?"

Kane thought again about Meg's husband. He shrugged.

"It's probably just some kid, looking for quick money," Clay said. "I could install a time lapse camera in the hallway, if you'd like, see if whoever it was comes back."

"No, that's all right. But thanks."

"I don't think it's anything to worry too much about. If it was someone looking for money and didn't find any, I doubt they'd come back."

"You're probably right."

"You might want to call your landlord, get the lock fixed."

"Yeah, I should do that."

Clay's eyes again went to the set of scratches on the right side of Kane's face. And again he looked away, quickly. He'd already peered far enough over the man's fence. He didn't want to look any farther.

"You can reach me anytime through my pager," Clay said. "The number's on the card."

"I appreciate that."

"There'd be no charge for the camera, if you change your mind. Just so you know. I meant what I said about the favor."

"Thanks."

Clay stepped forward then. He offered his hand. It was the size of an oven mitt. Kane took it. Clay's grip was firm but not at all forceful. They shook hands.

Then Clay left, and Kane was alone again.

The smell of Clay's cologne lingered, though. It filled the small front room. Kane wondered if whoever had walked through his place had been wearing cologne, too. If so, for how long had it lingered before fading away to nothing?

Kane kept a bottle of scotch in the cupboard in his kitchenette. He'd bought it a little over a week ago. There was enough left for maybe two glasses. He got it down and poured a glass and stretched out on his unmade mattress, the glass resting on his stomach. Even though his bedroom was in the back of his apartment, he could hear through the window in his front room the cars that passed on Nugent Street. He listened to them, the few that there were, listened to them approach, then go by and fade gradually away. These were the only sounds he heard. Winter night in Southampton. He was at the bottom of his second glass and, strangely, on the verge of passing out, when he heard from somewhere in town the sounds of sirens.

He thought about the broken lock on his door, then looked at the clock on the table beside his bed. It was twenty after nine. Clay had come by, what, a little after eight? He had stayed maybe ten minutes at the most. Could more than an hour really have passed? Kane wondered.

He thought then about getting up to fix something to eat. He needed food. He felt very weak. He thought, too, about maybe wedging his door closed with something, or maybe blocking it entirely with the short sofa in his front room. Someone—anyone—could just walk in while he slept. And then what would he do? He thought of Meg's tape sitting in the bottom of his bureau drawer. He should have put it somewhere else, he thought, somewhere it wouldn't be so easy for someone to find. He wanted to do that, he intended to do that, but he found that he couldn't sit up. He tried once, waited, a little puzzled at his condition, then tried again. But he couldn't move, not even a little. He was certain he'd only had two drinks. He was certain of it. Two drinks was nothing for him. It was barely a good start to a night. He couldn't be drunk, not yet, not this drunk, not on two drinks.

Things started to happen quickly then. He heard a humming in both his ears, one louder than the other. There was a throbbing deep down in his head. He felt that he was being pressed against his mattress by some great weight and at the same time being pulled into it. He felt himself sinking into it, being swallowed by it, as though it had become water and he could no longer float on its surface. His legs went numb. Then the numbness rose, spreading through him, into his groin, then into his torso, burrowing finally in his chest, like an animal in its hole. His lips felt rubbery, his face somehow foreign, as if it had been replaced by the face of another. He tried to lift his head from his uncovered pillow but couldn't. It had become quite heavy, amazingly heavy, as if water had rushed into his skull, filling it to the top, cold water swirling with white slivers of ice the size of teeth . . .

Something was wrong, Kane thought. *Something was terribly wrong.*

He blacked out cold then, unaware of the second wave of sirens moving through town, moving west, following the first wave of sirens, the wave Kane had been just conscious enough to make out.

It was nine forty-five, an hour and a half since Clay had left Kane in his two-room apartment. When the sirens finally stopped, the town slipped back into a dead silence.

FOUR

Miller was stretched out on his bed with the lights off. His knee was bothering him; it always seemed to hurt more when it got cold out. He needed to let it rest for a while and had lain down after coming home from work at seven. The plan was that Abby would come over at eight-thirty, after she got out of class. She took night courses at the community college in Riverhead. Miller had looked forward to seeing her all day, thought of little else. But when his phone rang as he was lying on his back, resting his knee, his first thought was that this was her calling, maybe to say she was running late, or maybe to cancel altogether. Maybe she had talked to someone who knew Miller, knew of his past. Maybe she wanted nothing more to do with him. He rolled onto his side, reaching out for the receiver, knocking his clock off the night table in the process.

"Yeah," he said. His own voice sounded groggy. He realized then that he must have dozed off. He looked down at the clock to see the time. But the clock had landed facedown. His room was dark, lit by the muted light coming through his windows. "Yeah," he said again. He felt out of it. Pulling himself out of sleep was like pulling himself fully clothed out of water.

"It's Reggie," Clay said. "You okay?"

Miller swung his legs out, his bare feet resting flat on the cold wood floor. He was sitting now on the edge of his mattress. "Yeah, I'm fine. What's going on?" He made an effort to speak clearly this time. The chill in his room helped him with that, helped to wake him up fast.

"If you're interested, we've got a job for you."

"Yeah, sure. What do you need?"

"There's a woman tends bar somewhere around here, we're not sure where. We need to find her, in a hurry."

"Tonight?"

"Right now."

Miller thought of Abby then, thought of her on her way to his place, on that long stretch of desolate road that ran between Riverhead and Southampton. When Miller had gotten back to his home the night before and told Abby what he had seen, told her about the dead boy that had been found floating in the Shinnecock Bay, all she could think of was what that weird customer at the deli had said to her, that old German professor who, on a good day, on a sunny summer day, gave her the creeps. *Dark forces.* Even thinking about that, about something out there in the night, something maybe even nearby, sent a chill down her back. Hearing from Miller that another boy had been found was more than enough to put a serious scare into Abby. She had clung to Miller as they slept, and in the morning, an hour after the slow winter dawn, as Miller drove Abby to her car in town, he sensed her hesitation at leaving him. Southampton Village was empty then, like a ghost town. He imagined her now, in this darkness, driving that long desolate road. She'd be coming to an empty house if he left right now, a house still for the most part strange to her. He didn't want to do that to her.

"You there?" Clay said.

"Yeah."

"Is there a problem?"

"No."

"We'll pay you the usual fee. All we need is for you to find her, then let us do the rest. Understand?"

"Yeah." Miller waited a moment, then said, "He's okay with this?" Miller knew not to utter the name of Clay's boss over the phone, particularly a cordless one.

"I wouldn't be calling if he wasn't," Clay said. "All we need is for you to find her, Tommy. Are we clear on that?"

"Yeah. Listen, I appreciate this. You won't regret it, I promise."

"It's not an audition. You don't need to impress us. Just find the girl and give us a call."

"So who is she anyway?"

"She knows the kid they found last night."

"Larry Foster?"

Clay was a little surprised by that, maybe even a little put off. He paused, then said, "Did you know the kid?"

"No."

"How'd you get his name?"

"A friend of a friend of a friend." Miller shrugged. "What's this girl look like?"

"I faxed over what we have."

The machine was downstairs, in Miller's father's office, which was pretty much exactly as his father had left it five years ago. Miller hardly ever went in there. Same thing with his parents' bedroom. One of these days, maybe, he'd get around to cleaning both rooms out, storing their things away.

"Does she have a name?"

"It's all in the fax."

"I guess I'll get going right now then," Miller said.

"I'm going to take the bars in Southampton. I need you to check out Hampton Bays. We don't have a lot of time, so cover as much ground as you can. And don't call attention to yourself. Don't ask questions, don't show off, just keep an eye out for her. If you don't see her in a particular bar, move on. If we both strike out, then we'll move on to Water Mill and Bridgehampton. Tonight, if we have time."

"Sounds good."

"And check in with *me,* got that? Whatever you do or don't find, check in with me. Understand?"

Miller nodded. "Yeah."

"Call me by midnight, one way or the other. Sooner, of course, if you think you found her."

"You got it, man."

"Remember everything I just told you."

"No problem."

"And be careful."

The line went dead. Miller hung up and left his bedroom. He moved as quickly as his knee would allow. He made it down the creaking stairs to his kitchen, pulled open the drawer to the right of the sink, and removed the pad of paper and a pen he kept there. He needed to leave a note for Abby. He felt bad about the idea of not being there when she showed, particularly with how spooked she had been that morning, when he dropped her off at her car. But there was nothing he could do about that. This was the chance he'd been waiting for, the chance he needed.

He wrote quickly, telling Abby that he had to do a job for his friend at the last minute and that he'd be back as soon as he could. She was welcome to wait for him here, if she wanted to, he added. Then he reread the note and thought maybe he should come right out and ask her if she *would* wait for him. He thought about maybe even going as far as letting her know that was what he wanted her to do. The idea of coming home to her later, of sleeping next to her for a second night, appealed to him. It'd been a long time since he'd had that. But there really wasn't time to rewrite the note, and anyway, maybe she wouldn't want to stay. His house was drafty, a stranger's house to her. She might not feel safe there, waiting around, listening to strange noises.

He tore the paper off the pad, grabbed a push pin, and walked into his father's old office. He ignored the trophies on the shelves, his trophies, and the photos on the walls, photos of Miller in his football uniform, of Miller in action. That had nothing to do with him now. A sheet of paper was in the fax machine tray. Miller grabbed it, headed back to the kitchen, put on his coat. Then he hurried out the back door, tacking up the note for Abby before crossing his driveway and climbing into his pickup. He took off toward Hampton Bays without even letting the engine warm up. His heater vents blew cold air for a good five minutes.

He followed Montauk Highway past the college and through the Shinnecock Hills. To his left was the bay, a flat sheet of darkness under the moonless sky. The first traffic light he came to was at the corner of Main Street and Ponquogue Avenue in Hampton Bays. The light was red. As he waited for it to turn, he looked over the page Clay had faxed to him. The lights from the dashboard were just enough to read by.

Colette Auster. Five foot ten, one hundred and thirty pounds. Athletic build, maybe a dancer. Twenty-five. Dark hair, pale skin. Leather bands around both wrists. Often wears black clothing.

There was a word that had been scribbled over. Miller strained to see what was under the heavy ink, but the quality of the fax wasn't good enough. He couldn't read the word. After it, though, was another word, a final piece of description.

Elegant.

The light changed then to green. Miller headed toward the western edge of Hampton Bays. He figured he'd start at the working-class bars there and make his way east, toward the Southampton border. There were maybe three or four bars on that side of Hampton Bays, and maybe a half dozen bars and restaurants in the heart of the village. It wouldn't take him much more than an hour to hit them all, to walk in and have a look around.

The first bar was a small roadhouse called the Barn. Miller stepped inside. There were no women there at all, not on either side of the bar. Miller didn't waste much time there. He drove to the next place. Sundowners. The only woman was a cocktail waitress. But she was blond and round, wore blue jeans and a pink T-shirt. Zero for two. It was then that Miller began to wonder if maybe he would have to do more than what Clay had asked him to do. What if tonight turned out to be this Colette Auster girl's night off? If Clay was as pressed for time as he had said he was, then

Miller figured he should get all that he could out of the time he had to search. That would be the smart thing to do. He wanted to impress Clay, he was desperate for that, even though Clay had told him not to try. He wanted that. He wanted Clay to know that he could be more to them than just someone from whom they occasionally got information. Miller wanted to be part of this business. He needed it, if for nothing else than the sake of his own soul.

Miller asked the cocktail waitress if a girl named Colette worked there. She told him no. He left, doubled back to the Barn, asked the bartender that same question. No. *Now I'm getting somewhere.* He drove past Sundowners again, stopped at Meghan's in town. No one there had heard of her. Miller tried three more places, got the same nothing at each one. Only forty-five minutes had passed and he was already through with the western edge of Hampton Bays and all of the places in the village. All that was left were the few bars between the village and the Southampton border. As he drove out of the village he thought of calling his house to see if Abby was there. He wanted to know how she was doing, if she was okay. He figured if she didn't pick up, he'd talk into his answering machine and tell her to pick up. If after a while she didn't pick up, he'd know she wasn't there, that there wasn't any reason for him to hurry home tonight. But he decided instead to keep going. The hope that she'd be there was better than the disappointment of knowing she wasn't.

Miller stopped at the first bar outside the village, a shack on Montauk Highway with ten tables and a five-stool bar called Al's. No girl fitting her description, no one who'd heard of anyone with that name. After that was the place set at the south end of the canal, where it opened into the Shinnecock Bay. But no one there had heard of her, so Miller left, heading for the last bar in Hampton Bays, a dive called the Water's Edge.

It was a large three-story wreck of a building set on the Hampton Bays side of the Shinnecock Canal. Every year or so the bar reopened with a new name. Whether each name change meant a new owner or not, Miller wasn't sure. The building had originally been a hotel, but that was decades ago. Miller had been inside a few times over the years. The bar and dance floor and booths filled the entire first floor. But what the two floors of guest rooms above were used for nowadays, Miller didn't know. All of the upstairs windows were boarded over.

Miller parked his truck, crossed the gravel lot, and entered the bar. A jukebox was playing a cover of "Take Me to the River." Heavy blues. He stood just inside the door and surveyed the long room. There was a scuffed-up dance floor with three dozen tables and booths set like a square horseshoe around it. There wasn't anyone dancing. Miller would have to cross the dance floor to get to the main bar, set along the wall on the other side of the room. A smaller bar wasn't far from the door, a coatroom beside it. But both were closed. To be expected for a weekday night. After he looked around for a moment, Miller took a few steps toward the dance floor, to get a better look at the main bar. It ran the length of the room. He paused when he saw that the bar was manned by a male bartender. He was tall, wore a black shirt and jeans. His hair was short and spiked. At the end of the bar Miller saw a woman holding a tray. She had dark hair but was petite with large breasts, large for her size. She was no dancer, at least not a dancer in the sense that Clay had meant it.

Miller was about to cross the dance floor to the bar and ask this girl if Colette Auster worked there when a door to a back storeroom opened and a woman walked through it.

She stepped behind the bar and said something to the male bartender. She stood beside him, put her mouth close to his ear. He laughed. She said something else, and he laughed again. She was laughing now, too. Miller saw that she was holding a bottle of liquor. She twisted off the cap, tossed it under the bar, then stuck in a speed pourer. She walked away from the bartender, the both of them still laughing, and poured the liquor into a waiting glass filled with ice. She moved skillfully, swiftly, Miller noted. Then she handed the glass to one of the customers seated at the bar. She smiled at him, a wild flash of a smile, friendly and confident. He couldn't take his eyes off her. Then she turned away from him, returned to her coworker, stood close to him, put her mouth to his ear again. Whatever she said made him laugh a third time. Then she turned away from him, abruptly, leaving him standing there alone. He called after her as she walked away but she ignored him, smiling with wild delight.

All the men at the bar—it was only men at the bar, Miller noted—were watching her. Some did so discreetly, their faces tilted toward the glasses but their eyes on her. Others didn't bother hiding it, didn't care. They wanted her to be aware of their attention. Miller could tell this.

Even from where he stood on the other end of the large room, Miller was positive that this was the woman he had been hired to find. It had to be. Everything that was on the list Clay had faxed him, this woman clearly possessed. The dark hair, the dancer's build, the height and weight, the black clothes and leather wristbands. But mostly the elegance. It was indefinable but obvious.

Miller watched for a moment more, studying not only her but every man there. Then he approached what was clearly her half of the long bar. It was of course the more crowded half. As always, whenever he was in public, Miller did his best to hide his limp. People didn't need to know how bad it was, that he had difficulty walking and that he couldn't really run, not very fast, not very far. He wanted the people around him, the people in that bar, to see his size, see a onetime football player, someone with whom they didn't necessarily want to mess. He wanted them to focus on that, not on a weakness as ripe for exploiting if needed as a bum knee.

Miller walked to the far end of the bar, where there was an empty stool. He stood beside it, leaning his elbows against the brass rail. All the men in a row to his right looked at him for a moment. Some stared longer than others. But they all turned away eventually, turned away to watch the dark-haired bartender make her way toward her new customer.

"How are you tonight?" she said. Her voice was low, raspy, and yet somehow girlish, too. It was a voice meant for a lucrative career in phone sex. Miller immediately wondered what it was she had whispered with that voice to her coworker. Her eyes were deep brown, soft, her stare intense, unflinching. She didn't so much look at Miller as get him in her sights and hold him there. Hers was a stare few men would want to end. Hers was a stare most men would swear was the start of something.

Miller ignored all that, or tried to, anyway. He held her stare. It seemed the thing to do. "I'm doing okay," he answered. "How are you?"

"Tired. But at least we're busy tonight. What can I get you?"

"Actually, I was wondering if you could help me."

"I could help you with something to drink, that's for sure."

"You weren't by any chance friends with a guy named Larry Foster?"

"Who?"

"Larry Foster."

She thought for a moment. "I don't think so. Never heard of him."

"Your name is Colette, right? Colette Auster."

She glanced down the bar, quick, then leaned forward, her face a little closer to Miller.

"I don't know anyone named Larry Fisher," she said.

"Foster. He told me you two used to hang out."

"Larry Foster?"

"Yeah."

"He's a kind of fat kid, right? Short, with blond hair?"

"Yeah, that's him."

Her brown eyes went cold. "Now that's a little funny, because the only Larry I know has dark hair and is skinny as a rail."

Miller said nothing.

"Who are you?" Colette said.

"I'm not a cop or anything like that. A kid was fished out of the Shinnecock Bay last night. His name was Larry Foster. I'm trying to find out what happened to him. I was told you two knew each other, thought you could help me out."

She leaned back, waited a moment, studying him, then said, "What's your name?"

"Tommy."

"Tommy what?"

He paused. He was almost afraid of telling her another lie and getting caught. *She had a way about her.* "Tommy Miller," he said finally.

"What do you care?"

"What do you mean?"

"If you didn't know what Larry looked like, then it's pretty obvious you didn't know him. What do you care what happened to him?"

"I'm just trying to help someone out."

"His parents hired you?"

Miller shrugged.

She waited, watching him again, then said, "You should probably get your story straight before you go around asking questions."

"I'm just trying to help someone out." Her stare was more relentless now than ever. Her eyes were a cross between a doe's and a shark's. "So you knew him, right?" Miller said.

"If it's the same Larry Foster, yeah. We took a class together at the college."

"Yeah, that's him."

"He's dead?"

"Yeah."

"How?"

"I'm not sure."

"But you said they found him in Shinnecock Bay."

"Yeah."

"So he drowned?"

"I guess, yeah. Can you tell me anything about him?"

She shrugged. "He was a weird kid. That's about all I knew about him."

"What do you mean 'weird'?"

"Weird. He was supposedly into some strange shit."

"What kind of strange shit exactly?"

"I thought he was just trying to show off, you know, just trying to impress me. He used to tell me he was into devil worship or some crap like that. I guess he thought I'd think that was cool or something."

"What did he tell you specifically?"

"I didn't really listen to him. He was just a kid. He seemed really lonely to me, really desperate."

"Can you remember anything about what he told you?"

"He said something about a chapel on the campus, somewhere behind the gym. I guess there's a skeet shooting range out there. Beyond it is supposed to be this old chapel, from way back. Larry claimed that he and some friends did satanic worship there. He asked me if I wanted to meet him there some night."

"Did you?"

"*No!* That shit really creeps me out. Anyway, I didn't really think he was serious. I just assumed he was trying to make himself out to be more interesting than he was."

Miller nodded, thinking about what he knew so far, about the two boys that had been found prior to the Foster kid, about what Abby had said that weird German professor had said. It seemed to fit, this possibility that some kind of fucked-up ritual or another was involved here. In the few jobs he'd done for Clay, Miller had already glimpsed his share of shit, enough to tell him that the East End of Long Island, as much as the tourist board would want you to think otherwise, is a place with its share of freaks.

"This chapel he told you about, it's on the campus?"

"Yeah, at least that's what he told me. He said it was behind the gym. I told a friend of mine about it, and he went to check it out. He's curious about that kind of crap. But the campus security chased him out of there, threatened to arrest him for trespassing. I guess they're a bunch of dicks, the security guys. I can only imagine they'll be even more so now that one of their students was killed. So if you go to check it out, you might want to be careful."

"Anything else you can tell me?"

She shrugged. "Not that I can think of. Like I said, I didn't really know him."

"Okay. Listen, thanks for your time."

"No problem."

"Sorry to be the one to bring you the bad news."

She shrugged again. "I've got to be honest, I'm not surprised. I mean, if he was messing around with that kind of shit, he was kind of asking for it, wasn't he? I imagine that stuff attracts some pretty fucked-up people."

"I would imagine, yeah," Miller said.

"So, do you want anything to drink?"

"No."

"It's on me."

"No. Thanks, though."

"On the job?"

"I just don't drink."

She looked him over, nodding. It seemed to Miller that she was deciding something. "You know, it's my night to leave early," she said. "Maybe you and I could meet up later. If I think about it for a little while I might remember more about Larry."

"I've got to be somewhere."

"You're on your way to check out that chapel, aren't you?"

"I wasn't really planning on it," Miller lied.

"If you wait for me, I could go with you. The security guards know me. They think I'm a student there. This way you won't get busted for trespassing if they stop you."

"Why?"

"Why what?"

"Why would you want to do that?"

She shrugged. "I'd like to help, if I could. Larry was a weird kid, yeah, but he was never anything but nice to me. And, I don't know, maybe I'm a little curious after all. It might be something I could write about. Who knows, maybe

there's a Manson family or something like that out here."
Her brown eyes got wide. "You and I could be famous."

Miller waited a moment, then said, "I'll think about it."

"I'm out by midnight. God knows I've got nothing else
to do."

Miller nodded. He wondered if his uncertainty showed, if
she could read him. Her stare seemed powerful enough to
see through him. He said, "Thanks again," and backed away
from the bar. All the men were looking at him. He felt his
face flush with blood but wasn't really sure why.

"Keep warm," Colette said.

"Yeah, you too." Miller walked to the other side of the
empty dance floor. When he reached the front door, he
stopped to zip up his coat. As he did, he glanced once over
his shoulder. Colette was talking to the male bartender. This
time she wasn't standing as close as she had been before.
The bartender's eyes were fixed on Miller but shifted away
when he realized Miller was looking at him. Whatever Colette was telling him now, the bartender wasn't laughing.
When she was done, she walked away from him and went
through the door to the back storeroom.

Miller stepped outside, got into his truck, and took out his
cell phone. He dialed Clay's number. It rang four times, then
rolled over to Clay's voice mail. Clay must have been out of
his service area. Miller left a message, telling Clay that he
had talked to Colette Auster and was heading to the campus
to check something out. He knew Clay would be sore that he
had talked to the girl, but he didn't care about that.

When nothing less than redemption is at stake, you don't
really give a damn who you piss off. The history of the world,
for better or for worse, was on his side, Miller thought.

Miller crossed over the canal in his pickup, heading
toward Southampton. Ten minutes later he steered
from Montauk Highway onto Tuckahoe Road,
heading north. A half mile down that road he turned right
into the parking lot of the college gym. There were two cars
parked out front. He pulled in near them, cut the motor and

lights, and was about to climb out into the cold when his cell phone rang.

He answered without even looking at the caller ID. He didn't need to.

"I thought I told you just to look for her," Clay said. The phone reception was poor, but Miller could hear well enough to tell that Clay wasn't very happy. Miller hadn't expected him to be.

"One thing led to another," Miller said.

"That's all you've got to say for yourself."

"You said you were in a hurry."

"I said some other things, too, but I guess you don't remember that. Where are you now?"

"Outside the gym, at the college. I just got here."

"Wait there. I'm on my way. Do you understand?"

"Yeah."

Clay hung up. Miller started his truck again for the heat. Less than five minutes later Clay's silver Intrepid pulled into the lot and parked beside Miller's truck. Miller cut his motor, climbed out. He and Clay met in the cold, standing between their vehicles. Though Clay outweighed him by a good sixty pounds of muscle, Miller was roughly the same height. They stood face-to-face.

"This is the kind of crap I'm talking about, Tommy," Clay said. He had calmed down some since his phone call. His voice was even now. It was just business at this point, just a matter of making himself clear. He'd had enough, that much he was certain was already known to Miller. It had to be. Miller knew what he'd done. He had to. The kid wasn't stupid, not by a long shot.

"I told you what I told you for a reason," Clay said.

"I thought I could save you some time."

"When we pay you to look, you're just supposed to look. You know that by now."

"I had to be sure it was her. Then she started talking. Once she did, I wasn't about to try to make her stop."

"You weren't *supposed* to talk to her at all, Tommy, that's the point I'm trying to make here."

"Look, I found some things out. That's what matters, right? Finding out what happened to the Foster kid. I'm sorry I didn't follow your instructions to the letter. But I found some shit out."

"If you can't do what you're hired to do, then you're no good to us, it's that simple."

"I know what I'm doing, Reggie. Christ, I could do this in my sleep. I grew up around people who did this for a living. You know that."

"Did you tell her you worked for a private investigator?"

Miller didn't say anything.

"Did you show off and tell her you worked for a private investigator?"

Miller shrugged. "Not in so many words."

"But she probably got the idea, right?"

"Yeah."

"Did you stop and think for a moment that maybe we wanted you to find her so we could tail her? And now that she's been paid a visit by someone who may or may not be working for a private investigator, she just might get a little nervous, maybe not do something she would've normally done, something that may have led us somewhere we needed to go. Did you ever consider this?"

Miller shrugged again. "I just thought I could save you some time."

"I clean up enough messes as it is, Tommy. I don't need to clean up yours, too. Do you understand what I'm saying?"

"Yeah."

"You're sure about this?"

"Yes."

Clay waited a moment, to make certain that it had all sunk into Miller's head. The cold stung his face. All he wanted was to be home. Sophia was there now. He hadn't seen her in, what, four days? Or was it five? She'd be on the day shift for another week. If he were home with her now, they could sit and eat together, they could talk, they could lie down together at the end of the day, like normal humans, like everyone else.

But there was work to do now.

"I need to know exactly what the Auster girl told you," Clay said.

"She said she didn't really know Foster, but that he used to brag to her that he was into some kind of devil worship shit, and that he and his friends used to meet at a chapel that's supposed to be behind the gym."

"There's a chapel back there?"

"That's what she said."

Clay shrugged, thinking about what he'd just been told. "What else did she say?" he asked finally.

"She told me that if I went to check the place out, I should keep an eye out for the campus security."

"Yeah, so?"

"Well, I mean, the police are calling this a suicide, right?"

"Yeah."

"And no one's even considering the possibility that this was anything other than that, right? I mean, there's been nothing like that in the papers, or on the radio or TV, right?"

Clay nodded. He hadn't told Miller anything other than that Colette Auster was a friend of the boy that had been found the night before, and that he needed to talk to her. Clay had felt that Miller didn't need to know anything more than that. There was no way that Miller could know about the bloodhound, what it had found and what that meant. Of course Miller had sources of his own, sources inside Village Hall, which was one of the reasons why Clay hired him from time to time. But he couldn't know that, not now, not yet.

"As far as I know," Clay said, "no one's considering it anything other than a suicide, cops or press. In fact, it's pretty clear that's what they want it to be."

"Yeah, well, this Auster girl was telling me that the campus security was made up of a bunch of pricks, that they had threatened to charge a friend of hers with trespassing just because she was on the campus but wasn't a student there."

"Tommy, what does this have to do—"

"She told me that if I went to the campus to check out the

chapel, I'd better look out for security because they'd probably be acting a lot worse than usual now that one of their students had been killed."

Clay looked at him, saying nothing.

Miller said, "I mean, she could have meant to say 'now that one of their students had died.' But she didn't. She said 'killed.'"

"You didn't say anything that would make her want to jump to that conclusion, did you?"

"No."

"You're sure?"

"Yeah."

"She could have just misspoke."

"Maybe. But it was almost as if she wanted me to go check out the chapel. Like she was baiting me. It was almost as if she wanted me to go there tonight. She even offered to take me there herself after she got out of work."

Clay said nothing.

"She knows something, Reggie," Miller said. "She *wants* someone to check that chapel out."

"Why, though?"

"I don't know."

"Did she seem afraid, like maybe she knew something but didn't want to say what?"

"I really don't think that girl is afraid of anything. She's something else, I'll tell you that much."

"What do you mean?"

"She knows how to play men. You should see it."

"Maybe she was playing you."

Miller nodded. "Maybe. But you've got to wonder why, right? What does she think we're going to find out there?"

Clay looked toward the gym then. After a moment he turned and looked out over the campus. Miller knew he was surveying the scene. The northeast entrance to the campus was directly across the street from where they were standing. Set a hundred yards back from the entrance was a small wooden booth. It was big enough for just one occupant. At night a security guard—campus police, they called themselves—sat in it, on a stool, checking incoming cars for parking stickers. From this distance Clay could just barely make out the man sitting inside. Parked not far from the booth was a Crown Victoria, one of the cars in which security guards made their rounds on the campus. This was the only security presence that Miller or Clay could see.

Clay turned forward, looking at Miller again. "You said on my voice mail that you found her at the Water's Edge."

"Yeah. Why?"

Clay shook his head, saying nothing.

"What?" Miller asked.

"Nothing." Clay was preoccupied now. He looked toward the gym again. "Go home, Tommy," he said.

"What are you going to do?"

"Go home." Clay walked around to the back of his Intrepid and opened the trunk. He removed a long Maglite flashlight, turned it on. The bulb was bright white. He turned the light off again and closed the trunk.

"I want to come with you," Miller said.

"No."

"Look, you wouldn't know any of this if it weren't for me."

"You really want to remind me of that?"

"I want to go with you. I want to know what's out there."

Clay closed his eyes at the words. Then he reopened them.

"Look, this Auster girl was right, Tommy. The college is private property, and this *is* trespassing. If they show up, I don't think you should be at my side. The cops aren't all that fond of you. And, anyway, you've already drawn enough attention to yourself as it is, don't you think? You're only good to us if as few people as possible know you're working for us."

"Most of the guys who work security here used to work for my father. They got fired when the new chief took over. If they started to give you trouble, it might work out better for you if I was with you."

"I'll take my chances." He started walking toward the gym, leaving Miller behind.

Miller waited a moment, then called out, "Look, all I want is a second chance. All I want is to make up for some of the things I've done."

Clay walked a few more steps, then stopped. He looked back at Miller.

"You think you can do that? Make up for the stupid things you've done in the past?"

"I hope so, yeah. And I'm not the only one, by the way."

Clay said nothing to that.

"I need this, Reggie. You know that."

Clay took in a breath. His chest swelled. Then he let the breath out. White mist shot straight from his mouth for a good foot, then rose fast in a cloud.

"You'll do everything I say?" he said finally.

"Yeah."

"I mean, not just tonight. From now on."

"Yeah."

Clay nodded. "All right, c'mon. But don't get in my way, okay?" He turned and started walking again. "And don't bug me."

Miller smiled. He followed Clay along the north side of the gym. It was a large building, built thirty years before, and looked more like an airplane hangar than the athletic facility of an institute of higher learning. But the college itself didn't look like much more than an air force base. Behind the gym lay a long field of scrub pine. There were no lights here, and the moon was just a whitish glow somewhere below the northeastern horizon. Clay switched on the Maglite, and he and Miller walked out onto the field. The ground was uneven, the soil sandy. At the far end, maybe a hundred yards away, was a row of dark trees. They had walked maybe a quarter of that distance when they came across a small building, half buried underground. It didn't to Miller look like a chapel. Clay got close to it, shined the light on it.

"It's a skeet shed," he said.

"What's that?"

"It's where they launch skeet from. This must be an old shooting range. Doesn't look like anyone has used it for a while."

Clay shined his flashlight toward the trees at the other end of the field. The light barely reached them. Still, it was enough to see something.

"Over there," Clay said.

Miller looked and saw it, the faint, ghostly outline of a structure in the shadows of the border trees. They started toward it. The terrain was hard going for Miller, hard on his bum knee, but he ignored the discomfort. He stayed behind Clay, making a point of stepping in Clay's footsteps. It seemed to Miller the thing to do. It wasn't till they were about twenty-five yards from the trees and Clay shone his light at the structure again that they saw it clearly.

It was small, barely more than a one-room building, made of gray stones. Two stories tall, it sat silent in those shadows. Its roof was two steep slopes that met at a sharp peak. Each slope was covered with tiles, many of which were broken or missing altogether. As they moved closer, Clay and Miller saw that the windows were boarded over from the inside. Miller thought of the bar where he had found Colette Auster, thought of its boarded-up windows. Clay paused to look around for a moment. Miller stopped behind him. Then they walked on again.

They reached the building, stood close enough to touch it. The front door was located on the side that faced south. Miller and Clay had approached it from the west. They looked at the front door, Clay shining his light on the padlock that secured it. The lock looked like new, but the hinge and the eyebolt from which it hung were well rusted. Clay aimed the light at the ground in front of the door. He spotted something, stepped to it, softly kicking at it with the toe of his shoe.

"What?" Miller said.

"It's a piece of metal. The U-bolt part of a lock. It looks like it's been cut."

Miller looked and saw it, glimmering in the circle of white light.

"There's no rust on it," Miller said.

Clay nodded, saying nothing.

"Should we take a look inside?"

Clay moved the light, swept the white beam up and down the building.

"Should we take a look inside?" Miller said again.

"No."

"But we've come this far."

"Breaking and entering is against the law, Tommy, you know that."

"But we've got to know what's in there."

"Not like this we don't."

"I could break a hole in one of the boards. It's only plywood. We could shine the light in, maybe see something."

"We're done here for now, Tommy. Let's go."

Clay started walking away.

"You're kidding me."

"There's a way to do things, Tommy."

"But we're here. We're this close."

"I've got a license to protect. Let's go, now."

Miller waited, took one more look at the dark chapel, then turned and followed Clay. They crossed the field quickly and returned to the parking lot. Clay unlocked his car door and tossed the Maglite inside. Then he reached into his back pocket, removed his wallet, and opened it. He pulled out two one hundred dollar bills and held them up for Miller to take.

Miller just looked at them.

"For last night and for tonight," Clay said.

"You could leave and I could go back there myself."

"Not while you're working for us."

"Keep your money then. If I see something weird, I'll call the cops."

"And tell them what?"

Miller said nothing.

"There's a way to do things, Tommy. Just trust me, all

right? We'll find out what's in there, without breaking any laws." Clay waved the money. "Take the money. You earned it. Go home."

"I'm not in this for the money," Miller said.

"I know. It'd almost be better if you were. But take it anyway, okay? Donate it to charity, if you want. Just take it before it blows away."

Miller reached out, took the two bills, slid them into his pocket.

"Is there anything more I can do tonight?" Miller said.

"No. We'll let you know if we need you."

"Maybe I could talk to the cops for you, find out what they know about the Foster boy."

"Something tells me you already did that."

"That was this morning. I could find out what they know now."

"Go home, Tommy."

Clay slid in behind the wheel of his Intrepid. He pulled the door closed, started the engine, and drove off. Miller watched him till he was gone from sight, then looked back toward the gym. He thought of what was behind it, what was just waiting there. He considered going back and taking a look. He stood there in the cold and considered that for a while. But then he thought better of it and climbed into his truck and got out of there.

He followed Tuckahoe Road to Montauk Highway, then turned right, heading east. He wondered if Abby was at his place waiting for him, thought then of calling her. If she didn't answer, he'd try her at her place. He was reaching for his cell phone when he realized there was a vehicle behind him. It was riding closely behind him. No one had followed him on Tuckahoe Road, and Montauk Highway had been completely empty in both directions when he had pulled out onto it. Now, though, out of nowhere, someone was behind him, riding close, right on his bumper. How could that be?

He left his phone in his pocket and kept his eyes on the rearview mirror. The headlights of the vehicle behind him were set high up, so it had to be another truck or an SUV or something like that, not a car. The lights were bright, clearly the high beams. They cut into Miller's eyes. He was coming up on the bar called The Still. It was just ahead, on the right. He was maybe twenty-five feet from its parking lot, doing fifty, just below the speed limit, when a car he had not seen before pulled out from behind the van, raced past it with its engine roaring, then cut in front of Miller, sharply, crossing the nose of his pickup, nearly clipping it with its back bumper. Miller hit the brakes, turned the wheel hard to the right, aiming for the shoulder of the road. But he had turned too hard, had oversteered. His truck skidded, for what felt to Miller like a long time but was really only two seconds, then went into a sideways slide. He lost all control of it then. The truck spun around and was facing backward when it went off the road. It sailed, almost smoothly at first, then cut through a sandbank and was popped up in the air by its own suspension. That was when the real ride began.

Miller felt the change in pitch, the change in the earth's pull on him. He felt that almost immediately. His left shoulder was slammed against the driver's door, and that was when he knew for certain that his truck was going into a roll. It happened fast, sickeningly fast, like a carnival ride. He watched the view out his front window tilt, turn upside down, then turn back again. It was all a blur. He braced himself, as best he could, his hands holding the wheel tight, his elbows locked so he was pushed back into his seat as far as he could go. But there wasn't anything more that he could do. He was a rag doll in the mouth of a wild dog.

He watched helplessly as the view through his windshield rotated one more time. His shoulder slammed against the driver's door again. His head snapped around like a boxer's speed bag. Then, suddenly, the truck landed on its wheels, hard. It bounced once, leaning again to the right, as if ready to begin another roll. There was a moment when Miller wasn't certain what was going to happen. He just sat there, holding the wheel, his senses reeling. That moment seemed to last forever. The truck continued its lean, and it seemed certain to Miller that he was in for one more roll at least. But then the truck fell back, landing squarely on its wheels. It bounced once more, and then was still, suddenly still.

Outside was a swirling cloud of dust and dirt. Miller couldn't see through it. His mind was still spinning, still in that roll. The engine had stalled but the lights were on, and the heater fan was blowing. Miller waited, his insides scrambled. He wasn't sure what he was waiting for now. It took him a moment to realize that he was holding his breath. He let it out, took in air. He was alive. He was alive.

But there wasn't time to celebrate that fact. He knew that much. He looked at his windshield, meaning to look through it. But a long crack that ran through it from top to bottom caught his attention. He looked past that, through the dust still churning in the air, and saw that a panel van had pulled over to his side of the road. It was the vehicle that had been behind him, following him closely, with its high beams on. Miller's mind was working well enough for him to understand that right away. The car that had cut him off, a black Volkswagen Jetta, had turned around and was speeding away, heading west on Montauk. Miller could hear its engine screaming. The panel van pulled ahead so that it was perpendicular to Miller's truck. It stopped there. The driver of the van didn't move. He remained behind the wheel. There was something about the way he was looking at Miller that Miller didn't like. It was an instinct. Miller reached up then and clicked on his high beams. The driver of the van quickly raised his right arm to shield his eyes, or maybe block his face. But in the second before that Miller had seen him, seen the man's ugly face. Then the van took off, did a fast U-turn, and sped west on Montauk, heading in the same direction as the Jetta, its tires squealing.

Miller listened till he couldn't hear the sound of the van any longer. It was all he could do. He was still badly stunned. He didn't know for sure how much time had passed when he first heard the sound of sirens in the distance. They were faint at first but grew stronger, coming from the east, from the direction of town. Miller figured that someone must have heard the crash and called the cops. He didn't really want to be around when they arrived. He had no way of knowing which cop would respond, so there was no way of predicting what kind of treatment Miller would get. He forced himself to focus. He saw that the truck was still in gear, so he shifted into park, then turned the ignition. The starter motor groaned, trying to turn the engine over. Miller cranked the ignition several times, the accelerator hard to the floor, in case the engine had flooded. Finally, though, it caught. But it was running very rough. Miller eased back on the accelerator, tapping on it only whenever the engine threatened to stall. After a moment of this the engine finally cleared out and began running smoothly, or smoothly enough. Miller shifted into drive and grabbed the steering wheel, easing down on the accelerator. The tires spun but the truck didn't move. He shifted into reverse, backed up a little, then shifted into drive again and tried the gas one more time. The wheels spun. He did this several times, rocking the truck back and forth till it finally grabbed hold of earth and shot forward.

On the shoulder of the road Miller paused for a second, listening to the engine. It seemed to be running fine now. He drove forward a short way, listening for the sound of the tires rubbing against the body. He didn't hear that. The truck seemed capable of forward motion, so far at least. That was all Miller cared about. The sirens were louder now, nearer. Miller had to leave. He pulled out onto Montauk Highway. The dark road was empty. He slowly got the truck up to fifty again. It took everything he had not to speed out of there, not to floor it. He detected a slight pull to the right, knew by that that the front end was out of alignment. But it wasn't so bad that he wouldn't be able to make it home. He drove the half mile to where Montauk Highway turned into Hill Street. It was there he saw the first patrol car, racing west. The car passed him in a flash, its lights flickering. Another followed fifteen seconds later. They were both part of the same commotion. A minute after that, Miller was turning onto Moses Lane.

He pulled into his driveway, parked his truck around back, out of sight from the street. He heard another wave of sirens coming from town. Probably emergency vehicles. He checked his watch. His vision was blurry in one eye, but he could see well enough to read the watch. It was nine forty-five. He listened till those sirens passed and had faded into the night before he tried to open his door. He felt pain in his left shoulder then. He'd been hurt before, in football, in the fight that ruined his knee. But this was a different kind of hurt altogether. It reached deep inside, deeper than anything he'd known before. But nothing was broken, everything moved like it should, and that was all that mattered to him. A bum knee was enough.

Miller tried his driver's door again. It wouldn't open. He checked to see if it was locked. It wasn't. He made his way across the seat to the passenger door. That opened easily enough. He climbed down and stepped back to look at his truck. The body was dented, the windshield cracked, there was dirt caught between the bumpers and the body. But the roof seemed to have taken the worst of it. The steel looked as if someone had danced all over it. There wasn't a part of it that wasn't dented.

Miller headed toward his back door. Abby's car wasn't anywhere to be seen, not in his driveway nor on the street in front of his house. The note he had left for her was gone, so he figured she must have been here and left. Maybe it was better, though, that she wasn't here, Miller thought. He didn't want her to see him like this. He didn't want to scare her off. Plus, his night wasn't over yet. There was the chance that whoever had come after Miller might go after Clay next. He had to warn Clay, had to tell him what had happened.

Miller walked toward his kitchen phone. It was mounted on the wall beside his refrigerator. He felt dizzy still, as if a part of him was back in the loose grip of his driver's seat, being spun around like nothing. He found it suddenly difficult to walk a straight line. It amazed him just how difficult that was right now.

He made it to the phone, barely, and dialed Clay's number. His hands were shaking badly. It took three attempts before he got the number right.

FIVE

Kane awoke in his clothes, facedown on the edge of his worn mattress, his only movement for a long time the uneven blinking of his eyes and the soft expanding of his stomach as he breathed.

The sky beyond his one window was overcast, the light that made it into his small room dim, almost solemn. *Early morning,* he thought. For a while he thought of nothing beyond that, thought of no one, was nothing more than a stranger to his own life. But that didn't last. Eventually he thought of Meg. It was inevitable. She was always the first thing on his mind when he awoke. He wondered as he lay there what she was doing right now, and when today she would get the chance—make the chance—to call him. He would give anything to be able to sit at her table and look at her as she stood naked in front of her work. Of course he didn't have much of anything left to give. But he kept his mind away from that, kept it instead on his most recent memory of her—her smell on him, the smell of the two of them. That was, what, yesterday morning? It seemed like a lifetime now. But as he lay there he remembered the night before yesterday morning, a night spent tearing at each other for hours, drunk, followed by him lying beside her as she drifted off, sweat drying, lips numb from hard kissing. He kept that fresh in his mind, as though it was all in the world that he had.

After a while his mind wandered from that, from Meg, wandered to the memory of his son, of the day he was killed.

Such thoughts were never far away, waiting always in the shallows, lingering just below the surface. But it was too early for that, Kane told himself, much too early. He always wanted his son with him, the memory of him, all memories, no matter what the pain. But this morning, for some reason, things were different. He felt that deep down. But what was different?

He was tired, beyond tired. He could barely move. He needed more sleep, that was for certain. Outside his window was a weak winter dawn. No reason for him to be up now. He lay there with his eyes closed, motionless except for his breathing, for the swelling and collapsing of his stomach beneath him. He wanted more sleep, chose to let it come if it wanted. Maybe he'd sleep deep enough to dream of Meg, dream of her eyes and her skin. He couldn't remember any dreams from the night before, which was unusual. He always dreamed, for better or for worse, always awakened in the middle of one, sometimes for a while, anyway, still lost in it. But there was no such spell this morning. Kane thought again about his sense that something was different. Something wasn't right. Something inside him, going off like a muted alarm, or a siren heard from a distance. Kane was focused on that thought, the thought of a siren crying in the distance, when he heard a noise come from down his narrow hallway.

His eyes opened again, he listened for the noise to repeat, heard it almost right away. A cupboard door was opened, then closed. That was the sound he had heard just seconds before. He was certain of it. Then he heard someone run the tap in his kitchen, heard water falling into the metal sink. The tap had been opened up full. The next thing that reached his ears was the sound of his kettle being placed upon his stovetop. It was followed by the soft pop of a flame coming to life, then the steady hiss of the gas burner.

Kane sat up. He felt like he was moving against a rushing current of water. There was an ache deep in his head. He moved to the edge of his mattress, paused there, had to because of a *whooshing* that sprang up like a sudden storm from the ache in his head. He closed his eyes, wincing against pain. When he opened them again, he saw on the floor not far from his bed an empty bottle. Then he saw a drinking glass, or what remained of one, anyway. It was in pieces, some of which had scattered across to the other end of the floor.

Kane heard more noise coming from the kitchenette. He forced himself to stand, careful of the pieces of broken glass, and made his way to his bedroom doorway. With each step he took, the ache in his head blossomed, spreading down the back of his neck. He thought of roots reaching through a dark, cold ground. He reached out for the wall, used it to support himself, to guide him along. He needed it. The plaster felt cold beneath his palm. It was only then that he became aware of the floorboards beneath his bare feet. They, too, were cold. The ache in his head began to throb, like a wound does, an echo to his heartbeat. His throat was dry, painfully so, and there was a bad taste in his mouth, the worst he'd ever known—foul, like he had recently bitten into something that had long since begun to rot.

Kane moved into the narrow hallway, wavering. Someone was definitely in his kitchenette. He could see a shadow moving, could hear whoever it was opening cupboard doors and then closing them. His first thought was that Meg had come to see him, had come to fuck him because she couldn't live without him as much as he couldn't live without her. She had been to his apartment only once before, back when they had first met. Upon leaving that late afternoon, she had told Kane that she would not be coming back, ever. Not enough light in his place, she had told him, too depressing for her. *Too much of a poor man's hovel, probably, is what she meant.* So for her to actually show up now, to put his tea water on for him, to show him uncharacteristic mercy, as it were, would have been a gesture that would have meant a lot to Kane. He was just about to speak her name, his heart, despite the swirling in his head, lifting with hope, when the shadow coming from the kitchenette moved again and a solidly built man stepped suddenly out into the hallway.

The man was heading for the bathroom door, directly across from the kitchenette. But he spotted Kane out of the corner of his eye and stopped abruptly. He turned and faced Kane fully, his shoulders all but filling the hallway. He seemed as surprised to see Kane as Kane was to see him.

"You're up," he said. Then, after a quick moment, after taking a good look at Kane, he added with uncertainty, "Or maybe not."

Kane muttered, "What are you doing here, Doc?"

Mercer stayed where he was. But he stood ready to move, ready to rush forward if necessary, if Kane began to fall. Kane was clear-minded enough to see that, clear-minded enough to know that it was more than obvious by the way he was standing with one hand on the hallway wall that he was struggling to keep from crashing down to the floor.

"I thought I'd better come check up on you," Mercer said. His voice was soft. He was fairly certain Kane wasn't in the frame of mind to hear anything louder than that.

"What time is it?"

"It's a little after four."

"In the morning?"

"No, Deke. It's four in the afternoon. You missed all your classes. Every one of them."

"Jesus. You should've called me, Doc."

"I did. A half dozen times. You didn't answer. I left messages on your machine, but you never called back."

"I was here," Kane said. He could think of nothing more to say than that. He'd never before in his life slept through a ringing phone. Maybe something was wrong with it, he thought. Maybe he had shut the ringer off by mistake. But he couldn't remember the last time he had touched it. He couldn't remember much of anything prior to a few moments ago, to waking up facedown on his bed, in his clothes.

"When you didn't answer your phone," Mercer said, "I thought maybe something had happened to you and decided to come by. Your door wasn't locked, so I let myself in. I'll tell you, if there'd been an empty pill bottle or something somewhere nearby, I would have called an ambulance. I mean, I couldn't wake you for anything. But the only thing nearby was an empty bottle. I was about to run a cold shower and drag your ass under it. I figured that'd wake you up, sooner or later." Mercer looked Kane up and down. He wondered how much longer Kane could stand there. He was holding on to the wall as if beneath his feet was a rolling sea. He could barely lift his head. Mercer watched this, feeling bad for the kid. But he had to think past that. This was life and death now, nothing less. Mercer took in a breath, let it out slowly, and then said the only thing he could say. It was a good enough place to start.

"You look like hell, Deke."

"I feel like it."

"This is how he got Bill. You know that, right? This is exactly how Dolan got Bill Young."

Kane lifted his head and looked at Mercer but said nothing. After a moment he lowered his head again.

"You remember what happened to him, don't you, Deke? To Bill."

"Of course."

"You should know that Dolan came by at the start of every one of your classes today, to check up on you. He knows you blew them off."

Kane nodded, saying nothing.

"Tell me the truth, Deke. Did you drink that whole bottle last night?"

"I don't know." He barely had enough air to get the words out.

"What do you mean, you don't know?"

"I can't remember. I feel like I just had surgery, like I've just woken up from surgery or something. I think I'm going to be sick."

"Do you need help getting to the bathroom?"

Kane shook his head. "I think I just need to stand still for a minute. I think maybe I got up too fast."

Mercer gave Kane a moment, watching him closely. Finally, he said, "Have you been having blackouts, Deke?"

"No."

"Time you can't account for?"

"No."

"Yeah, well, that's the thing with blackouts. You wouldn't know. Are you with your lady friend a lot?"

"Whenever possible."

"Has she said anything about you getting up at night, walking around, saying or doing things you don't remember?"

"I think she'd say something if I was doing something like that. She's not the type to let something like that go. She generally calls me on my shit."

Mercer nodded thoughtfully. "That's a good quality in a lover," he said. "Listen, that reminds me. When you didn't answer your phone, I called that other number. Some guy answered. I told him I had misdialed and hung up. I figured you might need to know that."

Kane was still looking down at the floor. He thought of Meg at home with her husband, felt even more now like he was going to be sick. Luckily, though, the thought didn't linger long. His mind could grasp very little, hold on to even less. He nodded once, then said, "Thanks for letting me know that."

"Look, Deke, I realize how much Bill meant to you, but you really don't need to do this."

"Do what?"

"Follow in his footsteps. Repeat his mistakes."

"I'm not."

"That's what it looks like from where I'm standing."

"What do you mean?"

"His writing career took a nosedive so he started teaching to make money. Then he started messing around with women he shouldn't have been messing around with. He went out of his way to lose everything. I watched him do it. You watched him do it. Now I see you doing everything you can to keep up that fine tradition."

"This has nothing to do with him, Doc."

"I think it does. I think it has everything to do with him."

"I don't see how."

"You couldn't imagine a life for yourself after your son

was killed, so you played out a scenario of self-destruction that was familiar to you. You stopped writing and came back here to teach. You started drinking like a dead Irish poet, took up with this married woman. You did everything Young did. It's like you needed to cause yourself harm for some reason and decided that the best way to do that was to do what he had done, to let what happened to him happen to you. A bad thing to block out the memory of an even worse thing."

Kane shook his head. "I didn't decide anything, Doc. It just happened that way."

"The unconscious mind is a powerful thing. We make a lot of things happen without knowing it, then let ourselves off the hook by calling it fate or luck or God's will."

"You think I wanted this to happen?"

"You tell me."

"My son died, Doc. You're telling me I wanted that to happen?"

"No, of course not. But that was four years ago. I'm talking about what you've done with your life since then. The things you've chosen."

Kane said nothing. Mercer took a step toward him suddenly.

"Did you cause your son's death?" he said.

Kane lifted his head. It took all he had. "No."

"Could you have prevented it?"

Kane said nothing.

"Could you have prevented it?"

"I wasn't there."

"He was scuba diving, right? That's what happened, isn't it?"

"Yeah."

"You were on vacation, all three of you? In Mexico?"

"The Yucatán. Yeah. Will had read about these caves, how the Mayans had thought they were the entrance to the underworld. He wanted to see that. I wanted him to have what he wanted, see everything he wanted to see."

"Do you dive, Deke?"

"It doesn't matter."

"Do you?"

"No."

"And your son was certified?"

"Yeah."

"You said he taught other kids how to dive, he was that good at it. He was an expert."

Kane nodded.

"So you weren't negligent in letting him go. You had no reason to think anything would happen to him."

"No."

"So it was in no way your fault."

"It doesn't matter, Doc."

"Why not?"

"It doesn't work that way."

"How does it work?"

"He drowned, for Christ's sake. Alone, in the dark. He got trapped and he drowned."

"And you can't forget that."

"No."

"You'll probably never forget that, right?"

"Right."

"And you can barely live with it, right? You can barely live with the memory of it."

Kane shook his head.

"You're going to have to learn to do that, Deke. You're going to have to find a way to live with it. You're going to have to find a way to live with the loss."

"And how exactly am I supposed to do that?"

Mercer shrugged. "I don't know. But drinking your body weight hasn't really done the trick now, has it? Nor has letting your marriage of fifteen years just fall apart. Or watching your career go down the tubes, or fucking this married woman, or pissing our bosses off. None of that has worked yet, has it?"

Kane said nothing.

"So what's left?"

Kane looked away, staring at the plaster wall beside him. After a while, he muttered, "I don't know."

Mercer took another step toward him then. "You're going to have to figure it out soon, Deke. Because I think you're about to run out of bottoms to hit."

"Am I fired, Doc? Tell me the truth."

"I haven't heard anything officially. But, yeah, you're probably done. Today was probably the nail in your coffin." He glanced at the tiny kitchenette—two-burner gas stove, a few cabinets, a small sink, barely enough room for one person. "Hard to imagine, giving all this up, huh?"

"You never struck me as the type to kick a guy when he's down, Doc."

Mercer said nothing, just looked at Kane.

"So what do I do now?" Kane said finally.

"You're out of booze. Do you think maybe you could go today without having a drink?"

"Yeah."

"It's probably not going to be as easy as that."

"I can try."

"That'd be a good place to start." Mercer waited a moment, then said, "Listen, Deke, I got a call last night from a friend of mine. He asked me if I knew anyone who might be able to help him out with something. It's pretty specific, and I'd thought about telling him about you, but I figured the last thing you needed was more trouble. I guess now that doesn't matter, though, huh?"

"What kind of help?"

"I'll let him tell you. I'll call him when I get home, set up a meeting."

"Is this a job?"

"No. But I think maybe in some way it might be good for you to do this. Just a hunch I have. I'll tell you this: I can't imagine it making things any worse than they are already."

The water in the teakettle started to boil then. Mercer turned to it, lifted the kettle off the burner, then switched off the gas. He placed the kettle on the other burner.

"I appreciate everything you've done for me," Kane said. "Despite all the evidence to the contrary. I appreciate you getting me the job in the first place. I want you to know that."

"Don't worry about it."

"I'll make it up to you."

"Just stop trying to drown yourself in your own shit. That'd more than make my day."

Mercer's coat was hanging on one of the hooks that lined the hallway. It was a workman's coat, heavy cloth lined with checkered wool. He took it down and put it on.

"Take a cold shower, Deke, wake yourself up. I'll call you in a little while, let you know where and when to meet my friend."

"Okay."

"If afterwards you want to come by, Joanne and I will be up. The guest room is yours, if you want it. I can make you something to eat."

Kane nodded. "Thanks."

"My friend's a good guy, Deke. You can trust him. You can relax around him. He won't steer you wrong." Mercer nodded toward the teakettle. "Make yourself some tea and sit tight. I'll call you in about a half hour. You'll answer this time?"

Kane smiled, despite himself, despite everything. "Yeah."

Mercer left then. Kane stayed where he was, listening to him move down the stairs. He heard the door below his front room open, then close. Then he heard a car start and drive off. He thought about taking a shower but decided to sit down for a moment instead. His head was ready to crack open. The throbbing was like something inside trying to get out, a reptile clawing at the shell of its egg. Kane made his way back into his bedroom, sat down on the edge of his mattress, his arms hanging heavy at his sides. Outside his window was the last light of day, not first light of morning, like he had thought when he first awoke. He could see that now, could tell the difference. After a while of looking toward his window, he looked down at the bottle, at the long, ghostly shadow it cast. He watched the shadow fade, then looked at the broken pieces of glass scattered across the floor. He wondered how that had happened, how they had gotten to be there.

Not long at all after that Kane remembered something about the night before. He remembered the last thought to cross his mind before passing into unconsciousness. From there it didn't take much for him to remember what had led up to that.

I t had been dark for a good three hours when he left for the meeting. While he had waited for Mercer to call, Kane picked up the bits of broken glass, tossed them into the garbage can under the sink, then went through the messages of his phone machine. There were the five calls Mercer had made throughout the day, plus two hang-ups and a message from Meg. He checked his caller ID to see who the two hang-ups were from. But the number had been blocked. He thought about that for a while, and then his thoughts went to Meg, at home with her husband. It killed Kane that he had missed her call. He hated it whenever a day would go by and he didn't get to talk to her. He listened to the message a few times before finally erasing it. It was all he had. But he couldn't save her message and erase the others, and there wasn't room for more than ten messages on his machine. It was the cheapest one Kane could find; he had let his wife keep everything in their house. The message from Meg was a quick one, telling Kane that she was sorry she had missed him, that she'd try him at his office. More important, it informed him that she didn't yet know when her husband was due to leave town next. She ended the message by telling Kane that she loved him and missed him. Nice to hear, but it wasn't enough. Not nearly. Kane was certain that she wouldn't be able to try to call him again till tomorrow. Still, a part of him wished that she would find an excuse to do that, even if it meant getting out of the house and calling him from a pay phone. Of course what he really wanted was for her to drive over to see him. It wasn't likely, he knew that, but he couldn't stop thinking about it, couldn't stop imagining her knocking softly on his door, imagining himself opening it, her smile as she walked toward him. He wanted that, to see her, to smell her. He felt alive when she was within reach. It was the only time he felt alive.

But more than that, he wanted to tell her what had happened last night, what he had just recently remembered—that his apartment had been broken into, that he believed someone may have spiked his scotch with something that had made him sleep sixteen hours, and that before that he had been visited by two detectives and a private investigator. She didn't know about any of this, but he wanted her to know, needed her to. He was used to sharing everything with her.

Despite the fact that he knew better than to expect such mercy from her, Kane found himself looking for Meg as he left his place. He looked for her as he walked around back to where his Jeep was parked. He even looked for her car as he drove through the village. But the streets were empty, for the most part—*empty of her, at least.* He gave up looking as he crossed Job's Lane and followed South Main Street to its end. There he turned right onto Gin Lane. A half mile west, on the left, was a large public parking lot. It was dark—no need for lights this time of year. Beyond the dunes on its southern edge lay the Atlantic Ocean. Kane imagined it as he steered into the lot. The lot was empty except for one car, parked nose first at the western edge. As Kane approached the car he could see that it was an old Pontiac, maybe early seventies, in mint condition. This was the car Kane had been told to look for, sitting with its lights on, like he was told it would be. Kane drove across the empty lot, parked, leaving a few empty parking spaces between the Pontiac and his Jeep. He left his motor running for the heat but switched off his headlights. The Pontiac's headlights went dark as well. But its dark yellow running lights remained on, as did its dashboard lights. The passenger door opened and a man climbed out. He swung the door closed, waited there in the cold and the dark for Kane. Kane watched him for a moment, felt a knot in his gut. Then opened his door and he got out to meet the man.

They walked toward each other, stopping halfway between their respective vehicles. Kane looked to see who was sitting behind the wheel of the souped-up car. He thought that maybe he should know that. He saw a woman, saw her by the soft green glow of the dashboard lights. She had a round face, pretty, exotic even. Her head was turned and she was looking at Kane. It seemed that she needed to see him, too. Though he only caught a glimpse of her, Kane's impression was that she was foreign. Maybe Arab, maybe Egyptian, something like that. Her hair was dark, with long, loose curls. Cut just below her ears, it accented the roundness of her beautiful face.

Kane looked at the man standing in front of him. The man was slightly built, like Kane was, more or less, but well dressed. Black denim jacket lined with dark fur, jeans, and black work boots. Expensive, well cut. *Money,* Kane thought. He was well groomed, too. Clean shaven, dark hair neat, recently cut. He wasn't much older than Kane, no older than forty at the most, Kane thought. He didn't smile but wasn't unfriendly. He studied Kane with steady eyes, attempting to size him up. They looked silvery to Kane, like polished steel, but maybe that was just a trick of the darkness.

Kane remembered what Mercer had told him back at the apartment, that Kane could trust this man, could relax around him. But Mercer didn't know what Kane knew, didn't know about yesterday, didn't know about last night. Kane could have told Mercer about all that when he had called back with the location and time of the meeting. But Kane kept silent about it instead. It was an instinct, a sudden hunch, and he obeyed it without thinking too much about it. This had seemed to him the thing to do. Maybe Kane just didn't want to sound crazy. Mercer already suspected that he was experiencing late-night blackouts. Would Kane really want to add paranoia to that? It mattered to him what Mercer thought. After Meg, Mercer was all he had. *No, I'll wait,* Kane thought, *wait till I find out more, find out* something. He needed to be smart now, smarter than he'd been in a long time. For all his faults, his drinking and wild grief and foolish attachment to Meg, he *was* smart, or at least once upon a time had been. A lifetime ago.

"Thanks for meeting me," the man said.

Kane nodded. His face was already getting numb. He'd only be able to stand a few more minutes of this cold. It violated him, cutting deep into his being. From beyond the dune to his left came the sound of heavy waves crashing in. He could only imagine how cold that water was tonight. *So cold it would burn.* He would have preferred they had met somewhere else, away from water and the memories it evoked. But he had gotten the impression that this meeting needed to take place out of the way. He didn't ask why. Still, there were out-of-the-way places around town that weren't anywhere near water, that weren't within earshot of waves breaking, waves falling. Weren't there? *Places out of reach of this freakish cold, at least.*

"Thanks for being on time, too."

"No problem," Kane said. "Mercer didn't tell me your name. I got the impression he didn't really want to say it over the phone."

The man nodded, then extended his hand. He was wearing fitted leather gloves. Kane had on a pair of green wool ones, old army surplus. He had bought them at the thrift shop in town for a dollar. "My name is Edmond Gregor," he said. "But my friends call me Ned."

Kane reached out and took the man's hand, shook it. The handshake was quick, the man's grip firm but not aggressive.

"You're Clay's boss?" Kane said.

"Actually, we're partners."

"And you're a friend of Mercer's."

"Yeah."

"How do you two know each other?"

"I took a few of his classes while I was at the college."

"You graduated from there?"

"Yeah."

"When?"

"A year before you started. I used to get into jams every now and then. Mercer always tried to help me out."

"Yeah, he's pretty good about that kind of thing," Kane said. "What did you study?"

"Criminology."

"So you've been in this business for a while?"

Gregor shrugged, leaving the question unanswered. He took a look around the empty parking lot, then looked back at Kane and said, "Mercer thought you might be able to help me out now."

"What do you need?"

"There's an old abandoned chapel on the campus, behind the gym. I'm told you know it."

Kane wondered what Mercer might have told Gregor about Kane's past. But Gregor didn't seem like the kind of guy who would care about any of that. "Yeah, I know it," Kane said.

"I own a private investigating firm. It's small, pretty much a one-man operation. I own it, Reggie runs it."

"Reggie?"

"Clay."

Kane nodded. "Oh, yeah."

"We've been hired by Larry Foster's family to find out what really happened to Larry. The police have labeled it a suicide, but we have very good reason to believe that it wasn't a suicide, or an accident, for that matter. According to another student of yours, Larry had claimed that there was something weird going on at that chapel. I need to know if what Larry claimed was true or not."

"What was it he said was going on there?"

"According to this student, Larry had talked about satanic ritual."

"Devil worship?" Kane almost laughed.

"I take it by your reaction that you don't think that's very likely."

"Well, I didn't know the kid all that well. But that just doesn't seem right to me."

"Why not?"

"He didn't seem like the type."

"What type did he seem like, then?"

Kane shrugged. "Not that, that's for certain. He wore the same blue sweater every day. He played acoustic guitar at the Catholic service on campus, I think. He wasn't what you'd call a brooder. He laughed at everything. Hard to imagine a kid like that in that kind of situation."

Gregor nodded. "That's why we need to know what is or isn't inside that chapel."

Kane read something in his tone. "You don't buy it, I take it," Kane said.

Gregor waited a moment, then shook his head. "No."

"Why not?"

"I have my reasons."

Kane expected more. He waited for it. When it didn't come, when it finally was clear that it wasn't coming anytime soon, he said, "Why doesn't Clay have a look around then? Why do you need my help?"

"If Reggie went, that'd be trespassing. The college is private property. I can't let him break the law like that. He has a license to protect. And I have a business to protect. You, on the other hand, being employed by the college, are free to take a walk out there. Plus, according to Mercer, you've done it before. Sneaked in, I mean."

"The chapel is all boarded up now. It didn't used to be, when I was a student. I'd have to break in to have a look around."

"Mercer gave me the impression that he didn't think that would be much of a problem right now. He didn't say why."

Kane said nothing to that. Waves crashed. His ears began to ache, as if someone had grabbed them and twisted.

"You know about the two other boys, right?" Gregor said.

Kane nodded. One of the boys, the one before the Foster kid, had been found in Peconic Bay. He thought of Meg's elderly neighbor bumping the body during his morning swim. Kane decided, though, not to say anything about his own connection to Peconic Bay. It was a detail that wasn't all that important. *Just a coincidence. Not worth mentioning here. No reason to interrupt.*

"Yeah," Kane said. "I've heard about them."

"Counting Larry, three boys found drowned in a span of ten weeks."

"You think they were killed."

"I don't know anyone who doesn't, except the police."

Kane thought about that for a moment, thought about his visit from the two detectives the previous morning. They had seemed convinced that Larry Foster's death was a suicide. More than that, it seemed they had come to Kane's office to locate evidence, any evidence, however slight, that might prove their theory.

"The other student," Kane said after a moment, "the one that Larry told about that satanic stuff. Who was it?"

"Colette Auster."

"Clay talked to her?"

"Someone did. Not Clay, though."

"Then why doesn't she check it out for you? From what I understand, she's all buddy-buddy with the security guys. And she has a way of wrapping men around her finger. If she got caught, I don't think she'd get into too much trouble, or stay in it for long."

"Ever hear of a bar in Hampton Bays called the Water's Edge?"

"Yeah."

"It's where she works."

"Yeah."

"Ever been there?"

"No."

"You sure?"

"Yeah. Why?"

Gregor shrugged. "Last night Clay went to wait for her there. He sat outside till seven o'clock this morning. She never left, not that Clay saw, anyway."

"So what does that mean?"

"It means we don't know where she is right now. We wanted to follow her, see what we could learn about her, see where she might lead us."

"Why?"

"Her name doesn't turn up anywhere. No one named Colette Auster ever went to Southampton College. No record of her at the DMV, no listing for such a name in the phone books for the past ten years."

"I was told she had once been a student at the college."

"Not under that name. So, until we know who we're dealing with, I wouldn't ask her to help us even if I did know where she was. I only work with people I know."

"You don't know me."

"Mercer says you're our man. That's all we need. That goes a long way."

Kane thought about all that. "I don't know," he said. He glanced at the vintage car, at the woman sitting behind the wheel. She was looking at him. Had she ever looked away? Had she not taken her eyes off him? Kane wanted to get out of the cold. It was close now to being all that he could think about.

"Look, I don't mean to rush you," Gregor said, "but we're pressed for time. We need to know as soon as possible what is or isn't in that chapel."

Kane looked at Gregor then. Despite the cold, despite everything that crowded his already troubled mind, he realized something, realized what was really at stake here.

"The funeral is the day after tomorrow, isn't it?" he said.

"Yeah."

"Up in Rochester."

"I think so."

Kane nodded. "Larry used to wear a cross all the time. On a chain around his neck." Kane decided to leave it at that. There wasn't anything more that needed to be said.

"So you understand what we're trying to do. We'd like to do more if we could, but we can at least do that much for his family."

Kane thought about what Larry's parents were going

through right now. He didn't want to think too much about it, though, not with the ocean within earshot.

"All we need is for you to get inside and make a video-tape record of whatever's in there," Gregor said. "That's all. I can tell you how to protect yourself, how to do this so no one will ever know you were there. I think you can understand that I don't want you to get caught, as much for our sake as for yours. You're removed from us, and by that I mean no one outside of Mercer knows we've even met. We're not connected, not formally. But if you were to get caught and find yourself in trouble, you could easily roll over on us and maybe get yourself off the hook. Needless to say, it's in our best interest that you get in and get out without any trouble, without anyone ever knowing."

"I wouldn't roll over on you," Kane said. "Just so you know." It seemed the thing to say.

"We'll make sure it doesn't come to that. But if you help us, then maybe we can help you. Clay told me you had some trouble at your apartment yesterday."

Kane nodded. "Yeah. Someone broke in."

"And nothing was taken?"

"No, not a thing, not that I can tell, anyway." Kane thought then about telling Gregor about the scotch, about sleeping away sixteen hours after just two glasses. But he decided not to, not yet.

"Listen, maybe we can help you with that," Gregor said.

"You mean if I do this for you."

"Even if you don't."

"Why would you want to help me?"

"Because you're a friend of Mercer's."

Kane looked at his watch. It was seven-thirty. Forty-eight hours ago he and Meg were starting their night together, starting off with wine, then moving on to vodka when that ran out. They had fallen together onto the bed in her front room even before the moon had begun to rise. He kissed and bit her neck. She was laughing in his ear. It seemed so long ago now. Long ago and far away, and getting farther away still. It seemed to Kane that it would be forever before he got to do that again, got to hear her laugh, feel her cool skin, fall with her onto the soft bed beneath the tall windows of her front room.

Kane looked up at Gregor then. He'd heard enough. He was shaking, his entire body fighting against the grip of that bitter cold. It had to be zero degrees now, probably even below that. Dark and cold and deadly. Like a cave, he imagined. *Like an underwater cave, the entrance to the underworld . . .*

Kane held Gregor's steady eyes. They were still silvery. Maybe not a trick of the darkness after all.

"So how exactly would I go about making sure no one knows I went out there?" Kane said.

He parked in the empty lot outside the Fine Arts building. Classes had been over for hours. Only the art studios in the other wing of the building were in use now. They would remain open till eleven, after which all the doors of the building would be locked tight by security. That left Kane an hour to get done what he had come to do.

He hurried inside the building, unlocked his office, stepped in, and turned on the light. He was carrying a black canvas knapsack. Gregor had given it to him. He lay the bag on the floor, opened it, and pulled out a pair of black shoes, then sat in his chair. He took off his sneakers, stuffed them inside the bag, and slipped on the black shoes, first the right, then the left. They were a size or two too large. Back in the empty parking lot, after he had instructed Kane on what to do, Gregor had pulled these shoes, along with the canvas bag, from the trunk of his Grand Prix. Kane noticed that there were several different sizes of the same kind of shoe in there, but he didn't ask why. This pair was the closest to Kane's size that Gregor had. But they fit well enough, and anyway, Kane would only need to wear them for a short time.

Kane waited for a moment, gathering himself. When he was finally ready, he pulled on a dark wool cap, zipped up his coat, and stepped to his door. He remembered that the videotape of Meg was in the pocket of his coat. He had figured it was safer on his person than in his apartment. He decided to stash it in his office for now, looked around for a hiding place. He went to his bookshelf and hid it behind a stack of literary magazines that were stored in his office. Then he left, the bag over one shoulder, locking the door behind him. He'd left the light on. That was part of the plan, part of his cover story. Though he knew his side of the building was empty, he looked down the dark hall before heading toward the exit. No one in sight, no one to see him leave. Once outside he started across the eastern edge of the campus, heading for the gym.

The campus felt deserted. Not much on this side, no reason for anyone to be here, especially in this cold. He walked behind the library, then behind the science building. In the shadows of the buildings, he felt as safe as he was going to feel. But then the shadows ended. Before him was the openness of the lacrosse field. But there weren't any lights, and the clouds had thickened in the past hour, blotting out the moon. He crossed the field as quickly as he could, came to Tuckahoe Road. No cars, not on the road or in the gym parking lot. Kane hurried across, walked behind the building, then stopped. Really, had no one seen him? He hadn't seen anyone. That wasn't unusual—the weather, the time of night, this being the desolate side of campus, he didn't really expect to see anyone. Still, he felt a little like he was alone at the edge of the world. He may as well have been out walking on the moon.

It took Kane two minutes to reach the chapel. He walked alongside a dirt road that had been made over the years by the maintenance trucks that were once used to transfer equipment back and forth between the chapel and the gym. The dirt road was really just two tire tracks that ran where the sandy ground was firmest. It clearly hadn't been used in years, was almost as overgrown as the rest of the field. Kane only found it because he knew it was there, had followed it years ago when he was a student out looking for diversion, for rules to break, for mischief to claim.

He removed a flashlight from the bag, a foot-long Maglite, and circled the chapel, aiming the light at all the windows, making certain they were indeed boarded up. They were. He stood then at its door. It was made of wood, ornate but badly damaged by years of exposure to the elements. Kane wouldn't have been surprised if the wood was rotted through. The door was held closed by a latch. Kane had been told to expect a padlock. A bolt cutter, for that reason, was in the bag that hung over his shoulder. But there was no lock. The latch was closed, the eyebolt turned. But no lock hung from it. Kane shined the light at the ground near the base of the door. There something shimmered in the bright circle. It was a padlock. New. Its U-bolt had been cut. Kane looked up at the latch again. Then he turned his head and looked over his shoulder. It was reflex. He saw the overgrown field to the south and the row of dark border trees to his immediate left. He turned his head and looked the other way. A hundred yards to his right was the gym. Another hundred yards beyond that stood the campus. He detected no motion at all, anywhere, and no sign of life on the campus except for the dull lights that lined the narrow road that wound through the grounds. Everyone was inside, keeping warm. He thought about Larry Foster's roommate somewhere on the campus, in one of those dorms that were long overdue for the wrecking ball. What degree of loss was that kid feeling right now? Had he and Larry become close friends?

Kane turned forward and aimed his light at the door again. Whoever had cut the lock and entered wasn't waiting now inside. They couldn't be. The eyebolt had been turned, and that could only be done from the outside. Still, his heart was pounding as he undid the latch and eased the door open. He was wearing leather gloves—they, along with the wool hat, had been given to him by Gregor as well. Kane wasn't worried about leaving fingerprints or small hairs or flakes of skin. He wouldn't have known to worry about that till Gregor had pointed it out to him. Kane's jeans were Levi's, very common. He was told not to worry about any fibers that might re-main after he left. *Just do everything Gregor said, and it would all come out fine*. He clung to that. It was all he had.

The door was lighter than Kane had expected it to be. It swung easily on its hinges. He shined his light in, swung it around the room quickly, just to be certain. No one was in-side. What would he have done if someone had been, if his fast-moving light had crossed someone just standing there in the darkness? Or worse, someone stretched out on the floor? He cleared his mind of that and slipped inside, closing the door behind himself. He swung the bag off his shoulder and placed it between his feet and crouched down. He opened it, pulled out a small camcorder, found the switch for the small floodlight that was built into the camcorder and flipped it on. The light it cast was weak, didn't illuminate much beyond what it was aimed at, and even that was more ghostly than bright. But it would do. He turned off the Maglite, stuffed it into his back pocket, then picked up the camcorder and pressed the record button. His heart was in his throat. It felt like a fist, closing and opening, closing and opening . . .

He stepped away from the door, brought the camera to his face, and looked through the eyepiece. The chapel was the size of his classroom, give or take. The marble altar had long since been removed. Kane knew that already, from having been there before. No one knew where the altar had gone. The window glass had been removed from the long rectan-gular windows long ago as well. Some of the panes of glass had found their way to the door of the chancellor's office. Handblown and lead-lined, the glass was supposed to have dated back a hundred years. The college itself, having been founded in 1962, was only forty years old. Old things, here and there, lent an air of heritage that the college otherwise lacked.

The chapel was empty now. It had been gutted since Kane was there last. Gone was the athletic equipment that had stood in piles all around. Gone, too, were the pews that had once been stacked along the wall by the door, and the hand-carved beams that had once decorated the vaulted ceiling. Perhaps these, too, had been recently installed somewhere inside the administration building. The room was just open space now, cold and echoing, a dark, gaping mouth without a single tooth.

Kane began to make his survey, to take note now of more than just what had changed since he had last been there. He wanted to get the job done and get out of there. He had come this far without being seen. He didn't want his luck to change, didn't want to push it. He only saw things as the light from the camcorder fell upon them. All else around him was just darkness, a curtain void of detail. His peripheral vision caught nothing at all. It was like having blinders on.

He began by the door, sweeping right to left. At first he saw nothing, just the square, gray stones of the wall. Damp, they glistened. Kane was halfway across that side of the room before something unusual appeared within the weak circle of floodlight.

He saw a design. He couldn't make it out at first. Then he saw it clearly. A circle with a slash through it. It was red. Kane lingered on that for a moment. His heart was racing now. He felt his breathing change. He moved the camera a little to the left. Just wall again. Then, something else. A pentagram, crudely drawn. It, too, was red. He held that in frame for a moment, then moved a little more. That was when he saw writing. Latin phrases. He held the camera on each phrase. His hands were sweating inside the leather gloves. His mouth went dry.

He moved the camera till it was aimed at the front of the chapel, where the original altar had once been. There he saw two stacks of milk crates supporting a long plank of wood. He knew right away that it was a makeshift altar. It could be nothing else. He held the camera on it. After a moment he moved his line of vision down to the floor. He saw something and stepped toward the altar.

Stains on the floor. A red trail of droplets. He zoomed in. Blood? He couldn't tell. Maybe just red paint, splashed from the writing on the walls. Hard to be certain. He knelt, moved the camera away from his face, was looking at the stains now with his own eye. He leaned close. He thought maybe that he should scrape at one of the stains, see if something would rub off. He thought of using a coin or something. He could bring enough of it back for Gregor to send out and have analyzed. It seemed the thing to do. Still, a thought was one thing, an action something else altogether. He wasn't made for this kind of thing, for handling what might be spilled blood, for creeping around in the darkness. He didn't want to get any closer to blood than he already was. Had someone been murdered here? On this spot? The thought sent adrenaline into his blood. *What was he doing here?*

He stood up as a chill spiraled up his spine. He shuddered, felt a slight pull in the muscles beneath his shoulder blades. He aimed the camera once again at the stains. After a moment he rubbed the tip of his shoe against one of the drops. He couldn't help himself. He dragged the edge of the sole back and forth across the stain. Nothing came off, from what Kane could tell, anyway. But that told him nothing. He thought maybe it would but it didn't. Still, this was as close as he was going to get. He rubbed the edge of his shoe across the floor, to get rid of anything that might have come up, that might have gotten caught on it—just in case.

It was then he heard a noise. From somewhere outside. He stopped and listened, looking toward the door. After a few long seconds he switched off the camera and floodlight. Total darkness crowded him now. He couldn't even see the camera in his hand. He stayed there for a while, listening, waiting. He thought his eyes might adjust to the dark, but they didn't. Blackness remained around him. He was lost in it, a part of it. He heard nothing, waited some more. A minute passed, maybe two. He hadn't moved a muscle, just stood there, listening, breathing, blind. Then finally he decided it was time to get out of there, whether or not he really had heard something outside. He'd gotten enough of what was here on tape. More than that, he'd pressed his luck as far as he dared.

Very quickly, though, Kane realized that the total darkness had completely disoriented him. He had no idea now where the door was. He had been looking at it when he shut off the light, but that didn't help matters any. He'd lost track of where he'd been looking. He hadn't moved, hadn't turned, and still he had no sense of certainty about which way to step. Doubt paralyzed him. Though he knew the floor was clear of obstructions, he found himself hesitating at the idea of taking a step. His feet felt heavy, his legs weak. The doubt only deepened. It was as if he had no confidence that, though he could no longer see it, the floor was in fact still there around him. He had to will his feet to take a step, command his legs to move. It took nothing less than that for him to start walking.

He headed in the only direction that made sense, straight ahead, moving slowly, one step at a time. Each time he felt floor beneath the soles of his shoes he felt relief. He extended his left hand outward, the camera in his right, held close to his stomach like a football. Eventually he touched something solid. Though he was wearing gloves he knew it was the stone wall. He had missed the door entirely. Panic rushed through him. Somewhere inside rose the irrational fear that he would never find the door, that he had somehow disappeared. His mind was racing now. He just wanted out of this blackness. It was all he wanted. He fought the panic as best he could, felt to his left a few feet. Nothing but the smooth stone. *Wrong way, wrong way*. He moved back to his right, step by step, still not believing fully that the floor would always be there for him. Finally, though, his hand found the door. The panic diminished, but only slightly. Still, it was enough for him to think straight. He felt around with the toe of his shoe till he found the canvas bag. He crouched to it, fumbled with it till he got it open. He should have turned on the floodlight, or used the flashlight in his back pocket. All the windows were boarded up, he had made certain of that, and the door closed. If anyone was standing outside, which he doubted now because he hadn't heard the noise repeat, there was no way that any light inside the chapel would be seen. Still, Kane wanted to be careful. *He'd come this far*. He slid the camcorder into the bag, pulled on the drawstring, then stood, swinging the bag over his shoulder. With his left hand he reached back for the Maglite, removed it, and felt along the door with his right till he found the heavy brass handle.

He was almost out now. All he needed was to make it back to his office without being seen. He could do that, easy. It was late, it was cold. No one would be around. He was more than halfway home now.

He pulled on the brass handle and the door swung open, moving even easier than it had before, when Kane had entered just minutes ago. It took only a split-second for Kane to understand why that was, why the door was so much lighter now, why it was opening so much easier this time around.

But of course by then it was already too late.

In that split-second a sliver of pale light crossed Kane's shoes as the large door swung open. He had been looking down, still wary of where he stepped, and saw that weak light rush into the chapel like moonlit water. He felt then free at last of the complete darkness that had clung to him like a glove, free of the disorientation it had caused him, the panic and fear that had run through every part of his being as he stood lost in it. Kane lifted his head, ready to step into the open outdoors, into the cold, arctic wind. Though the night sky was significantly overcast, that darkness had nothing on the darkness that had surrounded him for the past two minutes. He expected to see clearly by contrast, see the open field and the border trees and the low-hanging clouds that covered the broad Long Island sky from end to end. But he didn't see that, didn't see any of it. All he saw was the figure of a man—a *giant*, really— standing before him, all but filling the doorframe. It was then that Kane realized that this was why the door had swung open so easily, that this shadowed man had been pushing on it at the same moment Kane had been pulling on it. But before he could even think another thought, before he could do more than look up and glimpse the faceless shadow, something hit Kane in the chest, hit him with tremendous force. Not a punch but a shoving motion, maybe the broad sweeping of a powerful arm. Whatever it was, it was enough to send Kane off his feet and backward into the darkness of the chapel.

He stumbled, losing the canvas bag and flashlight. Next thing he knew he was flat on his back. The door swung closed, slammed, then bounced open again, but only slightly. A small amount of pale light made it through the gap that existed now between the door and its frame. That narrow, silver beam lay across Kane till the giant crossed it, blotting it out. Kane saw only darkness then, was back in it again, lost in it. But the beam of light reappeared a few seconds later. Kane quickly realized that the giant had moved around him and was standing now at Kane's right side. He could see only the shape of the man above him, couldn't see his face or even what he was wearing. The largeness of the man, the way he had filled the doorway, reminded Kane of Clay. *But this couldn't be him, could it?*

The man stood over Kane for a moment. Then, suddenly, Kane sensed movement. He didn't understand what it was, what the movement meant. All he saw was a blur in the dark, all he heard was the rustling of clothing. But then Kane felt something crash into him, crash into his chest, hard, and he understood finally the nature of the motion he had sensed.

The man stomped at Kane with his heavy boot, catching Kane dead center. Kane grunted as air rushed from his lungs. The boot came down a second time. Kane had brought his arms up, tried to protect himself. But it didn't really do much. Whatever air had been left in his lungs was forced out as the second blow landed on his crossed arms. Now Kane's lungs were a void inside him. They ached. He tried to breathe in, to refill his lungs, but he couldn't. His wind was gone.

Kane curled up slightly, rolled onto his right side. It was the only thing he could do. The boot came down a third time, and though it wasn't a stomp, there was nothing gentle about the way it landed. The hard rubber sole pressed against

Kane's shoulder with significant weight and force, pinning Kane to the cold floor.

He was still struggling to get air into his lungs. A new panic rushed through him, stronger than the panic he had felt before. Wild, furious, it was something he didn't recognize. *I'm suffocating. I can't breathe.* He gasped in a small amount of air, but it wasn't enough. He struggled to gasp in a little more. But that was all he could do, make short, frantic gulps at nothing, gulps that did nothing. His panic intensified, ruling him now. It was as if in a second he had simply lost his mind. His lungs burned, he felt blood rush to his face, rush to it but not leave. The void in his chest seemed only to deepen. It was as if both his lungs had collapsed onto themselves, collapsed into nothingness.

The man bent down then, grabbed something that was lying near Kane's head, stood up with it. It was the canvas bag. He opened it, searched through it as he listened to Kane gasp. He didn't move for a moment, just stood there, looking at the camcorder he had found inside. Rage moved through him, rage born of betrayal. He shoved the camcorder back into the bag, bent down again. Suddenly Kane felt hands on him. He felt them searching the pockets of his coat, then his jeans. The hands were powerful, fast. They handled him roughly, like he was nothing. Kane felt one of the hands reach deep into his hip pocket and seize his wallet. He felt the hand pull at it. The wallet didn't come out easily, though. The man pulled even harder, violently now. He didn't care about Kane. Kane knew that. The man's rage was evident to him. The wallet came free finally. A moment later a light came on, the bright white circle of a pocket flashlight floating in the dark above Kane. The light was shined into his eyes, cutting into them, painfully, then was gone. When Kane could see again, the light was illuminating his wallet. The man was holding it open, holding it up to the light. After another moment of stillness and silence, the wallet landed on the floor, not far from Kane's head. The flashlight went out, and Kane heard the sound of a cell phone opening, heard the sound of it being dialed.

Kane remained still, the heavy boot holding him down. He couldn't move if he wanted to. But he could breathe now—not deeply, not fully, not even enough. Still, the fear of suffocation was passing, the panic easing. *Just let it come, relax and let the air come.* Nothing else mattered to Kane right now but air, precious air.

Out of the darkness he heard a voice. Deep, but no accent. *Not Clay,* he thought. Still, clearly angry. Hellish, frightening, like the voice from a nightmare.

"It's me," the voice said. "Where the fuck are you? I'm out at the chapel. Call me back as soon as you can. It's important."

The lid of the cell phone closed. Nothing happened for a moment. No movement, no sound. Then the foot lifted from Kane's shoulder. An instant later, though, it was pressing down onto the side of Kane's face. Hard, harder than Kane could bear.

"Did she send you?" the man said. His voice was a hiss. The anger was unmistakable. *Hatred, seething hatred.* Kane could hear it, could feel it. "Did she send you? Huh? Are you fucking her? Are you fucking her, too?"

Kane didn't answer. He didn't yet have the air with which to speak. But even if he could, what would he say?

"Did she send you out here?" the man said. There was a kind of joy in his anger, Kane thought. No, not joy. *Pleasure.* "Are you her big hero now? Is that what's going on? You going to save her?"

The foot pressed down harder still. Kane winced against it but couldn't scream.

"She's going to be sorry," the man said. His hatred only seemed to grow. He seemed almost to want it, to want more and more of it. "Maybe I'll squish her head, just like this. Stick my dick down her throat and make her choke on it, then squish her head. What do you think?"

The man pressed down even harder, putting all his weight behind it. Kane winced again, didn't want to scream, but he couldn't help it. The sound came out of him, erupting from his throat.

The man laughed. "That doesn't hurt. You don't know hurt—yet."

The cell phone rang then, but it wasn't till the second ring ended that the man lifted his foot. Kane heard the lid flip, heard the man say, "Yeah." He could hear the voice on the other end, but not the words that were being spoken. Kane thought about moving, now that the foot was off him. But what would that do? He'd never been in a fight in his life, certainly not with a man the size of this giant. And Kane had no weapons, not that he'd know what to do with one if he had. But before he could begin to think through his doubts, to think that he really had no choice but to try, the foot came down on him again, this time onto his chest, pinning him. Kane braced against it as best he could, protecting the precious air inside his lungs.

"He's here," the man said. The voice on the other end said something. Then the man snapped, "No, not him. That *teacher* guy." He waited, then, impatiently, said, "Yeah, I'm sure. I saw his license."

Kane could hear the voice on the other end more clearly now. It was loud; whoever it was on the other end had clearly raised his voice. Still, though, Kane could hear no words. When the voice ended, the man spoke a little more calmly. But only a little.

"Yeah," he said. "A fucking video camera. Do I take it or what?" He paused, then said, "Yeah, okay. *Okay*. But what should I do with him? Toss him in the bay or what? He's pretty beat up, though. He'll have marks all over him—"

Kane tried to move then, tried to squirm free. He had to do something. In response, the man pushed down harder on Kane's chest. But he had to adjust his balance to compensate for Kane's movement beneath his foot. As he did, the phone drifted away from his face by a few inches. It was enough for Kane to be able to hear the words that the man on the other end was speaking.

"No, we definitely need him. Everything depends on him. Let him go."

The man caught his balance, returned the phone to his ear. The words were no longer audible to Kane.

"But what about *her*?" the man said. Anger lingered just below everything he said, everything he did.

The voice's answer, whatever it was, was a short one. Kane didn't hear the words. After they were spoken, the call was over.

The cell phone lid flipped shut then. The man returned it to his jacket pocket. His foot remained on Kane's chest, the pressure still on, the weight of him still pressing down. Nothing happened for a while. Kane listened to the breathing, his own and the man's. It was the only thing he could do. They were the only sounds in the room.

Then the foot rose from Kane's chest again. Kane knew what was coming, braced himself against it. But the target wasn't his chest this time. It was his head. Only Kane didn't know that, couldn't tell that in the darkness. The man's foot came down once, then again, then one more time, fast, one right after another. By the time Kane recovered his senses, he was alone in the chapel, the door wide open, the man long gone.

It took a while for Kane to be able to stand. Five minutes, maybe ten. He was shaken deeply, he was hurt—his chest, his head, his shoulder. When he did finally stand, he was even weaker, less on his feet than he had been when he had awakened in his bed six hours before. Enough light from outside was coming in for Kane to find his wallet and the Maglite. His wool cap had fallen off at some point. He found that, too. But the canvas bag was gone. And everything it contained. Gone.

Kane made his way to the door, made his way through it but didn't bother to shut it behind him. He retraced his steps across the uneven ground. He didn't care if anyone saw him now. He reached the gym, crossed Tuckahoe Road to the lacrosse field, made it from there to the science building. He walked slowly, stumbling at times, like a drunk. Each step he took jarred him, lit countless pains in him. He cut behind the library, through its long shadow, reached the Fine Arts building. Inside his office, he locked his door and sat at his desk, looking down at the black shoes. He knew he should take them off and dispose of them just as Gregor had told him to. *Put them in a garbage bag, along with the gloves and the wool cap. Weight it down with a rock or two. Drive over the bridge that crosses the Shinnecock Canal, toss the bag out your window and into the water, and just keep on going.* Kane remembered the words, remembered everything Gregor had told him. But his own sneakers were gone, were in the canvas bag with the camcorder and bolt cutter. And, anyway, he needed to sit first, to sit and think all this through, not that he had the first clue what the hell was going on, what it was he had now gotten himself into.

No, not what *he* had gotten himself into. What *Mercer* had gotten him into.

Kane looked at his phone. He wasn't in any condition to talk to Mercer, not yet. He stayed in his chair for a long time. The pain was less if he kept still. Eventually he realized that he was bleeding from the back of his head. He had to move then. He dug some memos out of the trash can beside his desk, used them to clean up the blood and stop the bleeding. There was blood in his hair, he could feel it, and down the back of his shirt and jacket. He thought about going to the men's room down the hall to get some paper towels and clean himself up, but he didn't want to run into security. They'd be coming around anytime now, to get the art students out of the studios and lock up the building for the night.

Kane was behind his desk, holding a wad of paper to the back of his head, thinking again about calling Mercer. He needed at least to tell him what had happened, how everything had gone wrong. Someone needed to know, and Kane wasn't about to call Clay or Gregor, not without figuring out first if this whole thing had been some kind of setup. He couldn't trust anyone, maybe not even Mercer. Mercer was the one to put this whole thing in motion. But why would he do this to Kane? *What reason would he have to want Kane to get beaten up like this? What in the world would Mercer gain from that?*

Kane couldn't make any sense of this, couldn't even begin to see beyond the little that he knew. It was like he was back in the chapel again, unable to see even his own hand in front of his face. He was that lost, that much in the dark right now.

The one thing Kane did know was that he couldn't go back to his apartment. He could be found there, by anyone, easily. But more than that, his lock was still broken. If someone came knocking, he couldn't sit in the dark and pretend he wasn't home till they went away. All they had to do was try the knob, open the door, and come on in. No safe feeling, that. Of course, he could barricade the door with his sofa, but the sofa wasn't all that big, and anyway they'd know that he was inside by the fact that something had been laid across the door. No, the only safe place for him right now was his office. That door locked, was locked now, and soon the whole building would be shut tight by security. He'd wait here, all night if he had to, trying to think this through. *But then what?* He was used to turning to people. Whom could he turn to now?

He decided that he should probably turn off his office light. If security saw it, they'd be made curious by it, come to investigate. Didn't they have master keys? That wouldn't be good. How would he explain what he was doing there, why he was beat up. Half the guards were ex-cops, still had their cop ways about them. Kane didn't want to deal with that, didn't want to go down that road. He was about to turn off his light, about to lean forward and flip the wall switch and sit there in darkness, when he heard a knock on his door.

He froze. His first thought was that this had to be security. Who else would be in the Humanities wing of the Fine Arts building at eleven o'clock at night? But he would have heard the jingling of keys if it was them, he thought, would have heard footsteps coming down the empty hallway. The doors were thin, and the walls, too. And the knock would have been different, wouldn't it? The knock would have been heavier, would have carried the clear and unmistakable sound of authority. The knock he had heard was soft, gentle, uncertain even. Whoever it was standing on the other side of his door had come up quietly, either doubted that Kane would really be inside at this time of night or didn't want to be overheard by anyone else in the building.

Whatever the reason, Kane had no intention of answering. He sat still, holding his breath and looking at the door, waiting for the knock to repeat or for the sound of whoever it was out there to turn and start to walk away.

Nothing happened for several long seconds. Holding his breath like he was reminded Kane of the nightmare of near-suffocation he had experienced back at the chapel. What a horrible thing it was, he thought, to die like that. It wasn't a thought he hadn't had a thousand times before. He breathed out as softly as he could, then took air in. Shortly after that came another knock, three soft raps, a single knuckle on wood, almost delicate. It was barely audible. But this time the knocking was followed by a whisper, a low and raspy whisper, a whisper that Kane recognized quickly. *A woman's whisper*.

"Hey, are you in there?" Colette Auster said.

SIX

Miller looked over at the clock on the table beside his bed, saw through the blue darkness of his room that it was just past eleven now. Abby had come by after work, they had eaten dinner together, then had gone up to his bedroom a little after nine. She was asleep now beside him, had found it quickly once they stopped kissing and lay still together. He was glad for that, that she had fallen asleep easily. He had turned the police scanner down so it wouldn't bother her like it had the last time she was here. They'd only kissed tonight—she was tired from a long day, which was fine with him because he didn't want her to see the violent bruise that covered his shoulder, didn't want to have to explain how he had gotten it. Tonight during dinner she'd noticed the bump on the side of his head, which, he had told her, he had gotten at work today, knocking his head against a shelf in the back room. She had believed him—why wouldn't she?—but he didn't want to push his luck, not if he didn't have to. Both injuries were on his left side, and his truck, which looked a little like it had been chewed up and spat out, was parked in front of her car in his driveway. She was a smart girl, he liked that most about her. There was a good chance that she would have put these things together and pressed him for the truth, and he didn't want a showdown of any kind or degree, not tonight.

Miller hadn't told her anything about what had happened, hadn't told anyone but Clay when he had come by the night before to make sure Miller was okay and get the whole story.

Clay had stayed for a while, told Miller to sit tight while he checked some things out, then left. Miller's reason for not saying anything to Abby tonight was that he didn't know for sure *what* had happened. Was the black Jetta just a drunk cutting him off? Or was it something more? A warning, or maybe something worse. There was no reason to burden Abby with it, any of it, at this point. But of course there was the other reason, the real reason, for keeping it from her. He wasn't fooling himself one bit. The last thing he wanted was to give Abby a reason—*another reason, like she'd need another*—to bolt on him. He liked her, liked talking with her, liked lying beside her in the dark, the smell of her lingering in parts of his empty house after she had left. He'd gone without companionship long enough, had paid his debt, or so he thought. Though it had only been twice so far that they had lain down together, it was enough to tell Miller that he was comfortable with her, and she with him. He knew enough about women to determine that much for himself. He wanted her around, didn't want to say or admit anything that would put that at risk, so he kept it from her. He wasn't all that happy about it, but there was nothing else he could do. And, anyway, it could have just been an accident. Clay was supposed to call him at work, let him know if he had found out anything to contradict that assumption. The call had never come.

Sleep didn't find Miller as easily as it found Abby, not that he had expected it to. He lay there and looked at the ceiling from ten o'clock to eleven, when it became clear to him that there was something he could do, something that would maybe give him some answers. If getting run off the road was a warning, or an attempt on his life, then he had clearly touched a nerve over at the Water's Edge. Maybe there was something he needed to know about that place that he didn't know. He looked over at the clock again. Its digits glowed clear and red in the watery dark: *11:07*. Only a few minutes had passed since he'd last looked at it. But those minutes had made all the difference. He had a purpose, a plan, an action to take. And following it wouldn't require honoring the promise he had made to Clay to sit this out.

He didn't want to disturb Abby, so he untangled himself from her limbs and got out of bed as carefully as he could. Under the heavy covers she stirred but didn't awaken. He gathered his clothes and boots off the floor, stopped at his desk, and wrote her a quick note, telling her that he'd be back as soon as he could, that he was sorry about this but that it was important, and that he hoped she'd understand. If he was lucky, he'd be climbing in next to her without her even knowing that he had gone. All he needed was to have a conversation, find out what he could from the one person in the world he could absolutely trust. An hour, tops. It beat lying there, sleepless, thinking. He placed the note on his pillow, looked down at Abby for a moment, at her closed eyes and the soft brown hair that spread across her pillow like rivers drawn on a map. He thought about the summer to come— windows open, sheets cool in the night air, her hair brushing against him in the solemn dark. Would she still be here then, he wondered, still be coming around to see him? Would she love him by then? Would he have told her everything, would she have forgiven him?

But first things first. He slipped out of his bedroom and crept downstairs, dressed quickly in his cold kitchen, pulled on his boots and coat, and left, making sure the door was locked behind him. As he drove his smashed-up truck toward town he realized that he probably shouldn't just show up where he was headed unannounced. There were rumors, persistent rumors that Miller ignored because it wasn't any of his business. Who was he to care what two grown people did behind closed doors? Still, he didn't want to cause any trouble. He was, after all, persona non grata in her circle. So he dug out his cell phone and dialed her number. She didn't answer, and he didn't want to leave a message on her machine, so he hung up and continued to drive toward her place. She lived alone in a large apartment on the top floor of a house on Lewis Street, a residential area comprised of a collection of a half dozen quiet blocks out by the hospital.

The house was a three-story nautical with large front windows and worn gray shingles. Miller pulled to a stop in front of it and saw that her windows were lit, that her car was parked in the driveway. He took out his cell phone and dialed her number again. Still no answer. He hung up, waited a moment, looking toward her windows. The light inside her place was dim, the warm, summery glow of candlelight dancing against her walls. Miller decided finally that there wasn't time now to be delicate. Lives were at stake, maybe even his. Her car was the only car on the gravel drive that ran the length of the house, so he had no choice but to assume that she was alone. There was of course the chance that she wasn't, that *they* were careful about their meetings, as careful as they should be, and that the man's car had been quite wisely parked elsewhere. Still, Miller didn't care. The trouble and embarrassment his knocking on her door might cause everyone involved was nothing compared to the life of the next kid. He was certain there'd be another victim, if one wasn't already floating facedown in some bay somewhere. Or about to be. Just to be careful, he drove down the street half a block, parked on the far side of her next-door neighbor's house, and shut off the engine. He got out and crossed the front lawn, the ground beneath his feet frozen solid, and rang her doorbell.

There was an intercom system. Miller looked at the speaker, expecting to hear her voice come from it. Instead, the hard buzzer sounded almost immediately. He entered, walked up the two flights of stairs, and knocked on her apartment door.

From inside, a muffled "Come in." She was obviously at the back of the apartment. Miller opened the door, stepped in, and called, "Hello."

"Back here." Her voice was less muffled now but still sounded far away. The apartment was so large, and a year-round rental. Miller wondered how she afforded it on a cop's salary.

"Kay, it's me," Miller said. He closed the door and walked into the center of the front door. Half a dozen candles were burning, and soft jazz—muted trumpet and piano—was playing on the stereo. Miller looked down the long, darkened hall that led to the back of the apartment. The hall itself was nearly as wide as a room. At the end of it was an open doorway, also wide, beyond which stood a bed. Covered with a plush white comforter and a half dozen pillows, it had a brass headboard and was higher off the ground than most beds Miller had ever seen. He walked to the hallway and called again, "Hello—" or started to, anyway. Before he could finish the word, he saw her.

She was standing in the doorway, wearing a tight-fitting white tank top and nothing else. The hem of the shirt stopped well above her belly button. Miller's eyes went to her naked lower half. He couldn't help it. He saw skin, tanned legs, though that was probably from the candles that burned in the bedroom. He also saw a narrow patch of dark hair. He looked away fast—it was his second reflex, the first being, despite himself, to look, to *see*—just as she realized he was not the man for whom her presentation was intended. From the corner of his eyes Miller saw her move quickly away from the door. A half minute later she reappeared, wearing a dark silk robe, pulling tight the sash around her waist.

"What are you doing here, Tommy?" Barton said.

"I'm sorry, Kay. I called out, thought you recognized my voice."

She remained in the doorway. If she was embarrassed, she didn't show it. Cool, always cool, that was Barton. A stray hair hung in front of her eyes. She brushed it away calmly. Miller stood frozen at the other end of the hall, his cheeks flush.

"I tried to call, on the phone," he said, "but you didn't answer."

"Yeah, I know. What's going on? What are you doing here?"

"I need a favor, Kay." He could barely look at her.

"It's not really a good time."

"It's important."

"What's wrong?" There was concern in her voice. She was, after all, the closest thing to family that he had left. It was a role she had always seemed more than willing to take very seriously.

"I need to ask you about something."

"Can it wait till tomorrow?"

"Not really."

"What happened to your head?" She could see the bandage clearly in the dim light. Like her skin, it glowed with an amber color, standing out in contrast to his dark head of hair.

Miller touched the bandage with the tips of his fingers, had almost forgotten it was there. "Nothing," he said.

"Are you okay?" It was more of a demand than a question.

"I just need some help, Kay."

"Are you in trouble?"

"I'm not sure."

She waited a moment, watching him, then took a few steps forward and said, "Where's your truck parked?"

"Down the street, past your neighbor's house. I figured better safe than sorry."

She knew what he meant by that and nodded to show her appreciation.

"We only have a few minutes," she said. "If he sees you here, he'll have a fit."

"Let him."

"You don't need that, Tommy. Neither do I. Tell me what is it you want." She stood with her long arms hanging at her sides. Miller could see the veins in her strong hands, remembered how her hands had taken his and held them several times during the day he buried his father. He looked at her face then. His embarrassment had pretty much passed. Her long hair was up in a ponytail. Still damp, it shimmered. Miller smelled perfume, and there was a degree of humidity and warmth in the air, from the shower or bath she had taken not too long ago.

Miller said, "There's a bar in Hampton Bays, called the Water's Edge. Have you heard of it?"

"Yeah, sure. It's by the canal."

"What can you tell me about it?"

"Why do you want to know?"

"I just do, Kay. Please just tell me."

She shrugged, then said, "It's owned by a man named Jorge something."

"Jorge what?"

"Castello, I think. He owns it through a company, which owns another company, which owns another company, and so on. Somewhere down the line, though, it ends at his feet."

"It used to be a hotel at one time, right?"

"Yeah, from what I'm told. A while back, though."

"The few times I've been there, there were more cars in the parking lot than I could account for by the number of people drinking at the bar. I got the feeling that maybe something was going on somewhere else inside that building, maybe upstairs."

"You always were a clever guy."

"What goes on there, Kay?"

"What do you think?"

"Sex. Prostitution."

"Yeah, among other things."

"You know about it?"

"Yeah."

"The other cops know about it?"

"Yeah."

"Then why is it still up and running?"

"Why do you think?"

"Because someone wants it to be. Someone with influence."

Barton nodded.

"Who?"

"I don't know. And even if I did I'm not sure I'd tell you."

"Why not?"

"Because I don't know why you want to know any of this."

"Why does that matter?"

"Because it does, Tommy. Because I know you. You're too eager for trouble. It's like a crusade or something with you."

"I'm not eager for trouble, Kay."

"Then why do you care what goes on at the Water's Edge?"

"I talked to a woman who worked there. One of the bartenders. Next thing I knew, someone was trying to run me off the road."

"When?"

"Last night."

"Where?"

"On Montauk Highway. Outside The Still."

"That was you?"

Miller nodded.

"You okay?" she said. It was a demand, but said softly this time.

"I'm fine."

"What was this woman's name?"

"Colette Auster."

Barton nodded at that, then said, "Why were you talking to her?"

"I was trying to find something out."

"What?"

"It's not important."

"You're working for that friend of yours, aren't you? That Gregor guy."

"No."

"You're a rotten liar, Tommy."

"I'm not lying."

"What is it with you and him?"

"What do you mean?"

"Why are you always trying to impress him?"

"I'm not trying to impress him, Kay."

"It looks that way to me, to everyone."

"I just want to work for him, that's all."

"Why?"

"Because I do."

"You're too old for that answer, Tommy. And you already have a job. You've got your parents' money. Why do you want to do the kind of work he does?"

"I have my reasons."

"I'd love to hear them."

"Why are you doing what you're doing, Kay?"

"What do you mean?"

"With *him*. This affair thing. You're beautiful, you're smart. Why are you sleeping with Roffman?"

"What makes you think I'm with him?"

"Kay, c'mon."

"Anyway, it's not the same thing, Tommy."

"You're a glorified chauffeur—*his* chauffeur. You were the head of your class, for Christ's sake. Is this all you want?"

"It's not about what I want."

"You're a real cop, Kay."

"You should go now, Tommy."

"I just don't want you to get hurt." He paused, then said, "He's married."

"I don't want you to get hurt, either, Tommy. People say things about your friend. None of it's good."

"Yeah, well, that's the thing about talk, it's rarely good. I'm sure you've heard things about me that weren't all that easy to hear."

"Is that why you want to work for him? To try to make up for the things you've done?"

Miller said nothing.

Barton looked down. Miller knew she was looking at his bad knee. Then she looked up at his face again. He knew what was coming next.

"He did that to you, didn't he. Your friend Gregor. Or Ned, or whatever his name is. He's the one who tore up your knee, right?"

Miller nodded.

"He took away your future. I'd think you'd hate him."

"I did, for a long time."

"But you don't anymore?"

"No."

"Why not?"

"I used to hurt people, Kay. I used to hurt women. We

had a club, back in high school, a bunch of us jocks, a stupid club. Girls who wanted to belong to it had to go through an initiation. It got out of control. It got out of control pretty fast."

"How did it get out of control?"

"There was no stopping us. There was no stopping me. I was a blue-chip athlete, I was college bound. People would let us get away with everything. My father, the other cops in town, my coach, the teachers, everyone. It went to my head."

"You were a kid."

"I was seventeen. I knew what I was doing."

"How did he end up hurting your knee?"

"Ned came out of nowhere one night, found us with a girl. He beat the crap out of me and two of my friends. Three high school football players, and he just tore us to pieces."

"And that's when he broke your knee?"

"Yeah."

"On purpose."

Miller nodded. "I didn't give him much of a choice."

"What do you mean?"

"I said some things, made some threats. I was a punk. You've got to know that. I told him that I'd come back when he wasn't around and hurt the girl. He did it to stop me from hurting her, or anyone, ever again."

Barton thought about all that, nodding, then said, "What did your father do? To Ned, after he hurt you? I'm sure he didn't just let him get away with what he did."

"He reacted exactly as you'd expect him to. He made Ned's life a living hell, for over a year. If Ned had run a stop sign, my father would have climbed all over him. He hated Ned. We both did. But Ned walked the line. He accepted that as the consequences for what he did to me, accepted it without complaint."

"You make him out to sound like some kind of a hero."

Miller shrugged. "He saved my life, Kay."

"I think your vision of him might be a little clouded, Tommy."

"I wouldn't be who I am right now if it weren't for him," Miller said. "It's as simple as that. You wouldn't like me if it weren't for him."

"That's not true."

"You don't know, Kay. I was a monster. I mean it, I was a monster. It took me a long time to see that. You have a lot of time to think when you're stretched out on your back in the hospital. I began to see everything differently. I'm not blaming anyone, because I made my choices, but they drill aggression into you, they tell you to take what you want, on the field and off, and then they protect you from the consequences. I fell for all of that. I believed everything was just mine for the taking. I wouldn't have ever thought otherwise if Ned hadn't done what he did. I would have only gotten worse. I'm more certain of that than I am of anything else in the world."

Barton said nothing for a long time. She stood there, looking at Miller intensely. He stayed where he was at the end of that long, wide hall and looked back at her.

"If I can, I'd like to make up for what I've done," he said finally. "For what I used to be. Can you understand that?"

Barton nodded. A strand of hair fell in front of her eyes again. She reached up, brushed it away, curling it behind her ear.

"Yeah," she said.

"He's not what you think he is. He's not what the cops say he is. You need to know that."

She thought for a moment, thought about that, about everything, then said, "He's been hired by the Foster family to prove that their son didn't kill himself. You know that, right?"

"Yeah."

"How is it going? Do you know?"

"Not very well, last I knew."

"Would he be impressed with you if you brought him copies of the coroner's report on the Foster boy, and the other two?"

"You have them?"

"I can get them. I can get a copy of the entire file."

"When?"

"Tonight. Now."

"You'd do that?"

She nodded. "I think you guys would find them useful."

"What about Roffman?"

"He'll wait. I'll tell him I had to run out for something."

"I don't want you to get in any trouble."

"There are advantages to not being taken seriously. No one will even notice I'm there."

"How will I get the file from you?"

"Wait for me in the hospital parking lot. I have to drive by it on my way back. I can swing right in."

"Are you sure about this?"

She nodded again, a short, quick nod. It was the only movement she made. "We better get going. He should be here any minute now."

Miller looked at her for a moment, thought he should say something to her, *wanted* to say something. Why Roffman? Why a married man? She was attractive, smart. Clearly willing to please, to light candles, wait bare-assed, make concessions. Miller didn't understand her choice, wanted to if he could. But in the end he didn't say anything to her, didn't say anything about any of this. It was her life, she was a grown-up, had to know what she was doing, what she wanted, what she needed. He had to give her that much, cut her that slack at least. It wasn't anything more than what he was asking her to do for him.

He turned and retraced his steps to her door, moving as quickly as his knee allowed. His heart was pounding. He hurried down the stairs and out to his truck, looking back over his shoulder for Roffman's car as he crossed the solid lawn. The street behind him was empty, no one out there, in this cold, but him now. He got in behind the wheel and made a U-turn, heading back toward the hospital. As he passed Barton's house he saw her crossing the front yard to her car. She was wearing gray sweats and Timberland boots and a heavy green parka, the fur-lined hood pulled up over her still-damp head. Miller kept going, pulled into the hospital parking lot a few blocks down, drove to the far end of it, and waited. He saw Barton's car, a dark four-door Volvo, new, drive by a moment later. It turned left onto Meeting House Lane, heading toward town, then left his line of sight.

Nothing for a moment, just a still night and dark, empty streets. Then a car appeared on Meeting House Lane, coming from the opposite direction of town, from the east. Miller knew by its headlights that it was Roffman's unmarked sedan. He watched it roll right through the stop sign and turn onto Lewis. As it passed the hospital parking lot, Miller caught sight of Roffman behind the wheel, or Roffman's silhouette, anyway. He was sitting up straight, rigidly, his eyes forward. Miller felt a chill. *A world full of monsters*, he thought then. *In one way or another, one shape or another*. He remembered what Abby had told him the other night, the talk she'd heard in town, and what that creepy professor, the old German man who was a regular at her deli, had said to her. *Dark forces*. Maybe he had meant that just to scare Abby, to have perverse fun with her. Maybe it was something more, maybe this old man knew something, or suspected something, maybe he had seen something. Maybe he was just old and knew the world. Whatever the reason, he had spoken aloud what everyone in town knew, consciously or otherwise, but would only whisper. They knew it without being told by those who were paid to protect them, protect their lives and property. This very knowledge, and what it would bring, was exactly what the cops hoped to avoid by covering up, by misdirection. It wasn't anything new. Miller had seen it, to one degree or another, before. The East End was a getaway for the rich. Years ago it was nothing more than a summer town. But now there was year-round trade. There was even more money to lose. Everything depended on those who came here from elsewhere. Would anyone really rush to this place if the truth of what was really killing young men got out?

Miller thought about them, about the three dead boys.

They were only a few years younger than he. He hadn't known any of them, had only read their names in the papers and didn't know anyone who knew them, only people who claimed to know people who knew them. Sooner or later, though, that distance would disappear. Southampton was a small town. Sooner or later one of these boys would belong to someone he knew, or *be* someone he knew. If he hadn't done something, done whatever he could, what would he have to say for himself then?

He wondered then what, if anything, Clay had found in the chapel, if it had been as Colette Auster had said it would be. His mind drifted and he thought about her, the way she had looked at him, her voice, everything she had said. From there he thought of the man he had seen in the van, the man's ugly face, and the black Jetta that sped away from Miller's crashed truck. He felt now that he was maybe on the verge of understanding these events and people, on the verge of seeing a connection, any connection. Soon enough, maybe, he'd read through the files and everything would begin to converge.

Roffman's sedan had disappeared from sight by the time Miller looked back at the road. He waited with his motor running for Barton to return. He placed his palm on the window beside his head and felt the cold coming off the glass. Someone was out in this same cold, this same darkness, hunting young men, killing them, leaving their bodies to be found. *Why? Who?* A monster, yes, clearly. But there was good news in that, or a kind of good news, anyway. Miller knew how a monster thought, knew about the dark things that drive us, thirsts that can't ever be quenched, or that we tell ourselves can't ever be quenched.

I can think like you, he thought. *I can think like you and understand you and because of this I can stop you. I can do this, do this much.*

Ten minutes later Barton's Volvo turned from Meeting House Lane onto Lewis Street, then made the right-hand turn into the hospital parking lot and drove straight toward Miller's beat-to-shit pickup. A minute later both cars were pulling out of the lot, Barton heading toward her apartment, and the man waiting there for her, Miller toward a warm and well-lit place to sit and read the bulky files that lay now on the seat beside him.

He didn't want to go back to his house and risk waking Abby, so he drove instead to his shop on Main Street. In the small back room, among the boxes of magazines to be returned the next day to his distributor, Miller turned on the dim desk light and sat down and opened the file. It was at least four inches thick, but he read through everything—the police reports, the coroner's preliminary and final reports on the first two boys, as well as the preliminary report on the Foster boy. He read, too, all the handwritten notes made in margins by the detectives, and the transcripts of interviews, or what passed as interviews, anyway, that the detectives had conducted in the last forty-eight hours. He read it all carefully but quickly, knew what to look for, what to pay close attention to and what to skim over. He had grown up hearing the jargon and the technical talk, could read a report better than probably half, if not all, the cops on the force. It wasn't that he was smarter, simply that he had been reading reports since he was a kid, first sneaking into his father's den and looking through them for the thrill of it, and then later with his father's approval and guidance, the kind of inevitable passing down of a trade that happens between some fathers and sons. When you do something for a long time, for as long as Miller has been reading reports, then you're generally better at it than someone who has, relatively speaking, only just begun.

When he was done reading, Miller leaned back in his chair, touched the bandage on the side of his head with the tips of his fingers, then rubbed his eyes with the heel of his palms. He needed a moment, deep inside he needed it. What he had read was disturbing and chilling. He hadn't expected it to be otherwise but knew he needed to shake that off before going any further. These files were more than just a col-

lection of facts, some bland, some gruesome. They represented the sudden ending of three lives. More than that,
though, more disturbing, they reflected, both subtly and not
so subtly, the agenda of those in power, the people for
whom, though not officially, the police in this town really
worked.

Except for the occasional squeaking of his chair as he
leaned back, Miller's shop was quiet. Dead quiet. It was as if
the world outside had disappeared entirely, swallowed up by
the winter darkness. He sat at his desk for a while, thinking,
sorting through the facts, considering the conclusions,
though of course there weren't many of those. Miller knew
now everything the cops knew, everything that *only* the cops
knew. Unlike them, though, he wasn't bound by what any
higher-up wanted. He didn't have to take into consideration
any bigger picture, didn't have to keep in mind local eco-
nomics, wasn't required to balance anything at all against
the lives of three boys. This wasn't anything new, the law of
the land catering to a wealthy few. Miller had seen it before,
many times. Gregor had fought it most of his life. But the
fact that it was as old as the world itself didn't make it any
less distasteful. Miller's father had been part of that machine, a facilitator of corruption. He had done what the
wealthy had wanted him to. But that was his father. Corruption was what got him killed in the end. Miller loved his father, despite what he did. Loved him then and loved him
now. So much had come out, had been written about in the
papers, after his death. *No one had any idea at all what he
was into.* But it was who he was, the role he played, the position he filled in a certain time and place in history. The man
was not by any means all bad—few people are. But Miller
wasn't his father, didn't have to care about anything but doing what he could to stop a monster, a shadow casting a
darker shadow that was not unlike the one Miller himself
had once cast.

He had promised Clay that he would only do what he
was told to do from now on, not show his usual "initiative."
But that all seemed pretty much irrelevant now. This had all

but fallen into Miller's lap, fallen right out of the night sky. He had only gone to Barton to learn what he could about the Water's Edge in order to better protect himself and Abby, if possible, to see who he had pissed off. Clay could hardly blame him for that. Well, *anyone else* could hardly blame him for that. Clay would probably find a way. Still, Miller knew he couldn't keep to himself what he now knew, regardless of how it would look, how Clay and Gregor might perceive it. Miller needed to share this information with them, not to gain favor, but simply because it would be the wrong thing not to do so. And they could just go fuck themselves if they had a problem with it. He'd do this on his own if he had to. It would go a long way to erasing his karmic debt.

Miller leaned forward and flipped the pages of the file over so he was looking once again at page one. He figured he'd read over it again, or parts of it, after he made his call and while Clay was on his way over from wherever he was right now. He reached for the phone, dialed Clay's cell. It rang two times, then Clay's hefty voice said, "Hello."

"It's me."

"What's going on?"

"I need to talk to you."

"What about?"

"Can you meet me?"

"Where are you?"

"I'm at my shop."

"What do you need?"

"I'll tell you when you get here."

"Are you in trouble right now, Tommy?"

"No."

"Then I'm kind of busy."

"I've got something I think you should see. It's important."

Silence, then: "Meet me by Agawam Lake in five minutes."

"Actually, I think you should come here."

"You know the deal, Tommy. You're no good to us if people see us together."

"Just meet me here, Reg."

"I don't have time to argue about this."

"Neither do I. I'm not dragging what I have all around town. You'll understand why when you see it."

There was another pause, a few crackles of static in the line this time. Then Clay said, "You're a pain in my ass, you know that, right?"

"Trust me, the feeling is more than mutual."

"I'll be there in a minute."

"You're in town?"

"I'm right around the corner."

"What are you doing there?"

Clay hung up. Miller placed the receiver back onto the cradle, walked through his dark shop to the front door. He only had to wait a little over a minute before he spotted Clay hurrying through the cold toward the door. Miller unlocked it, let Clay in, then closed the door again and spun the deadbolt.

"What's the big emergency?" Clay said. He brought in a burst of cold air with him. It clung to the fabric of his expensive coat, almost radiated from it.

"It's back here," Miller said. He led Clay to the back room.

"How's your head?"

"It's all right."

"Your shoulder?"

"It hurts."

"I told you I'd call you if I found anything out, Tommy. You were supposed to wait for me to call."

"Yeah, well, things don't always work out the way you want them to, do they?"

"I don't have time to play around, Tommy."

"Me neither."

He led Clay to the desk. They stood side by side. Clay looked at Miller, then down at the open file. He only needed a moment to realize what it was. He stared at it for a time, then looked at Miller.

"How did you get this?" he said.

"A friend."

"Is it stolen?"

"Does that matter?"

"It might."

"It's not stolen, not in any sense that you need to worry about. You're going to want to read it, Reg. When you do, you're not going to care how I got it."

"We have to do things by the numbers, Tommy. How many times do I have to tell you that?"

"Yeah, well, I don't have to do things by the numbers. That's the beauty of being me. It belongs to the friend who gave it to me. It wasn't stolen."

Clay looked at Miller again, then back down at the file. He stood still for a moment, regarding it, thinking. Finally he took off his coat, tossed it onto a nearby box, and sat down in Miller's creaky chair. He picked up the first few pages, started reading. Miller walked to a stack of three cardboard boxes on the other side of the small room, sat on top of it. After Clay read through a few pages, he started flipping ahead, looking, Miller assumed, for specific reports, the important ones, the ones that would give Clay what he'd need to accomplish, what he had been hired to do.

"You've read all of this?" Clay said.

Miller nodded. "Yeah."

"And you understand it?"

"Yeah, sure."

"Can you summarize it for me?"

Miller got up, walked to Clay, stood beside him. He leaned down, was shoulder to shoulder with Clay, like a tutor, went through the pile, locating the pages that mattered, pulling them out and setting them to one side.

"This is the coroner's report on the first boy, Jason White," Miller explained. "Nineteen years old, from Hampton Bays, found in Mecox Bay ten weeks ago. Five foot seven, one hundred and forty-five pounds. Healthy, well-fed male. The report indicates that no marks of any kind were found on the body, and there was nothing unusual in the toxicological screens that would lead the coroner to believe the death was anything other than by accidental drowning. You have to understand, most coroners are very careful about the conclusions they draw. They tend to be conservative. This coroner is clearly no exception. The most obvious answer is usually the correct one for these guys, and since most drowning deaths are accidental anyway, and without any reason to think otherwise, without the investigating officers giving any indications that the death might have been suspicious, the coroner doesn't bother to look any further than past the obvious cause of death. Also, determining whether someone did or didn't drown isn't as easy as you'd think. Usually the conclusion is reached by exclusion."

"What do you mean?"

"The circumstances of death are often more important than any physical findings. If a coroner can't find any signs of trauma or natural disease to explain a death, and the body was found in water, then he'll probably conclude that the victim drowned. There's nothing that can be done pathologically that will definitely say one way or the other."

"I'm not following, Tommy."

"Even the presence of water in the lungs isn't proof of drowning because lungs will fill with water when someone has a heart attack or overdoses from certain drugs. So someone could die of a drug overdose and his body can get tossed in the water, and though the coroner will find the drug in the tox screen, there's really no way of determining how exactly the victim died, the drugs or the water. Same thing with a heart attack."

"But where does the water in the lungs come from?"

"We're made of water, Reg. A failing heart causes increased pressure on the lung vessels, which causes fluid to rise. And to make things worse, if a dead body is submerged long enough, the lungs will passively fill up with water. And to complicate it even more, some drowning cases are what are called 'dry drownings.' When someone first starts to breathe in water, their larynx can spasm and close, and the death is actually caused by asphyxiation. Nothing gets into the lungs, not water, not air, and the victim suffocates rather than drowns. The larynx remains closed, and at the autopsy the lungs will appear perfectly dry."

"But this boy had water in the lungs, right?"

"According to the report, yeah."

"So I don't understand. Why wouldn't they just determine if it was actually water from the bay he had been found in that was in his lungs? I mean, maybe he had been drowned somewhere else and put in the water. You'd think they'd want to rule that out."

"There were no markings, no bruising to make the coroner think it was suspicious. Also, it's not a matter of simply getting a sample of the water out of the victim's lungs and seeing if it was salty or not. Again, water can enter the lungs passively postmortem. The coroner would have to run what's called a Gettler chloride test to determine the chloride content in the blood found in either side of the heart. If the blood from the right side of the heart has chloride in it, the victim drowned in freshwater. If the chloride content is higher in the blood from the left, the victim drowned in saltwater. But it's an expensive and time-consuming test, and without reason to run it, without the investigating cops asking for it to be run, the coroner just wouldn't bother."

"So Jason White's death was ruled accidental?"

Miller nodded. "It was Indian summer. He might have gone for a late night swim, didn't know how drunk he was."

"He had clothes on, though, right?"

"Yeah."

"Have you ever gone swimming in your clothes? With your wallet and cell phone in your pocket?"

"No, but his blood-alcohol content was pretty high. I imagine the coroner was thinking that someone that drunk might just do anything. He *was* last seen leaving a house party in Southampton."

"Did he have a car?"

Miller started flipping through pages, looking for a particular report. "The cops interviewed some of the kids from the party. They said Jason had said he was going to walk home."

"To Hampton Bays from Southampton?"

"Kind of far to walk, huh?"

"And he ended up out in Mecox Bay, out in Water Mill. That's a whole other direction."

Miller nodded. "Yeah, I know. It's up to the cops to fill in the blanks. The coroner only has the body and where it was found to work with. Of course, if you read the notes, it doesn't look like the cops tried all that hard to explain the kid's travels. Like I said, though, there were no signs of trauma, and the tox screens showed alcohol in his blood. The kids from the party confirmed that he was pretty drunk when he left. They tried to stop him, but I guess he slipped away when no one was looking. He was adamant about leaving, they said."

"Maybe he was supposed to meet someone," Clay offered.

"Could be. Or else maybe someone picked him up along the way."

Clay nodded, thinking about what the bloodhound had told him about the Foster boy's last walk. After a moment, he said, "How far was the party from the college?"

Miller searched for the notes from that interview, found them, skimmed through the pages till he located what he was looking for. "Yeah, that's right," he said. "About a quarter mile. The address is Little Neck Lane. That's right across Montauk Highway from the college, probably one of those small cottages along Shinnecock Bay. Some students take them as winter rentals because it's actually less expensive than living in the dorms, not to mention nicer. Landlords let them go cheap because they can get a fortune for them in the summer and don't want to leave them sitting empty all winter. Collect rent *and* have someone else pay to heat the place, not a bad deal at all."

"So what about the second boy?"

"Same thing, more or less. His name was Brian Carver, seventeen years old, five foot six, one hundred and fifty pounds. He worked at the McDonald's in town, left work one evening, and the next night his body was found in Peconic Bay."

"No connection between him and the Jason White kid?"

"Not that anyone found. The cops interviewed his family, his coworkers. Apparently Carver had some trouble with drugs two years before, went through a treatment program.

Nothing in the notes to say that the cops talked to anyone wherever it was he had received treatment. The general consensus of those who knew him was that the kid sometimes got depressed, but without any suicide note, and, again, without any markings on his body to indicate foul play, his cause of death was ruled accidental drowning."

"He worked. Did he own a car?"

Miller looked through the papers, then said, "No. His parents live on North Main Street. He used to walk back and forth to work."

"Did he go to the college?"

"No, he was a senior at the high school."

"And what about Jason White? Did he go to school?"

"He graduated from Hampton Bays High School a year and a half ago."

Clay nodded. "So no connection there."

"No."

"Okay, what about the Foster kid? What did the coroner find?"

"Yeah, well, that's where things get tricky."

"What do you mean?"

"The coroner has filed only a preliminary report, pending the results of further tests, one of which is the Gettler chloride test."

"So he's starting to think maybe this is too much of a coincidence."

"Yeah. And he's ordered a more complete toxicological screen, which takes more time."

"What does that tell you?"

"Two things. First, that he's not letting anyone rush him this time around. Second, that he might be looking for something to explain the lack of markings on the body. If you drown someone, they fight back. If they're restrained, they fight against the restraints. Either way, there should be markings on the skin. Deep markings, because once the water enters the lungs, the real panic, not to mention the real convulsing, begins."

"So a more complete tox screen might turn up some kind of drug in the blood that may have been overlooked in the first two boys?"

"Exactly. They generally only test for certain drugs. It's still a shot in the dark, though. I mean, there are a number of drugs that cause unconsciousness and disappear quickly, some even within minutes. But those are usually taken intravenously, and the coroner never reported finding any injection marks on any of the boys. But, yeah, he obviously thinks there might be something beyond the obvious in Foster's case, a pill or something he might have been given to drink."

Clay looked up at Miller. "How do you know all this shit, Tommy?"

Miller shrugged. "I've been trying to tell you for five years now, Reggie, I know some things about police work. I'm not just an errand boy."

"I guess not, huh."

Clay looked back down at the pile of papers spread out in front of them. "All right, so tell me, why is it the cops are so bent on calling the Foster boy's death a suicide?"

"Diversion, maybe."

"What do you mean?"

"Three accidents would maybe be a little too much to sell. Two accidents, a month apart, and then a few weeks later a suicide, maybe that's a little easier. Anyway, it'd keep the newspapers from printing the words *murder* and *Southampton* in the same headline, and buy the cops some time—till the tests come back, at least."

"Time for what?"

"The longer they can keep this out of the paper, the better, right? No summer people, no money. The mayor's a businessman. So are all the selectmen, the members of the town council. These boys were murdered, Reggie. There's no doubt about that. They were murdered and their bodies were disposed of in a way that would cover the killer's tracks nicely. Like I said, drowning deaths are almost always ruled accidental. It's difficult even in the best circumstances for the coroner to prove conclusively one way or another the cause of death. Whoever is doing this is smart, and getting confident. He waited only two weeks this time. He waited a month between killings before. He's getting good at what he does, he's escalating, he's calculating, picking his prey carefully. All that makes him a predator, and the thing about predators is, they don't stop. They can't. Do you think people would come rushing out here with their kids and their hard-earned money if they knew this was going on? The Son of Sam emptied the streets of New York for an entire summer. We're talking all of New York—Queens, Bronx, Brooklyn, Manhattan. People had to be there because they lived and worked there. They couldn't afford to go anywhere else. The people who come out here don't have to come out here. They can go anywhere they want, anywhere there isn't some twisted freak killing boys."

"So the cops stick their heads in the sand and hope no one notices."

"Or that it goes away entirely, yeah. They do what they're told, Reggie. Someone's telling them to keep this under wraps. They know what they have on their hands. You can see that by the notes. They've even given him a nickname."

"What?"

"John the Baptist. They've named him, and that in itself makes it pretty clear that he's real to them."

Clay flipped through a few more pages, but he wasn't really reading them now. "So it's clear by all this that they suspect that the Foster boy was murdered?"

"Yeah."

"Then we can use this to get the Foster family off the hook? We can leak the autopsy report to a reporter, force the cops to admit that the Foster boy was murdered."

"We can do that, yeah. But it's going to make a lot of people unhappy."

"Do you really care about that?"

"Not really, just as long as we do this carefully. Someone went out on a limb to get this for me. I don't want it coming back and causing that person any trouble."

Clay nodded. "No, of course not." He thought for a moment, then said, "Do the police have any suspects?"

"There are several references to a guy at the college, some writing teacher named Kane. Foster was in one of his classes. I guess the investigating detectives went to talk with him at his office yesterday and didn't really like what they saw."

Clay nodded, thought about his visit with Kane later that day. "Anything else?" he said after a while.

"The woman I talked to, Colette, she said that she and Foster took a class together at the college. Maybe they all knew each other, Kane and Foster and Colette. Maybe the class he taught and the class she and Foster took were one and the same."

"They were," Clay said.

"Are you sure?"

"Yeah."

"Kane's address is in the file," Miller said. "He lives right around the corner. Maybe we should go talk to him."

"He's not home."

"How do you know?"

"Because I was just there."

"What do you mean?"

"I was just at his place."

"What for?"

"We sent him to the chapel tonight to make a video record of whatever was inside."

"You guys know him?"

"A friend of Ned's knows him, vouched for him. We needed someone who wasn't connected to us, and since he already worked at the college, it seemed the way to go."

"So what did he find?"

"I don't know. He was supposed to meet up with Ned afterward, but he never showed."

"How long ago was that?"

"An hour."

"What do you think happened?"

"I don't know." Clay looked up at Miller then. "Let me ask you something, Tommy. The Foster boy, how big of a guy was he?"

"Not very."

"Same as the first two?"

"Pretty much, yeah."

"They were slight, probably not all that strong, right?"

"Yeah, probably."

"This Kane guy, he's on the scrawny side. You would generally pick on someone you could handle, right? If you were going to be lugging a dead body around, I mean, you'd pick someone in your weight class or smaller, right?"

"Yeah, probably. You think this Kane guy is behind all this?"

"I'm not sure what to think here." Clay looked at all the pages spread out in front of him. He was quiet for a while, then said, "Ned should see all this, Tommy. We should show all this to him."

"I figured you'd want to do that. But I'd rather the file didn't leave my shop, if that's okay with you. He can come here and look through it if he wants."

"That's fine," Clay said. He pushed his chair back and stood. "I'll call him from outside, have him meet you here as soon as he can." He grabbed his coat from the nearby pile of boxes, started to pull it on.

"Where are you going now?" Miller said.

"To have a look around Kane's apartment."

"I want to come with you."

"You need to be here, to show this to him."

"You wouldn't know any of it if not me for, Reg. You owe me."

"Is that why you showed this to me? So I'd owe you a favor?"

"No. But I'm more than just an errand boy. You know that now. I can help you out. Just give me a chance."

"Ned really should see all this as soon as possible. You can help out by being here when he gets here."

"You can call him when we get back. How long are we talking here, Reg? Ten minutes? There's nothing he can do with this information till morning anyway."

Clay buttoned up his overcoat. "You'll go over everything with Ned, just like you did with me?"

"Yeah, of course."

He looked at Miller for a moment more, then nodded once and said, "Yeah, all right, grab your coat, Tommy. And a pair of gloves, too. But try to stay out of my way, okay?"

"Don't I always?" Miller said.

It took less than a minute to walk from Miller's shop on Main Street to Kane's place on Nugent. Clay remembered what Kane had told him about the old lady who lived next door, so he and Miller climbed the stairs as quietly as they could. They entered through the unlocked door, switched on a light. Clay walked through the front room and started down the narrow hallway. Miller stayed behind and looked around for a moment, then followed Clay. The place was small; there wasn't much at all in it. Miller had expected more, didn't know why exactly, just did. It was hard to imagine someone who taught at a college living like, well, a student. Miller stood in the hallway, looked to his right, into the small bathroom, then to his left, at the kitchenette. A two-burner stove, a toaster oven on a counter, not much else. Clay had walked into the back room by then. Miller went to him, stood beside him. There was a narrow bed, a bureau, a few milk crates with some books. An empty bottle of scotch stood on the floor by the bed.

"What exactly are we looking for?" Miller said.

"I had hoped you'd know. You're the boy wonder."

Miller smiled. "He leaves his door unlocked," he said.

"The lock is broken."

"I didn't see that."

"I came by yesterday to see if he could tell me anything

about the Foster kid that might help. While I was here he told me that he had come home and found that his place had been broken into."

"Was anything taken?"

"No."

"Not much to take."

"Yeah." Clay looked around. "Aren't break-ins like this often just cases of drug addicts looking for money? I mean, looking at this place from outside, would a thief think there'd be something worth taking inside?"

"No, not really."

"Safe to say there'd be no security system to contend with. Maybe it was just some junkie desperate for whatever cash he could get his hands on."

Miller walked to the bed, looked down at the empty bottle, then at the bedside table. There was a lamp, a phone, and an answering machine. The indicator light on the answering machine wasn't blinking. No messages. After a moment Miller picked up the phone, looked at the receiver. "He has caller ID," he said.

"Scroll down."

Miller pressed the button marked with a downward-pointing arrow. His gloves were thick; it took effort not to hit any of the surrounding buttons. "Two calls in the last hour. A Bridgehampton exchange. Unknown name."

"What else?"

Miller scrolled down. "A call from a Southampton number. This one has a name. Meg Timmins. The rest are a bunch of calls in a row from Southampton College. All day yesterday, it looks like. And two blocked calls before that."

"Do you have anything to write them all down with?"

"Yeah." Miller took out a Moleskine notebook and pen from his coat pocket. He copied down the name Meg Timmins, along with the number and the time of the call. Then he copied down the number with the unknown name, and the times of both calls.

As Miller did this, Clay took another look around the bedroom, then finally walked back through the hallway. He paused, glanced into the bathroom, then into the kitchenette. He opened the upper cupboards, looked through them, found nothing but cans of soup. Then he bent down, opened the cupboard doors below the counter. A recycle bin, some empty bottles and cans, a newspaper. He picked up the newspaper, looked at it. It was last week's *Southampton Press*. No mention on the front page about dead boys. No mention anywhere inside, Clay remembered. He put the paper back, closed those doors, moved to the doors directly below the sink, opened those. A bottle of dishwashing soap, a can of Spic and Span, a spare sponge still in its plastic wrapper. Beside those, a plastic garbage container, tall, almost as tall as the cupboard itself. Clay grabbed it, pulled it out, looked inside. Just looking, just being thorough. He just stared into the container. After a moment he stood up straight.

Miller had stepped into the hallway, was watching Clay, saw the look on his face. "You find something, Reggie?"

Clay nodded. "Yeah. Look at this."

Miller moved in closer, stood beside Clay. There was barely room for the two of them in that narrow hall. He looked down into the garbage.

"Shit."

"Look around, see if you can find something for me to put this in," Clay said. There was a touch of urgency in his voice.

Miller began opening drawers quickly, found finally a box of plastic quart-size baggies. He pulled out the last one and opened it. It wasn't easy with his gloves on but he moved as fast as he could. Clay grabbed a fork from the dish drainer, reached into the garbage with it, carefully lifted out a black T-shirt, wadded up and caked with dried blood. Miller held the open Baggie directly beneath it, and Clay placed it inside. When it hit the bottom, the Baggie almost slipped from Miller's hands. "Careful," Clay said, urgency still in his voice. He didn't like that, didn't like how it sounded. He didn't want Miller to know that he was in over his head. Clay tossed the fork into the Baggie, and then Miller closed it.

Clay looked into the garbage container again.

"There's broken glass in here," he said. "Looks like a drinking glass. Maybe he cut himself, used the shirt to stop the bleeding."

Miller looked into the container, saw that the garbage it held reached a little over halfway up. The broken glass rested on top of it. The shirt must have been on top of that.

"I don't see any blood on the glass. No blood on the lining."

Clay looked at him. "What does that mean?"

"The shirt was already dry when it was put in there."

"How fast does blood dry?"

"Pretty fast. But if he cut himself and used this T-shirt to stop the bleeding or clean up, I think it would have still been wet when he tossed it in."

Clay nodded, thought about that, glanced at the Baggie. After a moment he said, "The autopsy report will have the Foster kid's blood type on it, right?"

"Yeah, of course."

"But you said there were no marks on his body, or on any of the boys, not cuts or anything unusual."

"Yeah."

"So this wouldn't have come from him."

"Drowning can cause the sinuses to hemorrhage. The lungs, too. It's possible that he would have bled from the nose."

"The shirt is pretty well covered. Would he have bled that much?"

"No, probably not."

"So what the fuck is going on here?" Clay muttered.

Neither of them spoke for a moment.

"C'mon, let's get out of here," Clay said finally.

"Where are we going?"

Clay didn't answer. Miller followed him down the stairs, then across the street to Clay's Intrepid. Clay had his cell phone out and was speaking into it.

"I need you to do a reverse lookup for me," he said. He popped open his trunk. Miller placed the Baggie inside. Clay closed the trunk, waved his hand in a way that Miller took to mean that he wanted the number they had gotten from Kane's caller ID. Miller opened his notebook, held it for Clay to see. Clay read the Bridgehampton number aloud. Someone had called from there twice in the past hour. They'd start there and work back. When he was done reading the number, he said, "Call me back," then hung up.

They sat inside Clay's car. He started the motor, turned on the heat. "This fucking cold," he said. He looked through the driver's door window at Kane's apartment, his dark windows. He didn't say anything. A little over a minute later his cell phone rang.

"Yeah?" He waited, then said, "You've got to be kidding me." He listened, then said, "That may explain why we couldn't find her anywhere. Yeah, I'll go right now. Give me the address." He waved again to Miller. Miller got out the notebook and opened it. Clay repeated the address aloud. Miller wrote it down. He knew Clay was talking to Gregor, that Clay didn't want Gregor to know Miller was there with him. Miller wasn't bothered by that, didn't blame Clay one bit. *One step at a time.*

"I'll call you with what I find out." Clay hung up, slipped the cell phone into his coat pocket.

"What's going on?" Miller said.

"The number that called Kane twice in the last hour belongs to a woman named—get this—Colleen Auger."

"You're kidding."

"Sounds pretty close to Colette Auster, doesn't it? That's her address. We're going to check it out right now."

"We?"

Clay buckled his seat belt. "You've met Colette Auster. I haven't. I'm going to need you to tell me if she and this Colleen Auger are in fact the same woman. I assume you're willing to do that."

"Yeah, of course."

"If we're lucky, this Kane guy will be there with her."

"You think they're in this together?"

"I think they've been playing us like a pair of plywood violins."

Clay shifted into gear, pressed down on the accelerator. Miller pulled the seat belt across his chest as the car lurched forward and headed down the dark, empty street.

SEVEN

Kane looked up, didn't recognize his surroundings at first. He saw darkness, small roadside motels and cottages whisking by faster than his eyes could focus. Then suddenly all that gave way and he saw that he was moving across a bridge above a narrow body of water. The area around the water was lit up like a border crossing. *The Shinnecock Canal*, he thought.

"Where are we going?" he said.

The inside of Colette's Cherokee was dim, the green dashboard lights turned low.

"You said you didn't want to go back to your place," she said as she drove. "And my place is definitely out of the question. So I figured we could come here. You need some looking after, I think."

"Where's here?"

She didn't answer. Once across the bridge she made a sharp right turn, steering the Cherokee off Montauk Highway. She made a couple more turns, then pulled into the parking lot outside a large, run-down building. Three stories, immense, a wreck of a place. When she parked, Kane saw the entrance, and the sign above it.

The Water's Edge.

"We'll be okay here," Colette said.

"I don't really want to be around people right now."

"We won't be. Trust me. I'll take care of you."

They entered through a side door, around the corner from the entrance with the sign above it. This door, concealed in the heavy shadow of several large trees, on the side farthest from the bright lights of the canal, wasn't marked in any way. Kane and Colette entered a dark, narrow hallway, at the end of which stood another unmarked door. She led Kane to it, knocked on it. It was opened by a large man dressed in jeans and a sweatshirt, wearing heavy boots. His head was shaved. He wasn't the largest man Kane had seen recently, but he'd do. The man looked at Colette, then at Kane, nodded once, almost indifferently, and sat down on a stool that stood just inside the door. There was a bulge in the man's sweatshirt, where it hung over his belt. Kane was fairly certain that it was a gun. Colette smiled at the doorman, a warm smile, devoid, Kane thought, of her usual tricks, of those things of hers that all men and some women fell for. It was a smile of sincere appreciation, of thanks. Nothing hidden by it, nothing hidden in it. But maybe that was the trick, that was what worked on this particular man. But Kane didn't think too much about that. He needed to sit down, needed to recover. It had only been a half hour at the most since he was pinned under a heavy boot in the chapel. He was still shaken, and every now and then new pains would report themselves to him, find their way across already crowded nerves to his brain.

Colette led him past the bald man and through the door, then up a set of steep, noisy stairs to the floor above. This hallway wasn't any better lit than the one downstairs. They walked past several closed doors, Colette leading the way, the floor creaking beneath their feet every now and then. Paint was peeling from the doors, flakes curled like dead leaves, and there were small brass numbers set at eye level, and new-looking locks. At the end of the hall Colette stopped at a door that was marked 14. She opened it, they moved inside, then she closed the door behind them, locking it.

The room was murky till Colette found the light switch, and then suddenly, a soft red glow, as incomplete as candlelight, surrounded them. Kane saw a bed and a chair, and next to the chair, a small wall-mounted sink with some folded towels placed on its edge. There was nothing else in the room, except for two windows on perpendicular walls, set not all that far from each other. This was obviously a corner room. One of the windows was boarded up, but the other was only partially covered. A small rectangle of night was visible through a single pane of dirty glass. By the fact that they had walked the length of the building, and that beyond this smeared window was unnaturally bright light, Kane was certain that this room looked out over the canal.

"What is this place?" he said.

Colette didn't answer. She sat him down on the edge of the narrow bed, looking closely at the cuts on his head. Maybe she was so preoccupied that she hadn't heard the question.

"The bleeding has stopped," she said. "I should try to clean you up a little."

She went to the sink, ran a towel under the faucet, then brought it back, sat beside Kane. The worn mattress sagged beneath their combined weight. She touched his head, turning it slightly, and applied the warm, wet towel to the area around his cuts, trying to clean the dried blood out of his hair. She could see two gashes, not very big, but big enough.

"How did you get these?" she said softly.

"I don't really want to talk about it."

She smiled. He didn't know why. Maybe it was at the way he had said that, with a kind of sighing grunt, like he was some kind of tough guy. He supposed she knew him well enough to see the humor in the idea of that.

"You look like you could use a drink."

Kane didn't say anything. He waited till she finished cleaning him up, then said again, "What is this place, Colette?"

"I work downstairs," she said. "I tend bar."

"Is this a hotel?"

She shook her head, went back to tending his cuts. He knew for certain then that she was trying to avoid the subject.

"You know, I was looking for you tonight," she said. "I thought maybe you'd want to get together and go out and have a drink, toast poor Larry."

Kane wasn't in a hurry for an answer, didn't want to push

her. Maybe she wasn't supposed to tell him what this place was. Anyway, he already knew more than he needed or wanted to know. This was someone else's business, he didn't really care one way or another. He decided to let his question drop for now.

"How'd you know I'd be in my office just now?"

"I didn't. I saw your Jeep in the parking lot, then saw that your light was on."

"What were you doing on campus? I mean, at this time of night."

"I model for the art students once in a while."

Kane nodded. She had the figure for it, and he didn't have a difficult time at all imagining her taking off her clothes in front of a roomful of people. She was bold, he knew that about her, had seen the way everyone in his class was drawn to her because of her boldness. Even the women. *Like a siren,* he had heard one woman, in her forties, divorced, taking the course as audit, say to another in the hallway. *Like a siren,* not said with contempt or rancor but with a little bit of awe, a little bit of envy. Colette's "fictional memoir" was full of sexuality, all of it frankly handled. Often, though, it wasn't flattering to her, and Kane had given her credit for that, for writing honestly about the fucks-ups as well as the fucks. If things had been different for Kane, if it hadn't been for Meg, for the hold she had on him, the hold he wanted her to have on him, needed, to keep him from falling to pieces— if it weren't for Meg, Kane probably would have acted around Colette a little more like all the others, like Larry Foster, poor Larry Foster, all the Larry Fosters. If it weren't for Meg, Kane would certainly have had some hope of contributing in a significant way to her "memoir."

"You were modeling tonight?"

She nodded, got up from the bed, rinsed the towel in the sink, sat next to him, went back to work.

"These are pretty deep. Maybe I should see if they have any bandages."

"Don't worry about it."

"You sure?"

"I'd rather you didn't leave. I don't feel so hot right now."

There was strength in Colette's hands, Kane noticed then, authority. She was strong, but strong in a precise way, not sloppy or rough, not careless. Meg was sloppy-rough, and he had the scratches on his face to prove it. Colette cleaned around his wounds, scrubbed around them, without touching them, without causing him much pain at all. Her strength—powerful hands lined with thick veins, forearm muscles that flexed with every movement—only emphasized his own overall weakness, made even more so now by the beating he had just taken.

"I think I need to lie down," he said.

"You okay?"

"I'd just like to lie down."

"Yeah, sure. Take off your coat."

Kane began to but stopped suddenly, wincing, drawing in a sharp breath.

"What?" she said.

"Just give me a minute."

"Let me help you." She placed the damp towel on the bed, then opened Kane's jacket as wide as it would go. This gave him enough room to slip out of it without having to wriggle so much. Still, it was slow going. When it was finally off, she tossed the jacket aside. Kane lowered himself down onto his back. He winced again, drew in a breath, more sharply than before. Once he was flat, Colette leaned over him and unbuttoned his shirt, opening it up. She saw several bruises on his chest—three of them, but so large they had almost merged into one giant mass. In the red light they looked like wide gashes, like flesh that had been cut and spread open.

"Jesus Christ," she said. "What happened?"

Kane didn't answer, just lay there, breathing.

"Who did this to you?"

"I never saw his face."

"*When* did this happen?"

"Just before you knocked on my door."

"At the college?"

"Not exactly."

"What do you mean?"

He paused, thought about saying nothing. But there was no reason to keep this from her.

"I went out to the chapel," Kane said.

"What for?"

"To find out if what you had said would be inside was inside."

"Why did you do that?"

"I was asked to go."

"By who?"

"Some private investigator. He was hired by Larry's family to prove that Larry hadn't killed himself."

"Why you, though?"

"What do you mean?"

"He just walked up to you out of the blue and asked you to do this?"

"No. Mercer knows him."

"Professor Mercer?"

"Yeah."

"He put you and this private investigator together?"

"Yeah. Why?"

She ignored the question. "So who did this to you?" She seemed almost afraid to ask the question for a second time, as if suddenly she was afraid of what the answer just might be.

"I didn't see his face."

"Did he come up behind you or something?"

"No, he stood right there in front of me. It was pretty dark in there."

"But you saw him? I mean, you could see the shape of him?" She stopped short.

"Yeah."

"Was he big?"

Kane nodded.

"How big?"

"Jolly Green Giant big. I thought at first maybe it was this guy I met yesterday, a guy named Clay. But Clay has an accent, and the guy who used me like a doormat didn't."

"He spoke to you?"

"Yeah."

"What did he say?"

"A lot of shit."

"What exactly?"

Kane shrugged. He didn't really want to think about it or repeat it.

Colette waited a moment, thinking, then said, "Was anyone with him?"

"No. He was alone. He was enough. He spoke to someone on the phone, though."

"What did he say?"

"He wanted to know whether he should kill me or not."

"And?"

"Obviously he didn't kill me."

"Do you know why he didn't?"

"I heard something about them needing me, that everything hinged on me. Something like that."

Colette paused to think again. Kane was grateful for the break, though it didn't last all that long.

"So what did you see in the chapel?" Colette said.

"Exactly what you had told them would be there."

Another silence. Kane looked around the sparse room, saw the peeling walls, the boarded-over windows. He thought of the numbers on the door and the armed man at the bottom of the stairs. He wanted to avoid talking any more about what had just happened to him and asked the first question that came to his mind, the question that Colette had twice so far avoided. Suddenly, without knowing why, Kane decided that he needed it answered.

"What exactly is this place, Colette?"

"It's just the bar where I work."

She got up, this time ran a clean towel under the faucet, brought it back and laid it across Kane's chest. This had worked before. The water was cold, not warm, and Kane would have moved in reaction against it if the cold wasn't less painful than what he would have felt trying to avoid it. Colette was careful not to move too much, careful not to touch the bruises on his chest directly, or even the area around them.

"God, that looks so bad," she said.

Kane wondered then if there was maybe something sinister in her avoidance. He'd already felt helpless once tonight, didn't really care to feel that way again.

He spoke as firmly as he could. "What are these rooms for, Colette?"

She shrugged, thought for a moment, then looked at him and said, "What do you think?"

He looked around the room again, not that he needed to. Bed, sink, chair. Boarded-over windows. Red light mounted on the wall. If he hadn't already known, it wouldn't have taken him long to do the math.

"It's a brothel," he said. He couldn't think of another word, at least not one that wasn't derogatory. He felt for some reason compelled to make where he was seem less notorious.

Colette nodded, looked at the unpainted walls. "It's amazing how many men are willing to pay top dollar to pretend they're slumming it. I don't know, maybe it adds to the thrill. The owner calls the decor 'A Bit of Old New Orleans.' I think that's being charitable, don't you?"

"And you tend bar here?"

"Yeah. The bar's just the cover, and a profitable one at that. I didn't know what went on up here when I was hired. I don't think I was ever supposed to find out. But I did."

"How can a place like this be in business?"

"The owner is connected."

"But don't people talk? I mean, customers, johns, whatever they're called. How can this be a secret?"

"The people who drink themselves stupid downstairs every night have no idea what goes on up here. Up here is a private-club kind of thing. Only a handful of people belong to it. Rich people, influential. They come from all over to get pretty much whatever they want. Who was it that said a writer should live in a monastery by day and a whorehouse by night?"

"Gabriel García Márquez."

"Yeah. I love him. When I found out about what went on

up here, I figured that maybe I'd write about it someday. It's the kind of story that can make a person rich and famous, you know?"

"If it's supposed to be such a secret, how did you find out?"

"Everyone who works here, everyone but me pretty much, is part of this big South American family. The son of the owner runs the bar. He was the one who hired me. I think he told me to impress me. He was drunk, and the next day he called me, all scared, begged me not to repeat to anyone what he had said. He made it pretty clear what would happen to both of us if anyone found out that he had shot his mouth off to me."

"How long have you worked here?"

"About six months."

"How long ago did you find out?"

"After I'd been here a month." She looked down at Kane's chest, then said, "Listen, I'm sorry I got you into this. It's all my fault."

"You know the guy who did this to me, don't you?"

"What makes you say that?"

"You asked some pretty specific questions about him."

She looked at Kane, looked at his eyes, then nodded. "Yeah, I know him."

"Who is he?"

"His name is Dean, or at least that's what he said his name was. Just Dean, nothing else. Like Dean Moriarty from *On the Road*. That's what he told me, anyway. He loved Kerouac, loved all things from the fifties. He had one serious Brando fixation. Too serious, if you know what I mean."

"How do you know him?"

"He's someone from my past."

"An ex-boyfriend."

"No. We used to be in the same business together."

"What business?"

"Drugs, mainly."

"You sold drugs?"

"He sold them. I ran them."

Kane nodded, said nothing.

"I hadn't seen him in over a year. I thought I'd gotten rid of him for good. Then one night he just walked in. I found out later that someone we used to know had seen me working here and tipped him off. He'd been looking for me for a while, but I've gotten pretty good at being hard to find."

"Why was he looking for you?"

"There was some unpleasantness between us. And some unfinished business."

"What does that mean?"

"I left him a little in the lurch, financially speaking. I took off with some money that was his, that he owed to someone else. That was the unfinished business."

"And the unpleasantness?"

"He used to want to fuck me."

Kane nodded.

"Nothing happened," she said. "I wasn't interested. He's pretty ugly. Be grateful you never saw his face. On top of that, he's pretty much as insane as they get."

"Insane how?"

"I think he must have done some serious steroid damage to his brain at some point. He's got a pretty freaky temper."

"That explains a lot."

"He's got a real reputation for violence. A real knack for it, too."

"He seemed to enjoy pouncing on me."

"He's a bit of a sadist."

Kane nodded at that, then said, "So one night he walks in here and finds you. Then what?"

"He told me that he wanted me to do something for him. That I owed him, and he'd make trouble for me if I didn't help him out."

"What did he want you to do?"

"He said he had a friend, some older man who liked to take photographs of young men, liked the young men to be unconscious while he took his photos, liked them to be naked. Dean wanted me to help him get a young man for his friend."

"That's an . . . unusual request."

"It wasn't a request."

"How exactly did he expect you to 'get young men'?"

"He had it all planned out. I was supposed to pick someone out, someone who trusted me. He and his friend had a
specific type in mind, but other than that, it could be anyone
I knew."

"Then what?"

"I was supposed to tell this kid to meet me for a drink.
Dean gave me something to slip into his glass. Then I was
supposed to tell the kid to wait a few minutes after I left
and then meet me down the road a bit. From there they'd do
the rest."

"So you did this?"

She hesitated, then nodded. "I didn't want to. I didn't really have a choice, though."

"You could have gone to the police."

"Not really."

"Why not?"

"Who was it that said the problem with living outside the
law was that you no longer had the protection of it?"

"Truman Capote."

"Yeah, well, there was nothing he didn't know, right?"

"You're in trouble with the police?"

She nodded again.

Kane waited a moment, thinking of all this, then said,
"So you did what they wanted?"

"Yeah."

"Larry was one of the boys?"

"Yeah."

"And the boy they found before him?"

Colette paused, then nodded again. "Yeah, him too."

"Did you know they were going to kill them?"

"No. They said the first boy had probably gone swimming after having too much to drink, just like the police
said. They said they'd only kept him for a few hours, then let
him go when the drug wore off. He wasn't found dead till the
next night."

"And you believed what they said?"

"I wanted to believe it. I needed to. I told myself what I needed to tell myself to live with what I had done. You can understand that, right?"

Kane nodded absently. "But when Larry turned up dead?"

"I started having my doubts even before that. I guess deep down I knew that the first boy hadn't been an accident. I knew there was more going on with Dean and his friend than just picture taking. There had to be."

"What made you think that?"

"We had only talked in person that one night, Dean and I. The rest of the times it was always on cell phones, and each time he called me, it was from a different number. Never on my home line, always my cell phone. I remembered, though, that his mother had a house in Riverhead. We'd gone there once, back when we were in business together, right after she had died. I don't think he ever knew his father. I decided to drive over there and see what I could see. This was the night after I'd met Larry at the bar and slipped what they gave me into his drink, then told him to wait five minutes and leave. I kept listening to the news on the radio, waiting to hear that he turned up dead somewhere, dreading hearing it. I couldn't sit around any longer. It didn't seem like anyone was home, and then I saw this white van back out from behind the house. I followed it, saw him toss Larry's body into the bay, saw it get carried away in the tide. I called the cops, told them where to look. I figured maybe, somehow, they'd trace it back to him."

"Why didn't you tell them where he lived?"

"Dean would have known that it was me. I didn't want to chance having him come looking for me. Making the phone call I made was bad enough. I didn't dare stay home. I never told Dean where I lived, but if I could follow him, then he could have just as easily followed me home from work one night. I didn't want to sit around and wait for him to knock down my door. So I asked Jorge if I could stay here."

"Who's Jorge?"

"The bar manager. The one who got drunk and told me about what went on up here. I figured this way I could stay here and still work and not have to leave, not have to run the risk of running into Dean on the road."

"Do you think he knows you're here?"

"I'm hoping he thinks I blew town again. Anyway, Ty's at the door every night till closing. And there's always someone in the back room just behind the bar. The men they have working here are pretty serious about their jobs."

"I don't understand something. If you're in such danger, then why did you go to the college tonight to model?"

"I didn't."

"What do you mean?"

"I didn't know you knew as much as you did. I didn't know you had gone out to the chapel, or that anyone had talked to you about any of this. I didn't know what else to say."

"So then why *were* you there?"

"I was looking for you."

"What for?"

"I called your place but you didn't answer. I was desperate, decided to come look for you. I drove by the college, saw your Jeep in the lot, then your light."

"Why were you looking for me?"

"Because Dean never mentioned this friend of his by name. Never once. He only referred to him by a nickname."

"What nickname?"

"The Professor."

It took Kane a moment to respond. He didn't see any significance at all, any connection to anything. He got the impression, though, that Colette thought he'd see it right away.

"I don't understand," he said finally.

"You sit here long enough, you start to think of all kinds of things. You start to try to fit the pieces together."

"I'm not following you, Colette."

"Dean had told me that if anyone asked me anything about Larry, about why he had disappeared for one night, *anything*, that I was supposed to tell them about the chapel, that Larry used to go there with friends and do Satan worship, that he had bragged to me about it. This is what made me realize that Larry wasn't coming back alive."

"Larry never said anything to you about the chapel or what went on there?"

"No, not once. Dean told me to say that. He told me exactly what to say, made me memorize it."

"But I saw it. I saw the writing on the walls, the drawings. There was even this little altar made of wood and milk crates."

"Pretty convenient, huh?"

"You think it was staged?"

"It's crossed my mind, yeah."

"But why? Why would they do that?"

She shrugged. "Diversion. Maybe a wild goose chase, to waste the cops' time or something. Like I said, Dean was very specific about what I was supposed to say to anyone who asked me about Larry. I think it's safe to say that he wanted someone to go there, to find it just the way it was."

Kane waited a moment, thinking about all that, then said, "I'm sorry, though, I'm still not following. What does that have to do with you looking for me tonight?"

"It was Dean who told me to pick Larry. The first kid could be anyone I wanted it to be, as long as he fit the description. It would work better if it was someone I knew, someone who trusted me. But he was very specific about Larry, knew Larry's name, knew a lot of things about him, his class schedule, what dorm he was in, that Larry had a thing for me. I finally asked Dean why it had to be Larry, and he said the Professor wanted him next, that he wanted Larry Foster or it was no deal. So whoever this Professor is knew Larry, knew that I knew him, that I would have easy access to him."

"So you were looking for me to tell me that."

"No. I was looking for you to ask you just how well you knew Mercer."

"What?"

"How well do you know Mercer?"

"This is ridiculous, Colette."

"Think about it. When I find you, you tell me that someone beat you up out at the chapel, someone who can only be

Dean, and that some private investigator that Mercer knows sent you there, that it was *Mercer* who put you and this private investigator together to begin with."

"This is crazy."

"Mercer would know about the chapel."

"A lot of people know about the chapel, Colette. Everyone who goes to the college or works there knows about it. Everyone who *ever* went to the college and who *ever* worked there knows about it."

"He knew Larry, or knew of him, anyway, saw him in the hallways every day, saw me talking to him, saw the three of us in your class."

"So did a lot of people."

"Dean said something about the professor having a German name. Is Mercer German?"

"I don't think so."

"You don't see a possible connection here?"

"I see a connection, yeah, but not the one you see."

"How well do you know him, though?"

"I know him very well."

"But how well do we really know anyone, what they're capable of? That's the thing with crazy killers, no one they know ever sees it coming. That's always the case, isn't it? That's how they get away with what they get away with for so long. He'd see Larry every day, Larry could have caught his eye, driven him crazy for some reason. Who knows what makes someone like that do what they do."

"First of all, it's just not possible, okay. Not in a million lifetimes. Mercer's not like that. He's married. To wife number four. I think I'd know if he had a thing for boys."

"Does he know about all your 'things'? Your kinks?" She glanced at the scratches on Kane's face. He ignored the shift in her eyes.

"Second," he said, "he's been busting his ass trying to keep me from getting fired. You make it sound like he's setting me up for something, that he conspired to get me to go out to the chapel. He's my friend, Colette, he's trying to help me."

"I used to see Dean do that all the time."

"Do what?"

"Keep someone close by. Keep them right there beside him, to take the fall for him if necessary. You don't know Dean. He's got serious steroid damage, yeah, but the part of his brain that thinks of ways to cover his ass works just fine. He knows how to pin things on people. I saw him do it a dozen times. A little coke in someone's car, a call to the police—boom, the competition, or threat, or whatever's eliminated just like that."

"But that's Dean. We're talking about Mercer."

"But if the Professor that Dean talked about is him, then that means they're working together. Dean could have taught him that little trick. Dean taught me a lot of shit back when we were in business together."

"This is crazy talk, Colette. It's just . . . crazy talk, that's all."

"He called someone from the chapel. Right? That's what you said. Dean called someone from the chapel, and the person on the other end said they needed you, that it all hinged on you, or something like that. That's what you said, right?"

"First of all, we don't know for a fact that it was your buddy Dean who did this to me."

"Who else could it be? I mean, c'mon, what are the chances that someone built like him would just show up out there while you happened to be looking around, then jump you and call someone and ask if he should kill you or not? C'mon, what are the chances of that?"

Kane said nothing. He was tired, past tired. And besides, what could he say? She was right—about this much, anyway, about the man who stomped him having to be the man she knew as Dean.

"I know Mercer means a lot to you," Colette said. "I know you look up to him and all that. And I'm not saying it is him. I'm not saying I'm right about this. I'm just telling you what I know and what I see. I'm just saying it's possible, that's all. Everything's possible, even the impossible. *Especially* the impossible. I mean, that's the thing about being alive, isn't it? About being alive in this world? For better and for worse, the impossible happens."

Kane didn't say anything. He didn't want to talk about this anymore, about any of it. Still, as he lay there, he found himself thinking over everything Colette had just said, looking more, or so he thought, for some way to dismiss it, some argument, some single fact, that would turn what she was considering into dust once and for all.

But the more he looked for that, for that one thing, the more he started remembering other things, things that only added to his confusion. The broken lock on his door. Mercer's visit to his apartment the following afternoon. Mercer's calling Meg's house, looking for Kane there the morning after Larry was found, bringing Kane in to talk to the two detectives. He thought about all this despite himself, despite the fact that he knew Colette was wrong, crazy wrong, out-of-her-fucking-mind wrong. Every part of him knew it, knew that she had to be. *Just had to be.* Mercer wasn't like that, wasn't capable of that. No one he knew, no one in his ever-diminishing world, could be.

And, yet, here was Kane, here was Colette. Dean had called someone. If not Mercer, then who?

Kane needed to find a way out of this, right now, his *mind* needed to find a way out, a way of escaping from these spiraling thoughts. He felt as if he was being led into a dark maze, and he wasn't up for that, not by any stretch of the imagination was he up for that. None of this made any sense, *none of it, none at all*—and, yet what from the last few days did? Or from the last four years?

His mind—tired now, way beyond tired—grabbed at the first sane question that floated by.

"What does Dean get out of all this?"

"What do you mean?"

"Why does he do this for his friend? Why does he go to all this trouble just so a buddy of his can fulfill some perverse fantasy?"

"Money, that's why. When I left Dean in the lurch, he lost everything, had to go back to Riverhead and lay low in his mother's house, take some crappy job just to pay the bills. The money that he's getting for this is supposed to be enough to get him back into the game. He blames me for losing everything. I think the only thing that kept him from killing me for what I did to him was the fact that he needed me, that he knew he could blackmail me into doing this for him. And, like I said, the guy's a sadist. Hurting people was sometimes part of the business. He was never squeamish about doing what he had to do."

"How much trouble exactly could he make for you? With the police, I mean. What could he tell them about you?"

"Enough."

"Then maybe you could get a lawyer, try to get immunity or something, testify against him and the Professor."

"Yeah, well, lawyers cost money. I'm a little short of that these days."

She lifted the towel from Kane's chest, looked at the bruises, then turned the towel over and lay the fresh side across him. He felt the coolness against his burning skin.

"I'm sorry you got dragged into this," she said. "I didn't think you'd be the one to go out there and look around. If I had thought that was possible, I wouldn't have said anything."

"It's all right."

Neither of them spoke for a long time. What was there left to say? Finally, though, Colette's raspy voice broke the silence.

"So where's your girlfriend tonight?" she said.

Kane swallowed, took a slow breath through his nose, let it out. "Home with her husband."

"So I guess you won't be going there, will you?"

"No."

"Back in the office you said you didn't want to go to your apartment."

"My lock's broken. I didn't feel like waiting there for anyone to just come by and walk in."

"You can stay here. You know that, right? You can stay for as long as you need."

"What about Jorge?"

"What about him?"

"How's he going to like the idea of me being up here with you?"

"He'll do what I say. He feels responsible for me."

"Why?"

"Because Dean found me here. Jorge doesn't know I have a past with him. He thinks Dean is some customer who got the wrong idea and won't leave me alone."

Kane nodded and looked up at the ceiling, the peeling walls, imagined the rooms just down the hall, imagined them to be just like this one. *Dilapidated chic*. He imagined what went on here—the men who paid, the women who performed for money, and the reasons, all the reasons imaginable, why either would do what they did.

"You know, when I woke up today," he said, "little did I know I'd end up under pimp protection."

Colette laughed. Her smile hovered above him. It was wild, glowing. Kane could tell by her laugh that he had caught her off guard.

"Look, maybe I'm wrong about Mercer," she said. "You know him, I don't. But, like I said, you sit here all night, staring at these walls, and you start to think about all kinds of things. Jorge won't even let me work my shifts anymore. Some kid came in two nights ago, asked me questions about Larry. After that Jorge told me it was too dangerous to have me behind the bar, that I'd have to sit it out till this all blew over or something was done."

"What kid?" Kane said.

"He told me his name was Tommy Miller. He was big, not Jolly Green Giant big, but big, you know, bigger than us. He walked with a limp. I just assumed that he was the private investigator you had talked to, or that he worked for him."

"I haven't seen anyone with a limp. Not yet, anyway."

"Yeah, well, you're pretty close to walking with one yourself. How's your head feel?"

"It hurts. But it's been hurting since I woke up today, so at least I'm maintaining a status quo."

"You should get some sleep. You should rest."

Kane looked again at the walls, the ceiling, thought of Meg, for some reason, felt—despite his condition, despite where he was, who he was with, what had been said and done—a tugging low in his gut, a yearning, a need *for something*.

"You know, you're right about these walls," he said after a moment.

"Maybe it's because they're so blank. We tend to want to fill in the blanks, don't we? Or cover them over."

"Melville's whale," Kane said.

Colette looked at him. "What do you mean?"

"*Moby-Dick.* What we project onto blank spaces tells us everything about who we are."

Colette said nothing, just watched his face.

"I need to get something from my office," he announced after a moment.

"What?"

He shrugged. "Just something. I can't leave it there for anyone to find."

"We can go back first thing in the morning. Get in before anyone shows up."

"Maybe I should go alone."

"No, I'll go with you."

"Shouldn't you stay here, where it's safe?"

"It's just to the college and back. It'll be all right. I need to get out."

"You're sure?"

"Yeah. The building will still be locked up that early. Do you have a key?"

"I think maybe they gave me one back when I started. If they had, it's in my Jeep, in the console between my seats. I'm usually still asleep when the first class starts. Usually asleep when it ends, too."

"Nice life."

Kane nodded. "It was, yeah." He waited a moment, then said, "Are you tired?"

"I'm fucking beat."

"Maybe you should sleep, too."

"Is there room there?"

"Yeah, sure."

Colette got up and turned off the light. In an instant the room was dark, as dark nearly as the chapel had been. Kane lay there and listened as Colette came back and moved in beside him on the narrow bed. He could sense that she was trying to be careful, trying to jostle the worn mattress as little as possible. He waited till she settled in—on her right side, facing him—then relaxed as best as his injuries would allow. It was cold in the room, except for where her warm breath touched the side of his face. She lay her hand on his stomach, low, just above the waistband of his jeans. "Is that okay?" she said. "Does it hurt?" He told her it didn't, wondered then if maybe she felt the same tug in her stomach that he had felt moments ago in his, if in general she knew the same need in the night as he. He could hear her breathing, and as he listened to it his eyes got used to the weak light that made it in through the dirty rectangle of window across the small room. Canal light. White-blue. He could see her face then, the shape of it anyway, make out her features, some better than others. Her brown eyes caught this ghostly light, reflected it in a liquid kind of way. Kane thought of water, didn't want to think of that, pushed it out of his mind. Always there, always just a thought away. He reached for something to replace that thought, anything, remembered staring at Colette's eyes all semester, forcing himself to look away from them again and again and again. Now, though, *this close, her face this close to his,* and no reason anymore to look away. Who would care now? Who could say anything?

He let himself feel her breathing for a long time, feel it touch his face, disappear, then touch it again—warmth, cool, warmth, cool. Steady, unending. He listened to it, heard only it. Maybe he fell asleep for a while. He had no idea how long. Maybe she had fallen asleep, too. But when he realized again where he was, who this was beside him, how much he needed to forget, he rolled his head to the side and faced her, found her lips in the dark. He felt her mouth open slightly, immediately, felt right away the same hunger, the same need, felt his tongue fall in to meet hers, fall into a dark, cool cave . . .

They kissed like that for a long time. Like two kids. Kane couldn't remember the last time he'd gotten lost like that, the last time he had lost all sense of time in *just making out,* all sense of anything but where his body touched another in the darkness, where that body touched his. Lips and tongues and hands, small sounds. After a while, though, Colette leaned back and began to undress him. Without a word, without urgency. It was just time now. She took off his shoes, the shoes Gregor had given him to wear, then undid his jeans, never letting her stare, *that stare of hers,* break for too long. *Eyes on his, a quick glance down at her hands as she fussed with a button, then eyes back on him, a soft smile, a knowing smile.* She pulled one leg free, then the other, dropped his jeans to the wood floor, where she had just a moment before dropped both shoes. Kane was still on his back, unable to move much, his shirt unbuttoned and spread open. She left it as it was, removed the damp towel that covered his chest, tossed it away, then she sat up on the edge of the bed and pulled her shirt over her head. One smooth, elegant motion. She undid her bra, dropped it to the floor, stood, kicked off her shoes as she unzipped her jeans, let them fall by the weight of the change in her pockets to her ankles. She stepped out of them, first her right foot, then her left, never once coming near to losing her balance. Her legs were long and smooth. Lean. She hooked the straps at the sides of her black lace thong with her thumbs, bent forward and pulled down, stepping out of that, too, with the same assuredness, the same grace. That alone was reason enough to want her. When she stood up again, he could see her tight dancer's back in the weak light, see the long bands of muscles, the line of her straight spine. Soft skin and dark shadows. He saw her long, elegant neck, wanted to kiss it, wanted to hold the back of it as he pulled her face to his and kissed her lips. He didn't care at all now about making sense of any of this, of anything. He only cared about his senses, what he could see before him, and the pleasure that was now just a moment away.

Colette turned and faced him, so he could see her, stood

there in the muted light, not posing, just standing there, hands hanging at her sides. Olive skin, breasts that were surprisingly full for a dancer, nipples hard in the cold.

"Go ahead, drink it in," she whispered.

Finally she came back to bed and straddled him, moving as carefully as before. She settled above him, leaning over him, resting her hands lightly on his shoulders. He felt her pubic hair brush against his. She asked again if he was okay. He nodded that he was, would have nodded even if he wasn't, who was he kidding? Not long after this he became aware that she was smiling, suddenly and wildly, at something, a thought, something. He heard the smile more than saw it, heard it above him in the darkness, heard her lips part and a soft, quick half sigh, half laugh. *A giggle, girlish, yes, and yet . . .*

"What?" he whispered.

"I just can't help myself," she whispered back. "I like my men helpless."

She sounded, of all things, *happy.* She reached between his legs with her hand. He felt her fingers search for him, felt them wrap around him as she aligned herself with him. Then she leaned back and sank down—one smooth, merciful thrust, and there he was, inside her. They gasped together, once. Neither moved for a moment after that. Stunned, like two birds that had flown into a window. *There was nothing else in the world but this here, this now,* Kane thought. He gave himself over to his overwhelming conviction that the world had fled them both. They lingered, motionless, letting the moment last, the moment that had made them gasp. The rest would come, of course it would, but first *this,* first *this feeling.* Finally Colette began to rock back and forth. Gently, searching for more now, more than just that first sensation, that first rush. Kane slipped even more deeply inside her. They both gasped again. Colette smiled, above him. *So happy.*

He stopped thinking then, stopped thinking in words, anyway. After a moment her hands left his shoulders and she leaned forward, resting her elbows on the mattress. Her face was above his now, her hard breasts—colder even than the air—pinned between them, pressing onto his chest. He felt pain, not a lot but enough that his mouth opened. Immediately Colette sealed her lips around it, before a sound could get out. It stuck in his throat but he didn't care. She kissed him, deeply, her dark hair falling around his face like a curtain, shrouding out all hint of the canal light.

Her felt her biting his lip, hard, felt the greed building in her, felt them moving together toward the same dark place, the same precious, fevered amnesia.

K ane awoke with a start and turned his head, looked for the small rectangle of window that overlooked the canal. Through it, a dark sky only just beginning to pale. Or was it maybe a pale sky just beginning to darken? He had made that mistake once before. He checked his watch: 6:15 AM. Looking at the window again, he could see that it was definitely the first moments of a slow winter dawn outside. He was relieved; they hadn't overslept. First real light was maybe a half hour away. Plenty of time to get Meg's tape from his office and get back here before the sun broke over the horizon.

He woke Colette. There would have been no way not to even if he had tried. Her left leg was over his legs, her arms across his stomach. She opened her eyes. They looked tired but no less intense. She smiled at him, fondly. Not a bad way to start a day. She asked what time it was. A morning whisper, intimate. He told her, then got up and found his clothes and began to dress. He had stiffened up during the night, bad, so dressing wasn't easy, particularly when he tried to put on the black shoes. But he did his best to hide all that from Colette. She moved even more slowly. Not a morning person, not that Kane was, but even less so for her, it seemed. He remembered when he was a bartender, going to bed at dawn, sleeping well past noon, writing in the afternoon, working on his book till his shift. A ghoul's life, his ex-wife, Patricia, had called it. When he was finally dressed, Kane went to the window and looked down at the canal, to see if the lights had gone out yet. They had. The predawn looked barren, rising gray washing over diminishing black. It seemed somehow colder out there, if that was possible, colder than the day before had been, and the day before that, and the day before that. He wondered if, when they returned here, would they crawl back into her bed, for warmth, for more sleep, for lack of anything else to do? He wondered if he would be here with her tonight, if they would repeat what they had done last night, and then repeat that, too. *So much to forget, to push away*. For the both of them. And nowhere else to go. But a lot could happen between now and then. Kane had to acknowledge that. The world, his world, was in flux. Nothing was as it should be, no one, it turned out, was as they had once seemed.

Kane thought about Mercer, tried to put it out of his head. Too early, too confusing. What if Colette was right? Anything was possible, even the impossible. What then? *What then?* His mind went to Meg, had known it would sooner or later. He thought about her waking up beside her husband in the next hour, walking around her kitchen naked, looking out at her tranquil bay, getting ready for her day's work. Kane could barely remember the last time he was there with her. How many days had it been? Or would it be better to ask how few days? No, not better, Kane thought. However long it had or hadn't been, Meg may as well have been in another country, there may as well have been countless guarded borders between them, no easy way back, if any at all. The one thing she didn't want was trouble. She'd made that clear, had everything to lose. Kane now had nothing *but* troubles. He'd have to stay away, regardless of what he had done last night, and might do again tonight. For her sake, for the sake of whatever future there still might be for them, he needed to stay clear of her.

But whatever he felt about her at that moment, whatever feelings were still strong, whatever feelings were maybe slipping, whatever trouble he was in, he had promised her that the tape would not come back to haunt her. He wanted to keep his word, to rest easy about that when he could rest, and face whatever it was ahead of him knowing he had at least done that much right, done that for her.

Kane looked back at Colette. She was dressed, had her shoes on, her coat across her lap. But by the way she was sitting on the edge of the bed, staring off, Kane knew something was on her mind. Her expression was complex, a direct contrast to the smile and look of pleasure he had seen in the dark above him last night.

"What's wrong?" he said.

She looked up at him. "I was thinking about something," she said softly.

"What?"

"Larry."

Kane said nothing. He watched her, watched the expression on her face. She looked pained now, as if she was on the verge of some kind of realization, one she'd really rather not have.

"What do you think they did to him?"

"I don't know," Kane said. "I don't really want to think about it, though."

She waited a moment, nodding absently, then said, "You know, maybe I should make an anonymous call to the cops, like you said. Let them know where Dean lives, what I know."

"What about talking to a lawyer?"

"I told you, I don't have the money for that."

"Maybe we can find one who'll do it for free. Or at least for cheap."

"Who?"

Kane shrugged. "I don't know." The only lawyer he knew was Meg's husband. That wasn't exactly promising, though, was it?

"Anyway, I can't imagine the DA just letting me walk away from this. I mean not even with everything I could tell him. I think legally I'm as guilty of murder as Dean and the Professor are. The DA would offer me a plea maybe, but not straight-out immunity. Certainly not with any lawyer who works for free trying to make the deal."

"You can't be guilty of murder if you didn't know they were going to kill the boys."

"I should have known, though. That's what they'll say. Especially after Brian."

"He was the second boy you chose."

"Yeah."

Kane wondered how she knew him, how she came to choose him, to lure him. He wondered, too, to what lengths he would go if someone had something on him, had him by the balls.

"Dean was blackmailing you," he said. "That should make a difference."

"When the cops realize who I really am, it won't matter."

"What do you mean, who you really are?"

She was too deep in thought to answer. Or maybe that was her way of avoiding the question. She seemed to have a real gift for that.

"If they arrest him," Colette said finally, "they will come looking for me. There's no doubt about that. If they do arrest him but he ends up for some reason walking free, *he'll* be looking for me. Either way, I'll have to leave here."

Kane couldn't help himself any longer. "What exactly is it you've done that's so horrible, Colette?"

"Just trouble in my past."

"With drugs."

She nodded. "Among other things."

"What other things?"

"Does it matter?"

"It might."

"We've got all day to talk about this." She nodded toward the window and stood. "We should get going before it gets too light out."

"Maybe I should go to the campus alone. Maybe you should stay here."

"No, I want to do this. If I sit around and stare at the walls and think, I'll go out of my mind. I'll just think more and more about poor Larry and what they did to him."

She looked at Kane as she put her coat on. Her eyes were soft with sorrow, glassy, tired. Kane remembered seeing her eyes in the dark a few hours before, how, reflecting the canal light, they had looked watery, and what seeing them like that had reminded him of. His son's death wasn't his fault, and still he could barely live with it, could barely hang on to anything good, even now, four years later. He could not imagine what his life would be if he *had* been to blame, even in the smallest way. Colette was facing something close to that now, facing having to imagine the unimaginable, a life of knowing someone—two people—were dead because of you, had suffered because of you. A life of guilt and regret, a life of nights in the dark, trying to forget.

"Where would you go?" Kane said. "If you left, where would you go?"

"I don't know. I mean, I'd have to leave here, I know that much. I couldn't just move to a different town. I'd need to go somewhere far away."

Kane let himself imagine that, imagine a place far away, a room or an apartment in some small town or unknown city, a life away from all this, away from everything, good and bad, that he'd ever known. He wondered then what would have happened had he found a teaching job elsewhere— upstate New York, Iowa, New Mexico, Kansas. Anywhere but back here, where he had started, where his onetime hero had blazed a trail of infamous self-destruction. Worn paths are so easy to follow. Too easy. Mercer had been right about that much.

"Why do you ask?" Colette said.

"Just curious."

She waited a moment, studying him, then said, "You could come with me, if you wanted. We could be two writers living in exile together. We could get jobs, write, read. We could tell people whatever we wanted to tell them about ourselves. Nothing more, nothing less than what we wanted to tell them."

In his tired mind Kane saw an apartment—above a pharmacy maybe, in some town out west—with a lock on the door, a bed under a window, a second way out if someone came knocking, a second chance at a second chance. He didn't want to look away from it, didn't want to break the sense of simplicity this imagined way of life promised.

Finally, though, he looked at Colette. She was watching him closely. The sorrow was still deep in her eyes. But Kane saw something else, too. Something he wouldn't mind seeing on a regular basis. A look of understanding. Acceptance, maybe. Recognition.

"What do you think?" she said softly.

"Exile sounds pretty good to me."

"We'll have plenty of time to talk about it when we get back. Well, all day, anyway."

They waited a moment, looking at each other. Neither said anything more. Finally they left the room together and walked down the hallway to the back stairs. It was already too light out, but there wasn't anything they could do about that. Ty wasn't at his post at the bottom of the stairs, but Colette didn't seem at all alarmed by that. She told Kane that the bar had closed two hours ago, everyone had gone home. Kane saw that the door below was dead bolted from the inside, a heavy-duty metal bolt. Not even Dean could make his way through that, Kane thought with a degree of relief.

He held on to the railing tightly as he followed Colette down. The railing was loose; one good yank by someone even just a little bit stronger and it would tear free. At the bottom of the stairs Colette pulled back the bolt and pushed the door open. She only opened it a foot or so, just enough to look outside. The parking lot was in front of the building, around the corner from this side door. They couldn't see the lot from where they were, only the cluster of trees that crowded this side of the building, making a kind of natural fence. Good for people wanting to make discreet exits, Kane thought. Better for anyone who wanted to ambush them. Kane wanted to ask if there was another way out, something more private. *There had to be, right?* But before he could say anything, Colette pushed the door open the rest of the way and led him out into the brutal cold. The door swung shut behind them, made a loud banging noise as it slammed against the metal doorframe. They then hurried around the corner to the front. There were no spotlights illuminating the parking lot, just the distant streetlights up on Montauk Highway. They glowed weakly in the gray light. Kane and Colette walked close to the front of the building, staying as near to it as they could for as long as they could. Then they hurried out into the open morning air, walking past the three cars still parked in the lot. *So not everyone had left,* Kane thought. *Someone was still inside, in one of those rooms down the hall, or maybe in one of the rooms on the floor above.* He felt an odd kind of desperation for whoever was in there, man or woman. Trapped by need, trapped by greed—whatever the reason, trapped, with no easy escape for either.

They reached Colette's Cherokee. The sky was still dark enough directly overhead for some stars to show through, but at the horizon stretched long bands of pale blue. There was just enough emerging light for Kane to see his own shadow. He was looking at it, faint, stretched out on the ground in front of him, when he heard a noise coming from somewhere behind him.

He didn't see what made the noise, didn't really know exactly what that noise was. But he didn't need to. When the two giant hands grabbed his jacket, grabbed him with the force of machinery, he knew exactly what was going on, and what he was in for.

It happened with the terrible swiftness of an auto accident. Kane felt himself being lifted off his feet and flung forward, as if caught by a wave, and then slammed hard into the side of Colette's Cherokee. There was nothing he could do, couldn't even brace himself for impact, it was all just too fast. He sensed immense power and weight behind him, like a racing city bus about to run him down, then felt that combined power and weight crash into him an instant after he was slammed into the steel fender. He was crushed, and his spine bent the wrong way for an instant,

bent farther than he would have thought was possible. His
limbs went limp, and then everything halted and he felt
breath on the back of his neck, felt it moving past his left
ear. Nothing for a moment, for a second or two, and then
suddenly he was pulled backward, hard, and flung forward
again, flung like he was nothing, a rag caught in the work-
ings of some automated industrial machine. He crashed
into the side of the Cherokee again, and this time what
smashed into him an instant later was specified, not along
the length but localized in one place. It was, of course, a
blow, the hard bone of a kneecap striking him in the lower
back. He felt his kidneys shift in their sockets, his head fly
back as if it was being yanked off. The blow landed again,
and then a third time, his entire body rattling. After that he
felt himself pulled backward again, then spun around, as if
in the grip of some carnival ride gone wildly out of control.
He was airborne then, nothing at all beneath his scrambling
feet, cast into a wild, terrifying flight. He came crashing
down after a long moment, just a bag of bones scattering
across the frozen dirt.

He heard shouting, scuffling. Colette's voice, and the giant's voice—Dean's voice. Deep, like something coming
up from the bottom of a dark well. Colette was screaming,
not from fear, not helpless, but angry, hateful. Kane was
facedown, forced himself to roll over and look toward the
noise. It was all he could do at that instant, all he could
manage. Helpless again, just like in the chapel. He hated
himself, saw Colette and Dean standing face-to-face, Dean
holding her by her wrists, his hands the size of oven mitts,
Colette's arms raised and held out in front of her, awk-
wardly, like an old-fashioned boxer. She was trying to pull
away from Dean, they were shouting at each other, but
Kane couldn't make out what was being said. There was
ringing in his ears, the long, steady drone of a hundred tuning forks. He tried to breathe, couldn't without sharp pain.
It took him a second, but he found what he needed to sit up,
did so slowly, then got to his feet, crouching like an old man
who had spent too long in a soft bed. Dean was shaking Co-

lette now, forcefully, yelling at her. She was yelling back,
angrily. Kane's legs were shaking, and he rose to an upright
position, or as close to it as he could get. He started toward
them, his eyes locked on them. His vision was blurry, he
wasn't thinking, didn't care about thinking, was past fear,
running on adrenaline and shame and the desire—deep in
him, wild in him, reckless—to never feel again the way he
had felt back in the chapel.

He cared only for that.

He threw himself into Dean, back into the wave. It was
like tackling a thick tree, and the impact of Kane's attack
barely moved Dean at all. Dean let go of one of Colette's
wrists, holding the remaining one tighter. Colette screamed
out, in pain this time, Kane could tell that much in the rush
and confusion. With his free hand, Dean grabbed Kane by
the collar of his jacket, pulled Kane forward again, sharply,
and lifted his knee, driving it into Kane's gut. Kane folded,
then was airborne once again. He landed this time on his
back, looked up through blinking eyes and saw the still-
mostly dark sky above him, the last remaining pale stars, and
his own breath, like white smoke, rising above him and then
dissipating into the cold air, gone for good.

He lost track of time, of everything but what he could
see above him and the feel of the stone-hard earth along his
back. But when his senses returned finally, in a rush, Kane
lifted his head in time to see Colette let her knees buckle
slightly and drop suddenly, lowering her center of gravity
just a little. They were back as they had been before Kane's
useless attack, face to face, Dean holding her by her wrists,
her arms stretched out before her. As she lowered herself,
putting her center of gravity below his, Dean leaned forward a little and tried to pull her toward him, like a parent
about to lift a resisting child. It was instinct, any man would
have done that, would have fought such resistance with
brute strength. But the instant she sensed that he was off
balance just a little, pulling at her as she pulled away, she
stopped resisting, straightened her dancer's legs suddenly,
and sprung upward and toward him. Her right hand was

open, her fingers grouped together and extended, and though he was still holding her wrist, she was able to use his own force against him and fling a jab up through his centerline and into his left eye.

He shouted, angry, caught off guard. His hand came up to his eye, instinctively, and she broke her right hand free and lowered herself again, like a boxer on the inside, like an in-fighter, and launched a swift openhanded uppercut into Dean's balls, striking him hard. He recoiled, shrunk a little, folding like Kane had, and grunted once as he dropped to his knees like a building going down. He still had Colette's other wrist, but she wasn't done. She reached for his face then, with both hands, dug into his skin with her nails, tore long divots from his flesh. This was just enough damage, done swiftly enough, for her to break free of his grip and rush straight to Kane. She knelt beside him, told him to get up, pulling at him with both hands, trying to drag him to his feet. It took all they both had to get Kane just to sit up. She told him then to stand, that they had to go. Her words, the ur-gency with which she spoke, were all he could hear, all he needed to hear. Somehow he got his feet under him, got him-self into a crouch, his heels against the hard ground. Colette took his right arm and wrapped it around her neck and pressed upward with her legs, lifting him. Suddenly he was standing, they were moving though he had no idea in which direction. He had to concentrate just to put one foot in front of the other, had to stare down at his own feet. He and Co-lette had taken a few steps, toward the Cherokee, Kane assumed, when their forward motion was suddenly inter-rupted. Dean collided into them both, coming out of nowhere, hitting them hard. Kane didn't know from which side he had been hit, only that he had been torn violently from Colette's embrace and sent flying again, alone again, made helpless again.

It all went to hell from there, happened even more quickly than before. Kane was adrift in space for a while, then finally realized that he was stretched out on his right side on the ground. He could hear screaming, far off, but he knew that was just a trick of his mind. Colette and Dean weren't more than a few yards from him. Then suddenly the screaming stopped. Kane thought maybe this was another trick his senses were playing on him, that his hearing had gone out again, or that the ringing of tuning forks had returned to drown everything out. But it wasn't ringing that drowned out the sound of the screaming. It was yet another sound, this one not inside his head but outside of it, reaching his ears from somewhere beyond the parking lot, the sound of an engine, from up on Montauk Highway maybe, roaring, like someone had gunned it, had pushed down hard on the accelerator. But Kane ignored that sound—what could he do about it, what did he care about that now?—and strained to find Colette in the confusion. He could barely lift his head now, felt the cold around him, felt it swallowing him. He saw Dean and Colette face-to-face yet again, but Dean wasn't holding her wrists this time. Both his hands were wound around her long throat, his thick fingers clasped together at the back of her neck, his thumbs pressing so hard against her windpipe that his arms trembled. Kane couldn't see Colette's face, but he saw Dean's, saw it in the early morning light, saw that it was indeed ugly, deformed even, made all the more so by the collision of rage and hate and fear upon it.

Colette was holding Dean's thick wrists, trying to pry free of his grip. But she didn't have anywhere near the strength. She reached out for his face again, tried to gouge at it like she had before. But this only made Dean even more angry. Kane, trying to stand, trying to break free of the invisible weight that seemed to press down on him now, press him against the cold ground, saw the emotion cross Dean's face like the shadow of a winter cloud. Dean leaned his head back, moved it as far as he could, putting it almost beyond Colette's reach. Her straining fingers reached him but could find no target, nothing to dig into. He was fast choking the fight out of her. Kane didn't hear the engine anymore, didn't hear anything but gagging, Colette gagging. He thought of the threat Dean had made back at the chapel, felt a swelling inside him, a rush of adrenaline. He wanted to get to his feet but was too weak, had taken too much. He hated himself, hated the uselessness, his weakness. Panic broke through him, rushed into his heart, but it did nothing to help him. All he could do was witness what happened next.

Colette, desperate now, searched for another way to hurt Dean, hurt him enough to break free. He was holding her too close for her to be able to knee him in the groin or kick him, so instead she stomped down on the top of his foot with her heel. But that did nothing. Dean's eyes had narrowed to hateful slits now, his mouth drawn tight like a trap that had sprung closed. He was seething, staring at Colette's face, seeming almost captivated by what he saw. A part of him did seem to wish he could stop. There was something about his face that made him seem like a man who was just a little baffled by himself. But if a part of him did want to stop, it went ignored. His mouth drew even tighter, the corners of it turning down sharply, like hooks, and he dug his thumbs into Colette's throat, dug with everything he had. Colette struggled against him, but Dean only pressed harder still. There was no gagging now, no sounds coming from her at all. She had long since run out of air, he had long since crushed her fragile windpipe. It was just a matter of her dying now.

She clutched at his wrists. There was nothing left for her to do. But gradually her struggle grew more and more feeble, till suddenly her body went rigid and she grabbed at his wrists with a burst of strength. She must have known it was almost over, that her life was almost over. Her brain, deprived of oxygen, must have been able still to grasp that. It was then that her nervous system took over and she began to shake violently, involuntarily, like a hanged man at the end of his rope. It was grotesque, a wild, vulgar twitching, not at all elegant. It seemed to go on forever. But then finally Colette went limp in Dean's hands, her head suddenly lifeless, hanging to one side as if it had been all but ripped off. Just like that she was dead, and Kane screamed. It was all he could do. The scream, hot with hate and anguish, burned his throat like vomit. He watched as Dean let her slip to the ground with a strange gentleness, watched as she lay at his feet in a heap, empty as an old coat. Dean let go of her finally, let her slip completely from his grip, and stood over her like a tower, looking down at her. He seemed almost surprised, maybe even conflicted, as if he couldn't believe what he was now seeing, as if he had nothing to do with it, had just himself come across this horrible scene. After a long moment he lifted his head and looked toward Kane. He hadn't heard Kane's scream, or had only just now heard it, had a delayed reaction to it. He looked at Kane with a kind of disbelief, a kind of pleading. There was silence now, no ringing of a mass of tuning forks, no gunning of an engine, just a spreading winter dawn with only the two of them under it, only the two of them left in the world.

Kane lay where he was, staring at Dean, waiting. There was no point in trying to stand now. It was too late to do anything to save Colette, not that he could have done anything. A new wave of self-hatred ran through him, and suddenly, he didn't care what happened to him, he didn't care if Dean walked over and stomped him to death. A part of him wanted that, wanted his life to end, wanted the shame and the sorrow, all of it, to end. He could see nothing beyond this, nothing at all, didn't care about anyone or anything. He'd been stripped to the bone one last time, had lost all that he could bear to lose. Enough was enough. He would die with Colette, die thinking of their one night together, her hands finding him in the darkness, her breath on his face, the soft sounds they each had made . . .

For a moment, a long moment, Dean did nothing, just stood there, staring at Kane. He seemed helpless, too, in his own way. But after that moment something clearly clicked in Dean's head, Kane could see it, see the sudden difference in Dean's expression. Dean moved suddenly, took a step toward Kane, one purposeful step, and then another, and then a third. Kane could tell that whatever confusion had clouded Dean's mind, had interrupted his rage, had passed. Dean stepped with force onto the hard earth, and Kane knew it was just a matter of seconds now before those feet would be crashing down onto his broken body again.

Bright lights swept across Dean then, a set of piercing headlights, Kane could tell that much. They stopped on Dean, lighting him up. He froze, looked toward the lights, raising his hands against them, his eyes squinting. He stayed that way for a moment, but only a quick moment, then turned and broke into a run. Kane couldn't see where he went, only saw him disappear from sight, very fast, Kane thought, for a man of his size.

There was nothing for a time, just stillness, and then suddenly someone was beside Kane, had rushed there, and was pulling Kane up off the ground. Kane looked for a face, couldn't focus at first, there was too much movement, everything was blurry, jumpy, but then he managed to lift his head enough to see the person who was beside him. He looked, concentrated as best he could, but didn't recognize him at all. Some kid with dark hair and a square face. He was being pulled along by this kid, held up by powerful arms. The kid had wrapped Kane's arm around his neck like Colette had, was carrying Kane, who could barely stand, along. He was big, this kid, bigger than Kane, and walked quickly despite a noticeable limp.

Kane said Colette's name. He had no idea where she was, where he was now in relation to her body. He didn't want to leave there. That was his only concern now. But her name came out in broken syllables. Each step they took together jarred Kane, made breathing evenly, let alone speaking, all but impossible. The kid said nothing, maybe didn't understand what Kane had meant by the incoherent sounds he uttered. The kid only cared about moving Kane along, getting him out of there. They stopped abruptly, and Kane heard the sound of a car door being pulled open. He felt a hand on the back of his head, pushing against it firmly. Kane couldn't have resisted if he tried. He was bent forward, pushed through the car door, fell in and lay across a back seat on his right side, his head pressed against the soft leather.

He heard a door close, then another open and close, heard

the kid with the limp calling to someone. The car shot forward, then skidded to a stop a second later. The passenger door opened and someone climbed in, the door closed and the car took off again. Kane braced himself for another stop but the car kept moving. The man in the passenger seat turned and leaned over the seat back and looked down at Kane. Kane looked up at him. His vision had cleared enough so he could see the face clearly. A large, dark moon, staring down at him. Though it was a familiar face, Kane wasn't made at all easy by the sight of it. He was in the middle of something he didn't understand, and how could anything at all comfort him after what he'd just seen, what he had been unable to stop? He felt motion then, felt the car moving at a great speed, making turn after turn. Left, right, left again. With each corner the car took, Kane felt himself being tugged in a new direction, held by a new and unseen force. The speed at which they moved never diminished, and Kane could do nothing but lie there in its solid grip.

Eventually, Kane said Colette's name again, got it out in one breath. The man in the passenger seat was facing forward now. Kane said his name, then said hers again, as clearly as he could. The man turned in his seat, looked at Kane, moved his head from side to side.

"I'm sorry," Clay said.

Kane closed his eyes then, tight. He had known she was dead, had seen it. But hearing it from Clay made it somehow official. Maybe Kane had been mistaken, maybe Colette had pretended to be dead, had fooled Dean. There were no maybes about it now. Colette was dead.

Kane kept his eyes closed, held them closed, and when he opened them again, the car was flying beneath a morning sky. It was full light out now, and the car was on a straightaway, moving at a steady speed. No more tugging, just the feeling of being carried along. He must have passed out, had no idea for how long or where he was now. Kane heard a voice from the front seat, Clay's voice. He was speaking on the phone.

"Tell Mercer we got him," Clay said. He was losing reception, had to shout to be heard. *"Tell Mercer we got him, to meet us there as soon as he can. We're almost there. Another ten minutes."*

Kane's stomach tightened. It was the last thing he knew for a while. He closed his eyes and slipped back into darkness, sank like a stone to the bottom of some vast emptiness and stayed there.

EIGHT

He drove his black Jetta toward Riverhead.

He was wearing a long black overcoat, thick black trousers and a heavy black sweater, black shoes, black leather gloves. He didn't usually wear black, was dressed today for the part. His hair was white, had turned so prematurely four decades ago. Coarse, it hung all one length now to his shoulders. His entire life he'd worn his hair short and neatly trimmed, wanted to look always like a man who had money and standing, a man of culture, a polished man. The women he'd known, pursued perhaps out of vanity, had valued that. But he had let his hair grow out during the past three months—a necessary evil, or so he had thought at first, till finally he came to admit to himself that he liked the way it made him look. Savage, part biker when he was in jeans, part mad puritanical minister when he was done up in all this black. But more than that, women seemed to like it. Different women. Younger women. Women perhaps looking for trouble, or for father, or for both. Of course he liked that. What man, really, wouldn't? Who didn't want to feel power? Who, stuck in daily life, didn't want nights of danger? He was handsome, had always done well with women in his circle—refined women, women with money, other men's bored wives. He'd made almost a second career out of the women he had loved. But this, the attention he was getting, this was something altogether different. Long looks—stares, even. Bold. At times downright *hungry*. He'd never known this before, and the only thing he could think of to explain it was that, with his white hair long, he appeared now maybe just a little dangerous. *If only they knew,* he thought. Of course he had never harmed a woman in his life, never would. Still, he smiled as he steered through the early morning toward Riverhead, smiled at the thought of this new self, this new image, and the abundant possibilities it seemed to promise him—once, of course, all *this* was done, once he had time again to indulge himself. A new start so late in life, but that was precisely what all this was about. Rebirth. A second chance. *Vita Nuova,* as Dante would call it. Maybe, he thought, he'd keep this look—the long hair, the black clothing, like some tragic poet or demented clergyman. Maybe this was the new him, not just a part for which he was dressed.

Once this was done, there'd be all the time in the world for women again.

He was tall, still strong for his age, strong enough to have carried this out on his own, easily. But he had realized early on that he'd do well for himself to find someone to do the work for him. A legman or henchman, that was what they were called in those old movies he watched well into the night. Years ago he had watched them for escape, unable to sleep. Now he watched them for inspiration, seeing himself in the men who do what needs to be done. He didn't really need someone to do the work, maybe he would have even enjoyed it, but he was thinking more along the lines of creating a buffer, finding someone who would allow him to remain behind the scenes, not as much as possible but entirely, a shadow among shadows. That was what he needed, and this very thought was one of the first things that came to him when he began to plan his project. The more he considered it during the months of deliberation, turning it over and over in his powerful mind, the more it seemed to him the smart thing to do. A risk, yes, that was true. It would require trust, and leave him, to a degree, vulnerable. But it was a necessary risk, all things considered—and for a number of reasons, enough reasons to make the gamble worth it.

No great achievement was without its risks.

As he approached Riverhead he thought that maybe he should have been more careful and chosen someone else. During his first meeting with Dean he had detected something, sensed something. It would have been difficult to miss. *The guy wasn't all there.* But Dean's obvious shortcomings, he thought, could work to his advantage in the end. He had spent months planning—maybe too long, but this was tricky stuff—and had found himself with not much time at all left for his search. Maybe Dean wasn't the best choice, but, really, he had been the only choice. Who else could they have asked? Who would even have considered such a thing? Colette had recommended Dean, had known him before, said she could predict what he would do in almost any situation, knew him that well. That was something of value, considering all that was at stake. Dean wasn't a very complicated guy at all, wanted only one thing from her, she had said. Of course that could prove most helpful, particularly when it came time to lead Dean to his inevitable end.

But just a few moments ago, Dean had called to tell the white-haired man that he needed to see him, that it was urgent. Dean had sounded frightened. There was no ignoring this, the man knew. First there had been the angry call from the chapel. And now this. Dean wasn't of much use if he couldn't control his emotions. There was no room for hysterics here, for sloppiness. Precision, care—*this* was delicate work. A lot to lose, a lot to gain. If he had known Dean was like this, if she had told him that the kid was prone to anger and depression and wild mood swings, then he would have bit the bullet and put his project on hold as he looked for someone else. Or so he thought now. But Colette had kept Dean's true nature from the man, mentioned many of Dean's faults but never said anything about his deeper emotional problems. The white-haired man and Colette had talked at length about his plan. Long into the night, many nights. She was in it as deep as he was, with him almost from the start. Why the omission, then? What exactly did her having held back crucial facts mean? He didn't know for sure, but there wasn't time to think about that now. Everything was in motion, no turning back. They were long past that.

Dean's house was a small clapboard cottage on the end of a dirt road, just south of Riverhead. It sat on the edge of Peconic Bay, far enough removed from the neighbors' homes to make it safe enough for the white-haired man to go there in daylight. He'd been here once before, had come then dressed in black like today, and if for some reason that didn't work, or if some neighbor took note of his license plate and later gave it to the cops—*all contingencies considered*—he had that covered: he was planning on selling his Jetta, he would say, and Dean had been interested in buying it. He had gone to the extent of running an ad in the paper for two weeks just to make that story ironclad. This, now, could be a second trip—again, *if* anyone saw him, took note, thought to mention it to anyone later on, after Dean was dead and the cops had had a look down in his basement. A second trip so Dean could take one more look at the car and make an offer, which of course would have been followed by brief but polite haggling over the price, to the benefit of neither. If the man still owned the Jetta by the time anyone came around asking questions, *if* they ever came around to ask questions, then he would say that he had decided to keep it, that the money he had been counting on that would allow him to dump the car and pick up the vintage Benz he'd had his eye on hadn't come through as planned.

And if for some reason he did have that Benz by then, if his luck suddenly changed with this act of karmic justice, well, then all the better.

He steered into the dirt drive that ran alongside the house, followed it to its end. The white van was parked in the yard directly behind the house, not far from the back door. It would be unseen from the road here, would make bringing "things" in and out of the house easier, and safer. He reached into his coat pocket, took out his chrome-plated .357, dropped open the cylinder, checked that it was loaded, then flipped the cylinder back and returned the gun to his pocket.

He would never go anywhere near Dean without it, had decided that right at the start. *Thinking moves ahead, taking all possibilities into account.* He got out and walked through the cold to the back door. The screen door was still attached, one of the hinges broken, the other barely hanging on. The house itself was a wreck, paint peeling, stone foundation cracked. An old washing machine lay on its side in the backyard, rusting. Looking around, he was aware that a tall man with long white hair, dressed in a long black Brooks Brothers overcoat, would certainly stand out in this setting. But there was nothing he could do about that. And his story would hold, he was sure of that.

He knocked on the screen door. It rattled against the door frame. A moment went by, no sign at all of Dean. He stood there, waiting, looked around casually. *Nothing to hide, no reason to bother with keeping his face hidden.* But Dean had sounded frightened on the phone. Something had gone wrong, something *was* wrong. What, though? What could frighten Dean? Too big to be afraid of any man, to dumb to be afraid of anything else. Something the white-haired man hadn't thought of, hadn't seen coming. But what could that be? He had covered everything, had thought of nothing else but this every day and night for months. Frontward, backward, inside and out, he knew every possible thread, every player, what they would do, what they would think. All this was nothing more than parts of an equation leading to the inevitable sum. Simple mathematics.

But he could feel it, standing there at that back door, he could feel a sense of dread. He tried to ignore it, told himself that he could think his way out of this, whatever *this* was, think his way past yet another sudden obstacle. He had to. *Remain calm, let your genius work.* He had been confronted by two unexpected obstacles so far, the first just days ago, when he got word that a critical player was on his deathbed. But he had within the hour thought of a way to succeed despite that, to keep his precious project from falling into chaos. The second obstacle was when someone came asking questions far sooner than he had anticipated. But he had dealt with that problem too, kept all this from coming tumbling down around him, could do it again if he had to. He wouldn't fail, not now. He had been growing more and more confident with each stage of his project that came and went as planned, and with each unexpected twist that arose but did not deter him. His old beloved arrogance was returning, he could feel it, like the presence of a long lost friend. A warmth, a sense of balance in a chaotic world. He had once been called a genius by men who could make or break a career. Then he had been stripped of that title. Now, he was out to reclaim it, if only for himself, for his own satisfaction and pleasure.

A quiet "fuck you" to those who had left him for dead.

He knocked again, waited. Then he heard footsteps inside. When Dean finally opened the door, the white-haired man saw right off the scratches on Dean's face. Deep, fresh, glistening. Dean turned his back to the man before he could say a word, walked through the small kitchen and disappeared. The man entered, closed the door behind himself, carefully followed Dean into the living room. The shades were drawn there, the room dark. The man kept his left hand in the pocket of his overcoat, the butt of the revolver in his palm. He stopped just inside the front room, looked around. They were, as far as he could tell, alone. But all the furniture was overturned, the place ransacked. Dean kept his back to the man, stood at the far end of the front room. He was breathing heavily, struggling to keep himself still.

A caged animal, ready to lose its mind.

"What happened here?" the man said. He kept his voice even.

Dean didn't answer.

"Did you do this or someone else?"

Eventually, Dean muttered, "I did it."

"Why?"

Dean half-turned, glanced tentatively toward the man. The scratches on his wrecked face looked black in the dim light.

"I think she's dead," Dean whispered.

"What did you say?"

Dean didn't answer.

"What did you just say?"

"I think she's dead. I think I killed her."

"Who?"

"*Her.*"

The man paused. He felt a flash of anger but contained it. "Colette?"

Dean nodded.

Through his anger the man thought of her—her skin, her mouth, her willingness to please him at all costs. These thoughts came quickly. For an instant he couldn't move or think of anything but his loss. *Where would he find another like her?* Then his mind began to clear, he willed it to clear, and there waiting for him was the realization that he had not seen this coming, hadn't even for a moment considered something like this.

A flaw in his planning? A failure of his genius?

"What happened?" the man said finally. He kept his voice clear of all emotion.

"I went to her place," Dean said. "I went to her apartment."

"When?"

"Last night."

"Why did you do that?"

"I needed to know that she was okay."

"She wasn't there."

"I know."

"She wasn't supposed to be there. She was doing her job."

"I know."

"So then why did you go?"

Dean shrugged. "In case she came back there for something."

"She was sticking to the plan, Dean. Like you should have done."

"I didn't know what else to do. I was afraid something bad might happen to her."

"You were jealous."

"I wasn't jealous. I just didn't know where she was and was worried about her."

"You knew she was with him. That's all you needed to know."

"I was afraid he might hurt her or something."

"What happened after you went to her place?"

"I waited. I got more worried and decided to drive to where she worked, thought maybe she'd be there. I saw her car out front and waited. I couldn't stop thinking about her being in there with him. And then I saw them leaving. I saw her with him, could tell they had been together, I lost it."

"Jesus."

"I couldn't stop myself. I went after him. She tried to stop me, got in the way."

"What did you do to her?"

Dean was staring at a spot in the floor somewhere between him and the man. His eyes were unfocused, and he spoke slowly.

"I grabbed her."

"And?"

"She kept fighting me. I just wanted her to stop fighting me."

The man didn't need to hear the rest. He held the grip of the .357 tightly. His palm was damp.

"What about him?" he said.

"Who?"

"Kane. Is he dead, too?"

Dean shook his head. "No. Someone came."

"Who?"

"That kid."

"The one with the limp."

"Yeah."

"What was he doing there?"

"I don't know."

"You're sure it was him?"

"Yeah."

The man thought about that.

"How did he find me?" Dean said.

"I don't know."

"Some black guy was with him."

"What black guy?"

"I don't know. Fancy clothes, big guy."

"They were together?"

"Yeah. I think they're onto us. I think we need to quit this right now. You said no one was going to find out."

The man thought for a moment, then shook his head. "No, they must be following Kane. If they are, then they suspect him, which is what we want. This will work in our favor. Trust me."

"I'm not going to prison."

"You want to live in this dump and mop floors for the rest of your life?"

"No."

"We're almost done. You'll get your money and get your life back. And I think it's safe to say that if they knew where you were, they would have been here by now, don't you?"

Dean nodded. "Yeah."

"Your license plates are registered to a fake address, right?"

"Yeah."

"So even if they saw it, it wouldn't do them any good. They were following Kane, they had to be. So we're going to stick to our plan, okay?"

Dean hesitated, then nodded. The man looked at the scratches on Dean's face.

"She did that to you?"

Dean nodded again. His hands were trembling. The man saw that.

"Where do you keep your booze?"

Dean nodded toward the kitchen. "In there."

The man turned, entered the kitchen, searched the cupboards till he found a bottle of bourbon. In his pocket was the vial of powder they had used on all the boys, and on Kane. He thought about how easily he could slip it into Dean's drink now, hand the glass to him, tell him to drink it, then wait till Dean dropped to the floor and put the gun to Dean's head, pull the trigger, then put the powder-burned leather gloves onto Dean's hands, put the gun in his palm, and leave. No time for a note, but that didn't matter. People didn't always leave notes, and for whom exactly would Dean have left one? He had no one, lived a horribly lonely life. The man had always planned on Dean's "suicide." It would be necessary to bring closure to the investigation. But not yet. He would need Dean for a while longer, even more so now that Colette was out of the picture.

The man stepped back into the living room, stopped, like he had before, just inside the door. He held out his hand, offering the drink to Dean, making him come and get it. Dean walked to him, took the glass, and drank down the bourbon in one gulp. *It would be that easy, when the time came,* the man thought. *A toast to their success, something simple like that.* The drink had calmed Dean some, but the rage was still in him, moving just below the surface. The man could sense it, had sensed it from the start.

Dean looked at the empty glass, then up at the man. His left eye was swollen a little, bloodshot. *Colette's handiwork, no doubt.* She had once spent a week in the county lockup, had learned how to fight there, fight dirty, had learned it the hard way. The man had always enjoyed her stories about her stay there—the other inmates, the guards. She had probably learned to embellish these tales a little, for his benefit—she was good that way, that was *her* genius. Forced sex, intimidation, flesh as currency. And the hose, the fire hose, the freezing water. She had a gift for knowing what a man wanted, and then giving it to him. Thinking about the hose now only brought the man back to the business at hand, to what was left, what now needed to be done, and quickly.

"Is the boy downstairs?" he said.

Dean nodded. "Yeah."

"We're going to need to kill him right now and get rid of his body tonight."

"He still has the cut on his forehead."

They were going to hold this boy for a few days, give the cut he had received during his capture time to heal a bit. They had held the others alive for twelve hours only so the drug would dissipate from their system, and had devised a way of containing them that would leave no telltale marks on their bodies. The device was in Dean's basement, would be there still after Dean was dead, to be found by the police.

Torture Chamber In Basement, the newspapers would report.

And if the cops connected all the dots, followed the trail left for them, they'd see the reason for the device and the dead boys, the reason the white-haired man wanted them to see, and at that point look no further, leaving him in the clear.

The cut on this boy's forehead up till now had been a problem, a cause for delay. Now, though, it was an asset, an excuse to move things along faster than originally planned.

"I figured out a way to cover for his cut," the man said. "To make it work for us. So we don't have to worry about that now. And even though we're still safe here, I think we need to pick up the pace. Just to be sure. So after you finish with the kid downstairs, we grab the last one, kill him, and then we're done, we're home free."

Dean nodded. The man watched him for a moment, then said, "Is the boy scared?"

"Yeah. Very."

The white-haired man imagined that, imagined the boy in the tub of water, his muscles weakened by the cold, scared out of his mind. "Good," he said. "When you're done, pack up his body, get rid of it after it gets dark, then go and wait for the last one. If things go our way, we could be done with all this by tomorrow night."

"And you'll pay me then?"

"Once you get rid of the last one, yeah. That was our deal. Just make sure there are no more screwups. Do you understand me? That's important right now. Just because we're down to the wire doesn't mean we can afford to get sloppy."

"Okay, yeah."

"Keep sharp."

Dean waited, took a few breaths, then, just as the man began to turn to leave, said, "What was she doing there with him, Krause?"

The Professor stopped mid-turn. He looked at Dean, could imagine the pain Dean was in, knew the torment Colette had caused him. But he couldn't care about that. He had a long time ago come to care only about his own pain. Still, he needed Dean to do his part, needed to humor the guy for now.

"Try not to think about that," he said.

"Just tell me. Please. What was she doing there with him?"

"She was keeping an eye on him. Leaving him with one more night he'd have trouble accounting for. And she was telling him what we needed him to hear."

Dean nodded at that, absently. The Professor hadn't answered his question, and knew it.

"I waited outside till morning," Dean said. "They were alone in that room all night. Do you think she fucked him?"

"She was just doing her job, Dean. Try to keep your mind on yours."

"The cops'll think he was behind all this. That Kane guy. They'll think he was behind the killings. Is that it?"

The Professor nodded. It was close enough to the truth. Dean didn't need to know more than that. If he did know more . . . well, that was why the Professor carried the revolver.

Dean seemed to find some comfort in the knowledge that Kane would suffer, and for the crimes Dean had committed. "Is this payback for something he did to you?" he said.

"No."

"So why him then?"

"Just the luck of the draw. Bad luck, in his case. Call me when you get back tonight, okay? No need for the last kid to suffer longer than necessary. He's just to tie up the loose ends. Kill him quick. Kill him like the others, but do it quick."

Dean nodded. The Professor watched him a moment. "You should put something on those scratches."

"I will."

"After you pack the kid up, you should maybe get some sleep. You look pretty tired. Don't want you falling asleep behind the wheel."

"Okay."

"I'll talk to you tonight."

Dean said nothing to that, just stood there and stared at the floor. The Professor waited a moment, then left and walked slowly to his Jetta, climbed in. His hands were shaking as he gripped the wheel and drove off. He didn't want to drive back to his apartment; he would only sit there and think of Colette. He couldn't give in to anger or grief. They were the enemy. A familiar enemy. He needed to keep clear, keep his mind sharp. He needed to see this through in his head, see it through all the way to the end, see all the possible obstacles and twists between here and there that he could.

He decided to go into Riverhead, stop at a coffee shop, order a cup of black joe. When he was done with his second cup he looked at his watch. It was almost eight. A half hour had passed since he left Dean's house. The boy was certainly dead by now. The Professor wished it had taken longer, wished that the boy's fear had lasted for days, as they had originally planned. There was a direct correlation between how much certain others suffered and how much better he felt. Still, he was pleased now that the kid was gone, relieved even, as if a dark point in his life that seemed would never end was at last over. Right now Dean was probably rolling the kid up in plastic, or maybe he had already done so, had already put the body in the van. He would have to keep the body there all day, under bags of ice till nightfall, when he would drive to Lake Agawam, in the heart of Southampton Village, and set that body, like the others, adrift in the icy water.

The Professor finished his coffee, waved to the waitress. She came over, poured him another cup. They shared prolonged eye contact, and then a quick smile. She had dark hair, like Colette, and filled out the uniform nicely. After she walked away the white-haired man cupped his hands over the steam that rose from its black surface, felt the moist warmth move past his fingers.

He had created Colette. She was an addict and sometime prostitute when he found her, and he had taken her under his wing and made her everything she was to become, showed her a world she hadn't known existed. She had belonged to him, a beloved pet, little more than that. Whether she had strayed on him or not, was looking to betray him, that didn't really matter. Pets often turned wild, bit the hand that fed them, as it were. She'd always had that potential, was always a little wild. That was the thrill. But he knew her past, and he understood her nature. She had agreed too quickly to be part of his plan, and how could you trust someone who so easily agreed to murder? But, despite all that, he had loved her in his own way, had passed countless long nights with her, and he would need to find someone to replace her soon, when all this was done, to be with him through the dark nights that lay ahead. He needed the comfort of a woman, always had, always would. The possibility of being betrayed was the price you paid for such comfort. He had come to accept that. But maybe, just maybe, if he got the right woman, made her just what he wanted her to be, got into her head, really got into it, then things might turn out differently this time . . .

He watched the waitress as he drank his third cup, listened to her talk to her customers, studied her, wondering what there was to stop him from doing again what he had done before.

Kane awoke in a strange bed, in a room he didn't recognize. A woman was leaning over him. She was black, had a small, narrow face. The window shades were drawn, but around the edges was the gray light of a winter day. The woman smiled at Kane. He knew it was meant to comfort him, but it didn't.

"You're okay," she said softly. "I'm just changing your bandage. You've got some cuts on your head."

"Who are you?"

"My name's Sophia. I'm a nurse. I won't hurt you."

"Where am I?"

"Just rest. I had to give you a few stitches. Other than that, and a few bruises, you seem to be okay."

Kane heard a noise then, coming from beyond the window. A steady, recurring hiss. It didn't take long for him to realize that it was the ocean.

"What is this place?" he said. There were shelves along the walls with books on them, a lot of books, and some framed prints by French Impressionists and a bureau and two chairs. This wasn't like the room at the Water's Edge. It was a guest room, in someone's home.

Kane remembered the drive then, how it was full light out when he awoke to hear Clay on the phone. How long had they been driving? He could be anywhere now, anywhere at all. Despite the plan he had made with Colette, their desire to escape here, he was uneasy at the prospect of having possibly been carried so far away from everything that he knew, for better or for worse. Leaving was one thing. Being flung to the edges of the world at the hands of men you barely knew and could not trust was something else altogether.

But the sheets on this bed smelled clean, and the blanket covering him was heavy, keeping him warm. He wasn't bound, wasn't handcuffed to the headboard. Sophia clearly wasn't here to harm him. She removed a fresh bandage from its wrapper, placed it on Kane's forehead carefully. He watched her face, listened to her breathing. There wasn't much else he could do. He was on that narrow edge between wakefulness and unconsciousness, teetering at best, more than likely to fall back into that darkness, and soon.

After a moment, he said again, "Where is this place?"

"Just rest. They'll be in to talk to you in a little while."

Her answer didn't make Kane feel any less uneasy. But it didn't increase his unease. That was something. Sophia stood, gathered her things together. She was tall, with long limbs and a long, elegant neck. Kane thought of Colette then, thought of her dying, his inability to do a thing to stop it. He closed his eyes as Sophia left the room, then finally drifted back into unconsciousness.

He slipped in and out like that all afternoon. At one point he heard two people talking in the hallway outside the door to this room. Sophia and Clay, he thought. Their voices were hushed, but it was clear that Sophia wasn't happy about something. Clay was never home, she said. He worked too much. When was he going to talk to Gregor, she said, tell Gregor that he wanted out? "It was Ned's idea to start this *thing*, this business. Then he gets married and leaves it all up to you to run. He left you holding the bag and doing all the work. *Enough is enough*." Kane half-listened to this. The conversation went on for a while, their voices never more than hushed whispers, but the intensity never waned, either. Kane passed out at some point, and when he woke again, the room was darker. It was still daylight, but the gray light around the edges of the shade was softer. He thought that he was alone till he realized someone was sitting in one of the chairs against the wall at the foot of the bed, not far from the window. It was a woman, he saw, a different woman, though, not Sophia but the woman who had been sitting behind the wheel of Gregor's Grand Prix. He could see her face clearly in the pale light. She asked Kane if he was okay, if he needed something. Her accent was French, but not soft, hard. She looked dark, Middle Eastern. She was wearing jeans and a black turtleneck sweater. Slim, holding perfectly still, confident, Kane thought. On the table beside the chair lay a copy of the *Jerusalem Post*. Kane told her that he'd like some water. She got up, stepped to him. A glass was already on the table beside the bed. She put it to Kane's lips, carefully, and tilted it. Water passed across his tongue and spread down his throat. It was cool, and when he'd had enough, he nodded. She put the glass back on the nightstand and returned to her chair. He fell back asleep watching her watching him.

The next time he awoke it was dark outside. The lights in the room were off, but the door was ajar, light from the hallway spilling in. Kane could see that he was alone. Both of the chairs were empty. From downstairs he heard voices, more than two, though he didn't know for certain how many. They were male voices, and they were evidently discussing something very important. One voice cut over another, and then another cut over that one. Sometimes the voices were raised, not angrily but emphatic, impassioned. It took a while but Kane recognized one of the voices as Mercer's. He felt his gut tighten again, swung out from under the blanket, and got up from the bed.

He was barefoot, the wood floor cold on his soles. He walked to the window, pulled the shade aside a little. He saw a small stretch of beach, and beyond it, the endless expanse of the Atlantic. The sky was overcast, there was no sign of the moon, but Kane could see the white tips of the heavy chop as they made their way toward land, then rose and folded at the shoreline. The hissing of the collapsing waves was loud now, like a lion's roar, each one just a little different in pitch and duration from the one before, and yet somehow all the same. Lazy and powerful. A roar and a yawn. Peaceful and violent.

Kane couldn't stay here. He knew that. It was all he knew, and it was enough. He couldn't shake everything that Colette—poor Colette—had told him, everything it had suggested. He couldn't answer how Clay and the kid with the limp—*Miller, isn't that what Colette had said his name was?*—had found them. He couldn't explain how Dean had found them. All he knew was that everyone had found them, and one right after another. Now Kane was out at the edge of the world, in some strange house, with Mercer and God knows who else downstairs, in heated debate. He couldn't imagine an answer to any of his questions that would be good news. He had to leave, didn't bother to try to think past that fact. He looked around for his shoes—the shoes Gregor had given him. They were nowhere in sight. On the chair at the foot of his bed, though, was a shoe box. He stepped to it, flipped the lid open. Inside were a pair of sneakers. He took them out, one at a time. Black Skechers.

Heavy for sneakers. Thick tread, like a boot. Slip-proof, the box said. And steel-toed. What the hell? He checked to see if they were his size. They were. He sat down, pulled the sneakers on, pulled the laces tight, tied them. All he needed now was a coat. It was still freakishly cold outside. He needed a coat, and a way out. He went back to the window. No roof to jump onto, no ledge. No way he was going to jump. This was only the second floor, but his head ached and his ribs and chest hurt. It was painful enough just moving around quietly, just breathing. He could only imagine the pain he would feel upon impact with the ground, even if he did land on his feet. He was about to look for a coat, and if he couldn't find one, take the blanket off the bed, wrap it around his shoulders. That would reduce his obstacles down to finding a way out. His mind was working on that very problem when he heard the sound of a door open and then close downstairs.

He stood there and listened. No voices, just someone walking across gravel. It was from outside, from the other side of the house, the front of the house. Kane heard the sound of cars starting up and driving off, gravel shifting beneath tires. When the cars were gone, all Kane could hear were the falling waves beyond the shaded window and a single set of footsteps roaming around downstairs.

Sophia maybe? The other woman, the beautiful woman with curled hair who had given him water, who had sat with him while he slept? He couldn't imagine either of them being enough to stop him, even in his condition. Or, for that matter, even trying to stop him. He could just walk out the door. What could they do? Yeah, but then what? Call the cops? Let them sort it out? Trust them to help him? Not likely. So then, the question: *once outside, once free from this house, where to from there?*

Kane heard footsteps on the stairs then. He thought about getting back into bed, pretending to be unconscious. But he'd had enough of lying helpless, of being on his back. He stayed by the window, looking toward the half-open door, listening to the footsteps. They reached the top of the stairs, started down the hall. The steps were uneven, and heavy. He began to doubt that these steps belonged to either of the women he had seen. He became fairly certain he knew to whom they belonged.

The footsteps stopped at the door. It swung open slowly. The light from the hallway widened, falling across the empty bed. Whoever had opened the door stepped through it then, looking around the dimly lit room. There was urgency in the way this person moved, surprise even. It was clear that he had expected to find Kane in bed, wondered for a quick second if Kane had somehow gone. But he found Kane fast enough, the room was small. And Kane saw him, too. It was the kid with the limp, and he stood just inside the doorway, staring at Kane. Neither moved.

"You're up," the kid said.

Kane waited, studying the kid. He wasn't as big as Clay or Dean, but, like Colette had said, he was big enough. Kane faced him, hid his fear.

"Where the fuck am I?" Kane said softly.

The kid didn't make a move, remained in the doorway, his hands hanging at his sides.

"Montauk."

"Where in Montauk?"

He wasn't sure if he should answer that. Kane could see this. Finally, though, the kid must have decided there was no harm in saying the truth. "Ned's house," he said.

"Your name is Miller, right?"

"Yeah. Tommy Miller."

"And you work for Ned?"

"Sometimes."

"What does that mean?"

"It's a long story."

"I want to leave here," Kane said.

"I don't really think you should do that."

"Why not?"

"Because pretty soon the police are going to be looking for you."

"Why would they be looking for me?"

"You should wait till Reggie and Ned get back, talk to them. And your friend, too. Mercer."

"Where did they go?"

"To check some things out."

"What things?"

"You should really talk to them."

"When will they get back?"

Miller shrugged. "I don't know. You're safe here, though. That's why we brought you here, so you'd be safe while they tried to figure everything out."

"What do they need to figure out?"

"You really should wait and talk to them."

Kane sensed that Miller wasn't going to give in. He looked around the room. He wasn't really sure what he was looking for. A weapon? Eventually he looked back at Miller.

"What time is it? Can you tell me that much?"

"Eight o'clock."

"How long have I been here?"

"Since this morning."

"My friend. Colette. She's dead, right?"

Miller waited, then nodded and said, "Yeah."

"The other guy, the one who killed her. What happened to him?"

"He ran off. Clay went after him on foot. He ran toward the canal. Clay couldn't catch him, and there wasn't really time to chase after him. We had to get you out of there."

"How did you know I was there?"

"We didn't. We were looking for the woman, went to her apartment. The guy who beat you up was waiting there. I recognized him, so we waited and followed him when he finally left."

"You recognized him from where?"

"He ran me off the road the other night."

"Why?"

"I'm not sure."

Kane nodded, thinking about that, then said, "You talked to Colette, right? A few nights ago."

"Yeah."

"Ned sent you there?"

"Reggie did."

"That big guy—Dean, I guess his name is—was black-mailing her."

"Is that what she told you?"

"Yeah. Why?"

Miller shrugged the question off. "Ned and Reggie weren't sure what had happened to you. They thought maybe you were up to something."

"Do they still think that?"

"They're not sure exactly what's going on. Mercer busted his ass all day trying to prove to Ned and Reggie that you didn't have anything to do with any of this."

"He did that?"

"Yeah."

Kane couldn't imagine what Mercer, or anyone, would say on his behalf. "What proof does he have exactly?"

"Apparently he called some woman you know, got her to confirm that you were with her at her place the night the Foster boy was dumped into the bay."

"What?"

"Her house has a security system. Once it's armed, it keeps track of how many times the doors are opened. Ned knows someone at the company that installed the system. Their records, I guess, should prove that you didn't leave her house that night. He's on his way to see about getting a copy, for that night and for the nights the other two boys were found. I guess you were there those nights, too—at least according to this woman friend of yours."

Kane wondered how Meg could know that, could recall the nights that he had been there, the dates. She barely knew what day of the week it was, barely knew anything except her work and eating and sex. He wondered if she was just saying what needed to be said to protect him. He wondered, too, if her husband had been there when Mercer had called.

"Where's he now?" Kane said.

"Mercer?"

"Yeah."

"He went with Ned."

"And what about Reggie?"

"He's waiting to pick something up from a friend of mine in the police department."

"What?"

"A copy of someone's police record."

"Whose?"

"A woman named Colleen Auger."

"Who's she?"

"You don't know?"

"Should I?"

"A number belonging to her was on your caller ID."

"You've been to my apartment?"

"Yeah."

"Why?"

"You disappeared after the chapel. Clay was trying to figure out what had happened to you." He paused. "And like I said, it was starting to look like maybe you were involved in this."

Kane was aware by now of the similarities between the names Colette Auster and Colleen Auger. He was fairly certain *they,* Miller and Clay and Gregor, were aware of it, too.

"What kind of police record does Colleen Auger have?" he said.

"We'll find out when Reggie gets back."

"How long till then?"

"My friend said she'd have to wait till the time was right to get the file. She's going to call Reggie on his cell phone when it's ready. That may be awhile."

Neither of them spoke for a moment. Kane needed to sit down but didn't move. He would stand there for as long as Miller stood there, face him fully, show no weakness, that he had nothing to hide. He felt a resolve in himself he didn't know he had.

"Listen, do you mind if I ask you a question?" Miller said. Kane shrugged.

"The woman who was killed this morning, whoever she turns out to be, you had spent the night with her, right?"

Kane waited a moment, then said, "Yeah. Why do you ask?"

"Did you two sleep together?"

"What does that matter to you?"

"Just that if you did, it means there's a murdered woman in the morgue right now who may or may not have your DNA in her."

Kane looked at Miller, hard. "You saw what happened. I didn't kill her."

"I never said you did. I'm just trying to figure out how much more trouble a guy can get himself into."

"What trouble exactly am I in?"

"That's what Ned's trying to find out. You know, if you weren't Mercer's friend, Ned would have had us turn you over to the cops this morning, let them sort it out. He's got a thing about not breaking the law. He says it's because he's got a license to protect, that he wants to stay in business. But it's more than that. Hell, I don't even think their PI firm does anything more than break even."

"So if it's not the license he's worried about, then what is it?"

"I'm pretty sure it has something to do with not wanting to become corrupt. He's obsessed with the whole thing, about as righteous as they come."

"Why's that, do you think?"

Miller shrugged, said nothing.

Kane thought about that, about everything, or tried to. His mind was tired, like an overworked muscle. Thinking was like moving something heavy. After a while he asked the only thing that seemed to matter now.

"When will Ned be back?"

"Shouldn't be more than an hour now."

Neither of them spoke after that for a few moments. Kane listened to the waves falling in on themselves, falling relentlessly. It sounded to him now like something creeping closer and closer, something trying to sneak up on him. As he listened, it slowly became clearer than ever that his life as he knew it was over. No going back.

But what life, if any, was awaiting him, lingering maybe somewhere ahead in this sudden darkness, he did not know.

"Do you need anything?" Miller said. "Something to eat or drink?"

Kane shook his head. "No. I'm good."

"You don't look so hot. Maybe you should lie down for a while."

Kane looked toward the window, pulled back the shade, saw the ocean, the white tips of the waves tumbling over in the dark, the steady momentum of the approaching high tide.

"No, I think I want to stand," he said.

"I'll be downstairs if you need anything."

Kane nodded. Miller waited a moment, then left. Kane stayed by the window, reached down after a moment, tugged on the bottom of the shade. It rolled up, and he stood there and stared at the water. This was like the other night, he thought, the night before all this started, when he sat on the edge of Meg's bed for hours and stared out at the dark stillness of the bay.

It was like that, but it was different, too.

Three hours went by before Kane heard a car pull into the driveway at the front of the house. Long time to wait around and think. He had stayed at the window for as long as he could stand, which hadn't been really all that long, and was sitting on the edge of the bed, looking at his left hand, when he heard the car pull in. There was a small tremor in his hand that came every now and then, caused his hand to shake for a half minute like some newborn bird. He stared at it when it shook, stared at it and waited for it to stop, and then stared it some more and waited for it to start up again. No pattern, no set time between spasms. It came without warning, then was gone. In a strange way it kept his mind active, gave him something on which to focus. But the sounds coming up from downstairs broke that spell, caused his attention to shift. He looked up from his hand as he listened to the door downstairs open and close, listened to muffled voices. The house had been dead silent up till then. He didn't hear Mercer's voice among those below. Gregor's and Clay's and Miller's. Kane listened to them for a while, heard the door open and close again, heard a car start up in the driveway and pull away. He heard someone walking around, then voices again. Male and female voices. Gregor and the woman who had given Kane a drink of water, maybe. They were speaking French, as far as Kane could tell. Spoke it fluently. Kane got up and walked to the bathroom. The hard soles of the Skechers squeaked a little on the polished wood floor. He ran cold water, splashed it on his face, on the back of his neck, ran his damp right hand through his hair. He looked at his reflection for a moment. He had to will himself to do that. He looked just like he felt. No surprise there. He grabbed a towel, dried his hands and face, then lay the towel on the sink and left the bathroom. He took two steps back into the guest room and stopped short.

Gregor was standing in the center of the small room. It was still dark in there, the room lit only by the light that spilled in from the hallway through the half-open door. Kane could barely see Gregor's face—Gregor was standing with his back to the light—but from Gregor's left hand hung a plastic garbage bag, and that Kane could see clearly enough. It was a large, dark bag, not even a quarter full. Whatever was inside it, though, hung heavy. Gregor was facing Kane, standing perfectly still, rigidly, even. Kane got the sense right off that Gregor hadn't come upstairs to check on him.

"We need to talk," Gregor said. His voice was soft, his tone solemn.

Kane nodded, but he had things of his own he wanted to talk about first. "Where's Mercer?"

"He went home, to make a phone call."

"Anything wrong?"

Gregor shook his head. "No, he's fine."

"What happened with your friend at the security company?"

"He won't be able to check till tomorrow. If he finds what we're looking for, he'll print it out, Clay will pick it up."

"My lady friend always used to turn the security system on every time we sat down to eat. That was usually around seven. Your friend is going to find exactly what Mercer says he's going to find."

"Yeah, well, we'll know tomorrow. In the meantime, I've called a cab. It's going to take you to a motel about a mile from here. You're going to spend the night there."

"Why?"

"The call Mercer needed to make was to a lawyer he knows. He's going to set up a meeting for you with this lawyer tomorrow."

"Why do I need a lawyer?"

"Because I've done everything I can for you. I've gone as far as I can go."

"I can't afford a lawyer."

"Mercer said he's going to take care of that."

"I don't understand. What's going on?"

Gregor opened the garbage bag, reached in, and pulled something out. He tossed it to Kane. It was a clear plastic Baggie. Inside was what looked to Kane like a dark T-shirt, rolled up. The T-shirt was stained.

"What's this?" Kane said.

"Last night Clay and Miller found it in the garbage in your apartment."

Kane looked at it. Even in the dim light he could see it clearly enough. It was a black concert T-shirt, and there was blood on it. Kane looked up at Gregor and muttered, "What's going on?" It was all he could think to say.

"Your friend Colette Auster's real name is Colleen Auger. She has a fairly substantial police record—solicitation, prostitution, assault, shoplifting, and drug possession. And apparently at one point she was a major addict, was ordered by the court twice to enter a drug rehab center. It just happens that one of the rehabs she went to was the same rehab that treated a boy named Brian Carver. Does that name ring a bell with you?"

Kane shook his head. "No."

"Brian Carver was the boy they fished out of Peconic Bay two months ago. The same bay, it seems, on which your lady friend, Meg, has a house."

Everything Colette had told Kane ran through his mind in a flash then. But he said nothing about that, nor did he address what it was Gregor was implying with his comment about where Meg lived. What at all could Kane say about that?

"Once we got a look at her police record," Gregor said, "and the mug shots that came with it—once we knew that Colette Auster and Colleen Auger were in fact one and the same—I sent Clay back to her apartment, to knock on her door this time and see if she had a roommate, and if not maybe talk to her neighbors. Maybe we'd get lucky. The last known address in her police record was out of date. Apparently, when she chose her new alias and moved, she failed to inform her parole officer. So we had a head start on the cops. But when Clay got there, it was clear someone else had gotten there first."

"What do you mean?"

"Her door was wide open. Someone had busted her lock, pried it right out of the door frame. Clay went inside, thought maybe someone might be hurt in there. Once he realized the place was empty, he looked around and found a few things."

"Found what?"

"Three different bottles of a prescription drug in the garbage. They were made out to three different names, all variations on Colleen Auger, each one prescribed by a different doctor. They had all been filled in a span of two months."

"What drug?"

"Xanax."

"That's for depression or anxiety or something, isn't it?"

"I'm told that, combined with alcohol, it also makes an effective date-rape drug. It can be ground up into a powder and slipped in a drink. The victim wakes up hours later, with a bad headache and a gaping hole in their memory."

"Where are these bottles?"

"Clay left them in her apartment. We don't remove evidence from murdered women's apartments. Especially women involved in serial murders."

"She was being blackmailed," Kane said.

"Is that what she told you?"

"Yeah."

"What exactly did she say?"

"Some guy named Dean, from her drug-running days, had found her where she worked. He threatened to make trouble for her with the cops if she didn't do what he wanted."

"Which was?"

"Get young men for a friend of his, a guy he called the Professor. He liked to photograph young men while they were unconscious."

Gregor nodded at that. "That would be Professor Krause," he said.

"Who?"

"An old man, wears black capes, has crazy white hair, was supposed to have known Einstein when he was a kid, got out of Germany on the day the Nazis closed it down. I'm sure you've seen him walking around town."

"Yeah, I've seen him." Kane thought about him—an old man, maybe seventy, maybe eighty, tall but frail, always with a cane, a badly stooped back, had taught at Princeton, or so the talk went. He'd been a fixture in town when Kane was a student, very hard to miss, even harder to understand when he spoke, his accent was so thick. "But how do you know he's the man Dean was talking about?"

"Colleen Auger's apartment had been pretty much ransacked. Her TV and stereo were missing. Clay found a printer but no computer. Beside the printer was a pile of papers that Clay said looked like some book or something she was working on. On top of the pile was a letter, written to that guy Dean, threatening to turn him and Krause in if they didn't pay her ten thousand dollars."

"Where's the letter?"

"Clay left it where he found it. The police will eventually

get her address, probably from the phone company, we hope as early as tomorrow. They'll find the letter then. They need to find it, they need to know what's going on. Like I said, we don't fuck around with evidence in murder cases—or in any case we're involved in, for that matter. My only problem with the letter is that it was printed out, not handwritten. The font and spacing was identical to the manuscript Clay found, but still . . ."

"She wrote on her computer," Kane said. "I can tell you that much."

"You know that for certain."

"I never once saw her handwriting."

Gregor nodded, thought about that.

"But I don't understand something," Kane said. "She told me she didn't know the Professor by name. She said Dean never called him anything but that."

"Apparently she was lying to you. About that, and other things, I think. Among her papers, Clay found a newspaper clipping. It was a story about Krause, his life, his escape from Germany. She obviously knew all about him. And the letter wasn't exactly the letter one would expect someone who was being blackmailed to write, is it? It's not the letter written by an innocent victim."

Kane said nothing.

"She called your number from her place last night," Gregor continued. "Clay saw her number on your caller ID; that's how they found out where she lived. So you can add that to the list of things the police are going to want to talk to you about."

"I had nothing to do with Larry Foster's death. I had nothing to do with any of this."

"Mercer believes that. But he also knows that you missed classes all day yesterday, that your behavior of late has been at best erratic. There are plenty of witnesses to that, and you know how the cops and the media eat up those kinds of details, get on TV and speculate. All you need is to look guilty these days, and your life is just about over."

Kane looked at the Baggie in his hand. "Someone's setting me up," he said.

"It looks that way, yeah. If not setting you up, then at least leaving you with a lot of things you'd have a difficult time explaining. Mercer said that when he saw you at your place yesterday afternoon, you looked like you were hung over. Only he had seen you hung over before, and this time you looked and acted differently. He said you claimed you could only remember having two glasses of scotch the night before."

"Yeah."

"Was there anything different about yesterday?"

Kane nodded. "Yeah."

"It felt different."

"Very different. I mean, I've drunk myself stupid before, felt like shit the next day, maybe couldn't remember some things. But like you said, it was like there was a hole in my memory, like someone had gouged it out of my head or I had fallen off the face of the earth for sixteen hours or something."

"So maybe someone had put something in your scotch."

"My door was open when I got home the day before. Clay looked at the lock, saw that someone had picked it."

"And since you were out cold, you have no alibi at all for that night."

Kane looked at Gregor. "I started drinking around eight, I think. Next thing I knew it was the next day, four in the afternoon."

"Clay and Miller are fairly certain the shirt was planted in your garbage. There was a good deal of blood on it, and we had Sophia look you over, but she didn't see any cuts on you, aside from those scratches on your face, and those clearly weren't deep enough to cause the kind of bleeding that would account for what was on the shirt. No, someone brought that into your apartment after the shirt had dried and put it in your garbage for the cops to find. That's the only explanation I can think of. You're lucky that we're the ones who found it. If you hadn't gone missing, we wouldn't have been looking for you, and the shirt would probably still be there, waiting."

"But I don't understand," Kane said. "Whose shirt is it? Whose blood is on it?"

"Foster was found fully clothed. So were Carver and the first boy. And none of them had a mark on them, no cuts, nothing. If our guess is right, if what we think is going on is what in fact is going on, then that shirt probably belongs to someone who hasn't been found yet. Someone no one knows is even missing. Someone who went missing either the night you were passed out or the night you spent with Colleen Auger."

"You think there's going to be another boy."

"I have no doubt of it. I wouldn't be surprised if he turns up in the next thirty-six hours."

"Why do you think that? Why the next thirty-six hours?"

"Because that's when the disposal company your landlord uses picks up the garbage at your apartment. Assuming you take out your trash on time, the bloody shirt wouldn't be in your apartment, or even the Dumpster behind it, after thirty-six hours from now. Whoever is doing this to you has to be clever enough to know that and take it into account."

"Jesus," Kane muttered.

"The cops already talked to you once, and we know that they've labeled you a 'person of interest' in the Foster case. My guess is it wouldn't take much more than an anonymous phone call to send them to your place. And there's already been a phone call like that in this case."

Kane considered all that, then looked at the trash bag hanging from Gregor's hand. It still hung heavy.

"What else do you have in there?" Kane said.

"The shoes I had given you to wear to the chapel. You had them on when Clay and Miller brought you here. There's a small amount of blood on the tip of one of them. You were supposed to throw these away after you were done."

"Dean jumped me that night."

"Where?"

"At the chapel."

"He was there?"

"He showed up right after I got there. He took your camera and my sneakers. I didn't have anything else to wear on my feet, and it's cold out there."

"Why didn't you get in touch with us?"

"I didn't know if I should trust you. It could have been a setup. It seemed like one, the way he just happened to show up. I wasn't thinking straight. He'd bounced up and down on my head pretty good. I went back to my office to try to think things through. That's when Colette showed up."

"And she took you to that bar?"

"Yeah."

"You know what goes on there."

Kane nodded. "I didn't before. But I do now."

"You'd never been there before."

"No."

Gregor thought about that, nodded, then said, "We found blood in the chapel."

"You went out there?"

"Mercer did. When you didn't come back. He was hell-bent on finding you. We tested the drops he found. That blood is the same type as the blood on the T-shirt. And, of course, what's on your shoes. The thing is, the drops Mercer found were spaced out very evenly around that makeshift altar. Not in a spray pattern. Not in the way drops would naturally fall from a wound. But like someone had poured it around carefully, poured it out a drop at a time."

"Then you think it was staged."

"Yeah."

"Colette said that whole Satan thing was maybe part of some diversion. Something to throw the cops way off the track."

"That might have been the one true thing she told you."

"But she told me about her past, that she had a police record. And in the morning she said she felt bad about what had happened to Larry, that she was afraid she couldn't live with what she had done. She was talking about going to the cops, but she was afraid of what Dean would do. Why would she tell me all that and lie about the other things?"

"I think it's safe to say that everything she told you was carefully chosen."

"But *why?*"

"Because I think she was working with whoever it is that's setting you up. Maybe she changed her mind and was trying to help you. Or maybe that was just all part of the act. I mean, if the cops asked you where you were last night, what were you going to say?"

Kane was shaking his head. He couldn't believe that, didn't want to. But more than that, he couldn't get his tired mind around it, around the idea of something so big, so carefully orchestrated, in place, working against him.

Gregor watched him for a while, said nothing. Then, finally: "You can show the T-shirt and the shoes to your lawyer, tell him everything, tell him we sent you to the chapel. Or you can toss them both into the ocean and forget about it. It's up to you. It's your life on the line."

"If I tell them you sent me to the chapel, wouldn't that mean trouble for you?"

"I can handle a little trouble, if I have to."

"I told you before, I wouldn't roll over on you. I keep my word."

Gregor looked at him a moment more, then nodded. "We shouldn't have sent you there. I'm sorry about that. We were desperate. We wanted to help Larry Foster's family, give them some peace. It was a mistake."

Kane shrugged. "Well, like you said, if I hadn't disappeared, Clay wouldn't have gone looking for me at my place. Things might have turned out a lot worse for me." He waited a moment, then said, "Were you able to do that? Help Larry's family?"

"We got hold of copies of the coroner's reports, leaked some information to a reporter we know. She's going to do what she can. But the funeral's tomorrow, and the preliminary report still says Larry's death was a probable suicide.

Unless something happens tonight to change that . . ." Gregor trailed off, was quiet for a time, then said, "It's an unpleasant thing, you know, having to sit around, hoping that a fourth boy is found dead so that you can earn your money. It's a . . . helpless feeling."

"Yeah," Kane said. "I wouldn't like that either."

Gregor tossed him the garbage bag then. Kane caught it with his free hand. He looked inside the bag, saw the shoes, saw the blood on the tip. He tossed in the clear plastic Baggie with the T-shirt and tied the open end of the bag into a knot.

"It's almost high tide," Gregor said. "Wait about an hour, then toss that into the ocean. The tide should take them out. Put a rock in the bag, and poke a few holes in it, just to play it safe."

"I appreciate this. I appreciate everything you've done for me."

"I'm doing it for Mercer, not you. And anyway, it isn't evidence if it's been planted. And you should know that everything we found might not necessarily be everything there *was* to find. Whoever is trying to set you up probably didn't just pin all his hopes of connecting you to this on a bloody T-shirt."

"What else could there be?"

"I don't know. I've never had a case like this before."

"Who would do this? Who would do this to me? I'm no one."

"Everyone's got enemies, whether they know it or not."

"It's certainly not the work of a friend, is it?" Kane said.

"The woman you're seeing, she's married, right?"

Kane nodded. "Yeah."

"Does her husband know about you?"

"No."

"You sure?"

"I don't think he's the kind of man to know something like that and let it go."

"Have you failed any students?"

Kane laughed.

"What?"

"If anyone in any of my classes deserved a failing grade, it was me."

"Mercer said you've had a rough few years." Gregor waited a moment, watching him, then said, "The driver wasn't too far away when I called, so the cab should be here in a few minutes. Liv's putting together some food for you, to get you through tonight and tomorrow."

"Liv?"

"My wife. It's important that you never call me or Clay. Do you understand that? Clay came to your apartment the other night, to ask you about the Foster kid. But as far as you and I are concerned, we have never met. You're okay with that?"

Kane nodded.

"Mercer will call you tomorrow morning."

"I don't have much money. Maybe enough for the cab, but definitely not enough for the room."

"The cab ride is no charge."

"You sure?"

"Yeah. And Mercer already put the room on his credit card, under his name. The guy at the desk will just give you the key, won't ask for any identification. He's a friend."

"Thanks," Kane said.

"I'm sorry about this, but I'm going to need you to wait down the road for the cab. I know it's fucking cold out, but that's the way it has to be. I've got a lot to lose, and I've already done too much as it is."

Kane nodded. He wasn't a fugitive yet, but there was the chance that he would become one soon enough. And the sooner Gregor cut ties with him, the better off Gregor would be. This house, his wife, his business—it was the wealth of Midas compared to what Kane had at stake. What was it Miller had said about Gregor? *He's obsessed with not becoming corrupt. About as righteous as they come.* So it was more than just things to lose, a wife to think about.

"I understand," Kane said.

"If we find anything else, anything else that isn't legitimate evidence, we'll let Mercer know."

"Thanks again."

"Don't worry about it," Gregor said. "Your stuff is downstairs."

Kane left the room, started down the steep steps. He held on to the railing as he went—or started to, anyway, then thought Gregor probably wouldn't want him to leave fingerprints and let go. He made it down all right without holding on. At the bottom of the stairs, on a Chippendale chair by the door, lay Kane's coat. Beneath it was a brown paper shopping bag. He picked up the coat, put it on, looked around the room. Small, cottage-style, old-world-looking. A stone fireplace and a sofa and some chairs, wood floors and whitewashed walls, shelves filled with books. No television, no stereo, no computer that Kane could see, anyway. Timeless. The way people had lived back in the twenties and thirties, when all there was at night were books and the company you kept.

Kane saw Liv, Gregor's wife, then, waiting just inside the kitchen door, her arms folded across her stomach, her thick, curly black hair framing that sturdy oval face. He nodded to her, nodded his thanks, for the food, for sitting with him during the afternoon, for everything, then picked up the bag and tucked it under his arm. He opened the front door, stepped through it and out into the freezing cold. He walked with both his hands plunged deep into the pockets of his coat. He got maybe ten feet, and then behind him the porch light, the only light to be seen, went out.

Montauk was desolate, little more this far out than a finger of land reaching into the Atlantic. The wind was raw, and Kane walked along the shoulder of the dark road, got maybe two hundred yards from Gregor's house, felt the cold in his bones, felt he couldn't last more than a few minutes in this, when he heard over the wind the sound of a car approaching behind him.

He turned. It was a cab, an old Checker that had been painted red. The paint job was cheap, the paint flat. The cab pulled to a stop just past Kane, and Kane climbed in.

The driver was an old, wiry Jamaican man, with silver bristles sprouting from worn skin and an unlit cigar between what was left of his yellowed teeth. He looked at Kane in the rearview mirror, said, "Cold, man." Kane nodded, held his coat tight around him, waited for the heat to find its way into him.

The cabbie drove Kane in silence to an empty motel in the dunes off Old Montauk Highway. The man behind the desk barely looked at Kane as he handed him the key. His room was around back, faced the water. Kane figured that Mercer had asked for that; maybe Gregor had told him to. It seemed something Gregor would consider. The room was cold and dark. Kane turned the heat on and waited in the watery blackness, waited for an hour to pass. When he could see the shift in the tide through his window, see each wave fall just short of the one before it, he walked out onto the beach, picked up a rock as he went, stood at the shoreline, untied the bag, put the rock in, then tied the bag closed again, tore a few air holes into the soft plastic with his index finger, and flung the trash bag as far out over the steely water as he could.

The ocean took it with a gulp. Kane stayed there for a moment, till each gust of wind that passed his face felt like the dull edge of an old razor, then went back inside the motel room and sat at the window and looked out, waiting for morning, for what would be found next.

Miller hung up the phone, got out of bed, quickly wrapped his knee with an Ace bandage—it was *killing* him, this cold—and pulled on his jeans and boots and went downstairs. He was alone tonight, so there was no need to write a note, not that there would have been time for that. He grabbed his coat, ran out to his beat-up truck, got in, and sped the half mile to town. He knew that Job's Lane would be closed off to traffic at both ends, so he turned his pickup onto Captain's Neck Lane and parked at the curb. The sign said no parking, but no one would care about that now. Every cop in town would be at the park, with more important things on their minds than handing out parking tickets. Miller hurried from Captain's Neck, crossed Hill Street, walked past the movie theater, then crossed Windmill Lane to Job's. His limp was bad tonight, but he did what he could to ignore it. A crowd was gathered on Job's Lane—workers from restaurants and those who had apartments in town, maybe twenty people wrapped in coats, all standing on the north side of the street, staring at the park. There were cop cars, a half dozen of them, forming an arcing blockade in front of the park's entrance. A fire truck and ambulance, too, and their lights, combined with the lights from the cop cars and the glaring floodlights the cops had set up beyond the blockade, by the shore of the lake a hundred yards away, lit up the bare trees and the night sky beyond, cast a glow over town like the glow of a carnival. Parked not far from the fire truck was a van, the logo of a television station out of Hauppauge printed on the side and a satellite dish mounted on its roof. Its sliding side door was open, and a reporter, in her own pool of harsh white light, was speaking, stone-faced, into a camera. Miller was too far away to hear anything that she said—everything was silent except for the occasional squawking police radio chatter—but he didn't really need to hear her, the near-quiet chaos spoke for itself.

Agawam Park was a stretch of lawn that ran from Job's Lane to the edge of Agawam Lake, a freshwater lake surrounded on two sides by handsome homes, most built early in the last century. At the far end of the small lake, directly opposite the park, was Gin Lane, a narrow strip of road that separated the lake from the Atlantic Ocean. The Indian summer that had ended with this cold snap had been a long one, so the surface of the lake had only just begun to freeze. Still, partially frozen or not, Miller thought, it was easily the least private place around for someone to dump a body.

Miller didn't see Barton. She would have stood out, lost in her slightly oversize parka. Beyond the perimeter of the patrol cars, a hundred yards away, uniformed cops stood next to detectives at the edge of the lake. No sign of the body yet, not that Miller could see. An empty stretcher but no EMT. Maybe the fire department had towed the boy to the shore and the EMT was trying to resuscitate him. They would think that there would be hope of that, of maybe bringing the boy back, what with the water as cold as it was. Miller had read of many cases where victims who had drowned in freezing water and had been dead for up to an hour were brought back to life. But that wasn't going to happen here, Miller thought. He was certain that the boy had been dead for a long time now, hours probably—drowned elsewhere, in water not nearly this cold, and then tossed into the lake.

Miller stood in the cold air for a few minutes, thinking he'd have to get warm soon, when he finally spotted Barton. She was walking down the sidewalk on the opposite side of Job's Lane, had a cardboard box in her hand. Inside it were a dozen Styrofoam cups—coffee, most likely. Steam rose steadily from the lids. He watched as she handed the cardboard box to one of the perimeter cops, took two out for herself, and crossed the barricade, stepping into the parking lot that ran alongside the park. Roffman's unmarked sedan was there. Miller hadn't seen it till now. Roffman was standing beside it, talking to two detectives. Miller knew them. Donahue and Ligowski. Both had worked for his father, had been as corrupt as his old man had been. But now, with the new chief, *walking the line*. Barton handed Roffman one of the two coffees. He didn't stop talking, didn't even look at her. They probably didn't acknowledge each other while on the job, to the point of rudeness, all part of their plan to keep their secret, however much of a secret it actually was these days, from slipping. She turned then and walked past the barricade again, turned right onto Job's Lane, heading back up the brick sidewalk, walking alone.

Miller knew then that she had seen him, that this was his chance to talk to her. He left the crowd and walked a parallel course on the other side of the street as Barton. Halfway up the dark block, out of sight of the cops and the crowd, she crossed and met him. They stood in the shadow of the library. She offered him the Styrofoam cup of coffee.

"It's yours, isn't it?" Miller said.

"I got it for you. On the chief."

Miller took the cup, felt the warmth coming from it, held it close to his chest. Every little bit helped. "Thanks," he said. "And for the call."

"I thought I'd better let you know, in case that girlfriend of yours was over and you were too busy to hear it on your scanner."

Miller looked at her. "How'd you know about Abby?"

"It's a small town, Tommy. I don't have to tell you that." Barton looked down the street. "I'll need to get back in a minute. You never know, they might need some doughnuts to go with the coffee, or someone might want some copying done."

Miller hated that, hated that she was treated like that by the men in the department. But that was another conversation.

"What can you tell me about this kid?" Miller said.

"He was found twenty minutes ago, floating facedown. His parents didn't report him missing till last night. The night before that he was supposed to be staying over a friend's house, but it turns out that was just a setup so his parents wouldn't know where he really went."

"And where was that?"

"To meet some girl, his friend says. No one seems to know who."

"How was his body found? Another call."

"No. Somebody walking his dog spotted him in the shallow water."

"What was he wearing?"

"That's the weird thing. This kid had no shirt on, no coat, nothing. Jeans and sneakers only. All the others were fully dressed, right? And they didn't have a mark on them, whereas this kid has a cut on his forehead. Not more than a few days old." She looked at Miller. "This wasn't some drunk kid out for a late night dip, Tommy. He didn't get that cut or lose his shirt falling off a bar stool. The story's going to break. By tomorrow everyone's going to know what's been going on here. There's no way Roffman can call this an accident or suicide. No way."

"Is the coroner here?"

"He's on his way."

Miller nodded, looked down the street. Clay had been on his way to the office of the *Southampton Press* when Miller had called him, on his way to the "morgue," as they called it, the basement storage room where copies of all the editions of the paper that had been published were stored in a data-base. Miller knew that Clay had a reporter friend who worked at the paper, and that she let him in at night when-ever he needed to look something up, something that couldn't wait till morning, or that was best looked up in pri-vacy. Clay had told Miller he was coming back from another look at Colleen Auger's apartment and would join Miller there as soon as he was done. So, like the coroner, Clay would be arriving on the scene any minute now.

"What else?" Miller said.

"That's all I know."

"How about the kid? What do you know about him?"

"He's eighteen. A senior over at the high school. Captain of the swim team, believe it or not. Record holder, even."

"Well, that's the headline then, isn't it? I take it he had his wallet on him."

"Yeah. Which means this wasn't a robbery that took a wrong turn."

"Bad luck for your boyfriend."

Barton ignored that. "Donahue just made the call to the kid's father. Apparently the kid was supposed to be at some friend's house for a few days, or at least that's what the par-ents thought."

"What's the kid's name?"

She reached into the pocket of her parka, dug for a note-book. "I have it written down here."

While she looked, Miller said, "Any idea what his father does?" He asked it for no particular reason, other than the fact that the more information he could bring to Clay, the better.

"I overheard some of the uniforms talking about him," Barton said. "Evidently he's a bit of a prick. A 'holy roller,' the guys called him. He works at the college, is the head of campus security, something like that." She opened the notebook, found the page. "Here it is." She had to turn the notebook to catch enough light to read her own writing.

"The kid's name is Dolan," she said. "Kevin Dolan." She flipped the notebook closed, returned it to her pocket. "That name mean anything to you?"

Miller shook his head. "No."

"Me neither. The kid's father may be a prick and all, but I wouldn't wish losing a child on my worst enemy. I don't think there's a good way for that to happen, but this way has got to be the worst. It just has to be. Parents want to protect their kids. His will probably spend the rest of their lives wondering what they should have done differently. And that kind of thinking has just got to drive a person to the edge, sooner or later."

"Yeah," Miller said absently. He thought of his own father then, the lengths that the man had gone to keep Miller from paying for the horrible things he'd done, to protect Miller from the consequences of his own actions. Misguided love, certainly, but no one could have told his old man that. He thought then of the lengths to which Gregor had gone to make certain that Miller did in fact pay, that he saw the error of his ways, or was at least given the chance to see that, to change.

And now, Miller, out in this cold, doing what he has to do, doing all that is necessary—all to honor both men.

He looked again toward the haze of blue-white light that hung above the park. As bright as morning—brighter even—though of course it wasn't morning. *False daylight.* The intense brightness only made the darkness that surrounded it seem all that more complete. *Plenty of places for John the Baptist, or the Professor, or whoever the hell he was, to hide in that blackness, hide while everyone stared dumbly toward that light.* Miller glanced at his wristwatch. Fifteen minutes to midnight. Seventy-two hours, more or less, since the Foster kid was found. Seven hours till actual daylight. And then what? How long would this go on? How soon would the next boy be found floating?

"The Foster kid didn't kill himself," Barton said then. Miller turned his head, looked at her. "You can tell your friend Ned that. Not that this won't be all over the news by morning. Not that the whole cover story won't come crashing down by lunch, for everyone to see. But he can tell the Foster family, have their lawyer call the coroner in the morning, demand that he change 'possible suicide' to 'homicide.' This way they can bury their poor kid in peace and maybe get on with their lives. That's what you guys were hired to do, wasn't it? Get proof that it wasn't a suicide."

"Yeah."

"So then your job is done?"

Miller nodded, thought about everything she had just said. "There's going to be trouble for Roffman, isn't there?"

"I would think so. He ordered the cover-up. He needs to cover *that* up now. I don't think he can, though. I think the best he can pull off is to make it look like all he did was allow the cover-up to continue. Either way, there are going to be a lot of stories in the papers, and probably an investigation. I mean, he was brought in to clean up your father's dirty department, ended up being just as corrupt himself. He didn't start out that way, just like your father didn't start out that way. But people with money want to live above the rules. They expect it, and they can make it hard for a man to keep saying no. That's the kind of story the papers out here love to print, and that people out here love to read. It's the kind of story they should read. There are people out here getting away with shit just because they have money. And Roffman's just a part in that machine. He takes as many orders as he gives."

Miller waited a moment, watching her, then said, "Are you in love with him, Kay?"

She smiled, vaguely. "You and I are family, Tommy, and I'll do anything I can to help you out, no matter what. But don't ever ask me that again, okay?"

"I just don't want you to get hurt, that's all. People are going to be digging up stuff on him, anything they can get their hands on. They might find out about the two of you. It could get ugly."

She glanced down the street, then looked back at him. "I should get back. Do me a favor, okay? Don't stay out in this cold for too long."

"Yeah, okay."

"How's your knee?"

"It hurts a little. Does when it's cold."

"You should get some of those bandages you can put in the microwave and warm up. And maybe stay off it for a while." She looked up at his face then. He remembered her beside him at his father's funeral, and then at his mother's two years later, holding his hand during both, standing at the graveside with him, smiling at him in a way that was meant to comfort him, tell him that everything would be okay. Everything both was and wasn't okay since his parents had died. But he hadn't expected anything more than that, anything other than a whole bunch of good rolled in with a whole bunch of bad.

"We learn what we can from the people in our lives," Barton said then. "That's what you and I do. Even the worst people we know can end up teaching us something about ourselves, about the way things really are. You can understand that, right?"

Miller nodded. "Yeah, I can."

"You're doing what you have to do, Tommy. With your 'friend' Ned, you're doing what you have to. It's the same for me with Roffman. I can live with what I'm doing because it became clear to me a long time ago that there just wasn't any other way. It's the way things are, that's all there is to it. 'Cause, you know, one of these days *I'm* going to be the chief of police in this town. And I'm going to know then just what to do—and, maybe more importantly, what not to do. Roffman's been a good teacher that way. So this'll all be worth it someday. And *they'll* be the ones getting the coffee and making copies. Just wait and see, Tommy."

Miller said nothing. What could he say to that, to her? Maybe, he decided then, they were much more than simply 'family.' Maybe, with their secret ambitions, the alliances they made with these very ambitions in mind, there was something more that they had in common.

Maybe they were nothing short of two of a kind.

Barton smiled, warmly, then said, "I should go. Don't neglect that girl of yours too much. Redemption is one thing, Tommy. Finding someone to sleep next to you at night is something else."

She turned then and left Miller in the long shadow of the library. He watched her cross Job's Lane, waited till she was far enough ahead of him, then started back down his side of the street, heading for the crowd gathered across from the park, staring with a collective expression of dread at what that false light was finally making visible.

C lay drove to North Sea, parked his car in the tiny lot behind the deli, climbed the dark stairs to his apartment. It was two in the morning, he was tired, needed more than anything now to get some sleep. The kitchen light was the only light on, the rest of apartment as dark and still as a tomb. He knew this meant that Sophia was asleep in the bedroom. Why wouldn't she be, at this time of night? Wasn't everything with a soul asleep now?

He took off his coat, poured himself a glass of orange juice, tipped a little vodka into it, sat down at the kitchen table. The Foster case was over—at least technically, anyway. They had gathered enough evidence to more than suggest that Larry had been murdered, one in a string of murders that were still ongoing. The dog that had picked up his scent and then lost it in the middle of the road; the police notes detailing their secret investigation, including their nickname for the killer; the coroner's reports indicating his own growing suspicion that this was more than what it may at first have seemed. And now this fourth dead boy, this Dolan kid, just like the others, identical to them, more or less, only a few minor differences. All this was more than enough to give the Foster family what they so desperately needed. All that was left for Clay to do was to write up the report, documenting his activities on their behalf, his time and expenses, his conclusions, attach the bill, and send it off to the family—not now, but in a few days, maybe even a week; waiting was the decent thing to do.

Or at least that would be all that was left for him to do were this not such an unusual case. It was, though, clearly had been from the start, for Clay and for Gregor. Not the kind of thing they got involved in.

Gregor had asked Clay to look into Professor Krause, find out what he could about the man, as soon as possible. This had surprised Clay at first, but then of course he realized it shouldn't have. The cops wouldn't find the letter in Colleen Auger's apartment implicating Krause till sometime the next day, after they found out where she lived. There was always the chance that they could even overlook the letter, miss it entirely or misplace it or even bury it, purposely. Anything could happen. Despite what Barton had told Miller, the cops could still choose to stall, make no comment at all to the press, or claim they couldn't discuss an ongoing investigation, that doing so would risk tipping off their suspect. They could say a lot of things, anything to keep the truth from coming out. And who knows, maybe they had found something else, stumbled upon something that would lead them to conclude, as someone clearly wanted them to, that Kane was definitely their man. Maybe something Clay and Gregor had been unable to intercept and weed out as false evidence. A letter naming Krause as the Professor certainly would confuse things, unnecessarily, in the cops' minds, weaken their case against Kane, and therefore could simply disappear. Hadn't Clay and Gregor done the same thing with the shirt they had found? Based on what Clay and Miller had seen, the lack of blood in the garbage, and Mercer's insistence that Kane couldn't be part of this, that Mercer would get evidence to prove that, they had dismissed the shirt as false evidence and disposed of it. What they had done in the pursuit of justice, the cops could just as easily do to pervert it.

But regardless of all this, of what the cops might or might not do, regardless of whether the letter was authentic or not, a lot could happen between tonight and tomorrow, and Gregor and Clay had to proceed as though the letter *had* been written by Colleen Auger. They had no reason to believe otherwise, as they had with the shirt. And it was the only lead they had right now to follow. But it was clear to them both that whoever was behind these murders was escalating, killing boys with increasing frequency now, leaving a shorter and shorter span of time between victims, with *each* victim that was found. It was safe then to assume— necessary, even, to assume—that there would be another, might already be another somewhere, another boy no one knew, or cared, was missing.

If they could locate Krause, then Clay could stake out his place tonight, watch his every move between now and morning. Even proving that he had nothing to do with this would be useful. If Clay channeled the information back to the cops through Miller and Barton, it could maybe save some time, avoid confusion. Clay knew that whenever Krause came into town to shop, he came in on the bus. Everybody knew that. So he didn't have a car. Did that mean anything? Not necessarily. Clay thought that maybe he could find Krause that way. The man stood out, came to town regularly, probably shopped European-style, bought everything he needed the day he needed it. A driver would certainly know him and remember what stop he was picked up at. But the bus company was closed now, and Clay needed to find Krause tonight, needed to stake his place out tonight, not start looking for him in the morning.

Gregor had checked the phone books, checked fifteen years back, which was as far as his library of local phone books went. But he found nothing, and it was decided then that Clay would cash in a favor with his friend at the *Press,* search their database for any reference to Krause, maybe find a copy of the article that Clay had seen in Colette's apartment. He went to the newspaper's office after being diverted to town to meet Miller and get the news about the Dolan kid, and see firsthand the crowd and the television reporter—the quiet before the chaos and panic.

Almost immediately Clay found in the database the article on Krause. Written twenty years before, it was a human interest story—a large photograph and fifteen paragraphs. In the photo Krause looked the way he always did—an old man with brittle, untamed white hair, wearing a black cape and wool scarf and dark suit, his clothes as old as he was. The photo had been taken in wintertime, during a snowfall. Blurred flakes hung suspended in front of a long face. Wrinkles, wiry eyebrows frowning over dark, squinted eyes, a hard-set and broad mouth.

The article reported that Krause had fled Nazi Germany when he was nine years old, taken out of the country by a neighbor shortly after Krause's own family—mother, father, and sister—had been captured by the Gestapo and killed. Krause's father was Catholic, but his mother was Jewish, and both had been active against the Nazis in the early years, vocal—too vocal. Krause had grown up on the Lower East Side of New York, lived in miserable poverty till a benefactor, someone from his youth who had survived the war and made it to America, had shown up in time to send Krause to Princeton, where he was reunited with Einstein, whom he had known casually in his youth. Later he taught mathematics at Princeton, till his health took a bad turn and he retired early and moved to the East End in 1998 to live a quiet life; a pensioner grateful for the opportunities his adopted country had afforded him.

But it was clear from the article that Krause had been haunted most of his life by the loss of his family. He had once taken a sabbatical from Princeton to return to Germany, to try to find out exactly what had happened to his parents and sister. He found records indicating that the

Gestapo had suspected them of belonging to an underground group and had taken them to a makeshift prison and tortured them for information. Though there was no way of knowing by which means his family had been tortured, Krause did learn that the method favored by the captain who had arrested them was water torture.

Clay could find nothing more on Krause in the database. But the mention of the Gestapo and water torture caused him to remember a book he had read in high school, about a man called Intrepid, the head of British Intelligence during the Second World War. Clay, a fan of the French Intellectuals who came out of the war, was drawn to Intrepid's story for its references to the French Resistance. He remembered now an account of a Gestapo interrogation technique—a long plank on a fulcrum, a large bucket of water at one end, the victim tied facedown, his or her head lowered into the bucket, held there till water was breathed in, then quickly lifted out. The angle of the plank was such that the victim's head was lower than the rest of his or her body, which allowed the lungs, with the aid of violent coughing, to drain. The men operating this device were, it had said in that book, well trained, knew just how long to keep someone under, and how much rest to give them between immersions. The torture could go on more or less indefinitely, the book had said. The water was always cold, often filled with ice, having the effect of waking the victim up with every dunking, preventing passing out and prolonging the ordeal.

Did Krause believe that his family had been tortured in this way? Clay wondered. Was this trauma what drove him to serial murder? But Krause had lost a father and mother and sister. Why, then, young men? There had been no mention in the article of Krause ever having been married. No mention at all of a life partner of any kind. A politically correct omission, maybe? The article was from the early eighties. Attitudes then weren't what they were now. Didn't serial killers generally kill members of the sex to which they were attracted? Was Krause then a homosexual? Could this be it, the motive, the reason?

Clay had access to the Internet in this basement room, and his friend, Pat, had run out to get them some coffee from the 7-Eleven. He decided to look deeper, find anything that he could on the subject, brought up a search engine, typed the phrase "Gestapo Water Torture," then pressed the enter button.

What he got was a list of pornographic Web sites, an entire subculture dedicated to what was called water bondage. He entered a few of the sites, navigated to the preview page, saw photographs of naked victims being held underwater, then photographs of them being lifted out again, gasping, water pouring from their hair. Most of the victims were women, being tortured by men or other women, though in some cases the victims were men being tortured by women. In all cases, the water containers were what looked like glass aquariums, large enough to completely submerge an adult person. Some of the victims hung upside down by block and tackle, were lowered head first into the water, others secured to the bottom of the tank by straps or manacles, the tank slowly filled by a hose as the victim struggled against the restraints. There was even a tank resembling the one made famous by Houdini, a Chinese Water Torture tank. All the photographs were clearly posed, set in basements that were made to look like dungeons. The torturers were invariably dressed in leather outfits, though some were themselves naked. One woman, dunking a man in a monk's robe, was even dressed like a member of the SS. Hanging on the wall behind them was a swastika flag.

These photos, clearly fake, so clearly posed, were unsettling to Clay, disturbing, but it was the last Web site that he visited that alarmed him. He had found this one when he typed into a search engine the words "young men water bondage."

This was a different Web site, he could tell that right off. All the victims were young men in their late teens and early twenties, many with a model's good looks, each one being held underwater by a pair of hands as someone else took the picture. The water sparkled, lit by sunshine—clearly someone's pool. In none of these photographs were the young men struggling against the hands that held them down. Many looked into the camera, which was either just above the water or beneath it, just a few feet away; they looked at the camera with docile, almost tranquil expressions on their faces. These photos, this Web site, had an eerie quality that the others did not. This looked more real than the other Web sites, less staged, less overtly over-the-top. These were young men, attractive young men, simulating a drowning death, not some wild fantasy of bondage and torture.

Later, back home, in his kitchen, Clay wondered if he had stumbled onto what was in fact happening to the boys who were being found dead. Didn't Kane claim that he had been told by Colette that the Professor liked taking photographs of unconscious young men? Could Krause be taking this a step further? Instead of simulating drowning for sexual gratification, as was clear by these Web sites that some did, could he actually be drowning these boys? For his pleasure? To release his grief? For another reason Clay could not yet think of?

Unable to locate where Krause was now living, there was nothing more Clay could do tonight except wait till morning, when Gregor would call a friend at the phone company and try to get a copy of Colleen Auger's phone records. Maybe they'd get lucky, do a reverse lookup and get to Krause, get to him before it was too late.

But in the meantime, while he could, Clay needed to sleep. He was exhausted. He stood up from the table, poured his orange juice and vodka into the sink—he'd only taken a few sips—then turned out the light, went into the bedroom, got out of his clothes, and climbed in next to Sophia. She didn't stir, never did anymore, had long since gotten used to his climbing in and out. He lay in the dark beside her, looking up at the ceiling, his mind, despite his exhaustion, racing. He lay there on his back for a long time, a good half hour, maybe more. He wondered how much longer he could keep this up, how much longer he could do this job. He saw ten kinds of ugliness in any given week—people at their most desperate, people at their worst, the hurt and those who handed out hurt, who for some reason, some flaw, just didn't fucking care about anyone or anything.

But if he quit, then what? He certainly hadn't gotten rich in the past five years, hadn't hoarded away enough money to take care of him and Sophia for the rest of their lives. And anyway, he couldn't do that to Gregor, no matter what Sophia said about him. Gregor had done his years in the trenches, had earned his place behind the scenes. Clay always figured that at some point he'd join him there, somehow, while they were still young even, the two of them secure in the knowledge that they had done their part, maybe even more than their part.

Clay finally realized that as much as he needed it, sleep wasn't in the cards. He sat up, moved to the edge of the bed, was considering maybe making another drink, actually drinking this one this time, when the quiet of his apartment was shattered by his phone.

The ringing sounded to Clay like something smashing to pieces across his floor. He reached toward the nightstand, grabbed the receiver before the second ring could begin. Sophia stirred, but he couldn't tell if she was awake or not. He spoke into the mouthpiece, in a quick whisper.

"Clay."

A male voice, with an accent—South American, maybe. Whatever it was, whoever he was, Clay didn't know the man, hadn't spoken to him before now.

"I need to meet with your boss," the voice said.

"Who is this?"

"My name is Jorge Castello. Do you know who I am?"

Clay nodded, then said, "Yeah."

"It is important that your boss and I talk, face-to-face. It is important that we do this right away."

"What about?"

"I have an exchange to make."

"What kind of exchange?"

"One hour. A bar called the Oceanside. Do you know it?"

"Yeah."

"In the parking lot. Him, and him alone. If not, I leave."

"I can't guarantee—"

The line went dead.

NINE

A deserted East Hampton beach club, boarded up for the season, on a strip of road that hugged the long edge of the ocean. Three in the morning. The parking lot was empty when Gregor arrived in his Grand Prix. He parked at the ocean side of the lot, where the asphalt was broken into chunks and dead beach grass stood half bent. He killed the lights but of course kept the motor running for the heat. The news had said the temperature at Montauk Point was a few degrees above zero tonight, warmer than it had been the last three nights, finally out of the negatives. *Small comfort,* Gregor thought. There were houses down the beach, in both directions. He knew that because he had been here before, a few times in his life. There wasn't anywhere on the East End that he hadn't been at least once. But these houses weren't much more to his eye right now than dark shapes set against a dark horizon. The sky was overcast, low clouds blocking out the stars and the late moon like a curtain. No streetlights for a mile in any direction, no floodlights on in the parking lot, not even any lights out at sea. A complete darkness then, and no matter how long Gregor waited for his eyes to grow accustomed to it, to find the available light, they did not. He could close his lids tight, open them again, and not detect that much of a difference between the two. The darkness remained till, a few minutes after Gregor had arrived, a pair of headlights appeared in the road. The car turned, the lights crawled across the parking lot, and a car rolled slowly toward him.

It was a twenty-year-old Benz sports coupé, white, in less than vintage condition. It parked about thirty feet away. The driver left the lights on, got out, walked around the back bumper. Gregor got out, stood by his door. After a moment they both started walking, meeting halfway between cars. They stood with their hands in the pockets of their coats, their shoulders hunched against the cold, white fog bursting from their nostrils with every exhalation.

The man was young, maybe thirty at the most, handsome. He was as tall as Gregor, had roughly the same build, wore expensive clothes—wool pants, three-quarter-length leather coat, dark sweater, and shoes. His hair was black, neatly trimmed, just like Gregor's, though not as thick. His complexion was darker, significantly so, and he moved with ease, an air of confidence, the way people with money, who have always had it and know they always will, can move. Gregor, as he always did, in all situations, carried himself differently, with more caution, moved more deliberately, as if deep thought preceded everything he did. There was a quality, too, to the way he stood that said he was ready at any moment for violence to occur, that he wouldn't be surprised by it. There was a good six feet between them, and there was clearly no need for that to change, no intention that either had to change it. They stood face-to-face, offered each other respectful nods, braced against the killing cold.

"Thanks for meeting me," Castello said.

Gregor scanned the parking lot, casually but carefully, then nodded toward the closed-up beach club. "Why here?"

"You live in Montauk. I wanted to make the gesture of meeting you halfway. It seemed to me the thing to do. Also, I felt our meeting should be in private. I was fairly certain you'd feel the same."

Gregor nodded, thought about that. Castello's accent was thick but his English was good. *Educated.*

"How did you know where I live?" Gregor said finally.

"I have my resources. Besides, I know a lot about you, have known a lot about you for a while."

"Oh, yeah?"

"I know that a friend of yours died five years ago, that you came into some money and started your PI firm with it. I know you own the only two cab companies on this part of the island, and that you have interests in some other businesses as well, one of which is a home security company in Southampton. I also know that you apprenticed under a private investigator named Frank Gannon."

"I worked for him a few times is all," Gregor said. A few times was enough. He kept his voice calm. Frank Gannon was a long time ago. A different life. *A ghost now*.

"Gannon did some work for my family," Castello said, "until he was killed."

Gregor wasn't surprised to hear that, ignored it. "You own the Water's Edge, among other properties," he said.

"That's my father, Jorge Sr. I'm Jorge Jr. I just manage the place for him, fill in behind the bar when necessary. In fact, that's where I was the night your man came in to talk to Colette."

Gregor doubted that managing and sometimes bartending was all the younger Castello did. There were stories about him, about things he had done, or was supposed to have done, to a young girl who had once been in his employ. The details of his actions, and the nature of the girl's employment, were sketchy, but there was no reason for Gregor to doubt them. He knew what the Water's Edge really was, knew the kind of family the Castellos were. But this was a topic for another time perhaps, another conversation.

"What man of mine was that?" Gregor said.

"Miller. A kid, really. But word is he does things for you now and then."

"Clay said you wanted to talk to me about an exchange of some kind."

Castello nodded. "Like I said, I know all about you. I know the things you've done, the people you've brought down. And not just since you've officially been in business, either. I know the things you did before that, before you came into your money and changed your name. Listen, there's nothing wrong with a man deciding he's someone else, wanting a fresh start. With the enemies you'd made, it was probably a smart thing to do. So, as we can both now see, I know all about you and you know all about me. And with all that we know about each other, I thought it might be best for the both of us if we tried to strike a bargain of sorts."

It took Gregor a long time to respond that.

"It's cold, man," he said softly. "Is there a point coming soon?"

"An hour ago, Colette Auster's apartment was cleared out. Everything that was in it is now gone, in the process of being destroyed. When my people got there, they found that her door had been broken in, and that some things were missing—her television and stereo and computer, the kinds of things a thief would take, or maybe someone trying to look like a thief. We assume that wasn't your man Clay's doing, that those things were already gone by the time he got there and had his look around." Castello waited, but when Gregor said nothing, he resumed. "Everything else that was there, however, everything she owned, is gone."

"Why?"

"My job is to protect my family, protect the business. I take it very seriously."

Gregor thought about the evidence, the prescription bottles and the letter naming Krause. It was all they had, not much but *something*. But he said nothing about that. Castello wouldn't care, couldn't even if he wanted to. Gregor knew the world in which Castello lived and worked, in which Castello's family lived and worked. He knew it well, knew that six feet was as close as he wanted to get to that world tonight, or *any* night, for that matter, or to anyone who moved in that world with such ease, made their living from it, got rich from it, was willing to protect it at all costs.

The letter, what it meant, what it would prove, was gone, as gone as if it had been tossed into the ocean.

"It's unlikely that anyone will even notice her absence," Castello said. "She came out of nowhere and then just disappeared, the way people who come out of nowhere do. I doubt anyone will miss her."

It took Gregor a moment to realize what it was Castello was telling him, just how far his act of self-preservation had gone.

"You got rid of her body," Gregor said finally.

"A dead girl in the parking lot is not very good for any business, particularly ours. Her body won't be found anytime soon. No dead body, no murder, so no police investigation. No investigation, no need for the police to find out where she lives and have a look at her things. Still, it's best that there's no trail, no possibility of anything somehow connecting her to my family. She was, I believe, up to something. No way of knowing what exactly, so better safe than sorry."

"What makes you think she was up to something?"

"She was staying in one of the rooms above the bar, for her protection. She had told me some tale about a customer who had threatened her. Like a fool, I believed her. What I didn't know till recently was that the man she was hiding from was a friend of hers, from the life she fled before she came to this one; a friend, it seems, she was getting ready to betray."

"How do you know this?"

"We have a somewhat elaborate security system in place."

"You mean you have video cameras monitoring the rooms."

"We like to think of it as insurance. Also, there's a market in South America for that kind of thing, tapes like that."

Gregor wondered if the men who went there, who kept this place a secret, men of obvious discretion and influence, knew that tapes of them fucking hookers were available for purchase below the equator. He made a mental note of that, certain that any of these tapes might just come in handy if it ever came to blows between himself and the Castellos.

"Do you know what she was up to?" Gregor said.

"She put this friend of hers, some guy named Dean, together with some professor she knew. She was, it seems, playing them both against each other."

"What was this professor's name?"

"She never said it. He was always Professor. 'Yes, Professor. Hello, Professor. I can't wait to see you, Professor.' The way she said it, you get the sense that her not saying anything more was deliberate. Whether they were being careful about hiding his identity because they were on cell phones or this was some game they played, some role they acted out, it's hard to tell. Some guy had stayed with her the night before she was killed, a guy named Kane. He taught at the college, but he wasn't the Professor."

"You know this for sure?"

"Yes."

"How?"

"The day before she was killed she talked to her beloved professor on the phone, talked to him about Kane. She was to keep Kane occupied for a night, tell him whatever she needed to tell him to keep him near her for twenty-four hours."

"Why?"

"Something about leaving him with another chunk of time for which he couldn't account."

"You have this conversation on videotape?" Gregor said. "You have her saying this about Kane to the man she called Professor?"

"Yes."

Gregor took a breath, let it out, looked toward the empty clubhouse, then back at Castello.

"It's safe to say," Castello said, "that Colette and her professor friend were working Dean, playing him, there's no mistake about that. But it's clear from her conversations that Colette was working this professor, too, or trying to anyway—working him against Dean, and Dean against him. I watched the tape of her conversation with that Kane guy the night he stayed with her. I heard everything they said, saw everything they did. She started working on him, too, told him some crap about me getting drunk one night and telling her about my family business. It was quite a performance."

"She knew all about what went on upstairs at your bar."

"Of course. She didn't just mix drinks."

"She turned tricks."

Castello nodded. "She came highly recommended to us by someone we trust. She was intrigued, said she wanted to give it a try. That was the thing with her, she'd do anything for the experience, I think so she could write about it. But also, she was a bit of a freak. You could see it in her eyes. She told me she wanted to work for us, did for a while, then said she'd had enough. But she wanted to stay on as a bartender, so I let her. She was good for the bar business, too. Men came in just for her."

"And she told you that she'd never had sex for money before, ever?"

"Yeah. Why?"

Gregor ignored the question. "So you emptied out her apartment in case there was something that might lead the police back to you."

"My father's the kind of man who doesn't tolerate failure."

"But you risked a lot just to indulge her, to indulge her artistic curiosity."

Castello shrugged. "What can I say? She had a way with men. You should see how she wrapped that Kane guy around her finger. I even had a hard time believing that what she was saying about me wasn't true. That was her gift. She could convince anyone of anything."

Gregor nodded. His face was beginning to hurt from the cold. "I'm still not sure what it is you want from me," he said.

"It's what I don't want, actually. I don't want to have to worry about you or any of your people coming after me or my family, coming after our business. In exchange for that courtesy, I'm prepared to give you something you might be in need of."

"And what's that?"

"I understand you've been hired by the family of one of the dead boys to find his killer."

Gregor didn't bother to correct the mistake. It was a small point of fact, and he *was* looking for the killer, so it didn't really matter.

"And you want to help me do that?" Gregor said.

Castello pulled his right hand from his coat pocket. In it was a slip of paper, shivering in the wind.

"Before we disposed of her body, we emptied out her pockets. She had her cell phone on her. We made a list of all the numbers in her address book and call history. My people tracked down each number, got the names and addresses of every person that the numbers belonged to. Most of her calls in and out were to and from cell phones, probably stolen ones, if they knew what they were doing, which I think they did. But there was one number, a landline, that she called several times. It's a Riverhead number. On this slip of paper is the name and address of the person to whom that number belongs."

"The guy she called Dean," Gregor said.

Castello shrugged. "Maybe. It's listed to a woman named Eva Kosakowski. She's been dead for about three years. Maybe it's this Dean guy's mother, maybe her house went to him and he never bothered to change the name on the phone bill. Anyway, Colette made several calls to this number the day before she died. We have her side of every one of those conversations on tape as well, and she's talking to him in some of them."

He paused, thought for a moment, then said, "I don't know, maybe she did all this so she could put it into that book she was working on. Maybe she did it just for the experience. I don't know what she thought she was doing, but it is clear by the phone calls we've heard that this Dean guy, with her help, captured those boys, brought them back to his place, and killed them there after a day or two, then got rid of their bodies. He was the muscle, the one doing all the work. The Professor, whoever he is, was contracting it, and Colette was the broker, brought him and Dean together. But this Dean guy's the one you need to find, the one you need to stop. Maybe he'll be more than happy to lead you to the Professor, make you the hero, get your name back in the newspapers."

Gregor looked at the slip of paper fluttering in Castello's hand. The last thing he wanted was his name in the papers.

He had constructed his whole life, before he had come into money and then after it, with the sole purpose of avoiding exactly that. He was out of that game, had never wanted to be in it to begin with.

But this, how could he not grab at this, despite what it meant, despite what it could do, what it *would* do, what it would signify.

"So I give you immunity," Gregor said, "promise that I won't come after your family or your business, and you give me that slip of paper."

Castello nodded. "Turn a blind eye and maybe save a life. Don't, and you and I end up having to look over our shoulders—me looking for you, you looking for me. I'd rather not have to do that, if possible. We're both men of resources, resources best spent elsewhere. It's my hope that you see this, too."

Gregor looked at him for a long time. "Why should I believe any of what you're telling me?"

Castello reached into the left-hand pocket of his coat and removed a videocassette, held it up.

"It's a copy, of course," he said. "And edited. It's all their conversations. For whatever reason, it seems they intended on killing five boys in total. That's what Colette says in her last conversation with the Professor. Five boys, and then they were done. Four have been found already, correct? So that leaves one more. Would you really want to take the risk of not checking out the address on this paper, only to discover tomorrow that a fifth was killed there tonight?"

Gregor said nothing, waited a moment more, felt the cold on his face, felt it cutting through his skin and into his bones. He could end this pain, with or without taking possession of the note, simply by turning around and returning to the warmth of his waiting car, driving to his home, climbing into bed next to his wife. He could separate himself from this cold, protect himself from it, sleep through it, safe and warm in his bed. But what about the fifth boy, what about his pain, pain he could even be feeling right now—*as Gregor stands there indulging his conscience*—pain this unknown boy was helpless to end?

He reached out then, took the slip of paper from Castello's hand. There wasn't time to debate this, no time to care about what this would do to him. Castello handed over the videocassette. Gregor took it.

Just like that, it was done.

Castello looked at Gregor, said nothing for a moment. *Did he know what this meant?* Gregor wondered. Finally, Castello spoke.

"There's something I don't understand, though. Why would they dump the bodies into the bay like that? There are better ways to dispose of someone, a lot of better ways. It's almost like they wanted the bodies to be found. But that doesn't really make sense, does it, considering how careful they have been with everything else."

Gregor didn't say anything. It was time to go. He turned, headed toward his car. Then Castello spoke again, and Gregor stopped. He listened without turning back. *The clock was ticking.*

"By the way, you might want to tell that teacher, that Kane guy, to keep what he knows about my business to himself. I'm sure he'd rather that the police didn't find a copy of a videotape that shows him fucking a hooker the night before she was killed. We can always direct them to her body, if it ever comes to that. The chief has some loyalty to my family. My father, you see, was able to do a favor for him once."

"I'll be sure to let him know."

"As long as we keep each other's secrets, we should all come out of this okay. Big thing, don't you think? Trusting another to keep your secrets. But what choice do we have in the matter? What other option is there? After all, we are civilized men, each of us with families and businesses we must protect."

Gregor started to turn his head to look back but stopped himself. There was nothing to say to that, no reason to look at Castello again. He continued forward, crossed the distance to his Grand Prix, calmly climbed in and hit the headlights, and got out of there.

A half mile down the road he stopped and pulled over,

looked at his reflection in the rearview mirror, at his eyes lit by dashboard lights. Then he took out his cell phone, flipped it open, and dialed Clay's number. It was only then that he looked at what was written, in distinct handwriting, on the slip of paper he held in his shaking hand.

Clay found the house, the last one on the end of a dark dirt road in a part of Riverhead called Flanders, a working-class community on the edge of Peconic Bay. He passed the driveway, the last one on the right, made a U-turn at the dead end, the bay just feet away, and coasted a hundred feet back up the road before he stopped. He adjusted his side-view mirror with the buttons on his door console and looked at the house. It sat alone about fifty feet from the edge of the bay, a dirt driveway running from the road past the house to the backyard. All the windows were dark, the driveway empty. Gregor had called from East Hampton, said he was on his way. Clay looked at his watch now. It would be a good twenty minutes before Gregor could get here. Too long to just sit and wait. Gregor had also told Clay that there was, if Castello was telling him the truth, one more boy. The boy could be in there now, Clay thought. He couldn't just sit there, watching the place like some security guard.

Clay grabbed his Maglite from under the seat—two-foot-long, hard metal casing, as much club as flashlight—and turned off the motor and got out. In the trunk of his Intrepid was a small safe that held his Ruger 9mm. He opened the trunk, then the safe, took the gun out, checked the clip, the safety, grabbed the slip-on holster from inside the safe, slid the Ruger into the holster, clipped the holster to his belt, then opened a canvas shoulder bag resting beside the spare wheel. In the bag were several pairs of hard rubber galoshes. He took a pair out of the bag, slid them over his dress shoes, then closed the trunk.

He walked along the edge of the road, walked on the dirt so the rubber wouldn't squeak on the pavement. No street-lights here, unbelievably dark, but that was a Long Island night when all the lights went out. But he could see well

enough and kept the Maglite off so no one would see him.
He reached the driveway, paused, looked around, then chose
the cover offered by the line of trees that ran along the
length of the yard. He followed that past the house and
stopped when he could see the back door.

No vehicle parked behind the house, the windows there
dark, too. He waited a moment, then approached the back of
the house, crossing the dirt driveway, stood not far from the
back door. Something in the yard, a shape in the darkness. It
took a moment for Clay to see that it was an old washing
machine, resting on its side. He looked back at the screen
door, clicked on the Maglite. A summer screen, one hinge
broken. He thought about pulling back the screen door and
trying the knob, but what if it was unlocked, what then? He
couldn't enter like he had at Colette's. Wouldn't be legal.
Walk the line. He stood there, looked up at the second-floor
windows. Nothing, no curtains, not even a shade. He looked
back at the door. After a moment he stepped away, spotted
the hatch to a coal chute nearby, went to it. Padlocked, not
that it mattered. Maybe the house was shut down for the
winter. Maybe nobody was here. Another dead end, another
diversion. But why would Castello do that? Clay shined the
light along the back wall, spotted the electric meter. He went
to it, heard faint humming from inside. Behind the glass,
very faint motion from one of the dials. The house was getting electricity. But he heard something else, too, a muffled
but steady droning, high-pitched. Clay recognized it at once.

The sound of water moving through pipes, somewhere
within this wall, or beyond it.

Clay listened for a good minute. The sound didn't dimin-
ish. So the house wasn't shut down for the season. Electric
service was still on, water was running. So someone lived
here. But the lights were off, every window dark. Why then
was the water running? And full blast, at that.

The only explanation Clay could think of made him not
care at all about walking the line.

He hurried to the back door, tried the knob with his
gloved hand. Locked. There was no curtain on the window,

so he shined his light inside. A small kitchen table, a counter, takeout containers piled in the sink. Nothing on the walls. He didn't bother to knock, didn't care who might be in there, tapped one of the panes of window, the one closest to the lock, with the butt of the Maglite. The glass broke, some pieces falling. He pulled out what shards remained in the frame, tossing them onto the dead grass. When the hole was big enough, he stuck his thick arm through, felt around, found the lock.

It was a deadbolt, not the kind with a latch but the kind that required a key to be opened from the inside. No key was in it. *Fuck*. Clay's heart was pounding, his blood cut with adrenaline. Carried by his certainty of what was going on inside, he stood back, lifted his right leg, kicked the door in.

He moved inside, left the door wide open, stood in the middle of the kitchen with the light aimed at his feet, his coat open so he could reach the Ruger if need be. At the other end of the kitchen were two side-by-side doorways. One opened into the living room, the other most likely led to the basement. Clay went to the open doorway, aimed the light through the living room. No one there. The only things in the room were a couch and a TV on a milk crate. He paused and listened. The sound of the water rushing through a pipe was muffled here, like it had been outside. He strained to locate the source. It wasn't coming from upstairs. The house was small; he'd hear water falling into a tub if it was the shower. The sound was too high-pitched to be a running toilet. The downstairs was just the kitchen and the front room. That left only one place.

He reached for the handle of the basement door, turned it, pulled the door open a few inches, enough to hear.

The sound was coming from down there.

He pulled the door all the way open, stepped onto the top step, shined the light down. The stairs looked safe, but still he moved carefully, stepping as lightly as he could, testing each plank before committing his weight to it. He heard the sound loudly here, but he heard, too, the sound of water falling into water, splashing. When he reached the bottom step, he swept the basement with the beam of light, saw the furnace, a bench press and set of weights, not much else. He swept the light into the farthest corner, caught something, stopped the light dead.

A bathtub, an antique, the kind with feet. Larger than modern bathtubs, and badly stained. Hanging above it was a garden hose, water falling from it into the tub. Clay moved toward it, could see that something was stretched over the top of the tub. Rubber cargo netting, like the kind in the back bed of some pickup trucks. It was connected to four eyebolts that had been screwed into the cement floor. The netting was stretched tight. Clay got close enough to it to see over the edge and into the tub. It was filled to the top, water spilling over the sides and running into a drain in the floor a few feet away. Clay shined his light on the tub, saw that something was inside it, under the netting. His heart skipped. He saw then what could only be a mouth, pressing against the rubber mesh, gaping.

Then it all assembled in his mind, assembled fast into something that both did and didn't make sense.

Someone was in that overfilled tub, being held down by the soft rubber netting, straining against it with everything he had, stretching it just far enough to keep his mouth above the water and get air.

So this was how they did it, how they drowned boys without leaving a single mark on their bodies, without having to hold them down by hand or restrain them.

Clay hurried toward the tub, shined the light into it, saw the face of a boy. His eyes were wide with terror. "Help me," he muttered. Water flooded into his mouth. He spit it out, breathed, struggled. *"Please."*

Clay tucked the flashlight under his arm, grabbed at the netting with two hands, thought he could pull it free. But it held fast. He gave up, removed a Benchmade knife from his trouser pocket, flipped it open, began to cut at the straps that connected the netting to the eyebolts in the floor. The rubber was taut but moved enough so the blade couldn't get a good bite. Clay dug with the knife, worked through the rubber till it gave way. Then he cut at another strap, and when it snapped free, he flung the rubber from across the top of the tub and grabbed at the boy as he lurched upward for air.

Gasping, hacking, the boy clung to Clay with the strength of the terrified. He was shivering, the water cold. Clay helped the kid from the tub—really, the kid just clung to Clay as Clay stepped back. The kid was wearing sneakers but the tread must have been worn out because when he put his feet down, he slipped on the wet floor. His grip tightened still more, and Clay held on to him, careful of the knife still in his gloved hand, till the boy was able to get his feet under him and stand.

He was sixteen, maybe eighteen, but no older, wore cargo pants and a T-shirt, over it a canvas army jacket, the kind, Clay noted, that tank crews wore in the Second World War. Every muscle in the kid's wiry body was rigid, his shuddering violent, like he was receiving electric shocks. His teeth chattered—from the cold, from fear, from exhaustion brought on by the strain of pushing against the netting. He could not have kept that up forever, Clay thought, would have given up at some point soon, when the cold robbed his muscles of strength, then slipped below the water and drowned.

Clay closed the knife, returned it to his pocket, held the Maglite between his knees, and took off his overcoat, hung it around the kid's narrow shoulders. The kid grabbed the lapels, held the oversize coat closed.

"Is anyone in the house?" Clay said.

The kid looked at him, was too busy trembling to answer. *"Is there anyone in the house?"*

The kid shook his head. "I heard him drive off . . . white van . . ."

"How long ago did he leave?"

"I don't know."

"Can you walk?"

Shuddering.

Clay reached down, rubbed the kid's legs roughly with his hands to get the blood flowing. Then he grabbed the kid

with one hand, his Maglite in the other, and led the kid—
dragged him, really—to the stairs. The kid did the best he
could, which wasn't much, but Clay handled him with ease,
used old bouncer techniques, didn't care how rough he was
with the kid, only cared about getting them both out of there.

He pulled the kid up the stairs, moved through the door
into the kitchen. The boy fell, Clay pulled him up, dragged
him on his feet toward the back door, which was open still,
just as he had left it, for this very reason, for a quick escape.
They crossed the short distance to the door, Clay about to
move them through it and start the long run to his car when
he detected motion, something rushing fast toward him from
just outside the door, a dark mass charging at full speed from
only feet away.

It flew into them with the force of a tidal wave. Clay, bur-
dened with the boy, was unable to resist the force of the collision and was sent flying backward, and together all
three—Clay, the boy, and the man who had rushed them like
a football player—fell to the kitchen floor.

It was Dean, had to be, Clay thought quickly. The force
that had knocked him down could only come from a man as
large and powerful as the one he had glimpsed outside the
bar at the canal this morning. He couldn't see Dean's face
now, not that it mattered; he hadn't seen Dean's face this
morning, had only seen enough to size the guy up, get the
sense that they were, physically, at least, an equal match.
This was unusual for Clay; he towered over most men, outweighed them often by a hundred pounds, seldom was confronted by anyone who was close to an equal match to him,
in size, anyway. Gregor could hold his own with Clay on the
mat, but Gregor had a lifetime of tricks at his fingertips. This
was different, this was size and force, giant against giant. Ti-
tans, then, the two of them, entangled in sudden violence on
a kitchen floor.

They had hit the floor hard, the three of them, and the
house trembled as if it had been struck by lightning. The boy
was knocked backward, torn from Clay's grip by the force
of Dean's tackle. He tumbled across the tile, came to an

abrupt stop against the stove, hit it so hard that a cast-iron frying pan that had been sitting on one of the burners fell to the floor, just missing the kid's head. The Maglite, still on, skidded away, too, and came to a stop against the floorboard below a cabinet, casting a long, widening cone of light along the floor.

In that light, struggling for dominance, taking chunks out of each other, were Clay and Dean.

Dean had landed on top of Clay but didn't get to stay there for long. Clay had wrestled in high school, was used to fighting on the ground, and he immediately slipped his hips out to one side, got out from under Dean, pulling Dean till he rolled and they ended up on their sides on the floor. Clay was getting ready to continue the roll and mount Dean, throw his leg over Dean's hip and climb over him and sit on his chest like a schoolyard bully. But there was something about Dean that Clay had not encountered before, on the mat in high school, or in a fight, ever. There was a ferocity in Dean, the ferocity of a trapped animal, swift and relentless. *Instinct at work, not thought, pure animal instinct.* But there was something else, too, something that caught Clay off guard, overwhelmed him for an instant—a rage, wild and unstoppable, as unstoppable as some piece of heavy machinery gone suddenly out of control.

Dean didn't waste any time, clawed at Clay's face, or tried to, just went straight for it, screaming, loud, angry screams, but not just angry, something else again, the tantrum of a boy, or maybe the panic of a boy lost—whatever the case, something primal, something sent flying up from depths, too powerful to be contained.

It was then that Clay saw Dean's face, saw it as he grabbed Dean's wrists and held his hands back, his fingers fractions of an inch from his eyes. Dean's face was scarred, horribly, a cluster of small burn marks on his cheeks and forehead and neck and even his lips, random like stars in the night sky, as though someone had long ago systematically burned him with, Clay could only assume, cigarettes.

The sight of Dean's face, the thought process it set into

motion, slowed Clay enough for Dean to pull free and scramble to his feet. *He moved so fast.* Clay rose too, got up on one knee, reached back for the Ruger, cleared it of the holster, was about to bring it around and take aim when Dean stomp-kicked him square in the chest, sending Clay back and into the refrigerator, hard. The refrigerator rocked backward from the force of Clay's weight, then teetered forward enough for the top freezer door to open. Baggies of frozen meat, as hard as rocks, rained down on Clay.

He still had the Ruger in his hand, was able to aim it in Dean's direction, where Dean had last been, covering his head with his left arm as the last of the freezer contents came down around him. He didn't dare fire blind, the kid was somewhere back there, couldn't risk hitting him with a stray shot. This hesitation was just enough time for Dean to rush Clay, grab his gun hand, try to pry the gun free. Dean knelt on Clay, pressed his knees into Clay's ribs, put his full weight into it. Again, the freakish strength, hands like machine parts, a sudden, savage power. As they struggled for control of the gun, Clay adjusted himself, got out from under Dean's knees, put his foot into Dean's stomach, and pushed. Dean flew off him but held on to the gun, tore it from Clay's hand. He landed on the floor, hard, on his back, and Clay rose to his knees, then got to his feet, and rushed after him.

Dean had the gun by the barrel, not by the handle, and fumbled as he tried to adjust his grip. Clay didn't waste any time. He rushed Dean, threw himself onto him, mounted him, one foot on the floor and one knee on the floor, and grabbed at the gun with both hands, tried to wrestle it free, keep the barrel pointed away. Dean fought back, quickly kicked at Clay's head with his powerful leg, connecting with his shin, knocking Clay off his balance and against the stove. The kid was on his feet then, and bolted, still in Clay's overcoat, toward the door. He was running, Clay could hear his footsteps on the dirt driveway, but that didn't matter, he didn't care about that, couldn't care about that, what the kid knew, what the kid could tell them, fuck that, just fuck it all now. Clay turned the barrel of the gun to one side, and just as he did, just as its aim cleared him, the gun fired, the bullet shattering the window over the sink. The smell of powder was in the air now, a little smoke, too, and as Dean and Clay struggled, they scrambled to their feet, the two giants rising together till they were finally standing, their hands locked on the gun between them. The instant they were up, Dean shoved Clay, threw all his weight into him. Clay shoved back, and like that they went around the kitchen, clumsily, violently, crashing into the counter, against cupboards, back again into the refrigerator, sending it back and into the wall, cracking the plaster. Wood was smashed, holes kicked into walls, the small kitchen being taken apart piece by piece. Finally Dean got control of the situation—*so strong, so fucking strong*—and pinned Clay against the stove, bending him backward. Dean had a firm grip on the gun, a better grip than Clay had, and was turning it, trying to aim it once again at Clay. Clay kneed him once, in the groin, a clean shot, solid enough, but Dean barely flinched. *No balls?* Dean suddenly let go of the gun with one hand, threw an elbow at Clay, hitting Clay in the face once, then again, then a third time. It was like getting hit by lightning again and again. Clay's legs weakened but he remained standing, wasn't going down, not for this guy, not like this. Just as quickly as he had let go and thrown his elbows, Dean had both hands on the gun again, had found an even better grip, was turning the barrel, lining it up on Clay.

It was only a matter of time now, Clay knew this. Dean was strong, stronger, as hard as it was to believe, than Clay was. He knew that sooner or later Dean would get control of the gun, pull it free again or turn it, while still in Clay's hand, against him, or else start flinging Clay around the kitchen again till Clay hit his head on something hard and softened or exhaustion took over. Whatever the case, there was nothing else that Clay could do, no way out but this.

Clay hung onto the gun tight with both hands, gave it one last jerk toward him. Dean responded by jerking back, and that was when Clay shot forward, riding the momentum of

Clay's tug, bending at the waist, throwing his head forward, turning it so the top of his heavy skull struck Dean flush in the nose. Clay heard a snap, like a pin shearing and Dean flinched, softened a little, but that was about all. Still, it was the distraction that Clay was after. He let one hand slip from the gun and reached down to his trouser pocket, grabbed his Benchmade knife, pulled it free, and flipped the blade open with his thumb. It locked with a deep click. Clay could cut Dean's hands or wrists, quickly, one sweeping motion, cut the tendons, "defang the snake," as Gregor would call it, make it impossible for Dean to hold on to anything. Dean was all they had, the only connection to the Professor. He couldn't kill Dean, didn't want to, but he couldn't let Dean kill him. So this was the thing to do, cut clean, cut fast, and even if he could only drag the blade across Dean's knuckles it would be enough to end the standoff.

But Dean, with two hands on the gun to Clay's one, was able to overpower Clay more quickly than Clay had expected. He moved as if he sensed the absence of Clay's other hand, moved like a wrestler just waiting for an opening. He pounced at his chance, turned the gun the rest of the way around, till Clay could see into the barrel, see that it was aimed at his shoulder. His heart pounding felt like hooves against the inside of his sternum. Clay realized his mistake at once, realized the advantage Dean had grabbed, said fast, didn't know what else to do, "Don't, man. Don't." It just came out, but Dean ignored Clay's plea. It was all beyond reason now. Clay saw that Dean's finger was on the trigger, saw it contract, just once, the smallest possible gesture imaginable, but it was enough.

The gun fired, kicked against their mutual grip, and Clay saw a flash of white light and blue sparks, felt heat as the bullet tore into him, through his shoulder muscle, hit bone and stopped. The sound of the gunshot was like two hands clapping over his ears. He heard nothing after that, nothing at all, though he knew he screamed out, felt it rise up in his throat, felt it escape his mouth. He felt, too, his legs weaken, felt himself dropping as if the floor had been ice that cracked beneath him. He was going down now, fast, crumbling, and did the only thing he could then, the only thing he had left to do: He thrust upward with his right hand, just once, a wild motion, no real aim to it, and sank the four-inch blade into Dean's gut, sank it in just below the sternum, penetrating at an upward angle, till the blade was gone and the hilt of the handle hit bone and stopped. Dean grunted, spit blood almost instantly, grabbed on to Clay out of reflex, grabbed on to his shirt, preventing Clay now from falling, delaying it for a brief moment. However long the moment was, it was enough for Clay to witness the changes that came over Dean's face—a look of shock, then a dull grimace as the pain, what had to be an incomprehensible pain, rushed through him. Clay had no choice but to see this; they were in an embrace, their faces were only inches apart. In one second, Dean's mask of menace and rage was gone, replaced by a vacant look of surprise and, oddly, Clay noticed, a sudden, almost childlike sadness.

They stood for a moment, frozen, almost holding each other up. Clay's shoulder burned, as if it had been split open by a red-hot knife. He felt blood spread over his hand, its slick warmth letting loose in him a violent chill. Dean's knees gave out slowly and he slumped to the dirty kitchen floor. Clay followed him down, barely able to stand himself, holding the knife with one hand and the gun by the barrel with the other. Dean gave it up now without a fight, was bleeding from the mouth by now, coughing up blood. They reached the floor together, Clay landing sitting up, his back to the stove against which Dean had him pinned, Dean falling onto his left side, curled up against the pain in his gut, his hands shaking, his skin quickly turning white.

Clay did nothing but sit there and breathe, or try to, his skin tingling with sweat. He was bleeding too, but it was nothing compared to Dean. Blood flowed from him, spread across the floor. Clay watched Dean bleed out; there was nothing else he could do. His cell phone was in the overcoat the kid was wearing, and maybe he could have stood to reach the phone mounted on the wall, maybe he could have made it, but there wasn't really any point. Clay had cut one of Dean's arteries, that much was frightfully clear, and it was only a matter of seconds now, maybe a half minute at the most. Dean's eyes began to flutter, like a man fighting sleep. The look of surprise and deep sorrow never left his face. Clay thought for a moment of asking why four boys were dead, what was the point of all this, the reason. He thought of asking where Krause was at that very moment. But there was no point in that, either. Dean couldn't have answered even if he wanted to. Fifteen seconds went by, no more than that, and Dean, like the boys he had murdered, like Colette, and God knows who else, was silenced forever.

TEN

In Southampton, Kane awoke from a dream of his son. he lifted his head off the pillow, didn't know where he was at first, then realized he was in his apartment, had been there for over a day now. He wasn't sure what had awakened him, but he lay still, with his head raised, as if he had been alarmed by some noise. He waited that way for a moment but heard nothing. He was awake now, so he sat up and moved to the edge of his mattress and stared at the window that overlooked the back parking lot, and the overcast sky hanging dead above it.

It was still daylight out, and though he had no idea what time it was, Kane figured, by the weakness and the angle of the light, that it was probably late afternoon. The day before, Mercer had called Kane at the motel in Montauk, just after sunup, only hours after Kane had been dropped off there, and told him that it was all over, that it was safe for Kane to come back. That was all Mercer was willing to tell him over the phone. Kane had caught the train from Montauk to Southampton, then walked the mile to his apartment in town and had yet to leave. Most of his time was spent listening to the radio, trying to get an idea of what exactly Mercer had meant when he said it was over. Had they found the Professor? Had they found Dean? Was Kane in the clear, free to go back to what was left of his life?

At first there was nothing at all on the radio, no mention of anything that Kane needed to hear. Then, toward the end of his first day back, Kane heard a newscaster—a female, with a deep, steady voice—report that a man had been found stabbed to death in the kitchen of a Riverhead home. The dead man's identity had yet to be released, but the police did issue a statement indicating that this man was in fact a suspect in the recent murders of two young men, and that he had been killed, they believed, by his last would-be victim prior to that victim's daring escape.

There wasn't much more than that for the rest of that first day, and not wanting to leave to get the paper, afraid that one step out his door would land him somehow into even more trouble, Kane had no choice but to wait as patiently as he could for more news to break.

He had slept for only a few minutes at a time that night. His apartment felt foreign to him, cold, not that it had ever really felt otherwise. That night it just seemed even more so, like it was a place he had once stayed at, long ago, decades ago maybe, had stayed at only briefly, not for two years, and was now only revisiting—out of nostalgia, perhaps, for a different, not better, time. Without his routine of obsession and self-destruction to give his life its structure, Kane felt lost, unsettled. He had in his place nothing alcoholic to drink, and it took all he had that night to keep from running out and spending the last of the money in his pocket on a bottle of scotch. He watched the clock till the liquor stores were closed, then watched the clock till the bars were closed. It wasn't discipline that kept him from leaving, it was fear of what might happen to him out there in the openness of the village—on the sidewalk, crossing the street—what piece of bad luck might accost him, send him back into chaos, make once and for all a ruin of his small life.

The morning of the second day brought nothing new on the radio. Kane listened all day, sometimes sitting on the edge of his bed, other times in the secondhand chair in the front room. He listened to the radio, to sounds coming up from the street. Sometimes he'd hear a car door close and he'd go to the window and look down onto Nugent Street. It was never anyone he knew, never anyone coming toward his downstairs door. Kane began to wonder if his phone was broken or out of service, if maybe he had forgotten to pay the bill, didn't understand why no one was calling him. He checked his phone several times during the day, each time hearing a dial tone loud and clear. He thought now and then of calling Mercer but always decided against it, figured Mercer would get in touch with him when he had the chance. Kane knew better than to even think of trying to call Clay or Gregor. Gregor had made his feelings on that clear. And there was no way of knowing, short of leaving his place, if Meg's husband was still home, so that was out. There wasn't anyone else for him to call, no one else in his life, aside from his ex-wife, but that would only remind them both of what—of all—they had lost, and there really wouldn't be any point in that.

It was in the middle of the second afternoon that Kane gave up listening to the radio—the news was now saying nothing at all about the dead man in Riverhead—and stretched out on his bed to get some sleep. He dozed off, slipped quickly again into a dream of his son, and woke with a feeling of alarm, uncertain for a second time where he was. It wasn't long after that his phone finally rang.

He was still sitting on the edge of his mattress, looking out at the late afternoon sky. The number on his caller ID was one of the college numbers. Kane answered it on the second ring.

"Yeah."

"It's Mercer."

"What's going on?"

"I'll be around in ten minutes. I've got some things I need to tell you."

"Anything wrong?"

"I'm leaving now. I'll be there in ten minutes."

The line went dead. Kane put the receiver on the cradle, waited a moment, then got up and went into the bathroom and ran some cold water on his face. He didn't look at his reflection in the mirror above the sink, knew he'd only see a tired man, all the worse for wear. It was more than enough just feeling that way, he didn't need a visual to go along with it.

Kane waited in the front room, standing by the window. He saw Mercer's old Volvo wagon pull up and park, watched Mercer enter through the door below, listened to him coming up the stairs. It was just starting to get dark now, the sky softening into night. Across the street was the IGA. People walked into it, walked out of it. Kane watched them, wondering if any of them at this moment feared for their lives, felt the need to hurry to the safety of their cars, then speed to the safety of their homes, hide inside, watch out their windows. *Probably not, but, if so, then he wasn't alone in this.*

Mercer knocked, Kane opened the door, let him in, asked if Mercer wanted any coffee or tea, walked as he did so into his narrow hallway—retreated to it, really—and stood by the stove. He felt for some reason suddenly a little foolish in front of Mercer. Perhaps it was because the man had worked so hard to save a life Kane had worked so hard to destroy. Whatever the reason, standing in that dark hallway, with a good ten feet between them, was something Kane obviously needed.

"I'm fine," Mercer said. He stayed close to the door, stood with his back to it. "I only have a few minutes."

Kane put the kettle on the burner anyway, lit the gas. *Something to do.*

"Have you been listening to the news?" Mercer said.

Kane nodded. "Yeah."

"The man the police found was Dean. I don't know if you've heard that. Only his name wasn't Dean. It was Eric Kosakowski. Dean Moriarty was an alias, one of them anyway. Apparently the guy had quite a record."

"Ned tell you this?"

"Yeah. He just called me a little while ago."

"Do they have any leads on who the Professor is?"

"They're working on something, that's all I know. The police don't even know he exists, so they aren't even looking for him. The only reason we know of him is because of what Co-l___ told you, and the only reason we know she didn't make it ___ecause Ned has apparently seen some videotape of her ___ to someone she calls Professor on the phone."

"What videotape?" Kane said.

"He didn't say, and I didn't ask. But that makes us the only ones who know he's out there. The guy, whoever he is, knows what he's doing, I'll give him that much."

"So what's being done to find him?"

"There isn't much anyone can do at this point. Ned's going to keep looking, following his one lead, whatever it is. But with everyone who ever spoke to the guy dead, he isn't very optimistic."

Kane thought about that, then said, "What about me? Any more planted evidence turn up?"

"So far, no. Ned's person in the department is keeping an eye out, though. Let's hope what they found was all there was to find."

"But the person who did that, who planted evidence against me, is still out there."

"Yeah."

"So what do I do?"

"Ned wanted me to tell you that if you see something you don't like, anything, you can call him."

"And that's it?"

"It doesn't sound like a lot, I know, but—"

"Everyone else goes on with their lives, and I spend my days and nights looking over my shoulder for a psychopath?"

"Not everyone's going on with their lives, Deke," Mercer said. He gave that a moment to sink in, took a step toward Kane. "Trust me, Deke, I understand what you're feeling right now. You're afraid. I'd be afraid, too. But you're not alone in this. Good people will be looking out for you."

"It's just that I feel so . . ." Kane's voice trailed off, his eyes, a little glazed, fixed on the floor between them.

"You feel so what, Deke?"

Kane shrugged, didn't look up. "I feel so helpless. So fucking helpless."

"What do you mean?"

"I was helpless in the chapel, when Dean was kicking the crap out of me. I was helpless when he killed Colette."

"He was twice your size, Deke. And, from what you've

told me, you've never been in a fight in your life. What could you have done to stop him?"

"Nothing. That's exactly the point."

"What do you think you should have done?"

Kane shook his head, said nothing. Mercer waited a moment, watching him. The only light source in that hallway was the blue flame of the gas burner. It cast more shadows than light. But it was enough for Mercer to see Kane by.

"I guess you must have felt pretty helpless after your son died, huh?" Mercer said.

Kane was still looking at the floor between them, his eyes glazed, his mind far away. "You have no idea," he said softly.

"Anybody would have felt helpless then. There was nothing you could have done. Nothing anyone could have done."

Kane nodded. "I know." He nodded for a while, absently, then drew a breath and said, "I used to think it was guilt that was making me do all the things I've been doing. For the past four years I've been calling what I feel guilt, letting it run my life. I mean, what else could it be, right? What parent wouldn't feel guilt, wouldn't go out of his mind with guilt? And I used to think for sure it was grief that was keeping me from writing. I hadn't finished mourning yet, and all that crap, so I was blocked. But I'm beginning to think now that it isn't really any of that, that it wasn't guilt or grief that kept me in this tailspin."

"What was it then?"

"Anger, maybe. Rage."

Mercer's eyes narrowed. "Toward yourself?"

"No."

"Who then?"

"That's the thing. There was no one to blame, no one to get angry at. There was nowhere to go with the fury I was feeling. Something I didn't want to happen did happen, and there was nothing at all I could do about it. Not a fucking thing. And that just ate at me, day and night. It ate at me the first night, was still eating away at me after the first week. A year went by and it was still eating away at me. Then two years, then three, then four."

Mercer watched Kane, saying nothing, standing still by the door.

"It wasn't fair that he was taken away from us like that," Kane said. "He was gone and we'd never get to see him again. That was hard enough to get our minds around. But the fact that it was no one's fault was something we just couldn't comprehend. We just couldn't stand it. So, from the moment we were told that he was dead to right now, right here, I have felt nothing but anger and rage and fury and helplessness. It's an odd mixture, Doc. It fucks with your head. Like dying of thirst in the middle of the ocean."

Neither of them spoke for a long moment. A few cars passed by below the front window. From across the street, outside the IGA, a child was crying. Distant-sounding, echoing across the wide-open parking lot. It stopped abruptly. Kane stared at the floor for a while, then finally looked at Mercer and said, "I take it this wasn't all you came to tell me, was it? The message from Ned. You've got some other news, too, don't you?"

"Yeah, I do."

"I'm fired, aren't I?"

"Yeah. Sorry, Deke."

"I figured they'd get around to making it official before they closed down for the break. Who gave my finals?"

"I did."

"My students all did okay?"

Mercer nodded. "They asked about you. I told them you were out sick."

Not a lie, Kane thought.

"I appreciate everything you've done for me, Doc. I don't just mean at the college. With Ned and Clay, too. It's safe to say I wouldn't be standing here right now if you hadn't done what you did."

"You'd have done the same for me."

"You wouldn't have needed me to."

"You did the only thing you could, Deke, the only thing you knew how to do. You know that, right? It's amazing how what our heroes do, we can end up doing. What they value, we value, what they despise, we despise. Where they fall short, we sometimes fall short too, despite ourselves, despite having seen them fall short. There's a story in all this somewhere. In everything that has happened to you. Maybe writing it will help you let out the rage you can't let go of, make you feel a little less helpless."

"I can't imagine putting one word on paper, let alone trying to write another whole book."

"You did it twice before. And you did it well. Better than I could have." Mercer waited a moment, watching Kane. "I should tell you, Deke, I got a little nervous when they dragged Dolan's kid out of the water the other night."

"What are you talking about?"

"The kid they found in Agawam Lake the other night was Dolan's son."

Kane's face was blank. It took him a moment to speak. "You're kidding me."

"No. I confirmed it with Ned just a little while ago."

"They mentioned finding a kid that night on the radio but they didn't give a name."

"It was Dolan's son. Kevin."

"Jesus."

"I'll be honest, I thought maybe you were involved in all this after all, that it was some kind of elaborate revenge scheme or something, to get back at Dolan for getting you fired."

"You thought that."

"For about a second, yeah. And then I came to my senses. After that I was more concerned with what some desperate detective might make of it, that he'd see it as some kind of twisted way for you to work out the death of your son. Someone might think that—someone who didn't really know you, someone looking for a motive, any motive, to explain why someone would ritualistically drown boys. You've got to admit, it's a pretty big coincidence. You have to wonder if whoever was trying to set you up knew all this about you. If he did, then he did his homework."

"But who would know that?" Kane said.

"That's the million dollar question."

Kane tried to think but couldn't. He'd been given too much bad news too fast, and his still tired mind was reeling. He felt as if he had been stomped in the head once more by Dean. Now that he had been fired, Kane had no income with which to pay his rent and bills, to buy food. But with the Professor, whoever he was, still out there, these concerns seemed now almost ridiculous, perfectly absurd. Kane had no idea where he was standing suddenly, where in his life he was, where he even thought he should be. Everything was foreign to him, his life itself a foreign city through which he didn't dare roam.

Kane finally asked the only question that mattered to him. "How's Dolan doing?"

"He's out of his mind. But what do you expect, right?"

Kane nodded, remembered the moment he had gotten the news about his son; the torture that began then had yet to cease. *If there had only been someone to blame.*

"Poor guy," Kane muttered. There was simply nothing else that he could say.

Mercer reached into his coat pocket. "Listen, Deke, I've got something for you." He pulled out a small plastic bag, tossed it toward Kane. Kane caught it, barely.

"What is it?"

"Just something I thought might come in handy."

Kane opened the bag, looked inside. In it, still in its packaging, was a small voice recorder. Kane took it out of the bag, glanced at it, then looked up at Mercer.

"It's digital," Mercer said, "so you don't have to worry about tapes. It records up to eighteen hours. I know you said that when you're working on a book, a lot of ideas come to you in the middle of the night. This way you won't have to turn on the light and write them down, you can just lie there in the dark and talk into that, then go back to sleep."

Kane hadn't been awakened by ideas in a very long time. And the only things that came to him in his sleep were dreams of his son. But he didn't bother telling Mercer that.

"Thanks, Doc."

"There's a story in all this, Deke. I mean it. Like I said, it's just amazing how you followed Bill Young's footsteps, followed them footprint by footprint straight into hell. Like you were on some kind of holy crusade. The mentor-student dynamic is a pretty powerful thing. It's the stuff of myths, you know? Definitely, I think, a subject worthy of your talents."

Kane said nothing, just looked at the mini-recorder. After a while he nodded.

"In the bag is a slip of paper with the number Ned wants you to call," Mercer said. "If you see anything you don't like, anything, just dial that number. And then call me, okay? I'll get here as quickly as I can."

On the stovetop beside Kane, the water in the kettle began to roil, just a moment now from full boil.

"I have to get going, Deke. I'll call you later on tonight, make sure you're okay. Tomorrow I'll help you get your things out of your office." Kane nodded, thought of Meg's videotape hidden on his bookshelf. He had forgotten all about it till now. Once it had been his most prized possession, something he couldn't bear to lose. Now he'd probably just throw it out, into the ocean like he had done with the garbage bag of evidence Gregor had given him.

"Thanks, Doc."

"Watch your back, Deke. Okay?"

"Yeah."

Mercer left. Kane listened to him go down the stairs, then out the door. A moment later Mercer's car started up across the street, then pulled away and drove off. Kane turned the gas flame off, and the windowless hallway went dark. He moved the kettle to the other burner, walked out of the dark hall and into his front room, stood at his window, watched the night fall, the lights in town come on, watched them cast both light and shadows along the length of Nugent Street.

Sophia was standing in the front room of her apartment in North Sea, looking out the window at the empty road, when the phone rang. Clay was still asleep in their bed. She turned her head and could see him through the open door at the other end of the room. There had been daylight in the overcast sky when she went to the window, but it was night now, the apartment dark and still. She turned on the standing lamp by the couch, hurried to the phone on the nearby coffee table, picked up the receiver on the second ring.

"Hello."

"How is he?" Gregor said.

"He's fine." Sophia made no effort to hide the coldness in her voice. "He's sleeping."

"When did he take his last pill?"

"About four hours ago."

"So he should be waking up soon."

"Probably."

"I need to talk to him."

"He'll be out of it for the most part."

"I'm not far away. I can be there in a few minutes."

"I should give him another pill. He'll be in pain. Can it wait?"

"Not really."

"Then I guess you're coming over."

"Thanks."

The line went dead. Sophia hung up, looked at Clay. The ringing of the phone had awakened him. He was flat on his back, the white bandage on his right shoulder bright against his dark skin. He rolled his head to one side and looked toward her, squinting against the light.

"Was that Ned?" Clay said. He was groggy, murmured more than spoke.

Sophia walked to the bedroom door, stood there with her long arms folded across her stomach. She nursed people back to health for a living, was used to pain and suffering, saw it every day. But that was different; those people were strangers. During the past two days she'd often watched Clay as he slept, sat in a chair or stood in the doorway and listened to his every breath. She could think of nothing else to do. No rounds, no other patients, no paperwork, nothing to distract her, give her momentum, tire her out. Only Clay, lying there, and their apartment around them, as silent as a library.

"Yeah," she said. "He's on his way over."

"What time is it?"

"Five-thirty."

"Night or morning?"

"Night. How do you feel?"

He shrugged with his one good shoulder.

"You're lucky, Reg. You know that, right?"

"I know."

"It could have been a lot worse."

"I know."

She waited a moment, watching him, then said, "You won't be going back to work for a long time. If you don't want to tell him that, I'd be more than happy to."

"Ned knows that," Clay said. He opened and closed his eyes, spoke softly, breathed evenly. "He's been shot before."

"When?"

"A long time ago."

"It's a shame."

"What?"

"That it wasn't fatal."

Clay smiled at that as best he could, said nothing.

"If you ask me, Reg, you shouldn't go back at all, ever."

He nodded. "I'm a little dopey, sweetie. Can we talk about this later?"

She shrugged. What was the point talking about it at all? They'd talked about it and talked about it, argued about it, shouted at each other about it. And still, every night, he went out. Loyalty, to his friend—so-called friend. She would never understand it, didn't care to.

"Do you need anything?" she said.

"Some water."

She nodded, left the room. He lay in the quiet dark for a while, looked at the ceiling, ignored the throbbing in his shoulder, the sickening lightness in his head. When Sophia came back, she held a half-filled glass to Clay's lips, watched him take a few sips from the bent straw.

"Here, you should take another pill."

"I need to stay sharp."

"The kind of pain you're going to feel in a few minutes isn't the kind that makes someone sharp."

She held out her palm, a pill resting in it. Clay closed his eyes and nodded. She placed the pill in his mouth and put the straw to his lips. He took a long sip, swallowed. When he was done she placed the glass on the nightstand and stood by the edge of the bed.

Clay looked up at her. "I love you, you know that, right?"

"I love you, too. Very much. It'd be a lot easier if I didn't."

"Would you leave me?" Clay whispered.

"In a heartbeat."

"You'd be nothing without me," he teased.

"Probably."

Clay breathed in a few times, testing how far his chest could expand before it triggered pain in his shoulder. Not very far at all. He glanced at the bandage.

"How bad?" he said.

"Bad enough."

"I don't remember much after getting shot. I don't remember how I got here."

"Ned brought you. And that kid, too. That wannabe."

"Tommy."

Sophia nodded. "They helped get you up here. It took the two of them."

"You should have taken a picture of that."

"It's not a joke, Reg."

Clay nodded. "Sorry. Did the bullet pass through?"

"No."

"Is it still in me?"

"We got it out."

"We?"

"Ned and I."

Clay said nothing.

"He's a pretty cool customer, your friend. I'll give him that much. He learns fast. And his hand didn't shake once."

"Any damage to the bone?"

"The bullet nicked it. With no X-ray we can't be sure if it's fractured or not. We're going to need to find a way to have a doctor look at you soon."

Clay nodded again. "How many stitches?"

"Ten. Ned's wife showed up with a suture kit. He helped me stitch you up."

"A full house, huh?"

"It was a real party. Wish you could have been here."

"Me, too."

Sophia took a breath, let it out, then said, "What do you think he wants now?"

"Ned?"

"Yeah."

"I don't know."

"Does he expect you to run his business for him from your sickbed?"

"Of course not."

"You need to heal, Reg. You need time to rest. Christ, someone shot you. I don't even know what happened. No one's told me anything. Ned just said you were on a case, wouldn't tell me anything more than that."

"That's for your own protection."

"What are you talking about, 'my own protection'? What does that mean? Is somebody after you?"

"I'm not really up to this right now, Sophia."

"Yeah, well, I'm a little tired, too, Reg. I need you to tell me. Is somebody after you?"

"No. It's just that the less you know right now, the better. Okay?"

"No, it's not okay. I'm done being a good sport. I need to know what's going on. I need you to tell me right now."

Clay closed his eyes, opened them. He took a breath. Sophia watched him.

"What's going on, Reggie?"

He was awake now, as awake as was humanly possible, had willed himself that way.

Sophia kept her voice soft, kept the anger out of it. "What happened, Reg?"

"I killed a man, Sophia." He looked up at her. "I killed a man."

Neither of them said anything, just looked at each other. A car pulled into the driveway then, swung around back, came to a stop. Clay and Sophia listened as a car door opened, then closed, listened to the sound of footsteps on their back stairs.

"Are you in trouble with the police?" Sophia whispered.

"I don't know."

The footsteps stopped, and then there was a knock on their kitchen door.

Sophia didn't move.

"Let him in," Clay said.

She nodded, left the bedroom, walked through the kitchen, opened the door, let Gregor in. She barely acknowledged him, told him that Clay was in the bedroom. Gregor walked back there. Sophia filled a glass with water, drank it at the sink. There wasn't anywhere in the apartment she could go where she wouldn't hear everything that they said.

So she put the glass down on the counter and returned to the front room, stood at the window, and looked down at North Sea Road.

Gregor asked Clay how he was feeling. Fine, Clay said. Sophia rolled her eyes in disbelief. *Tough guys.* Then Gregor and Clay got right down to business, spoke in soft, conspiratorial voices. Sophia listened hard, tried as best she could to follow what was said.

"There's no sign of that kid anywhere," Gregor said. "I found your overcoat a half mile from the house. It's safe to assume, since no one has found his frozen body on the side of the road anywhere, that the kid made it home okay, wherever that is."

"Do the police have any idea who he is?"

"No."

"Did they find anything in the house?"

"Just the bathtub, a lot of porn, and some clothes. I was hoping they'd find pay stubs or something. Colette had told Kane that Kosakowski had to take some crap job to make ends meet. I was hoping maybe someone he worked with would know something. Or where he worked might give us an idea where to look for the kid. Maybe he was a janitor at a school or something. But the cops found nothing."

"What about Krause?"

"Yeah, well, that's where the news gets even worse."

"What do you mean?"

"He's been bedridden for the past two weeks. Emphysema. He's under a nurse's care, whacked out of his mind on morphine. He should have died a week ago; they've given him last rites twice already. According to his nurse, he couldn't hold a phone in his hand, let alone talk into one."

"So who was Colette talking to?"

"Exactly. She could have been talking to anyone, for all we know. *Professor* could have been a pet name. Whoever he was, he seemed to be something of a mentor to her. That's clear in their conversations. And there's always the possibility that she could have been talking to no one at all."

"You mean like an imaginary friend?"

"Not really. She had to have known about the cameras. She worked there. How could she not have known? So it all could have been an act, all part of the plan to pin this on Krause."

"I'm not following."

"Castello handed over the surveillance tapes pretty quickly, don't you think?"

"You think he's behind this?"

"Kane said he heard Kosakowski talking to someone on the cell phone out at the chapel. Maybe it was Castello he heard."

"But why would he want to kill a bunch of boys? Why would he go to the trouble of making it look like a serial killer? Doesn't he have resources of his own?"

"Maybe the boys knew too much. Maybe Colette told them something she shouldn't have. Maybe he needed to take care of this in a way that wouldn't get back to his father. I don't know. I don't know what the fuck is going on. All I do know is that Krause had nothing to do with it. He couldn't."

Sophia heard silence for a moment. And then, when Gregor finally spoke again, his voice was even more hushed than before.

"Listen, Reg, I've taken care of everything. Okay? Your clothes, the galoshes, the overcoat, the knife, they're gone, I've taken care of all that. So you don't have to worry about any of it. You were never there. The police think that a would-be victim got free and killed Kosakowski. They seem determined to believe that, actually. As far as they're concerned, that's that."

"The kid knows otherwise, though. He saw my face."

"He hasn't come forward yet, Reg. And I don't really think he will. I would imagine he'd rather not have to explain how he got in that basement in the first place. It's safe to say Colette didn't lure any of the boys out with the promise of candy. I figure she must have made arrangements to meet this boy before she was killed. Either way, he might just keep the whole nightmare to himself. But if for some reason he does come forward, or tells someone the story and they come forward, and the cops put two and two together, you were with me and Miller the entire night, on a case. The paperwork documenting that fact has been taken care of, so it's done, nothing more to worry about."

"That isn't exactly going by the book, Ned. You're destroying evidence, like I'm guilty and you're trying to protect me."

"I don't need you to tell me you were acting in self-defense, Reg."

"But destroying evidence like this, covering up, that was the kind of shit Frank Gannon did. You said you weren't going to end up like him, no matter what was at stake. Are you sure you want to do this?"

"The cops would make real trouble for you, Reg. I guarantee it. It's amazing, what they'll ignore and what they'll pursue. I don't care what it does or doesn't mean. I'll do whatever it takes to keep them from making trouble for you. They'd only be doing it just to get at me. Unfinished business and all that."

Sophia turned her head then, looked toward the bedroom door. She could see Clay, lying on their bed, looking up. All she could see of Gregor was his back as he stood just inside the bedroom doorway.

"This is how it starts," Clay said. "You know that. The deal with Castello, then this. This is how it starts."

"You don't have worry to about that, Reg. Just get some rest. I'll come back in a couple of days."

"What about all the jobs we had lined up?"

"I'm taking them."

"You sure?"

"It's time for me to stop hiding."

"You could hire Miller, start him out on some of the easier cases."

"That's what I wanted to talk to you about. I wanted to know if you thought he was ready or not."

"He's still a kid, but if anyone was born for this work, it's him. Born and bred. And his friendship with Kay Barton is certainly a plus."

"I'll swing by his house after I leave here, ask him if he wants to do a job for us."

"Which job?"

"Actually, I was going to have him keep an eye on Kane for a while."

"Why?"

"The blood on the T-shirt you found in Kane's apartment is O negative, the same blood type as Kevin Dolan. I got the results yesterday."

"You don't think Kane was a part of this after all?"

"No. His girlfriend's security system clears him."

"So what will watching him do?"

"I don't know. It's a long shot, I admit it, but it's all we have. Kane's always been a connection, and right now he's the only one left alive. If Krause was supposed to take the blame all along, then why the bloody shirt in Kane's apartment? It just doesn't make sense."

"Maybe it's not supposed to."

"What do you mean?"

"Maybe it's all just some giant mess left behind for the cops to try to sort through, to keep them busy."

"A trail of confusion."

"Maybe."

Gregor said nothing. Sophia could tell by the way he lifted his head and looked toward the wall that he was thinking about that.

"What about Kosakowski's phone records?" Clay said. He was still fighting, still willing himself into a lucid state. "Was there something there to help?"

"The only numbers he called from his landline were a few dozen 900 numbers and a Chinese takeout place in Riverhead. The rest were all calls to and from cell phones, some stolen, the rest the disposable kind."

"He planned this well, whoever he is," Clay said.

"Yeah."

"How'd you find out about his phone calls?"

"Miller got it from Barton."

Clay nodded, decisively, or as close to that as he could get. "So then Miller watches Kane, and we wait. For as long as it takes. You're right, it's all we have."

"I wait, Reg. You rest. It's going to hurt, you know that, right? And it's going to take a long time."

"Yeah, I know."

"You're on the payroll, of course, for however long it takes you. Tell Sophia if she needs anything to just call."

"You're well-off, Ned, but you're not rich."

"It doesn't matter."

Clay nodded. His eyes were opening and closing again. Whatever will he had summoned to clear his mind was leaving him now. He reached up with his left hand. Gregor stepped to the bed, took Clay's left with his right, held it for a moment.

"Thanks," Clay said.

"What are brothers for."

Clay swallowed, opened and closed his eyes a few times, then said, "Listen to me, brother to brother. Stick to doing things by the book. My first illegal entry in five years and I get myself shot. Isn't that how it goes?"

"Get some rest, Reg."

"Miller might be out with his new girlfriend tonight. I think he was going to take her out for dinner. I don't know where, though."

"I'll find him."

"It's a long shot, you're right. The Kane thing, I mean. But I guess since we're the only ones who know about any of this, it's up to us, huh?" He was drifting now, his voice trailing off.

"I'll come by in a few days, Reg."

Clay said nothing more, just looked up at Gregor through barely open eyes. Sophia watched them.

Eventually Gregor let go of Clay's hand. It hung there in the air, adrift. Gregor took it again and gently set it down on Clay's stomach. He waited a moment, then turned and walked out of the bedroom. He spotted Sophia at the window, looking over her shoulder at him, and stopped. Neither of them said a thing for a moment.

Then, finally, Gregor said, "I'll find him a doctor, if you don't think you can. One who won't ask questions."

"I wouldn't know who to ask."

"I'll let you know tomorrow."

"Thanks for your help. For saving his life, everything else you did."

"No problem."

"Of course, his life wouldn't have needed saving in the first place if it weren't for you."

There was nothing Gregor could say to that. It was, after all, when it came down to it, the truth.

"He saved a life. That should matter to you."

"You're as dangerous now as you were before you retired. Reggie's told me all about you. You were bad news then, and you're bad news now."

"I'm not the enemy," Gregor said.

"You're mine."

He nodded back toward Clay. "I meant I'm not his."

"Not yet. Give it time."

Gregor just looked at her for a moment. Her stare was hard. Everything about her was rigid.

"If you need anything, you know where you can reach me."

He waited, maybe for her to say something more. She couldn't read him, never had been able to. Clay was devoted to him, she knew that. Blindly, she had always thought. It seemed now that Gregor was just as devoted to Clay. But what was devotion, blind or otherwise, when it led to this?

At last, when she said nothing more, Gregor nodded to her and walked through the kitchen and out the door.

Sophia waited at the window till the Grand Prix pulled out onto North Sea Road, heading toward Southampton. She watched it until its red taillights disappeared into the darkness.

K ane sat in his front room, in the dark, till he realized he'd need food if he was going to be holed up in his apartment indefinitely. He waited until just before the supermarket was all but empty now, and Kane put on his coat and went down his stairs and stood for a moment on the sidewalk. He looked up and down before crossing the street. *Looked for what, for who?* He felt a little foolish, but what else could he do? The night air was still, the temperature holding steady at thirty degrees. Balmy, compared to the last few days. The supermarket was all but empty now, and Kane moved through the aisles quickly, grabbing things and totaling them up in his head as he went along. The forty-some-odd bucks in his pocket was all he had to his name. Not a lot at any time, but especially now. He felt, again, like he was in some foreign city, out of money, no way to leave and nowhere to go.

As he waited behind an elderly woman in the checkout line Kane looked through the tall windows to the parking lot beyond, keeping his eye out. He still wasn't certain what he was looking for, or who. The kid at the register was young, tall and lanky, clearly still in high school. Around the age Kane's son would be right now. Of course Kane's mind went there. A young girl was bagging up the cans of soup and boxes of pasta and jars of tomato sauce that Kane had selected. Winter food, filling and cheap. The girl had curly blond hair, was pretty, with a round face and pale skin. She glanced at Kane now and then. He didn't know why at first, then remembered the scratches on his face. The girl told the boy at the register that today was the first day of winter, which meant tonight was the longest night of the year. She said that she always thought Halloween would be better if it was celebrated tonight instead of in October. The boy didn't seem to have an opinion either way, was occupied with counting out the right change. Kane got just under seven dollars back. He wondered if the change he had in various drawers at home, combined with what he was holding in his hand, would be enough for a small bottle of cheap scotch.

He left with the change in his pocket and three heavy bags in his hands, hurried across Nugent Street, not a car in sight, and entered his apartment. At the top of the stairs he opened the door, immediately heard a voice coming from his bedroom. A female voice, filtered through his phone machine. It was Meg. He dropped the bags in the doorway, left the door wide open, and hurried through the narrow hallway to his bedroom. He reached the nightstand and grabbed the phone just as she hung up.

His first instinct was to call her back, but he stopped himself. Her husband could be home still, she could have called while he was in the other room, or from a pay phone. Kane hit the play button on his answering machine, waited as the tape rewound, then, after a few clicks, her voice again.

She was speaking in a hushed, low tone. She was home, he knew then, and so was her husband, somewhere.

"I'm sorry I missed you," she said. "He's still home, will be for two more days. I can't stand this. I hope you're okay. I'll try you again tomorrow. In the morning, maybe. Or maybe later tonight, if I get the chance." A brief pause, then: "Hope you're not with another women, though if you are, I guess I probably deserve that. I miss you, can't wait to see you. I love you. Bye."

She hung up. Kane realized then that she had no idea at all what he'd been through these past few days. *How odd,* he thought. He looked at the machine for a while. Normally he'd listen to the message several times, just to hear her voice. *Like a drug.* But he didn't this time. He reached for the erase button, pressed it. Gone. Then he looked out the window, at the back parking lot. Beyond it, a few hundred yards away, was Job's Lane, and across from that, the entrance to the park where Dolan's kid had been found in the lake. Kane thought about that for a long time, wondered if Meg, in her house, standing naked in front of her paintings, knew anything about *that* at least, about what had gone on these past few days in the very town in which she lived. Kane doubted that. She rarely left her house, got all that she needed—all the "entertainment" she needed—from her own mind and her own body. To be so content, if that was even the word. Kane saw her in his mind, imagined her day, from morning to night. She liked to think of herself as single-minded, strong-willed—and yet so willing to compromise. An odd mix, maybe—or maybe, in fact, really very common, Kane thought. She had so much to lose, had made that clear at the start. And yet she *had* started, took up with Kane, took the risk. So maybe then there was something worse than loss. Not having? Or maybe they were the two sides of the same coin. Whatever the case, there was *something* greater than the fear of loss, had to be, otherwise why would Meg risk loss at all?

Eventually Kane looked down at his nightstand, saw the digital recorder Mercer had given him sitting by the answering machine. He picked it up, held it for a while, looked at it, familiarized himself with all the buttons. Then he pressed Record, held the device close to his mouth, spoke into it.

"A novel," he said, "about loss." He paused, thought for a moment, then continued. "About grief and self-destruction and, who knows, maybe even redemption. Maybe. Dark and frightening, set during a week of record cold. Maybe someone trying to deal with a shadow, a secret he has to keep or maybe tell. Shadow Self, all that Carl Jung stuff. Mercer would like that. But definitely about loss, all kinds of loss, all kinds of people dealing with it and reacting to it in all kinds of ways. Maybe the loss of a son to drowning, so a water theme, water everywhere, the hero unable to escape the memory that haunts him."

Kane thought for a moment more, considered the word *hero* to be the wrong word, was reluctant to use it, but these were just notes, thoughts off the top of his head. He hadn't tried to think in this way in a long time, think in terms of emotions and ideas as they might relate to a story. It both did and didn't feel good. Nothing more came to him—*enough for now, take it slow*—so he clicked off the recorder and slipped it into the pocket of his coat. He looked again out the window. The municipal lot was poorly lit, full of empty parking spaces and the long, tapering shadows of bare trees. Fingery shadows. Eventually, Kane remembered his groceries in the open doorway, turned and left his bedroom, passed through the narrow hall, his mind now full of thoughts of structure and characters and mood. Elusive things, all of them, strangers now—but once they had been all he knew, all he could think of, day and night. Thinking of them again, it was difficult now to put them aside. His old obsessive mindset was coming back—well, not coming back, it'd always been there, just focused elsewhere: on Meg, on self-destruction. He'd felt like a fraud for the past two years, teaching writing but not once thinking about it. Now his thoughts raced with it—*so much for taking it slow*—and he found himself trying to imagine a conclusion to this story he was considering, what it was he would be working toward.

But just as he reached the end of his hallway, his mind full of this, he looked up fast and stopped short.

Someone was standing in his open doorway.

Kane's heart stopped, every muscle in his body flexed. It was a man in jeans and an army field jacket, work boots and a dark wool cap. A tall man, as tall as Clay, though not as wide, not nearly. He stood just outside the door in the darkened hallway Kane shared with his neighbor. Kane looked at the man for a while—*rugged, a workman, it had to be,* was his first impression—before even seeing the man's face. It took a moment more before Kane even realized the man's face was a face he hadn't seen in years. The face of an old friend, long lost.

Kane's heart pumped again, and a surge both of boyish joy and overwhelming confusion rushed through him as he stood face-to-face with his former teacher.

"Bill!" he said. "Jesus Christ."

Bill Young was in his sixties now—early sixties, Kane figured. But he didn't look any worse for the years, or the wear. A handsome man years ago, he was handsome still—elegant, with alert, piercing gray eyes the color of the Atlantic in winter. Regal, to say the least, even dressed as he was. Still the giant, even after all these years, that he had once seemed to Kane.

"What are you doing here, Bill?" Kane looked Young up and down quickly, unable to remember ever having seen Young dressed in this manner before. Young had never once, as far as Kane could remember, worn jeans. He was a man of standing and intellect, had always dressed the part.

"Long time, no see," Young said. He remained in the doorway, didn't enter. He had his hands in the pockets of his field jacket, which was zipped all the way to the top. He stood casually, smiling like an old friend, pleased with himself, with surprising his former student like this.

"I don't believe it," Kane said.

"I was wondering if you'd like to go out and get a drink. You look to me like a man who could use one. I heard about you getting fired. I thought you might like to talk about it with someone who has been there."

"How'd you find out?"

"I know a woman in the art department. She's been keeping tabs on you for me. I'd been meaning to get in touch with you sooner, but things have been crazy. I've been on sabbatical, working on a project."

"I thought you fell off the face of the earth for good."

"I did, for a while. But I'm back now. What do you say to a drink?"

Kane nodded. Young's timing couldn't be better. Kane needed to get out but was afraid to leave. Foreign city, and all. But he'd feel safe with Young.

"Sounds good," Kane said.

Young looked down at the bags. "I could help you put these away."

"No, I've got that," Kane said. He walked to the door, grabbed two of the bags. He'd forgotten how tall Young was. Strong, not like Clay, but still strong, stronger than Kane, anyway. Young grabbed the third bag, handed it to Kane, remained in the hallway outside as Kane went to the counter in the kitchenette, put the bags down. Nothing needed refrigeration, so he left them there. He was still in his coat, so nothing more to do, nothing to stop him. They left together, walked down the stairs to the sidewalk.

Young led Kane around to the back parking lot, walked with his head down. Kane wondered why the wool cap; it wasn't that cold, at least not like it had been. Young had thick white hair—women had loved it, Kane remembered—but none of it, not that Kane could see, showed from under the edges of the cap. Maybe Young's hair had fallen out, Kane thought. Maybe he had taken to wearing hats, whatever hat the season allowed, to hide his baldness. Young was as vain as he was brilliant. But it didn't matter now. The hat, the workman's clothes, they didn't matter. Ten years can change a man. Kane was different. Very different. Young had to be different too. But Kane didn't think too much about that. He felt a spring in his step, liked the coldness of the air on his face suddenly. Moments ago, Kane was a rat in a hole. Now, an old friend had returned, just in time.

A five-year-old Crown Victoria was parked next to Kane's Jeep. It looked like an unmarked police car, not the kind of vehicle Kane would have expected Young to drive. Young had always owned sports cars, was obsessed with speed. Drunk, he had once crashed an old MG and miraculously walked away. This was in Kane's third year of college. The Crown Victoria was in good condition, clearly well kept. Clean on the outside and in, no sign of crashes. Again, men change, are sometimes forced to change. Kane knew this. Still, it was the *last* car Kane would have expected Young to be driving.

They got in, Young steered toward the western exit of the municipal lot, through the long shadows, pulled out onto Windmill Lane, headed west, away from the village. He held the steering wheel with two hands, was wearing expensive-looking leather gloves. Kane noticed a sticker on the windshield, on the upper corner of the driver's side. It was the same sticker he had on his Jeep—a Southampton College parking permit. Same sticker but different color. Student stickers were red, faculty blue, administration green. This sticker was green.

"Is this your car?" Kane said.

"No. I borrowed it for tonight."

The first left turn off Hill Street was Captain's Neck Lane. Young took it. The road was wide, ran south for about a mile to the ocean. The streetlights that lined it were positioned far apart. Ahead, a pocket of light, a pocket of darkness, then another pocket of light and another of darkness. It went like that all the way to the end.

This was a residential neighborhood, wealthy. No bars or restaurants down here. Did Young live here now? Had he recently gotten lucky with a book deal? Was he living in a gardener's cottage? Was a woman he was in love with waiting for them somewhere down this road?

"Where are we going?" Kane said.

"I need to stop somewhere first. I need your help with something. It won't take long."

Young drove slowly, carefully, passing under a light and then into darkness. On the dashboard stood a plastic Jesus. Young was a famous atheist, had written books with atheist heroes, men forced to make their own justice in a godless universe. His novels were frank, hard-hitting, had been all the rage for a while in literary circles. But tastes changed,

Young fell out of favor, lost his confidence, then lost everything, had gone out of his way to lose it, like Kane had.

"You hanging out with the holy now?" Kane said.

Young glanced at the Jesus, then looked forward again. He smiled. "No."

Kane waited a moment, then asked the one question that mattered.

"Are you writing?"

"Sort of," Young said.

Kane smiled. "What do mean, 'sort of'?"

"You'll see. You'll understand."

"You still at the community college?"

"I'm on sabbatical. But, yeah, I'm still there."

Kane couldn't imagine that, a man like Young teaching at a community college, a man with his credentials, his ego, teaching Freshman Composition and Introduction to American Literature. But the community college in Riverhead was the only other college in the area, and maybe Young, like Kane, had a reason to want to stick around the East End. Kane wondered, too, if that was where he was headed, if that college was where he himself would go now that he had been fired. It would be a fall, certainly, not as bad as the one Young had taken, but bad enough. Still, it beat tending bar somewhere.

Captain's Neck Lane ended, and Young made the right onto Dune Road. A narrow road on a narrow strip of land, it extended west for a few miles, the Atlantic on one side, Shinnecock Bay on the other. There were houses along this road, on the ocean side, built on the dunes, grand summer places, some looking like European villas, others old, sturdy New England homes. Others still were modern, bland-looking geometrical structures of wood and glass. This strip of land was visible from the college, and at night, with the streetlights and houses lit up, it had always looked to Kane like a long, glowing bracelet of green stones.

Up ahead was Road D, a short paved road that ran perpendicular to Dune Road for a hundred or so feet and stopped at the edge of the dunes. Young made the left turn onto it. In the headlights, at the very end of the road, sat a black Volkswagen Jetta.

Young drove to it. Kane glanced at the side of Young's face, didn't understand what was going on. Young parked beside the Jetta. No one was inside, as far as Kane could see. He looked at Young again.

"What are we doing?"

Young shifted into park, reached down for the door handle, jerked it up and opened the door.

"You'll help me, right?" he said.

"With what?"

"An old friend in a jam is asking you for help. Do you help him?"

"What are you talking about, Bill?"

"Do you help an old friend in a jam?"

"Yeah, of course."

Young nodded. His mood was suddenly serious, the friendliness that he had displayed back at Kane's apartment now seemingly long gone. "Follow me then."

He got out. Kane waited, then got out, too, and met Young by the back of the car. The wind was blowing out here, it was a different world from back in the village, colder, wilder. Young reached into the pocket of his field jacket, took out a pair of cloth work gloves, handed them to Kane.

"Put these on," he said.

Kane looked at the gloves, then up at Young.

"It's really cold down by the water," Young said. "You'll need them."

Young walked to the end of the pavement, stepped onto the sand. He took a few steps, turned when he realized that Kane wasn't following him.

"It's okay," Young said. "Just follow me."

Before Kane could say anything, before he could ask again what the hell was going on, he saw Young's line of vision shift suddenly toward the road. Kane looked over his shoulder and saw the headlights of an approaching car on Dune Road. After a few seconds a beat-up pickup appeared, passed by without slowing down. There wasn't anything be-

yond Road D except a few more beach houses. Dune Road
came to an end a few hundred feet down, at the inlet that
gave access from the ocean to Shinnecock Bay. Where did
the driver think he was going? The truck disappeared from
sight quickly, and, from what Kane could hear over the wind
and the sound of the ocean beyond the dunes, kept on going.

Kane turned forward and saw that Young was already walking toward the ocean, had decided, it seemed, not to wait for
Kane. By the distance he had already traversed, Young must
have turned the instant the pickup had appeared. Kane didn't
follow but just stood there for a long moment. Finally, though,
he pulled on the cloth work gloves Young had given him and
walked to the edge of the pavement, crossing onto the sand.
His curiosity had gotten the better of him. And his sense of
loyalty. Young had taught Kane everything Kane knew. Young
had been his friend when Kane had needed one the most, when
the woman he had met during his second year got pregnant,
and then, during his third year, when she gave birth to his son.

Kane saw Young's footprints, and another set of prints
running alongside them, smoother than the ones Young was
now leaving. Kane figured someone had been here earlier
and the wind, constant here, though sometimes gusting, had
begun to erase them. *Was that person still here? Was Young
walking to meet whoever had made these prints?* Kane followed, stepping every now and then into Young's footprints.
He couldn't avoid that; the path leading between the dunes
was narrow. The sand was soft, seemed to get even softer as
he walked. It wasn't long before Kane's calf muscles started
to burn from the effort. So out of shape, Meg his only exercise. He was twenty feet behind Young but didn't hurry to
catch up. He still had no idea what they were doing out
there, so he walked cautiously, his eyes on Young up ahead,
his ears open, though all he heard was the hiss of the ocean
and the roar of the wind. Young stepped out from between
the two dunes onto the open beach, heading straight for the
dark water. After a moment Kane was on the open beach,
too. He looked up and down, east to west, saw nothing in either direction but beach and dark houses. He looked toward

Young again, saw him standing at the edge of the ocean, his hands in the pockets of his field jacket, his head bent forward, as if he were looking down at something at his feet.

The tide was going out, waves crashing in and then receding quickly, as constant as traffic, loud. The beach was flat, then dipped suddenly just before the surf, ran from there at a sharp angle to the water. As Kane approached the drop, he could only see Young's torso. He was standing still, looking down. Seven or eight waves came in and rushed out again before Kane finally reached the crest of the drop. Once there, he could see Young from head to toe—could see, too, that there was something at Young's feet, something wrapped in clear plastic.

It was a body.

Kane stared at it. Young was looking out over the ocean now, his back to Kane, his hands still in the pockets of his jacket. Kane once again looked up and down the beach, a little desperately now. He didn't know whether he was hoping to see someone or not. But there was no one. He looked back at Young. The sound of the waves filled Kane's head. He couldn't think, took one step off the crest, misjudged the distance down, stumbled to the wet sand, almost fell but caught himself. The sand was packed down by the waves, was hard beneath his Skechers. Kane waited a moment, looked again at the body, dumbfounded. He put his hands in the pockets of his jacket, didn't know what else to do, could think of nothing to say. He felt the recorder in the right pocket. He'd forgotten it was there, had forgotten everything—everything that was possible to forget.

The very edge of the waves as they rolled in reached the body and rushed around Young's feet, churning into white foam. As the waves rolled back, Kane heard hissing from the sand. The water was shallow, not enough to move the body. But it was deep enough to reach Young's ankles. It had to be cold, Kane thought, the water had to be freezing. But Young just stood there, showed no reaction at all when each wave came in.

"What's going on, Bill?" Kane said finally.

Young didn't answer. Kane took a few steps toward him. He was still a good ten feet away from Young and the body, didn't really care to get any closer. But Kane wanted to see Young's face, needed to, so he walked a kind of half circle around Young. When he had a view of Young's profile, Kane stopped.

Much of Young's face was in shadow, but what Kane saw was enough for him to know that Young was deep in thought.

"Bill, what's going on?" Kane had to speak up to be heard over the constant waves and wind, the cave of sounds in which they both now stood.

"I read your books, Deke," Young said. His eyes were fixed on the horizon. "They were good. You rely a little too much on repetition, but you would have grown out of that eventually, I think. I was pleased to see that I had influenced you. The language, the careful scene structure. Seeing that made me feel a little better about things. I wasn't so much of a failure if I had taught you so well. The feeling didn't last long, but . . ."

Kane said nothing, looked down at the body. He couldn't see through the plastic sheeting, couldn't see anything but the vague shape of a lifeless human form stretched out in the dark. He looked back at Young's face.

"Whose body it that, Bill?"

Young ignored the question. Or maybe he hadn't even heard it. "Colette read about you in the alumni newsletter. You were the first graduate to get published, so it was a fairly big deal. She gave me your books when they came out. I was proud of you."

Young seemed tired, Kane thought, like someone finally at the end of a very long trip—or near to the end. *A few steps more to go, but so tired.*

And then another, different thought came to him.

"You knew Colette?" Kane said.

Young nodded. "Yeah. That's how I knew what had happened to you. That's how I knew about your son's death, your bad case of writer's block, where you lived. I'm sorry about your boy, by the way. I'm sorry for the whole thing, I really am."

It took a moment, a long, confusing moment, but then Kane realized finally what it was Young was telling him, what all this meant. His heart came to a crashing stop in his chest, shattering to pieces.

A chill moved through him, colder than the night air around him, colder than anything he'd ever known.

"Oh, Jesus," Kane said softly. He could barely form the words, barely give them enough air with which to leave his body. "You're the Professor."

Young looked at him, then nodded and looked back out over the water. "I wasn't sure you knew about that. Colette told you?"

Kane said nothing.

"I was, it seems, a fool to have trusted her as much as I did. I'd known her for years, thought I knew her. I got her the job at that bar, used to frequent that place, back when I had money to spare, when I was someone. In her eyes I wasn't such a failure. She was in awe of me, even with my life, even with what it had become. She was going to write a book about me, about our affair. Salacious, full of details, real Henry Miller stuff, thought *that* might put me on the map again. In return, I taught her everything I knew. I even sent her to take classes with you, thought she might learn something from one of my own disciples. But it seems that she had her own plan. I really thought I knew her better than that. Her betrayal wasn't a twist I had anticipated. I should have seen it coming but didn't. So I had to make some quick last-minute changes because of her."

"You had her killed."

"No, that was all Dean's doing. But it forced me to move out from behind the scenes. I had to break into her apartment afterward and get some things. Lucky I did, too. She kept a journal on her computer; the file was sitting right there on the desktop. My name was everywhere. The whole plan, everything. A detailed record, like the whole thing was some research project of hers. I read through it all before destroying it. She made it sound like she was conflicted, like she wanted to stop me but was afraid. Like she had gotten in over her head and needed to do something about what was happening. That was pure fiction, I assure you. She was as involved in this as I was. She was tired of hiding from him. From her old chum Dean. If he was dead, he couldn't make trouble for her for what she had done to him. She'd be free. Killing a few dirty-minded boys in the process wasn't a problem for her. Hell, I think she even liked it. Deep down she had a contempt for all men, felt she was so much smarter than all of them, had control of them. She needed that, for obvious reasons. But, in the end, getting rid of Dean wasn't enough for her. She wanted to get a book out of this. She wanted to tell it all and be the hero, make herself look good. I should have known she'd do something like this. Looking back, it fits perfectly, it's her character, she couldn't have done anything other than that. It was her nature. But I couldn't see that. I was blinded—by her, by my own hate. It was a flaw that proved almost fatal to me. Almost. But all this doesn't matter now. Her notes, everything she wrote is gone. All that is left for the cops to find is part of her memoir, the boring part dealing with her troubled childhood and sexually abusive father. Like the world needs another book on that subject."

"You wrote the letter naming Krause, didn't you? You left it for the police to find."

Young nodded thoughtfully. "It was always supposed to be Krause. I even pretended to be Krause. Colette had introduced me to Dean as him. I dressed the part every time I went over to Dean's house, in case his neighbors saw me. For all Dean knew, I was Krause."

"You put that shirt in my apartment. And the blood in the chapel."

"It wasn't personal, Deke."

"Whose blood was it?"

"The Dolan boy. We took him the night you passed out. That way you'd have no alibi. Colette kept you busy the next night, for the same reason. Like I said, it wasn't personal. Krause got sick, and I needed to come up with something fast. What with what had happened to your son, and your bad behavior of late, you fit the bill pretty well. A clever use of a minor character, if you will. That's always the sign of a careful writer. I taught you that, remember? If there was any other way to end this, Deke, I'd do it, you know that, right?"

Young looked at Kane then. There was real remorse in his face, in his shadowed eyes. Kane could see it.

"It all has to fit neatly," Young said. "The cops need to buy this."

"Buy what?"

Young removed his right hand from the pocket of his jacket. Kane didn't pay attention to it at first, his mind was too busy taking in all that he had just heard, trying to see where it was going, what it was Young was referring to, what he meant about the cops needing to buy this. But then Kane saw in his peripheral vision something shiny in Young's hand and looked down, looked at Young's hand for a long time as his brain struggled to process the irreconcilable contradiction of a genuine expression of regret on a man's face, an old friend's face, with a gun held firmly in his hand.

Kane's thoughts all stopped then.

"Do me a favor, take your hands out of your pockets," Young said.

Kane froze. He didn't know anything about firearms, had never touched a gun in his life, but he'd seen enough TV and movies to recognize a .357 when he saw one. Young's arm was extended, locked at the elbow, the gun aimed at Kane's forehead. Kane winced as if he were looking into the noonday sun.

"Take your hands out of your pockets, okay?" Young said. "Let me see them."

Chaos, like a sudden virus, ran rampant in Kane's mind. Still, amid all those thoughts tearing into each other, colliding like atoms in a vacuum, one thing, one rational idea emerged.

Carefully, Kane felt for the recorder Mercer had given him,

pressed the record button in with his thumb, then took his empty hands from his pockets, held them away from his body.

"I don't imagine that you have any weapons, but do me a favor, zipper the pockets closed, okay?"

Kane pulled the zipper on each pocket, sealing them, then held his hands out again.

"I need you to come over here and unroll the plastic for me," Young said.

"What for?"

"Just do it, Deke."

Kane hesitated, looked at Young's face, then the gun. He breathed once, twice, then a third time before he was able to move. His feet felt heavy, his legs numb. Finally he stepped to the body, knelt down beside it, searched the clear plastic till he found an edge, then stood, pulling as he rose. The body inside was heavier than Kane had expected it would be. The cloth gloves Young had given him didn't grip the plastic well; the sheeting slipped from his hands several times. Finally, though, Kane curled up enough of the material to get a solid grip on it and pulled again. The body rolled over once, then again, and finally rolled free of the plastic.

It landed on its back. Half of the left side of its head was missing. There was smeared blood on the plastic in Kane's hands. He tossed it aside, felt a chill colder than anything he had known in his life. Kane looked at the body, saw the exposed bone and brain, the dried blood covering its face. He wanted to look away but couldn't. He had expected to see the face of a boy, a face that would remind him of his own son. But this wasn't the case. What Kane was looking at didn't make any sense at all.

And then, suddenly, horribly, it did make sense, in its own way, made sense of everything, or at least began to.

Lying dead on the wet sand was Dolan.

He was dressed in jeans and an army field jacket and work boots, dressed like Young, *exactly* like Young. Young removed his cap then, coarse white hair falling to his shoulders. He shoved the cap into the pocket of his jacket. Anyone who may have casually seen Young with Kane tonight, seen them leaving his apartment and getting into the Crown Victoria, might think Young was Dolan. Kane knew this, understood that this was the whole idea. He knew, too, that the black Jetta parked on Road D belonged to Young, and the Crown Victoria—with the administration sticker on the windshield and plastic Jesus on the dashboard—to Dolan. Kane stood there, unable to do anything but stare at Dolan's lifeless face, dotted with blood and clumps of wet sand.

"Did you write your books with an outline, Deke, or did you do what I taught you, start with a character with a problem, a problem that needed to be solved, and find the story as you went along, letting it come from all the characters involved?"

Kane looked at Young. Was this what he really wanted to talk about now?

"What?" Kane muttered.

"You know, in the past ten years I haven't been able to finish a book. I started many, over a dozen, would get as far as a hundred or so pages sometimes, think I was on to something—and then they'd just die on me. I'd lose what I thought I had, then spend months trying to start a new one. Those wouldn't go anywhere, either. I'd lose the feel or have to admit to myself that I didn't have a clue what it was the hero wanted. A hero without wants and you're fucked from the start. So I endured false start after false start, year after year. I thought I was washed up, that whatever it was I had was gone, never to return. And then I remembered something. I remembered that *my* teacher, years ago, had lost his wife to cancer, a painful and protracted death, and for close to a decade he had been unable to write. Not a single word. He took the usual route—drinking, fucking. He even went to war, thought that might help, that might give him something to write about. But nothing. And then finally he awoke in the middle of a particularly dark night and realized that the problem was he hadn't mourned his wife, that grief was in him but he refused to let himself feel it. And since he wasn't feeling anything, wasn't *letting* himself feel anything, he couldn't write. If you can't feel, you can't write. It's as simple as that."

The urge to vomit came over Kane suddenly. He didn't know if it was a delayed reaction to the sight of Dolan or something else. But his gut was empty, everything about him felt empty—his head, his chest, his veins, everything. Hollow. He tried to see Young's face. Everything that was still recognizable about the man was lost in shadow now. Lost for good.

"It's the risk we face," Young said, "comes with the job. One day your mind will dry up and you won't be able to write anymore, not like you used to. Christ, even Updike has slowed down. But to have it taken away, to have it ripped from you prematurely, unfairly, that's something else. There's just no living with that."

Kane thought of the recorder running in his pocket.

"You hired Dean to kill all those boys, Bill. Why?"

"You can figure it out, can't you, Deke?"

"I want you to tell me."

Young shrugged. "I wanted him to feel loss."

"You wanted who to feel loss?"

"I wanted the man who had taken everything away from me to know what loss is, what real loss is."

"You're talking about Dolan."

"It's a rage that never goes away, Deke. It's always there. You can't feel anything else. You try to drink it away, fuck it away. If there was a war, and if I were younger, I would have gone off to fight it. I would have done anything. Then one night I woke up, remembered what my teacher had gone through, saw the parallel. He was grieving his wife. I was grieving my *life*. He felt rage against God for taking his wife. But that wasn't a luxury I allowed myself. I couldn't blame it on a god I didn't believe in. And, anyway, there was *someone* to blame, someone who was *actually* to blame for my loss. Rage requires action, rage needs the score to be settled. Since my complaint was with a flesh-and-blood man, and not some bearded father figure in the sky, there was something I could do about it."

"Dolan got you fired from the college."

"He did more than that. He ruined my life. How do you mourn the loss of a life, Deke? Not *someone,* but a *life*? I live in a three-room apartment. I teach at a community college. I can't write a fucking word. The last ten years have been madness. And there was, I realized finally, only one way to put an end to it."

"By killing the son of the man who wronged you."

"You barely survived the death of your son, Deke, and his death was an accident. Colette saw the shit your life had become because of that. But what if someone had killed your son, had willfully murdered him, gone out of his way to murder him. And what if that someone was walking around, living a better life than you, thinking he had done God's good work—what would you have done then?"

"That's different, Bill."

"Is it? You haven't written a word in the four years since your son's death. You're full of grief and rage. I can see it in your face. It's like looking into a mirror."

Kane ignored that. "This doesn't make sense, Bill. You have all these poor boys killed so you can kill Dolan's son and get away with it. You set it up so the cops waste their time looking for some serial killer, and then you hand them clues leading to Krause. You do all this so you can hurt Dolan for ruining your life and walk away scot-free, and then you go ahead and kill Dolan anyway? It doesn't make any fucking sense."

"I didn't just do this, Deke. I did my research, read all there was on the subject. I waited for the right situation, thought it through. I read in the paper that some idiot kid in California got drunk and walked into the ocean and drowned. That's when I began to put this together. I was on sabbatical, had been told to get my act together or I was going to be fired. No Dolan there to push my dismissal through. So I was sitting in town, not far from your apartment, actually, trying to think of a way to do this, to kill Dolan's son and cover my tracks. Then one day I saw Krause in town. A creepy old man, a foreigner, people would be quick to believe he could do something like this. I remembered his story—everyone knew his story. It was perfect. But he was an old man, weak. How could he pull it off? I knew from my research that most serial killers work alone, but there were some who worked in pairs. So I needed someone strong enough, someone who would have his own reasons for hurting young men. Colette had told me about Dean. I knew she was hiding from him, that she'd want him out of the way so she could live her life again. I told her my plan, and she saw what she could gain from it. The fact that Dean's mother was a sometime prostitute who used to put cigarettes out on his face made him perfect for the job as a physically strong but morally weak henchman. I had everything in place. But the killings couldn't just stop cold with Dolan's kid. I knew that. A clever cop might wonder why that was and start looking for something to explain it, maybe look into the family's past for someone with a grudge. I needed this to be clean, needed it to be perfect. I couldn't replace rage with fear. That wasn't going to help me one bit. Even with Dean dead and all evidence pointing to Krause, as I had originally planned, there needed to be a fifth boy, I needed the killings to end there. But then Dean got himself killed early, and the fifth boy got away, and there was the chance this boy would talk, tell the cops all about Colette. She was the one who lured him out so Dean could grab him. She'd arranged it before she was killed. She lured all the boys out. So there were suddenly two things that could connect me to this—my history with Dolan and Colette. Two things too many. Certain people knew about her and me, knew that she sat in on my classes. Add to that the fact that Krause, the old kraut, it turns out, is on his deathbed, and suddenly everything that could go wrong *was* going wrong. I'd come too far to turn back. I needed to come up with something that would satisfy the cops, give them reason to close the case. I needed to give them someone else with a grudge against Dolan, someone to blame all this on and call it a day."

It took him a moment, but then Kane spoke, his voice low, barely audible over the sound of the waves.

"Me," he said.

"You were right there, Deke. Right when I needed you to be. Distraught over losing your job, you confronted the man responsible for your getting fired, the man who went out of his way to get you fired. He represented yet another bad turn in your tragic life, it was more than you could bear, so you killed him, then killed yourself. No one will think twice about it, bother to look past what's right there in front of them. The fact that you were once considered by the police to be a 'person of interest' in the murders of all those poor boys, one of whom was a student of yours, another your enemy's son—well, that will only add more confusion to an already difficult-to-fathom case. They'll be overwhelmed, and when people are overwhelmed, they tend to grab on to the easiest answer and leave it at that. Thus, of course, the concept of God. And if for some reason they don't, if for some reason they look deeper, they'll find in you a man whose only son had drowned four years ago, whose life had become little more than chaos. A man with demons that needed exorcising. A fascination, if you will, with drowning. Like I said, it wasn't personal, Deke. You just turned out to be the best man for the job."

Kane stared at Young, at what he could see of him in the darkness. He said nothing. What could he say?

"You would have known what it was like," Young said. "Sooner or later. He got you fired because he hated you, hated what you did with your personal life. He was a holier-than-thou little prick. You would have sat there in that apartment of yours and started to fantasize about revenge, about setting things straight. Not right away, but eventually, after years of setbacks. It eats at you, you know, a bite at a time, till there's nothing left for you to do but to bite back. I'm saving you from all that, Deke. I'm saving you from hell on earth."

"You're just trying to get away with murder, Bill. That's all. You're just fucked up and blaming everyone but yourself for your problems."

"I'm sorry you think that way. But don't believe for a moment that you wouldn't have ended up here. You did everything that I did. *Everything*. You would've gotten here sooner or later, would have seen Dolan in town one day, remembered this simple wrong he'd done to you and the bad turn your life had taken because of it. Where are you going to go from here? Back to tending bar? Back to that crappy apartment of yours? You would have realized one day—one night—that this dullard who had hurt you wasn't ever going to have to pay for what he did to you. No justice in this world but what we make. One night you would have woken up, realized you had to do something about him, that nothing was going to be right till you did. You couldn't live in a world in which he existed, in which he was rewarded for the bad he did."

Kane kept silent. Waves came in, washing over Dolan's body. It didn't budge. Neither Kane nor Young moved or even spoke for a long time. What more was there to say?

"I need you to face the water, Deke," Young said finally.

Kane couldn't move. He knew what Young wanted, knew what was next. His frantic mind grabbed at a detail he had once read in the newspaper or seen on some television show.

"They have ways of knowing if someone fired a gun or not, Bill. They'll know I didn't kill myself."

"The gloves you have on now are the gloves I was wearing when I put the gun to Dolan's head and pulled the trigger. They'll find the powders burns they need to call this a murder-suicide. It seems I have a mind for this, Deke. I'm moves ahead of everyone. Have been from the start."

Kane spoke softly, said the last thing he could think to say.

"They'll find you. You don't realize that right now, but they will find you. This'll all come out."

"Not as long as there's someone to blame. That's all they need. That's all they'll be looking for. Just someone to blame."

Young took two steps forward, closing what remained of the distance between himself and Kane. The gun came even closer to Kane's face now, and out of reflex Kane turned his head away, couldn't have stopped himself if he tried. He realized then that he had given Young exactly what Young wanted, a clear shot at Kane's temple. It wasn't long after he realized this that he felt cold steel press against the side of his head, not on his temple but just above the back of his ear.

Kane's mouth and throat went suddenly dry. He tried to swallow but couldn't. Every inch of his body tingled, every muscle tensed. He heard the ocean and the wind, thought suddenly, strangely, of his ex-wife, Patricia, thought of her alone in their home, getting the news that Kane was dead. The image triggered a flood of sorrow in Kane, and regret. It paralyzed him.

"I'm sorry it had to come to this," Young said. "It's the only way. I promise, in the book, I'll make you as much of a hero as possible."

Kane opened his eyes and looked at Young in disbelief. *What did he mean by that?* Kane suddenly saw a light, not the flash of the gun being fired but something else, something steady. What looked like the beam of flashlight caught the side of Young's face. Kane could see his profile clearly. The beam danced—maybe whoever was shining it was in motion now, but Kane didn't care about that. Young turned his head quickly, looked back toward the pass that ran between the two dunes, where the light was coming from. The gun barrel slipped from Kane's head, moved enough so it was aimed past him, out over the dark ocean.

Kane saw his chance and took it.

He grabbed the barrel of the gun with one hand and Young's wrist with the other, pushed upward, pointing the gun straight up into the night sky. He didn't move gracefully, was wild and reckless, frantic, but it was the best he could do. Young responded by grabbing hold of the collar of Kane's jacket with his free hand, pulling Kane away from him as he tried to yank his gun hand from Kane's grip. Young was just too big, too strong, his arms too long. And he moved way too fast. Kane lost hold of Young's wrist and the gun only seconds after grabbing it. He had it, and then it was gone. Once he was free, Young turned on his heels, spinning around and pulling Kane with him. Kane stumbled into the surf, the sneakers Gregor had given him, heavy to begin with, made even heavier by the freezing water that suddenly filled them. Young completed his turn and flung Kane away from him. Kane fell on the soaked sand. A wave came in and washed over him. He was flat out on his stomach, rose to his hands and knees fast, gasped for air as white foam churned around him. The water was so cold it felt like something solid was smashing into him, smashing his hands, his chest and groin, his face. His ears and nose ached instantly. Kane looked up, saw through the wet hair hanging before his eyes that Young was moving toward him, the gun still in his hand. Kane knew Young wanted to get the barrel as close as he could to Kane's skull so the angle of the wound and the powder burns on Kane's skin would lead the cops to the conclusion Young was counting on them reaching. Young made three long strides, kicking up the rushing water as he went, and had the barrel just inches from Kane's face, close enough for what he needed, when out of nowhere someone sailed through the air and tackled him from behind.

Kane couldn't see who it was, only saw the collision itself, heard the dull thud of bone knocking against bone. The stranger had hit Young with tremendous force, and both were airborne for a moment, then separated as they began to fall toward the sand. The stranger had made a controlled tackle and landed on his knees beside Young, who landed face first in the water. The stranger immediately tried to stand, to gain an advantage, but the instant he rose to his feet, he cried out loudly and reached down protectively to his knee. He tried to shift his balance onto his other leg, but a wave came in, knocking him down.

Kane realized at that moment that the stranger was Miller. He saw Young scramble to his feet, saw that Young was empty-handed now. He must have dropped the gun in the water when he was tackled. Despite his hurt knee, Miller struggled to get up, but Young didn't let him get too far. He grabbed Miller by the collar of his coat, pulling him off balance again. Miller fell forward into the water, and Young climbed onto his back, placed both hands on Miller's head, and pushed down.

Kane saw Miller's head disappear under the water.

Miller fought back, tried to get above the water by pushing himself up to his hands and knees. But Young pressed with all his weight, didn't let Miller's head rise above the water long enough for Miller to gasp more than a second's worth of air. A wave came in, a large one, the water covering Miller entirely and rising to Young's chest. It was a wave that didn't seem to end. Then, finally, it moved out, and the water dropped low enough for Miller's face to be exposed to the cold night air. But Miller was too busy trying to cough out the water he had inhaled to catch his breath.

Kane heard the horrible sounds of someone drowning. Another wave came in, covering Miller, and after that Kane heard nothing but the sound of the wind and the waves. He sat there, listening, stunned once again into helplessness.

Then, suddenly, an overwhelming rage began to grow in him and he heard nothing at all. He felt ill again and thought of what had been done to him in the chapel, thought of Colette, of his son, his still-mourning wife, felt the illness grow even more. He wanted to explode, to disappear, wanted small shreds of himself adrift in the vast ocean. He couldn't bear another death. He didn't even care about his own life, would have preferred it to be over anyway—what could there be for him after all this? The wave receded, and Kane heard Miller coughing again. Kane saw the beach and the water and the night sky again, felt the terrible, killing cold around him. He saw Young leaning forward, his arms locked and his hands on the back of Miller's head, Miller thrashing beneath the white foam.

And then, suddenly, Kane was on his feet and rushing forward. He felt a surge of adrenaline burst from his chest and into his limbs, felt his scalp tingle, knew nothing else. He came up behind Young and wrapped his arm around Young's neck, grabbed his own wrist to lock his hold down, and pulled Young off Miller, pulled with everything he had.

Young scrambled backward like a crab, and Kane dragged him that way for a few feet. But Young's weight was too much for Kane, and he was slick with water. Young slipped from Kane's hold, and Kane tripped and fell backward onto the sand. The instant he landed, Kane got to his feet again, but Young was just as fast, and they rose together, faced each other in water to their thighs.

Young didn't waste any time, came right for Kane, trying to grab at Kane's jacket with huge hands. Kane did the only thing he could do, did it without really thinking, did what he had seen Colette do outside the Water's Edge. He dropped low and swung his fist upward, smashing Young in the groin with a solid hit. Young cried out and folded, dropping to his knees. Kane shoved him, knocking him backward into the water. Young landed below the surface but got up on his elbows fast, raising his head above the water. He was taking a breath, his eyes closed tight against the cold water, when Kane stomped down, drove the hard sole of his Skecher into Young's stomach.

Young grunted, and Kane stomped again, this time knocking the air out of Young's lungs. He dropped on top of Young, driving his knees with all of his weight behind them into Young's chest. Young brought his arms up to protect his chest, but his head slipped beneath the water, and Kane, all rage and hatred, mounted Young like a schoolyard bully and grabbed his long hair with both hands, holding his head under. Kane could just see Young's face below the surface, felt Young struggling, his eyes closed tight at first, then opening wide in wild panic. Kane leaned forward and locked his arms at the elbows. He was panting, breathing in through his nose. He saw Young's mouth open, but Kane didn't ease up. He felt Young convulse as his lungs drew in the first rush of water. Young's legs kicked, his feet breaking the surface. Kane felt no pity, felt nothing at all, only his rage—not stagnant now but flowing, something powerful, something white hot that rushed through him and spilled into the turbulent ocean.

Kane hung on. And then, suddenly, beneath him, Young

went lifeless, his face frozen in a look of panicked shock, his eyes bulging, his swollen tongue filling his gaping mouth.

Still, Kane held on, held Young's head under. It wasn't until he knew Young was dead that Kane let go and rolled away.

He sat in the surf, waves hitting him from behind, water churning around him. He sat with his arms hanging at his sides, his head hung low, his chin touching his chest. He couldn't lift his head, didn't want to. Eventually, Kane began to feel the brutal cold, his hands aching as if they'd been smashed between two pieces of blunt metal. He knew he couldn't last long in this cold, in soaked clothes. He knew that but didn't really care.

And then he heard coughing and remembered Miller.

He lifted his head, found what it took to do that, saw that Miller had crawled onto the beach, was on his hands and knees, struggling to clear the icy water from his lungs. Kane got to his feet, his clothes unbelievably heavy, his body weak, and staggered out of the water and onto the soft sand. The thin cloth gloves that Young had given him started to freeze upon being exposed to the air, so Kane took them off, dropped them as he walked. He reached Miller, knelt beside him, placed his hand on Miller's back, stayed there with him as he coughed. Kane was trembling, violently. So was Miller. They only had a minute or two at the most before the cold would kill them. There was no doubting that.

Kane waited till Miller finished coughing, then told him that they had to go. Miller nodded, and Kane wound Miller's arm around his neck, then stood. They struggled together across the soft sand, following Young's footprints. They stumbled and fell several times, and each time they did, Miller cried out, cupped his hand over his knee. Kane got them back on their feet, guided them toward the pass between the two dunes. He noticed that the wind was already erasing the footprints the three of them had made on their way out to the water. It wouldn't take long before the tracks disappeared entirely.

As they made their way between the two dunes, Kane

spotted Miller's beat-up truck ahead, parked across the narrow road from Dolan's Crown Victoria and Young's black Jetta. Kane kept his eyes on Miller's truck as they moved toward it. *Only need to go that far, that was all.* They reached the road, and the solid pavement felt strange beneath Kane's feet, like the surface of a different world. He got them to the truck, opened the passenger door, helped Miller in as quickly as he could, to keep the warmth that remained inside from escaping. Then he hurried around to the driver's door and climbed in behind the wheel.

There was no key in the ignition. Miller had to dig it out of his pocket with shaking hands. Once the key was free, he handed it to Kane. Kane started the engine, turned the heater fans on full blast. The motor was still hot enough that warm air poured from the vents. Kane sat there for a while, shivering, his teeth chattering. Miller, too. Neither of them said anything. Then Kane remembered the recorder running in the pocket of his coat. The zipper was frozen; he had to pull hard to get it started. It hurt the tips of his fingers to hold the small metal tab. But he got the zipper open, reached in, felt that the wool that lined the pocket was only damp. A rush of hope moved through him as he grabbed the recorder and took it out and looked at it.

It was still running, the red record light still glowing. He closed his eyes, switched the recorder off, then dropped it onto his lap. His jeans were frozen, the material so cold that it burned, so hard with ice that the seams cut into his skin. He opened his eyes after a moment and looked over at Miller.

Miller was staring ahead, through the windshield, at the two cars parked side by side in the lot. He took several breaths, then said, "Which one did you come in?" His voice was hoarse, and he wheezed when he spoke. Kane looked at the cars for a moment, then finally understood what Miller was telling him.

"There are some rags under the seat," Miller said.

Kane reached down, found a clean oil rag and grabbed it, then opened the door and hurried through the cold to the

Crown Victoria. He used the rag as a glove to open the door, could barely move in his clothes but leaned in anyway and wiped down the seat, the dashboard, couldn't remember if he had touched either of them but didn't care, wiped them both, wiped everything that would have been in his reach as Young drove him here. Then he ran the rag over the inside door handle, swung the door closed and wiped down the outside handle, too. He hurried back to the truck, climbed in, shut out the cold, and looked again at Miller.

He was barely conscious now. Kane knew that the heat coming out of the vents wasn't going to be enough. Miller needed more; freezing water had touched his lungs. The warm cab of a truck wasn't going to cut it. He shifted into gear, steered the truck to the end of the lot, then turned onto Dune Road and sped toward town. He parked the truck behind his apartment, helped Miller up the stairs, then down the hallway to his bathroom. He turned on the shower, made sure the water was cool, not hot or even warm, then got Miller under the stream and held him there. None of this was easy. Miller was only barely conscious, and he outweighed Kane by fifty pounds. Kane reached down, strained to put the plug into the drain. Once he got it, he helped Miller sit, cut off the shower, and let the water pour from the faucet to fill up the tub.

Kane hurried to his kitchen, found the slip of paper that Mercer had left him, with Gregor's number on it. He grabbed his phone and dialed. When he came back to the bathroom, Kane saw that Miller was passed out. He waited till the tub was filled, then shut the water off and opened the faucet in the sink, let it run hot, to fill the room with warm steam. He made sure Miller was okay, that he wouldn't slip under the water, then went into his bedroom, stripped out of his wet clothes, found a towel, and was about to dry off when he stopped.

He saw his reflection in the dark glass of the long window. Ghostly, unreal, shadowed, he was nearly unrecognizable to himself. He stared at what he saw, searching for something he could recognize. *Who was this man now?*

Whose life was this? Finally, when he'd seen enough, Kane dressed, leaving his soaked clothes on the floor as he walked out of his dark bedroom. His hands still hurt, so he stood at the kitchen sink and let tepid water run over them. He remembered his last morning at Meg's house, sitting on the edge of her bed and staring at his useless hands. How many days ago was that? he wondered. He couldn't remember. But it didn't really matter. *What could matter now?*

It would take at least another forty-five minutes for Gregor to make the drive from Montauk to Southampton, so all that was left for Kane to do was watch over Miller. He turned off the faucet in the kitchen sink and crossed the narrow hallway to his bathroom. The small room had quickly filled with thick steam, but Kane could see though it well enough to observe that Miller was still unconscious. Kane entered the room, then closed the door to keep the warmth in and sat on the floor. He listened to the water running and sat with his back against the door, watching Miller, waiting silently for him to awaken, determined to be there at his side when he finally did.